THE SILENCE OF SCHEHERAZADE

DEFNE SUMAN

TRANSLATED BY BETSY GÖKSEL

HEAD
of ZEUS

An Apollo Book

Originally published in 2016 as *Emanet Zaman* by Doğan Kitap, Istanbul, Turkey, and as Η Σιωπή της Σεχραζάντ by Psichogios Publications, Athens, Greece

First published in the UK in 2021 by Head of Zeus Ltd
This paperback edition first published in the UK in 2022 by Head of Zeus Ltd,
part of Bloomsbury Publishing Plc

9 7 5 3 1 2 4 6 8

A catalogue record for this book is available from
the British Library.

ISBN (PB): 9781800246973
ISBN (E): 9781800246980

Typeset by Divaddict Publishing Solutions Ltd
General map by Jamie Whyte
Smyrna map and illustration page 1 by George Poulimenos

Printed and bound in Great Britain by
CPI Group (UK) Ltd, Croydon CR0 4YY

Head of Zeus Ltd
5–8 Hardwick Street
London EC1R 4RG
WWW.HEADOFZEUS.COM

To those who have been exiled from their homeland

Whether it's dusk
or dawn's first light
the jasmin stays
always white.

G. Seferis, 'The Jasmin'

Many stories can be told of Friday's tongue, but the true story is buried within Friday, who is mute. The true story will not be heard till by art we have found a means of giving voice to Friday.

J. M. Coetzee, *Foe*

Author's Note

As the twentieth century dawned, the Ottoman Empire was losing power and land. For the last seven hundred years, the sultanate had ruled territories from modern-day Greece to Bulgaria, from North Africa to India, and the wealthy, elegant port of Smyrna on the west coast of Asia Minor was famously one of its most vibrant and cosmopolitan cities. Here, Muslim Turks and Orthodox Greeks had lived and traded harmoniously alongside European Levantines, Armenians and Jews for centuries, and all religions and cultures were respected. But the rise of nationalism in the nineteenth century and the end of the First World War would see the dissolution of the Ottoman Empire, with Britain, France, Italy and Greece fighting over the spoils. For the time being, Smyrna remained under Turkish administration, but as nationalist and independence movements gathered strength, so the city's multi-cultural fabric was about to be ripped apart, unleashing the most catastrophic of stories.

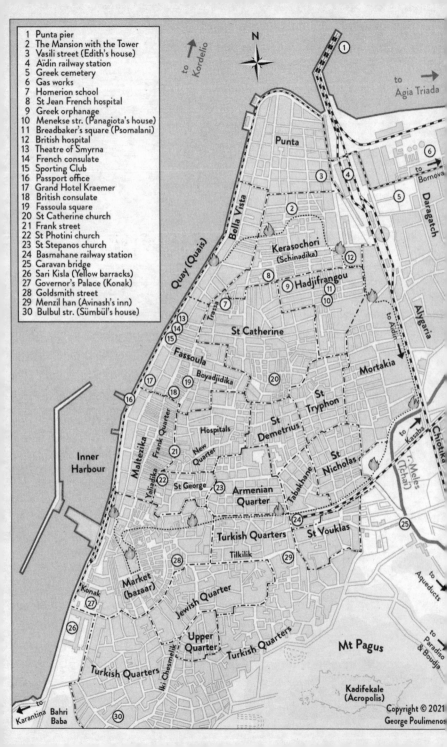

1 Punta pier
2 The Mansion with the Tower
3 Vasili street (Edith's house)
4 Aïdin railway station
5 Greek cemetery
6 Gas works
7 Homerion school
8 St Jean French hospital
9 Greek orphanage
10 Menekse str. (Panagiota's house)
11 Breadbaker's square (Psomalani)
12 British hospital
13 Theatre of Smyrna
14 French consulate
15 Sporting Club
16 Passport office
17 Grand Hotel Kraemer
18 British consulate
19 Fassoula square
20 St Catherine church
21 Frank street
22 St Photini church
23 St Stepanos church
24 Basmahane railway station
25 Caravan bridge
26 Sari Kisla (Yellow barracks)
27 Governor's Palace (Konak)
28 Goldsmith street
29 Menzil han (Avinash's inn)
30 Bulbul str. (Sümbül's house)

N

to Kordelio

to Agia Triada

to Bornova

Punta

Bella Vista

Quay (Quais)

Kerasochori
(Schinadika)

Hadjifrangou

Daragatch

to Aïdin

Alygaria

St Catherine

Mortakia

Trassa

Fassoula

Boyadjidika

St Tryphon

St Demetrius

St Nicholas

to Kasaba

Chiotika
(r. Meles (Tchai))

Inner Harbour

Maltezika
Frank Quarter
Yaliadika

Hospitals

New Quarter

St George

Armenian Quarter

Tabakhane

St Vouklas

Turkish Quarters

Tilkilik

Market (bazaar)

Konak

Jewish Quarter

Upper Quarter

Turkish Quarters

Mt Pagus

to Aqueducts

to Paradiso & Boudja

to Karantina

Bahri Baba

Iki Chesmelik

Turkish Quarters

Kadifekale (Acropolis)

Copyright © 2021
George Poulimenos

Part I

THE GATES OF PARADISE

When I emerged from the ashes of the paradise lost
They said my name was Scheherazade.
One hundred years have passed since my birth
But the end of my silence
Has not come.
Though my tongue be hesitant
I will tell all,
Everything,
That death may find me
In the tower of this wreck of a mansion.

The First September

My birth, on a sweet, orange-tinted evening, coincided with the arrival of Avinash Pillai in Smyrna.

According to the European calendar, it was the year 1905. The month was September.

When the passenger ship carrying the Indian spy approached the port, I had not yet been born, but through the opening in my mother's womb a slender beam of light had begun to seep into the dark pool where I had lived for months. She couldn't get up and walk. Not because of the weight of me, but because of the opium she was inhaling from the pipe wedged between her middle and ring fingers. She'd turned her face to the window and was watching the curtains flying drunkenly in the arms of the wind.

The previous year – or was it two years ago? – she'd danced a waltz with one of the engineers from the Aydin Railway at a midsummer party held at the Bournabat Club. The man had whirled her around on the polished-wood floors much like those curtains were flying around just then. What was the man's name? She remembered his high British cheekbones, the house he lived in at the northern end of the quay and the soulless skill of his steps, but somehow she couldn't recall

3

his name. Mr...? Mr Somebody. What? A strange name. Not ordinary. She raised her head and took another puff of the pipe between her two fingers. Purple rings wavered in front of her dark eyes. Mr Somebody slid away, across the polished-wood floor.

Avinash Pillai, standing on the second-class deck of the elegant *Aphrodite* as it waited out in the gulf, was unaware of my mother, or me. He was busy sniffing the air like a wild animal, his eyes closed, his nose lifted towards the dappled firmament. As the sun set, the land was expelling the breath it had been holding all day. The young Indian man, fed up with the smell of coal and cold iron which had permeated the days-long sea voyage, was inhaling the pleasant aroma of flowers and grass. Rose, lemon, magnolia, jasmine and deep down a touch of amber.

Avinash's nose was long and delicate, as noble as an Ottoman sultan's. As he identified each fragrance, he savoured its tone and essence as if it were a tasty morsel with which he was breaking his fast. Especially the roses. Even with his eyes shut, he could distinguish a white rose from a red one. Somewhere ashore, in the city whose pink lights were dancing on the sea, lived a man named Yakoumi. Neither the beautiful city nor its legendarily beautiful women interested the young man. His entire mind was set on the dim room which Yakoumi had mentioned in his letters. In the workshop behind his pharmacy the elderly chemist extracted oil from the petals of the rarest roses brought from the four corners of the empire.

'What is this captain waiting for now?'

'That freighter will move away and make room for him probably.'

On the brightly lit upper deck, the first-class passengers

– gentlemen in frock coats and bowler hats, with expensive cigars splitting their lips – grumbled as if they had not already patiently voyaged from Alexandria to Rhodes, from there to Leros, then to Chios, and finally to Smyrna.

'Not so, Sir. That freighter will not move. Don't you see, it has drawn up to that barge. It's coal. That one's got to be loaded yet.'

'I'm not talking about that one. I'm talking about the ship that's loading the bales of tobacco. It's been standing there for twenty minutes.'

'This ship won't go into the harbour, gentlemen. Its waters are shallow, and captains who don't know this are always running aground on the rocks. There's nothing for it but to wait for the rowing boats.'

The sounds coming from the quay – the ringing of tram bells, the rattling of carriage wheels, the clanging of horseshoes – reminded the gentlemen of pleasures they had forgotten during the sea voyage. Some of them even swore that they could hear the laughter of women drifting out of the nightclubs along the quay. Surrounded by whistling pilot boats, multi-coloured sailing boats, and freight and passenger ships passing each other and then vanishing on the china-blue waters, the gentlemen checked the time on their pocket watches every minute on the minute.

'To be this close to shore and not able to step out upon it is intolerable, my dear friends. Where could the rowing boats be?'

Avinash had walked to the afterdeck. When he was certain that no one was watching, he clasped his palms together over his breast. As he was now working in the service of the British Empire, it was important to give the appearance of a European. However, he was also the grandson of a hermit who awaited God's mercy as he lived out his final years in a monastery in the foothills of the Himalayas. It was time to give thanks to the mighty Creator who had protected him throughout the difficult days and stormy nights, first from Colombo to Port Said, then on the dark train to Alexandria, and from there to Smyrna on the *Aphrodite*.

He turned his face towards the sun, which was melting into the sea like a scoop of red ice cream, and closed his eyes.

'*Om namah Shivayame*. Oh, mighty Shiva. We give thanks to you for protecting us from being shipwrecked and from disasters, horrors, illnesses and epidemics, and for bringing us to the shores of this lovely city.'

He had said his prayers ever since childhood. And not only to the god Shiva, whom his family favoured, but also to the Protector, Vishnu, and, of course, to the Creator of the Universe, Brahma. He believed that the gods were friendly beings, even Shiva the Destroyer, and that they loved him. Before them he was himself, without a mask, without deceptions. He asked their mercy for any offences he might unknowingly have given, and he felt in the depths of his heart that these divine beings forgave and protected him.

'Oh, great Shiva, divine power that destroys and re-creates! Help me, that all my works may go well on this new page of my life. Be near me, that my duties be successfully completed; bestow strength, skill and understanding. Protect my mother, father and siblings from accidents, catastrophes, sickness and plague, that I may accept what happens with patience.'

A strong wind suddenly swept across the deck. This wind, which always picked up just before twilight, was famous for the way it could cool even the hottest of days in a matter of moments. Sometimes, like a good-hearted giant unaware of his own strength, it stirred things up too much, unintentionally capsizing the fishing boats and causing a sack of curses to be unleashed upon it. But that evening it was at its most benign. After stroking the flaking green paint of the ship's rail, it snatched up the young man's bowler hat and carried it off to the empty chaises longues at the foot of the stairs. At first Avinash didn't react. He kept in mind the manners he'd been taught by his grandfather; even when agitated – particularly when agitated – one should finish one's prayers properly. It would bring bad luck if he were to run after such worldly troubles before bidding farewell to the gods. Hastily, he touched his hands to the space between his two eyebrows, to his lips and lastly to his heart.

'Oh, mighty God, you are great, you are capable of miracles. We entrust ourselves to you. *Om namah Shivayame.*'

Then he raced over to the chaises longues to retrieve his hat. He felt guilty that he'd cut his prayers in half, particularly at the point of request.

The wind, as if to remind him that life was too short to waste on feelings as weighty as guilt, swept the hat a few steps away, tousling his raven ringlets. Avinash's curls were as thick and heavy as the plaits of the Armenian girls who were hanging their clothes out to dry; even if the ship were to capsize, his hair would not be disarrayed. The wind whistled and crept down his front, inside his silk shirt. The colour of Avinash's skin was the velvet brown of Eastern slaves, but in appearance he was superior to the Europeans who were strolling along the quay all dressed up, holding onto their hats. He was not a maharajah – he was travelling second class, yes – but he strode the earth more elegantly in his pointy-toed shoes than the gentlemen on the upper deck. He wore an emerald earring in his right ear, a matching green silk cravat, and a handkerchief of the same shade in his pocket. Just like the Europeans.

The wind made another tour around Avinash, howled in his ears and then took its spicy breath to the other side of the harbour, to the rooftop terrace where my mother and I were living the last of our interconnected hours. Through half-closed eyes, my mother glanced suspiciously at the dancing tulle curtains. Was someone there? But the top floor of our mansion was a long way from the passenger ship *Aphrodite*, well beyond the sights of the young Indian man that evening.

God winks at us with coincidences. The Indian spy Avinash arrived in the city that same evening, and it was he who, years later, brought me the story of my birth. It was by chance that he discovered my story, thanks to an old photograph, when he was looking out over the city from the deck of another ship, just as he had on the night of my birth.

Again, it was the month of September.

But that was a very different September.

It was different because, on the night I was born, the city's domes, minarets and tiny houses with ceramic-tiled roofs shone like gold. Seventeen years later, the city would be vomiting flames like an angry monster. And the wind, that playful wind that had made the young spy angry by tossing his hat back then, would carry terrible smells to the deck of the ship: the stink of kerosene and melting tyres, of charred, century-old sycamores, of the milky juice of figs scattered on the streets, collapsed churches, pianos, gilded books. Worst of all would be the acrid reek of scorched flesh blowing across the deck of the *Iron Duke* as it transported Avinash, with my mother in his arms, far from the flames and the unendurable sufferings of the city. Everyone would be covering their mouths with handkerchiefs; some would be leaning over the railings to be sick. The stink of frazzled flesh, of cats caught in narrow passageways, of seagulls with their wings on fire, of desperate camels and horses, of people rushing out of their basements and attics where they'd been hiding like cockroaches. Fingernails, bones, flesh – burning.

The same wind that had once tried to teach Avinash that life was too short to waste on feelings as heavy as shame would now allow fate to have all the wretched souls gathered on the quay witness that not only water but also air could drown a person.

But before then, much will take place.

For now, let's stay on that sweet, orange-tinted evening when I was born. Let me put pressure on my mother's narrow cervix and leave Avinash to call out the names of villages and districts he had hitherto only studied on paper, like a schoolboy asked to recite. Up ahead was Kokaryali, then Goztepe, Karantina, Salhane, Karatash, Bahri Baba. You couldn't see it from where the *Aphrodite* was anchored, but beyond the customs house there was a modern building in the shape of a horseshoe. People called it the Yellow Barracks, the Sari Kisla, and Avinash knew that six thousand Ottoman Nizam-i Djedid soldiers were stationed inside it.

This was important.

It was part of his mission to make contact with these soldiers. The Secret Service was keeping a close eye on the soldiers in all Ottoman cities, from Salonica to Smyrna. He was to live in the Turkish district and mingle with them in the coffeehouses and markets. He was to attend the meetings of the Europeans and gather intelligence on the tricks of the French and the Italians. A knot formed in his stomach.

What if he failed to carry out his duties properly?

What if he heard but could not understand the foreign languages he had learned at school?

'You are talented, determined, young; in two months you'll begin to speak better than the natives.'

That was his Oxford professor.

'We chose you for a reason, son. Trust us. You are perfect for this special mission.'

For now, this mission was a knot in his stomach.

Beneath his silk shirt, two rivulets of sweat trickled from his dark armpits. Glancing around the empty deck, he stuck his nose into his collar and smelled himself. Throughout the voyage he'd been very careful not to eat spicy food, but he could still detect a slight whiff of garlic on his skin.

This upset him.

The first thing he needed to do was find a place to stay and cleanse himself. Leaning out over the railings, he observed the deck below. Trunks were being loaded onto the rowing boats that had surrounded the *Aphrodite* like pirate ships. As soon as he got ashore, he had to find a bathhouse.

'One of our men will meet you at the pier to ensure that you have no difficulties passing through customs. But that's all. After that you're on your own. It's better that way. Head straight for Basmane train station when you leave the pier. When you get to the Street of the Goldsmiths, ask for the Yemiscizade Bazaar. Then wait for us to contact you.'

Meanwhile, as his stomach was aching at the thought of beginning a new life in an unknown city, my mother, a native, born and bred in Smyrna, was moaning desperately as she twisted in the increasingly violent pangs of my birth. The opium had lost its effect by now. The baby in her belly had turned into an animal with sharp claws, tearing her flesh from inside. She slowly, slowly stood up; like a drunken barrel, she rolled to the door of the glassed-in room where she had been imprisoned for exactly three months, one week and five days, and leaned against it. From the turret, the vibrations of her screams reached the sitting room downstairs, where the Armenian midwife sat with a bag of gold in her hands and a huge weight of responsibility upon her, larger even than herself.

Across from Midwife Meline sat my grandmother in a velvet armchair. Coffee cup in hand, she gestured towards the ceiling with her finely pointed chin.

The time had come.

Thus, full of secrets, my life, which was to span more than a century, began.

The God of Fleeting Moments

The people who gave me the name Scheherazade found me unconscious in a garden smelling of honeysuckle just before dawn one morning. My hair was tangled in the roots of the mulberry tree under which I was lying. My legs were a mass of festering wounds from the flames that had engulfed my skirt, but it was impossible not to notice the serene smile on my face. They assumed I was watching a lovely dream behind my closed eyes. They couldn't understand how I had got through the locked gate and into the garden.

I remember it all. This was a different September. The acacia trees were in bloom, schools were about to open. I was seventeen. My birthday week had just come to an end. The kite stuck in the mulberry branches – it was red, like everything else that night – was fluttering in the wind blowing from the mountains to the sea. The earth beneath me was soft, moist, inviting. Angel fingers moved over my cheeks. A door slammed somewhere far away. Then I heard the 'tak' of a cartridge being loaded. The double-barrelled shotgun would definitely blow my brains out. Let it happen. Everybody was shooting everybody that night. The sea was clogged with bodies, every one of them bloated like balloons.

We had mingled with death too much to be afraid of it in those days.

The surprising thing was life itself. The sight of children in red and green dresses splashing around among the corpses as the ocean currents drew their little bodies downwards. The boys and girls whose hair was floating like seaweed, singing their last breath as they hung onto the chains of the European ships and begged the captains to take them aboard. How they clung to life! I did not have that much strength left in me. I was debilitated, weak, used up, finished.

My ribcage collapsed into the earth. I didn't even open my mouth.

If I had opened it, no sound would have come out, but I did not yet know this.

Heaven was at the end of the double-barrelled shotgun.

I closed my eyes.

In the distance a child was crying.

Behind my closed eyes I saw a woman. She was standing on the deck of a long, narrow ship. Two thick plaits were wound around her head and a fringe hid her frowning eyebrows. Avinash Pillai was standing directly behind her, his dark arms encircling her waist, pressing her tightly to his chest. The sea was flickering with yellowy-orange flames. The hatless woman, leaning her head on the Indian man's shoulder, was crying.

The woman's name was Edith Sofia Lamarck.

She was my mother.

I did not know this at the time. Avinash Pillai told me years later.

Charles Lamarck's youngest child was born in Bournabat, in a stone mansion with a large, sloping garden full of camellias, bougainvillea and various kinds of roses set in the middle of a vast tract of land. When she was a child, Edith believed that this garden, which on one side was bordered by a poplar forest, was paradise itself. Bournabat was surrounded by mountains which merged with the blue of the sky. Cherry trees and pomegranate trees greeted passers-by.

Little Edith used to lie among the blue, purple and pink hydrangeas that had been planted by her grandfather with his own hands – 'These are my grandchildren,' he would say – and watch the clouds. One of those clouds carried Kairos on its back. Kairos was the god of mortal time, time which flew away. He was in love with the Amazon queen Smyrna, who founded the city that took her name. Every day, Kairos travelled across the blue skies on the back of a cloud, greeting the queen's great-great-grandchildren. Smyrna was as beautiful as she was powerful, and equally just. In archery, she had no superiors. Like other Amazon women, she had cut off her right breast at puberty in order that it not interfere with the drawing of the bowstring. Edith dreamed of her as she rode her horse along the golden shores, her long black hair rippling. If she ever had a daughter, she would name her Smyrna.

Sometimes she would run down to the far end of the garden where it opened onto the forest and bury her face in the rosemary and wild thyme that the washerwoman Sidika had planted, inhaling the aromatic herbs until she sneezed. The garden was full of fruit trees and vines. After he'd turned his business over to his son, Edith's grandfather, Louis Lamarck, had become very interested in vineyards; he devoted every minute of his retirement years to growing grapes. Swings hung from the iron poles of the vineyard, their ropes plaited like the hawsers of the ships in the harbour. Edith's father and their butler, Mustafa, had made them in the carpentry shop.

When Edith swung high enough, she would snatch at a cluster of her grandfather's grapes and, despite her mother having forbidden it, would pop the warm and dusty yellow Muscat grapes, drunk with their own sugar, into her mouth unwashed.

The mulberry tree was right in front of Edith's bedroom and left its fruit on her balcony. She used to nourish silkworms in tiny nests of mulberry leaves beside her bed. Her nanny from Bursa had taught her how to sing lullabies to the caterpillars. The nanny insisted that the silkworms only understood Greek, so Edith sang Greek songs to the silkworms every night. And every morning she would raise the leaves and peep in with curiosity and fear. In midsummer the Greek servants would spread a blanket under the huge tree and ask little Edith to lean over the balcony and shake the branches with her slender arms. The white, honey-filled mulberries would patter down onto the blanket with a sound like summer rain.

One day she discovered that the unripe figs she'd picked left a white liquid on her hand, as white as the milk that came from the teats of Grisha, the cat who'd had kittens in the garden. Sidika explained that the milk was the fig's blood. The fig needed it to grow, so that it could swell up like a breast. Sidika was a refugee from Crete. She had blonde, almost white hair and blue eyes, and she was tall and slender. She spoke a dialect of Greek that no one except her husband Mustafa understood, not even her sons. Sidika would give Edith cinnamon buns and herbal pies when she ran away from her mother's guests and hid in the hut at the edge of the garden.

Because Edith was so much younger than her siblings, she grew up separately from them. She was a child who knew how to play by herself. Her sister, Anna, and brothers, Charles Junior and Jean-Pierre, were away at school in France for eight months of the year. During those months, Edith was the only child in the huge mansion. It wasn't that she didn't have friends. On the contrary, Bournabat was a child's paradise in those years. In the tangerine-scented sunset, the children would have bicycle races on the road and play hide-and-seek and marbles; they waited for the halva seller more eagerly than they did for their fathers disembarking the evening train. Kosta, the halva seller, who lived in the small village at the centre of Bournabat, came past the Lamarck mansion every evening and would give the children candy floss. To the ladies who'd had their lounge chairs brought out front and were stretched out upon them, drinking coffee, he would offer cones of nuts, Turkish delight, and sugar lumps.

Edith's best friend was Edward Thomas-Cook, the neighbours' son. Together they would scramble over the iron garden gates and search the huge mansions for ghosts. On endlessly long summer afternoons they would find a shady spot and act out scenes from the books they were reading. Edward had a large family and was often forgotten among his two elder brothers and his ailing younger sister. Their house was always full of relatives and guests, all of whom Edward addressed as 'auntie' or 'uncle'. Edward wasn't like other boys. For example, he would rather read books with Edith than join the football team. As well as *The Adventures of Tom Sawyer* and *Treasure Island*, he had also read Edith's favourite book, *Little Women*. At Edith's insistence, he had even cut off her two long plaits with his own hands so that she would resemble the book's heroine, Jo, whom Edith adored.

Edith had another friend besides Edward: her father, Charles Lamarck. Monsieur Lamarck was actually old enough to be her grandfather. Perhaps for this reason, their relationship was based on mutual tenderness and understanding. And perhaps also because of this, her father spoiled her unnecessarily, as was frequently pointed out by Edith's mother, Juliette. As the time of the evening train's arrival neared, Edith would sit on the edge of the ornamental rock pool with her little white hand up to its wrist in water lilies and goldfish, keeping her eyes on the garden gate as she waited. Juliette would pass through the garden on her way to one of the neighbours' for tea, and without slowing the steps of her dainty feet wrapped in satin slippers, would say, 'Darling Edith, please wash and tidy yourself before I return. I have spoken to Nanny. She is preparing your dress with the blue ribbons. We have a guest for dinner and I would like everyone's face to have a smile upon it.'

Words streamed out of Juliette's mouth at a running pace. As she paused to catch her breath, her blue-green eyes would linger on Edith's face for a moment, awaiting acknowledgement, and then she would avert her gaze as if she had seen something quite different. Her daughter's black eyes must have triggered some dark insecurity in Juliette's soul, for when looking at her daughter, a deep crease would appear between her eyebrows. When the same crease appeared on Edith's brow before she turned twelve years old, the mother was more upset than the daughter.

During those years, she would complain to guests who came to tea, 'Do you see, Madame Levon, Edith has wrinkles already. At her age! I tell her to rub her face with rose oil every night, as a precaution, but she pays no attention.' As if by repeating the complaint continuously, the irritating crease would go away.

Every evening, Monsieur Lamarck would take his dreamy daughter, waiting for him beside the rock pool, in his arms and pet her, calling her his 'miniature'. Edith was really quite small. Her features were perfect, as if carved with a fine blade; her face was like a water droplet. She remained the smallest child in her class until she took a step into adolescence. Her teeth were perfectly aligned, like pomegranate seeds, and there was a gap between the front two, which made her completely adorable and which also, according to Sidika the washerwoman, protected her from the evil eye. That gap was Edith's good fortune. In the evenings, after a tiring day at his chandlery business, a single glance into his little daughter's coal-black eyes and thick lashes was all it took to fill Monsieur Lamarck with joy. Father and daughter would walk arm in arm around the vast garden looking at spiders which had made webs among Grandfather Lamarck's dusty vines. They would speak of the stars rising behind Mount Nif and of the moon painting the violets silver.

Charles Lamarck had countless theories regarding space and time. For example, that the universe might be shaped like a horseshoe. If this were so, if one stood at one end of the horseshoe and took a photograph of the other end, one might see Caesar making love to Cleopatra or Marie Antoinette's milky-white neck hanging from the guillotine. Just as Edith couldn't figure out how the moon could show only one face to the world, she didn't understand the horseshoe, but the possibility of taking photographs of the heroines whose stories she adored appealed to her. Most of all, she loved the way her father decorated his theory of the universe with her favourite historical figures.

Monsieur Lamarck indulged his daughter, spoiling her with wooden music boxes inlaid with mother-of-pearl, emerald-encrusted combs, dolls from Paris with real hair. On her tenth birthday he gave Edith a white pony brought from London, and on her thirteenth a shiny black Arabian thoroughbred. Father and daughter would mount their horses and ride to the district's summer palaces, to Narlikoy and Kokluca, sometimes catching their breath at one of the outdoor cafés. Once they roasted a lamb and distributed the meat to a tribe of nomads who had set up their tents there and to locals who had gathered for a picnic.

With father and daughter being so close, Monsieur Lamarck's sudden death shook no one as much as it shook Edith. On a summer's day so hot that time itself seemed to slow down, the poor fellow's heart just stopped as he was eating his lunch all alone in Kraemer's restaurant. Charles Lamarck breathed his last right there. His head fell into his rare, bloody steak and his salad bowl was overturned by *The Charterhouse of Parma*, which he always carried in his inside pocket and which had been lying open on the table at the time.

In the year following this sudden death, the intimacy between father and daughter – which she had not been pleased about when her husband was alive and well – came to Juliette Lamarck's aid. Edith left school before her final year and was not seen in public for the whole summer. Now she was wandering around, all skin and bone, with a pale face and dark circles under her eyes. She never set foot outside the house. With a skilful twisting of words, Juliette connected all this to a deep depression brought on by the loss of her father.

'Where is Edith? Ah, *ma chérie*, Charles's death affected her greatly. Don't even ask... She had to abandon school because of her health. When the doctor said that the heat here was not good for her, what could I do? I sent her to the thermal baths at Baden-Baden. She was there all summer.

Now she must rest. That is the reason she has not been seen in society. Naturally, this cruel turn of events has shaken us all, but one must return to one's life, must one not? My sons, bless them, immediately took over the work. Dear Anna is expecting another *enfant* – yes, don't even ask! Twins this time! *Mon Dieu!* They've moved into a house like a small castle in Boudja. Did I tell you already? My son-in-law is such a gentleman. British aristocracy, you know. Oh, yes, you have met him. Of course. *Ah, oui.* You asked about Edith, yes… My dear, this little daughter of mine is a bit over-sensitive. And of course she and her father were very attached to each other. There is nothing to be done. I spoke to that famous nerve doctor who resides at the Huck Hotel. He says to leave her alone. He came from Vienna to write his memoirs here. I met him at a reception given by the Thomas-Cooks recently. And do you know what he said…'

Eventually, even Juliette herself came to believe what she was saying. It is possible that she was actually telling these stories in order to convince herself and not her friends. And there was a kernel of truth in there. For sure, Charles had died at exactly the right time. If Juliette had planned it, she couldn't have organized it better. If her husband had lived, he would not have acted with reason; with his soft heart he would have revealed Edith's shame to society and that would have been a disaster. Juliette had saved not only her daughter's name and honour but that of the whole family. She had kept them all from being disgraced. Certainly, Edith would soon recover from her depression and make a successful marriage. As soon as the neighbours' son Edward completed his education in New York, those two should waste no time in becoming engaged.

Let's leave her making such plans.

* * *

One winter's morning, just when Juliette believed she had destiny under her control, out of nowhere a lawyer from Athens arrived carrying a leather briefcase from which he extracted a document and delivered a blow to the precarious balance between mother and daughter, turning it upside down.

Before the Leather Briefcase

Edith was reading the newspaper when her mother entered the dining room in her swirling pearl-coloured dressing gown.

It was one of those rare days in Bournabat when the sun was nowhere to be seen. The sky had darkened and forbidding rumbles could be heard from the hills. The wind was equally angry, taking its fury out on the thin, bare branches of the apricot and sour-cherry trees in front of the window.

In defiance of the storm outside, the Lamarck dining room smelled of toasted bread and wood smoke. Butler Mustafa had lit the yellow enamel stove in the corner after morning prayers and one of the maids had placed a record on the gramophone – a Mendelssohn sonata for violin and piano. Juliette required that music be playing in the house when she woke. She had no patience left for the silence which had been mandated following her husband's death. She had purchased gramophones for each of the downstairs rooms as well as one for her bedroom.

Edith's gaze, lifted from her newspaper, slipped by her mother in the doorway and focused on the oil portrait of her father hanging on the wall. Her father used to say that introverted people were most at peace in wintertime. Just as the shape of a tree became apparent once the leaves, blossom and fruit had fallen, so could the depths of a person's soul be revealed in winter's silence. What a shame that winter was so short in this city whose residents lived their lives outdoors or in front of open windows. She remembered with nostalgia the long, howling, winter nights at the convent school in Paris, when the girls would sit together around the huge fireplace in the library, reading books. The convent school was no more than a dream now. The classmates alongside whom she had sat, all in a row, leaning on their elbows, had graduated last spring. She had not been among them.

Sighing, she again buried her head in the newspaper. It reported that the Comédie Française would be performing in Smyrna. The Consul had spoken in person to Jules Claretie, the director of the world's oldest and greatest theatre company, and had obtained a promise that they would stage a production at the Sporting Club the following year. *La Réforme* newspaper had made this a headline story to emphasize the pre-eminence of French culture among the elite of the city.

'*Bonjour, ma chérie.*' Juliette leaned over to kiss her daughter's right cheek, glanced at the newspaper over her shoulder, and then asked in a vivacious voice, 'Did you sleep well?'

Edith nodded without raising her head. There had been a strong earthquake in the capital of Jamaica. The streets of Kingston were filled with the debris of ruined buildings and people with terrified eyes. She peered intently at the paper so as to see the black and white photographs more clearly.

'Just look at the weather – how dark it has become! It is as if not clouds but threatening armies are approaching. I declare I am in distress this morning.' Juliette took her place at the table and placed a smile upon her face, which looked naked without its make-up. 'Have you seen your brothers or had they already left when you got up? Where are Gertrude and Marie – still sleeping?'

Edith glanced around at the empty chairs and shrugged. She had only now noticed that her sisters-in-law had not come down to breakfast that morning.

Without waiting for an answer, Juliette continued. 'Ah, *bien sûr*, I remember now. They were going into the city today. Gertrude's cousin has arrived from Amsterdam. They were to meet at the Café de Paris. You should have gone with them, my dear Edith. Gertrude and Marie must be considered your sisters now. But isn't the weather horrid. *Krima!* What a shame! Listen to what I propose. After breakfast, let's go up and see the baby together. What do you say? She's begun to smile, did you know that, Auntie Edith? Between you and me, she's looking more and more like your brother. I haven't said as much to Marie, in order not to hurt her feelings, but little Daphne is the picture of her father. She even looks rather like me, I think. After all, your brother greatly resembles me.'

Edith murmured something unintelligible. Juliette reached for the bell which was sitting on the dining room table beside her silver fork. One of the servant girls immediately dashed out of the kitchen with a thermos of coffee and stood beside Juliette. Her white cap had slid to the side a bit, over her right ear. Noticing her mistress's glance, her hand went nervously to her head. After her husband's death, Juliette had ordered that all the servants must wear a uniform. Bringing a tailor from Smyrna, she had had uniforms sewn just like the ones she had seen in a *Good Housekeeping* magazine in the American settlement in Paradiso. The white caps and aprons were to be washed daily, the navy-blue uniforms twice weekly.

Zoe, standing at attention with the thermos of coffee in her hand, prayed that her mistress would not notice the ink stain on her frilly white apron. That morning, she'd gone to light the candles in Monsieur Lamarck's study and had just sat down at his desk to write a brief letter to her sweetheart on the island of Chios when she'd heard laughter in the hallway. It was Gertrude and Marie, preparing to catch the 8 a.m. train into Smyrna. Zoe had jumped up anxiously and the inkwell had spilled into her lap.

At any rate, this morning Juliette was in no state to bother herself with the stain on Zoe's apron. Without the daughters-in-law at the table, the tension between Edith and herself was all too apparent. She felt like a wild animal caught in a snare. Furthermore, the crease between her daughter's eyebrows depressed her. She reached for her coffee cup as if her life depended on it.

'*Merci*, Zoe. You may bring in my breakfast. Edith, have you eaten, dear?'

'I have not eaten, nor will I eat.' Finally, Edith raised her head. 'Zoe, would you please refresh my coffee. Then kindly go into the garden and ask Sidika to roll me two cigarettes. Thin ones, please.'

'Certainly, Mademoiselle Lamarck.'

Juliette, hoping to revive her fading smile, rotated the circular wooden platter in the centre of the table. Jams – sour cherry, rosehip, strawberry – honey and butter revolved in front of Juliette, but there was nothing there that she desired.

'And why not, my dear Edith? Drinking coffee on an empty stomach is not healthy. At least eat a croissant. And where did this cigarette business come from? What would your father say if he saw you lighting a cigarette at the table like a nightclub hostess?'

She waved her silver spoon at the oil portrait hanging over the gramophone. Inside the gold-plated frame, the tiny buttons on Monsieur Lamarck's jacket strained against his considerable belly as if they might burst. He was turned towards Edith, his eyes fixed on the corner where the enamel stove stood.

'But he can't see me, can he? So I'm okay.'

Juliette observed her daughter over the rim of her china coffee cup. In spite of all the nervousness, the coffee drunk on an empty stomach, the cigarettes, even that damned crease between her eyebrows, Edith maintained the freshness of her nineteen years. Something between jealousy and pride stirred inside Juliette. If Edith gained some weight, held herself straighter, rubbed some rouge on her cheeks and went out into society, she could easily land a fortune. Perhaps it was not even necessary to wait until Edward returned from New York. She herself could talk to their neighbour, Helene Thomas-Cook, and the two of them could arrange an engagement between the children. Or had Edward received news of the scandal and was this what was delaying his return? To be sure, the shame had happened right under his nose.

Zoe came into the dining room through the garden door, put the cigarettes right next to Edith's plate as if she were hiding them, and sped out again. Sidika had also sent in a plate of orange-flavoured biscuits. Edith took an ivory cigarette-holder from the pocket of her black dress; she'd worn nothing but black for two years in order to spite her mother, who had opened wide the curtains and windows and filled the house with guests as soon as the obligatory forty-day mourning period had come to an end. Edith inserted the cigarette into the holder, lit it with the gold lighter she had taken from her father's study, and exhaled smoke through her delicate nostrils.

'You could at least smoke American cigarettes, daughter. Must you smoke the tobacco of peasants? Next week, let us go together to Paradiso and buy you some decent cigarettes, since you enjoy the evil stuff. And you have not yet seen Paradiso. You will be amazed at the beautiful city the Americans have created.'

'And where do you think American tobacco comes from, *Maman*?'

Lowering her eyes, Juliette cracked the top of her egg with her silver spoon. She had no idea how to forge a relationship with this rebellious daughter. It was exhausting. Since Edith's childhood, she had tried to love her but somehow had never been able to find favour. She had dressed Edith in Parisian frocks and emerald-studded combs, had taken her to eat pastries at Café Kosti and accompanied her on carriage rides along the quay. Anything Edith desired from the toyshops on Frank Street had been bought without hesitation.

When Juliette's elder daughter, Anna, returned to the Bournabat mansion from her studies in France for the summer holidays and saw silk scarves the like of which had never been purchased for her, and rosy-cheeked dolls piled in a corner of her little sister's room, she threw a tantrum. 'It's so unfair! I had only two dolls and had to wait until Christmas for a third. You tied my hair back with ribbons, not emerald combs. I can't believe you would do this, *Maman*. It's because I'm not as beautiful as Edith, is it not? There's not a scrap of fairness in your heart.'

Anna was right. It hadn't even occurred to Juliette to dress Anna up and take her to the quay to eat cake. She was a stout, heavy-boned girl, with hair like a mouse's. When Juliette had been handed her as a swaddled newborn, she'd taken one look at baby Anna, saw that she resembled a Breton peasant with her red face and potato nose, and began to cry. Meline, then a novice midwife, had found it very moving that a young mother would cry upon holding her first child and left them alone in the room. Whereas Juliette was actually crying because she had agreed to marry a man her father's age and had given birth to a child who looked exactly like him.

She was still very young. With two sons following closely after Anna, each born one year apart, all her energy was used up. When Edith was born seven years after the younger son, Jean-Pierre, Juliette not only had all the time in the world but also an adorable daughter whom she could play with like a doll. However, Juliette never held her, kissed her, inhaled her smell. In spite of her cuteness, Edith was not a cuddled child. 'A child needs compassion as well as love. Without compassion, she becomes ill-tempered,' Charles used to say. Juliette did not understand what he meant. She gave this daughter whatever she wanted, took her with her everywhere. What more should she do?

Mother and daughter sat for a while without speaking. The ticking of the wall clock was irritating. Placing her jam knife on the edge of her plate, Juliette rose to her feet. Feeling Edith's eyes upon her, she walked towards her husband's portrait. Taking Mendelssohn off, she put on 'Nobody', a record she had recently bought in Paradiso. She turned the handle to rotate the turntable. After a few crackling sounds, from the tulip-shaped mouthpiece came Bert Williams' entreating song.

'*Voilà!* A very appropriate piece. Perfect for today, when

life seems full of clouds and rain. What do you say – am I wrong?'

Edith was absorbed in the smoke rising from her cigarette to the chandelier on the ceiling. One day she would board a ship from Smyrna harbour and escape to Marseille. From there she would go to New York – the New World – alone, with a single suitcase and a one-way ticket. One morning, without telling anyone, she would slip out of this house. Then, just like in the song, she would get lost in the crowd and become Nobody. Not a Lamarck, not a Levantine, not a French lady nor a European one. Naked. A person must first become a nobody and after that they could become anything.

Juliette raised her birdlike voice. 'Guess who's coming to afternoon tea.'

When no sound was forthcoming from Edith, Juliette answered her own question joyously, as if each syllable spelled happiness.

'Avinash Pillai.'

Edith continued blowing smoke into the emptiness. Juliette's chin twitched involuntarily. Whenever Edith used to drift off like this as a child, Juliette would want to slap her face. And now that urge was swelling inside her again. She would clasp her hands behind her back and satisfy herself by yelling.

'Snap out of it, young lady! Given the privileged life you lead, you have no right to wear such a sour face. Go to the poor districts of Smyrna and see the babies who have not so much as a piece of cloth to cover their bare bottoms and then tell me if you have anything to sulk about.'

Except for that one time, she had always managed to curb her anger, had never laid a hand on her daughter. That last time though... Oh, Monsieur Lamarck, how he had spoiled this girl. How much shame had she brought! How much! Ah, *Dieu*.

'Yes, *oui*. I have invited Avinash Pillai to dinner this evening. I hope you will join us. You know who he is, of course.'

'Yes, a gemstone merchant.' Edith's alto voice became thicker after smoking.

'Ah, yes, that's what you think!'

She waited in vain to see if her daughter's interest had been piqued, and then, unable to endure the silence that hung in the air like the cigarette smoke, she continued.

'His precious-stone business is just a front. It is true that he has an assistant who shuttles between Smyrna, Alexandria and Bombay, bringing trunks filled with rare gems. What diamonds, emeralds and rubies there are in those trunks! Also therapeutic stones – blue agates, quartz, apatite – which is why sorcerers gather at the dock whenever one of his ships is unloading. The witches begin their bargaining even before the rowboats have thrown over their ropes. There's a lot of trade among the Muslims, and even the Sultan's men know of his fame. I requested that he bring us a few pieces. If you like something, we will buy it. He came to a tea party given by Auntie Rose the other day and we spoke then. A very interesting individual. Can you believe it, he lodges at an inn in the Muslim district. He's been here over a year, but we've only just learned of it – for obvious reasons. Listen to me now; guess what the jewel seller is really occupied with!'

Edith closed her eyes. Was there somewhere in the world where one was not allowed to speak a word until noon? Maybe she should hide herself away in a nunnery. Ha, ha, ha! They had thrown her out of a Catholic high school and now she wanted to shut herself up in a nunnery!

'Edith *mou*, listen. The man is a secret agent! A real-life spy! Do you hear me? And do you know who he works for? The British! I couldn't believe it either at first, but it seems that British spies can come from India. They even choose Indians on purpose, so that they will arouse less suspicion when they mingle with Muslims. This one is actually an Oxford graduate as well. I didn't realize that Oxford even accepted Indians, but it seems they have done so for quite some time. Monsieur Pillai told me this himself. The rest Auntie Rose heard from a reliable source.'

Edith blew out a stream of smoke.

Juliette was buzzing with the pleasure of so much gossip; her cheeks, already shiny with the geranium oil that she applied every morning, had got pinker, and her blue-green eyes were wide. 'So what do you say – an interesting case, no? Wouldn't you like to meet this gentleman tonight?'

'I would not.'

As she watched Edith extinguish her cigarette on her plate, Juliette sighed. She had lost her appetite. She wouldn't even be able to eat the flaky pastry Zoe had placed in front of her.

'Why not, Edith dear? What will you do instead – continue pacing around upstairs like a ghost? Are you aware that your complexion has turned a ghastly white, like an Englishwoman's, because your skin never sees daylight? I honestly don't know what I can tell people any more when they ask about you. It's been a year...'

Edith finally lowered her gaze from the chandelier and turned towards her mother in a fury. Her whole face – her small mouth, retroussé nose, high cheekbones, slanting black eyes and thick lashes – had hardened. 'Why don't you just tell the truth!' she fumed, her voice unexpectedly deep for one with such delicate features.

Juliette clashed her cup into its saucer and exhaled. Her

voice had already assumed the deep tone she used with the servants, and her chin had sharpened.

For no particular reason, Edith felt she had won a victory.

'Look, daughter, my patience can last only so long. I have been careful, I have shown sensitivity, but I get nothing from you. What is the purpose of so much anger? Yes, I know we went through a very difficult time. But...'

Her daughter's eyes blazed.

'One can't die with the dead. One can't question God's will. It's time for you to get yourself together, resume your life. You are not a child. It is to your benefit to show yourself in society. You heard yourself a few days ago that Lucy Gillard has become engaged. At your age, eligible bachelors can disappear in a moment. If we wait too much longer, you'll be left on your own, I swear it. Come, let us see a small smile.'

Juliette pushed back her chair, wiped her mouth with the linen napkin and walked over to Edith. She reached out her hands. Before she could touch her, Edith sprang back like a cat. She knew what would happen next. When she used to pout as a child, her mother would pinch her cheeks and tighten them, forcing her to smile. She deftly grabbed the second cigarette that Sidika had rolled, her ivory holder and the gold lighter, crossed to the other side of the table and hurried out into the hall. The biscuits remained on the dining room table.

Just as she reached the stairway, the front doorbell rang. Halfway up, she waited, listening.

At the door, a foreigner was asking, 'Is Mademoiselle Edith Sofia Lamarck available? It is necessary that I speak with her on an extremely important matter.'

Katina's Dream

Grocer Akis took one last sip of his coffee. His waterpipe had gone out. The coffeehouse apprentice appeared beside him, holding tongs to stir up the coals.

'Not necessary. I'm going.'

Everyone in the coffeehouse objected as he stood up.

'Hey, stay for one more game, *vre* Akis! Your shop won't run away. God's share is three. You'll see – maybe this time around your luck will change.'

Akis looked at the open backgammon board beside the cup holding the black dregs of his coffee. He had just lost two rounds. Rubbing his black beard, he stuck his head out the door and glanced in the direction of the British Hospital. Except for the halva seller passing with his tray, there was no one in sight. He turned back to the coffeehouse. It was buzzing inside and smelled of burned coffee, apple peelings and feet.

'*Endaksi*. All right. One more round. Just one, then I have a lot of work to get on with.'

'*Malista*, Akis *mou*. Sure. We all have work to do. Let's play this round and then we'll all leave together.'

The men sitting idly and drowsily in the coffeehouse

were relieved that Akis was staying. His neighbour, Hristo, called to the apprentice. 'Pavli, my boy, run and refresh Kyr Prodromakis's waterpipe and his coffee.'

Akis gave his hand that was holding the dice a kiss. '*Ade*. Good luck.'

When Katina appeared in the square with the baby on her back half an hour later, Akis had won the third round and begun the fourth. He didn't notice his wife under the arbour knocking on the steamed-up window. Katina's headscarf had slipped down around her neck, her damp red hair was sticking to her head, and her cheeks and nose were red with cold. On the other side of the steamed-up window, the men were rolling dice as if they had forgotten the world outside. At the risk of waking her baby, Katina took the ring off her finger and tapped the glass.

Pavli left the coffee on the coals and came out to the arbour. '*Kalimera*, Kyra Katina. How are you?'

Katina gave no answer. Pavli hastened inside.

'Kyr Prodromakis, Auntie Katina is outside.'

This time no one said a word when Akis got to his feet. It was ten thirty. Clearly the rain was not going to stop. Three labourers who were laying cobbles on Menekse Street left the coffeehouse with Akis. Akis, a former wrestler, led the way. Katina, small enough to fit in his pocket, walked beside him with the baby on her back. Behind them were the three seasonal workers from Chios with pickaxes on their backs.

They passed through their small neighbourhood square. Because of the delicious smell of bread that always wafted out of the bakery on the corner, it was known as Psomalani, Bread-Baker's Square. As soon as the weather warmed up, residents would take over the square with their children, their chairs and their divans. It had a young sycamore tree with a fountain under it and a neighbourhood police station, and it was encircled by a low wall alongside which the girls would play skipping ropes and eat sunflower seeds.

That morning the square was deserted because of the rain. The wet cobbles which had been laid the previous week shone like mirrors under their feet and the side streets were rivers of mud. To get into their houses, people had to first jump over ditches that were streaming with water. The sleeping baby on Katina's back didn't make a sound.

Akis's grocery shop was on Menekse Street, which opened onto the square. It was the bottom floor of a two-storey stone building with a narrow roof. The top floor was their home. In the back was a storage room, a small stony area for the water pump, and a courtyard where Katina hung their clothes to dry.

Searching under his sash for his key, Akis asked, 'Did you take the boys to school?'

'A long while ago.'

'So what have you been doing until now?'

'What should I have been doing? I went to Fasoula to the market, bought some meat to make *yahni* for dinner. Oh, and I've run out of saffron at home, so put some aside for me – I'll lower the basket down for it. I'll add some to the pilaf this evening. Then I stopped by Kyr Yakoumi's. He gave me some lavender oil. It seems that if I rub some on the soles of your daughter's feet, it will help her sleep. He sent some frankincense oil for the boys, for concentration. From there I walked to Berberian's Bakery. The only way I can get this girl to sleep is to keep walking. I have to tie her on my back like the peasant women do and walk around.'

Akis looked at the baby. She was in a deep sleep, her

white-capped head resting on his wife's shoulder, her nose and cheeks red and her mouth open. All of a sudden he wanted the evening to come quickly so that he could take his daughter in his arms.

'Go on home quickly now. Don't let her catch cold. Why ever did you take her out in this storm?'

'What else could I have done – leave her at the coffeehouse? She was making a huge fuss at home, but then she fell asleep before I'd even got as far as the French Hospital. Mrs Hayguhi sent you a pastry, by the way. I'll bring it to you with your coffee. Or do you want to eat it with *subye*?'

Akis shook his head as he raised the shop's shutters. 'Bring the coffee. No *subye* seller will come by in this rain.'

Katina pushed open the blue wooden door next to the shop entrance and went in. Taking care not to make squeaking noises on the stairs, she tiptoed up to their home. At the top step she took off her shoes and shoved them towards the wall. The woodstove in the centre of the room had gone out, but the house was still warm and smelled of the clean white laundry she had ironed early that morning. As she was taking off her headscarf, she looked in the mirror behind the icon at the baby on her back. Still sleeping. She could sleep until lunch was ready.

While Katina was lowering the baby into the cradle in front of the bay window, the little girl opened and closed her red lips. Katina's heart filled anew with love and awe. Every time she looked at the baby, she was overcome by the feeling that she was witnessing a miracle. She covered her with a blanket, then touched the half-moon fingernails of each of her daughter's slender white fingers one by one. Before going to the kitchen, she made the sign of the cross three times over the cradle.

'Lord Jesus, Holy Mary, protect Panagiota from the evil eye, from accidents and from disasters. Amen.'

She hadn't told Akis, but this morning after she'd dropped the boys at school, before going to the market, she had stopped by the Church of Agia Ekaterini. She still couldn't believe her daughter was alive and well. For a whole year now, she'd been going to the church to give thanks to Agia Ekaterini, who had touched Panagiota with her holy hand and was thus her daughter's protector, and to the Holy Mother Mary. Immediately after the birth, she had sold the bracelets from her trousseau to make a votive offering. Akis didn't believe that Panagiota's birth was a miracle, a blessing from the Holy Mother. He had only grumbled about the offering, but if he knew that Katina went to the Church of Agia Ekaterini every morning to make a donation, he would raise the roof. It was best to keep these visits secret from her unbelieving husband.

Katina had thought that both she and Panagiota had died during the birth. 'Thought' is not the correct word; she was sure of it. As blood coursed down between her legs like a red river, she had risen into the sky like a feather. Down below, on the floor of the bedroom, women were holding her legs and with one voice shouting, as if reciting a prayer they didn't believe in, 'Push, Katina. Persevere. Push. *Ela*, come on, Katina *mou*. Just a little more.' The baby was struggling with all its might. Katina was pushing, the women were holding her legs tightly, forcing them down. The baby's head was not visible.

The young midwife Marika had fallen to her knees in the middle of the red river, her face dark with fear and hopelessness. She'd been there for forty-eight hours. Checking the cervix with her hand, she murmured, 'The cursed thing is sealed as tight as the Sultan's treasury.'

They should have gone to the hospital right away. The head

midwife Meline would have known what to do, but as luck would have it she had been called outside the city to attend a birth at a rich person's house and had still not returned. One of the assistants had run to the Turkish district to fetch Old Aybatan. Taking no notice of its being midnight, the elderly woman immediately got up from her bed, prepared her bag, threw a shawl over her head and shoulders and rushed to Akis and Katina's home on Menekse Street. Katina was able to endure the second twenty-four hours with the help of the herbs that Old Aybatan dipped in alcohol and dribbled down her throat, drop by drop.

From where she was perched once she had left her blood-soaked body and floated up like a feather after forty-eight hours, she saw Old Aybatan whisper something in the midwife's ear. She couldn't hear her, but she knew what she was saying. 'You can't save the baby now; save the mother.' The baby had died. Katina wanted to speak, but, as in a nightmare, when she opened her mouth, no sounds came out. She wanted to say, 'Let me die.' Like people who freeze to death, she wanted to surrender herself to the hereafter as to a sweet slumber. A shining white tunnel appeared before her. It arched like a rainbow across the sky and at the other end her little daughter was waving to her. The little girl looked exactly like her mother, and this made Katina very happy. Her sons took after Akis's family – dark, strong, heavy-boned boys – but her daughter was tiny, with red hair and freckles, just like her mother. Katina took a step towards her, into the brightly lit tunnel.

Down below, around the body she had abandoned, something was happening. From far, far away, she heard Midwife Marika say something in her ear. 'Stay with us, Kyra Katina. We're taking you to the hospital.' They shouldn't have bothered. What a wonderful freedom it was to be without a body! Everything seemed to be made of light. Katina touched the wall of the tunnel. She was progressing step by step towards its end. The light of the wall poured from her fingers like phosphorescence. Even her new body was composed of light, like everything else. Her hands, her arms, her whole body became one with all she touched. Katina was light; the tunnel itself, the daughter waiting for her at the other end, everything was light, everything was connected. No one was separate from anyone else. Separation was just an illusion. Ah, how could she have lived so many years without knowing this simple truth. What a shame! Watching with awe as her hands, her arms, her body turned into light, she continued her journey.

There was no doubt that she was going to heaven.

All her life she had tried to be a good Christian. As well as going to church every Sunday, she had also gone without fail on saints' days and holy feast days. Whenever her prayers had been answered, she had always given the offering she had promised. Before Christmas, Easter and Holy Mother Mary day she had fasted for forty days, said her prayers without missing a single one. She was certain that Mother Mary was waiting for her and her little daughter at the end of the tunnel.

She wanted to say, 'Don't take me to the hospital,' but couldn't find the breath to speak.

From the sky she looked down. The dark red river between her legs had consumed the whole world. Suddenly her heart tightened. Was that her blood? Katina was walking in the light of the tunnel, but down below people were screaming, roofs were collapsing, and the screeching of birds with their wings on fire mixed with the shrieking of humans. This was a nightmare. Flames were swallowing life in every corner.

That had to be hell. It was even worse than its description in the Holy Book. 'Mother Mary, Panagia *mou*, keep my sons safe from the devil's tricks, forgive their faults and their sins. Keep them from the nightmare I see below. Open the doors of heaven for them.' With this prayer in her heart, she lost consciousness.

A long while passed. When she opened her eyes, a divine light in gold, blue and green was playing on the wall. Dust motes dancing in the air above her bed had taken on the same colours. A cool salty breeze carried the scent of magnolia blossoms through the window into the whitewashed, high-ceilinged room. So this was heaven. Gazing with half-opened eyes at the fig leaves rustling in front of the window, Katina remembered what her mother had said about magnolia blossoms. 'When you put the flower in a vase, you must suffocate it a bit with a piece of thread. Otherwise the perfume will suffocate you.'

At the memory of her mother, the little freckle-faced girl Katina had left at the end of the tunnel came into her head. Her hands instinctively went to her stomach. She had returned to her earthly body. She could hear the murmurings of patients on the other side of the curtain. She was not in heaven but still on earth. Sorrow spread through her like the liquor Old Aybatan had dribbled down her throat. Her stomach was deflated; her womb ached subtly. She felt very lonely without the being who had lived inside her for nine months.

Turning from the window, she closed her eyes and let her sorrow flow onto the pillow. The emptiness of her stomach was like a fist striking her from the inside. The little red-haired, freckle-faced girl at the end of the tunnel appeared again. She was waving to her mother. Then, smiling, as if to remind her that all was light, she disappeared into the white eternity.

'Panagia *mou*, Mother Mary, put me back in that tunnel. Take this body from me. Let me be with my daughter.'

It seemed that God and his angels had other plans concerning Katina's death, for no answer came from any of them. Instead, the curtain opened and a European nurse in a pink uniform appeared beside her bed. She was carrying a baby wrapped in a yellow blanket. She was a tall, smiling-faced woman. Her blonde hair was gathered in a tight bun and her round white face shone like an August moon. She spoke Greek with a cute accent. 'Good morning, Kyra Katina,' she said. 'I am Nurse Liz. Are you ready to meet your daughter?'

Katina looked with shock at the nurse and at the yellow blanket which was being handed to her. The baby had a full head of hair. Her face was bright red, her eyes shut tight. As Nurse Liz placed the baby in Katina's arms, her tiny mouth opened and she began to cry at the top of her voice.

'Your daughter is very hungry,' said the nurse with a smile as she settled the baby in Katina's arms. 'The hospital's wet nurse fed her while you were unconscious. Seeing that you had woken up, I grabbed her immediately and brought her to you.'

As if under a spell, Katina looked at the red-faced infant in her arms. Not a sound was heard in the room.

'You had a difficult night. You were unconscious when Marika brought you here. Thank the good Lord, our head midwife Meline came to the rescue like a godsend. The angels must be protecting you and this little one. I don't know how Meline got the news of your situation in the pitch dark of night, especially as she'd gone to attend a birth outside the city. As soon as she arrived here, she shut herself up with

41

you in the delivery room. She didn't want any of us around and she delivered your baby all by herself. While we were upstairs, she even washed and swaddled it as well. What a marvellous midwife she is – she can even revive dead babies.'

Exhausted, Katina nodded. While the nurse was speaking, the baby had found her mother's nipple and had begun to suck with her tiny mouth. Nurse Liz's face lit up. 'Just look at that! It's as if she learned to suck in the womb. She knows exactly what to do.'

It was only after the nurse had left her alone to go and see to some other patients that Katina could touch the baby's lips, her black hair, the soft little ears that seemed they might melt in her fingers. It was unbelievable. Her daughter – mouth, nose, bones and flesh – was lying in her arms. It was a miracle! So this was the reason Mother Mary, Almighty God and the angels had not taken Katina's soul. A miracle! Mother Mary had touched this infant with her holy hand. With wet eyes, Katina made the sign of the cross and whispered in her baby's ear. '*Na ziseis, moro mou.* Live a long life, my child.'

With the baby at her breast, half crying, half laughing and continuously giving thanks to the Blessed Mary, Katina erased from her memory the sight of the little daughter waving farewell to her at the end of the white tunnel as she hovered between life and death.

The Leather Briefcase

'Is Mademoiselle Edith Sofia Lamarck available? It is necessary that I speak with her on an extremely important matter.'

The foreigner who stood with his hat in his hands at the entrance to the Lamarck residence looked more like a vulgar provincial than a lawyer. Butler Mustafa, who had opened the door, took him for a soap salesman from Aydin. In spite of the cold and the rain, the man was wearing an oversized cream-coloured frock coat. Although his reddish-brown moustache was trimmed short and his shiny, pomaded hair had been carefully combed back, there was still something unrefined about him. Perhaps this was because he was leaning slightly to one side, upon a silver cane, or perhaps it was because the legs of his trousers, purposely cut long to compensate for his short stature, fell over the heels of his pointy-toed shoes.

Edith walked back down the stairs. It didn't escape the butler's eyes that the uninvited guest seemed startled at the sight of her. But the man quickly recovered, and, holding his hat behind him, bowed low to the ground, saying in strongly accented French, '*Mademoiselle*, may I introduce myself. My name is Dimitrios Mitakakis. Do I have the honour of speaking to Lady Edith Lamarck herself?'

'Yes, I am she. How can I help you?'

The man observed Edith's flat bosom, thin body and pale face and pulled at his moustache. Her unruly hair was gathered into a bun and she looked as if she'd only just got out of bed. The only sign that she was a mature woman was her deep, self-confident voice.

'*Enchanté, mademoiselle*. I have come from Athens to meet with you. I am an attorney.'

Edith extended her hand to be kissed. Just as she was about to welcome her visitor into the reception room, the double-door of the dining room opened and Juliette dashed out in her pink dressing gown. Seeing a stranger standing in the hall, she made a show of closing the top of her gown and tying the sash.

'Yes?'

Unbuttoning his frock coat, Mitakakis again repeated his name and introduction.

'Ah, no doubt you are seeking my sons. They left for the city on the eight o'clock train. You have come to Bournabat in vain. Do you know the location of our business in Smyrna? It's on the quay.'

'That will not be necessary, *madame*. I have come to meet with Mademoiselle Lamarck.'

Juliette untied and retied her dressing gown nervously, glancing from her daughter to the lawyer and back again. Her left hand rose instinctively to her neck and her blue-green eyes widened. After a short silence, she said, 'But what dealings could you have with us? Following my late husband's sudden death, the business was turned over to my sons. Monsieur

Lamarck had a heart attack and left us two years ago. Surely you have heard about that.'

'Yes, forgive me. Of course, I am aware of that. Please accept my belated condolences on your loss, Madame Lamarck.'

When nothing further was said for some time, Juliette drew in a long breath. The attorney was perhaps reluctant to speak in front of the servant.

'Fine. Let us proceed to the library in that case. There we can speak comfortably. I will be happy to assist you in any way I can. Mustafa, ask the kitchen to prepare coffee, *se parakalo*. Monsieur Mitakakis, would you prefer Turkish coffee or, as they say here, "European" coffee?'

Her nervous laughter reverberated through the emptiness of the high-ceilinged hall. Edith remained standing there, stubborn and frowning. The lawyer continued leaning on his cane, grinding the black and white stars of the hall floor with the pointed toes of his shoes. Finally, without lifting his eyes from the floor, he murmured, 'I have come to speak privately with Mademoiselle Edith on a certain matter.'

'And what is that matter?'

As her anxiety intensified, Juliette's voice became more strident. The lawyer raised his head and perused the faces of the two women standing opposite him. They put him in mind of the symbolic masks used in the plays of the Ancient Greeks. The mother's face, stretched into a tight smile, was like a mask for a comedy; the daughter's face, with its downturned mouth, was for a tragedy. Yet there was something familiar in her frown.

'Unfortunately, it is by law not permissible for me to share this information with you, Madame Lamarck.'

'But...' A red flush began rising up Juliette's throat and face.

45

Sensing that her mother was becoming agitated, Edith took a step forward. 'Please come this way, Monsieur Mitakakis. We will go into the library.'

After he had handed his hat and jacket to Butler Mustafa, the lawyer from Athens, leaning on his cane, followed Edith to the library, which lay to the right of the spacious hall. If Juliette had intended to follow them and press her ear against the door, the eyes of the butler upon her convinced her to go to her room and get dressed. What kind of business could a lawyer, especially a lawyer from Athens, have with Edith? Could the girl have become involved in some matter her mother was unaware of and got herself into another calamitous situation? After all the scandal and humiliation, would she now have to go through all that again?

Upon entering her bedroom, Juliette grabbed the bell on her mirrored dressing table lined with bottles of cologne and rang it furiously. Then she sank onto the satin-covered stool in front of the dressing table and waited for her maid. She turned her back to the mirror, not wishing to look at herself so early in the morning. It was as if her reflection in the silver-framed glass might tell her the most terrible things. Standing up, she put a record onto the gramophone and absentmindedly turned the handle. In the back of her mind she knew very well the connection between Edith and Athens, but she prevented her thoughts from going there. It was a very old matter, a matter that had long been closed. She had ensured that her daughter was raised in a peaceful environment. And who would dare make such a claim after all these years?

Turning her face from the window, she was startled to see that her bed had not been made. The imprint of her head on the feather pillow looked like a volcanic crater. She reached for the bell on her dressing table and rang it for a second time, even louder and more violently. Anger helped, masking her swiftly rising fear for a time. She touched the large green and blue enamel stove in the centre of the room. Tepid! Have pity! In a fury, she left the room and stood at the top of the stairs. As the shrill ringing of the bell reverberated around the empty stairwell, there came the sound of two pairs of running feet. Her personal maid Irini and the housemaid Zoe both appeared on the bottom step at the same moment. Since they had run from two different directions, they almost crashed into each other.

'How many times must I tell you that it is forbidden to run in this house?'

The women bowed their lace-capped heads.

'What is going on, may I ask? I have been ringing for you, Irini, for one hour. In which part of hell were you?'

'*Signomi*, forgive me, *Madame*. I was collecting laundry from Sidika. I was over at her shack.'

'And why has my bed not been made? Zoe? The stove has gone out. Why are all these shameful things happening today? Did you change your apron?'

The sight of the servants obediently walking up the stairs with bowed heads soothed Juliette somewhat, but as soon as she entered her room, the question of why that poor excuse for a lawyer downstairs wanted to see Edith came back with a vengeance, just as an agonizing toothache will return even after oil of cloves has afforded a brief respite. Her anger swelling, she turned to Zoe.

'Change the sheets as well!'

'We changed them two days ago, Madame Lamarck.'

'Are you questioning me, Zoe? If I say change them, you will change them. I can no longer smell the mastic on them. Tell Sidika not to iron my laundry again without washing those hands of hers that stink of cigarettes and to add more lavender to the wash water. I only tolerate her because she is Mustafa's wife – one cannot even understand what she says.'

'As you request, *Madame*.'

Scratching her cheek, Juliette walked towards the window. In the garden below, Mustafa was talking to the gardener in front of the arbour. Suspicions grew within her: what were they talking about? The rain was coming down heavily. She watched the bare boughs of the sour-cherry tree being battered by the wind for a while. No, she was worrying over nothing. She must think other thoughts. For example, about this evening's tea party. Who would attend, she wondered. Had fewer guests come to her most recent tea parties? Of course not. Obviously, it was simply a coincidence. What a day for such a downpour! Hopefully, the Indian spy would keep his word and come that evening; she would ensure he stayed for dinner too. He would definitely attract the ladies' attention. Edith had acted like such a mule at breakfast – the slovenly girl hadn't even shown any interest in the spy, whereas when she was a child, she used to go around saying, 'When I grow up, I want to be a spy.'

Ah, when Edith was a child…

She turned to Zoe, who was making up the bed. 'Light the stove too. You're going to make me ill. Have you been smoking opium or what? Both of you have your heads in the clouds.'

The women continued working silently.

'Irini, come and help me with this corset. Don't dawdle. It's noon and I am not yet dressed. Did you bring my beige dress? No, not that one! My goodness, Irini, do you think I'm going to be playing golf? The plaid one with the blue sash at the waist. I will wear that for now. Before evening tea, you will prepare the blue-green silk. I swear, you have already worn me out.'

In the library downstairs, the aroma of Monsieur Lamarck's pipe tobacco lingered still. Dimitrios Mitakakis stretched his plump, hairy hand towards the fireplace as he watched the blue-tipped flames consume the logs. The room had a convivial atmosphere, which gave a person confidence. With the fire crackling, one could even forget the wind beating at the windows. The carved walnut desk in the back corner still seemed to be in use, with papers and inkstands upon it. Volumes of French, English and American literature bound in red, burgundy and black lined the glass-fronted bookcase that extended the entire length of one wall. Some of the books had yellowed writing along their spines; others had titles inlaid in gilt so shiny that they could be read from a distance.

As soon as Edith had tugged the tasselled bell-pull that connected the library and the indicator board in the kitchen she collapsed into the brown leather armchair in front of the fire, without waiting for her guest to seat himself first. She was biting her lower lip, which was now flaky as a result. The leather briefcase lay open on the side table between the two brown armchairs. It was full of documents and she stared at the Greek letters on the top one, trying to decipher what this important matter that concerned her could be. She longed for another cigarette but could not find the second one Sidika had rolled for her in her pocket.

They didn't speak until the servant who had brought in the coffee on a silver tray had left the room. Dimitrios Mitakakis had sat down on the other leather armchair. With a gracefulness unexpected from such a short, stout body, he turned towards Edith.

'Mademoiselle Lamarck, I shall speak briefly and openly. I anticipate that what I am about to say will cause you considerable shock.'

He busied himself looking through the green cardboard folders in the briefcase on his lap. The girl, her head tilted slightly towards her shoulder, was waiting calmly but expectantly for him to continue. Her face was drained of colour, her eyes dark. How different this pale-faced child was from the spoiled, self-centred, rich girl he had imagined on his journey from Athens to Smyrna. Perhaps his business would proceed more easily than he had feared. It was good that the mother had been left outside. The girl had a frowning face, but there was something soothing in her silence. She wasn't making small talk just to fill the silence. He took a sip of his coffee and cleared his throat.

'I have brought you news of an inheritance.'

Edith knitted her thick eyebrows.

'If you accept the will of my late client, a considerable fortune as well as a house, Number 7, Vasili Street, will come into your possession.'

The lawyer waited to see what effect his words would have. A deep crease appeared between the girl's eyebrows. When she offered no response, he felt obliged to add, 'Of course, you may refuse the inheritance.'

Setting her coffee cup on the side table, Edith leaned towards the man. 'Where on earth is Vasili Street?'

The lawyer was relieved that the young woman had switched from French to Greek.

'In Smyrna. Very near Punta Station, the Aydin Railway terminus. The people there call that neighbourhood "the

English houses". I presume you are familiar with Aliotti Boulevard? Yes, *vevea*, of course. Vasili Street is one of the roads that crosses it. Mostly British, Italians and wealthy Greek families reside in this neighbourhood.'

Upon arriving in Smyrna the day before, his first business had been to locate the house and ascertain its condition. The railway passed very close to the property, and the neighbourhood seemed to be filled more with bachelor British engineers than with families. The house, which had been locked up for years, was in a dilapidated state, as was the garden, but now was not the time to mention this.

'I do not understand. After my father's death, all of his assets were shared out. No one mentioned such a house to me. There must be a mistake. I have an older sister, Anna Margaret, whose husband is in Smyrna. He owns a considerable number of properties in Bournabat and Boudja. His name is Philippe Cantebury. Is it possible that it is he whom you are seeking?'

Dimitrios Mitakakis took a cigarette from a silver case hidden in his waistcoat pocket. During his client's final days, as the man suffered through the grip of pneumonia, he had attempted to prepare the lawyer for this meeting with the girl, but Mitakakis had always closed down the subject, not wanting to tire the poor man on his sickbed and also wishing to demonstrate his skill as a lawyer. Now, sitting opposite Edith's frowning face in the Lamarcks' tobacco-scented library, he was squirming, not knowing how to tell her the truth.

'May I also have a cigarette?'

'Ah, certainly. Excuse me, I should have offered you one earlier. I did not consider. Please take one. You look so young.'

So it seemed the women of Smyrna smoked cigarettes in the company of strange men.

Edith waved his remarks aside with her hand, inserted the cigarette into the ivory holder she took from her pocket, and, not waiting for the lawyer, lit it with her father's lighter.

'Mademoiselle Lamarck, this is a rather complex matter. I wish that you could have received the knowledge from someone other than myself – from your mother perhaps.'

'Shall I call my mother?' The furrow between the girl's eyebrows deepened.

'Oh, no, no. That is not necessary.'

After handing the green cardboard folder to Edith, the lawyer rose to his feet. With one hand in his pocket, he limped to the window and gazed out at the gardener chatting with the Turkish butler in front of the arbour.

'This document?'

Dimitrios Mitakakis turned round. Throwing his cigarette into the fireplace, he stood across from Edith, clasped his hands in front of him, bowed his head, and spoke.

'It is thus, Mademoiselle Lamarck. My client, the late Nikolas Dimos, that is, the individual who has bequeathed this property to you, himself... How can I express it? It is his assertion... It was his assertion... We lost Monsieur Dimos very recently, may he rest in peace. Ahem. To tell the truth, little lady, "assertion" is a mild word for this claim. To say that my late client was quite positive on this point would be more accurate. And now that I see with my own eyes, I am without a doubt convinced that my client was correct.'

The girl's eyes had grown large and her chewed fingernails were buried in the leather of the armchair like claws. Taking a deep breath, the lawyer raised his head.

'Mademoiselle Lamarck, I have come here to inform you that your true father was my late client, Nikolas Dimos.'

Tilkilik Days

Avinash woke at dawn. The call to prayer was sounding from the Mumyakmaz Mosque next to the Menzilhane Inn where he was lodging. He had slept well, in spite of the dogs howling in chorus throughout the Tilkilik neighbourhood. He lay on his straw mattress with his eyes closed, listening to the sweet, sad call of the muezzin echoing through the emptiness of the morning.

He sometimes met the muezzin, Nuri, on his way to and from the market. He was a youthful, good-natured man with a thin, pale face. From their chats, Avinash learned that Nuri went regularly to the Sufi Dervish lodge, and one evening Avinash went too, as a guest, to attend a session of spiritual music-making. There he discovered that Nuri was a talented flute player. When the young muezzin blew into his reed pipe, the sounds he produced seemed to hold all the mysteries of the world. Listening to him, Avinash's eyes filled with tears. He remembered his grandfather's words: 'Music forges the purest connection between man and God.' *Raki* was also drunk at the lodge's musical gatherings. His superior at the Secret Service, Maximilian Lloyd, found this the most surprising detail and noted that Avinash's infiltration of the

Muslim cult was a great achievement. Avinash preferred to remember the night not as a professional success but as a divine experience that satiated his love for music and for God.

When the call to prayer came to an end, he rose and shoved the straw mattress against the wall. With the mattress out of the way, the room was as bare as it had been on the day he arrived. A year had passed since he'd come to live like a monk in this empty room at the Menzilhane Inn.

On the evening of his arrival in Smyrna, as soon as he debarked from the ship, Selim, who had been hired to do the footwork by his servant Ravi, had found this inn. He was a resourceful boy. Avinash had warmed to him when they first met at the harbour. The son of a refugee from Crete, he very conveniently spoke both Turkish and Greek. When asked, he would say he was eighteen years old and would soon do his military service and become engaged to his sweetheart Zeyno, who lived over by the Hatuniye Mosque. However, Avinash did not believe he had completed his fifteenth year.

While Ravi was supervising the trunks, which were able to pass through customs with ease thanks to the British Consulate having bribed the official, the boy was explaining the business of Smyrna port to Avinash. The wide shore road was full of offices, agents and warehouses, and a little further on there were European-style shops and hotels. A gentleman like Avinash would surely like to stay in one of those hotels.

While he was talking, Avinash lost himself in observing the carts, the tables, the peddlers with their baskets, the bags spilling out into the middle of the street, the leather packages, the barrels, the crates, the bales of wool, the camels waiting calmly amid stacks of logs and iron, and the porters wearing colourful waistcoats, short, baggy trousers, and fezzes on their heads. Smyrna harbour was a vast organism made up of people of every colour and race, every kind of living, breathing being and all manner of material things. Ferries were sounding their horns, dogs were barking and anchors were clanging. Oarsmen's shouts mixed with curses from the harbour porters. And then a horse-drawn tram entered the fray! The conductor tried to clear a way through by ringing the bell hanging from the ceiling as the horses stood there shaking their heads in disapproval at the piles of stuff blocking their road.

After they had locked up the trunks that had been loaded onto a single-horse cart ready to be taken to an office building at Yemiscizade Bazaar reserved in Avinash's name, they followed Selim on foot. He led them to a tranquil place, a travellers' inn set around a rectangular courtyard shaded by fig and lemon trees. The boy had quite strongly resisted bringing them there. He had tried to settle Avinash in one of the European hotels at the quay or in one of the converted office buildings at the Kemeralti Bazaar. Failing those, he suggested trying the grand old mansions between Tilkilik and Basmane that now served as hotels. It was possible that Selim received commissions from these establishments. When Avinash insisted on a traditional inn in central Tilkilik, a now sulking Selim led him to the Menzilhane Inn, at the top of Kecheciler Street.

This was exactly the sort of place Avinash had dreamed of. The great confusions of the narrow streets jostling with carts did not intrude here. Peace descended on you as soon as you stepped into the courtyard of the inn, effacing the world outside. The only sounds were the cooing of pigeons and the plash of a fountain. Unlike the buildings in the bazaar, this inn was designed to accommodate travellers. There were just three or four shops at the front, facing the street, and the rooms arranged around the courtyard were sparsely appointed but meticulously clean.

The Menzilhane Inn reminded Avinash of the time he had spent in Rishikesh with his grandfather. The monastery where his grandfather had stayed had had a cool, shady courtyard like this one. Even the vine-wreathed arbours were the same. The monastery was located on the banks of the blue-green River Ganges in the foothills of the Himalayas beneath peaks that were perpetually snow-capped. It had been built for old men who wished to spend the last years of their lives in meditation and prayer, and Avinash had spent the year before university there, with his grandfather.

Having risen from his simple bed, Avinash went out to the courtyard, rinsed his face in the ice-cold water of the fountain, splashed his neck and armpits, and washed his teeth with bicarbonate of soda. In the muggy pools of the neighbouring gardens frogs had long since awakened and begun to croak. Grey clouds, having drawn their loads from the sea, were scudding towards the mountains, bathing the city in an unusual leaden light.

Although this was Avinash's second winter in Smyrna it was the first time he had experienced such cold, grey weather. He was pleased with the change. He enjoyed spending time inside on dark days. He remembered his small room at Oxford. From the kitchen of the accommodation where overseas students like himself stayed there used to rise aromas that his time in England had made him forget – pickled cabbage, garlicky yogurt, salted fish, curried vegetables. These smells wafted into the corridors, the bedrooms, the living rooms, the souls of the people.

He returned to his room, took off his boots and placed them beside the door opening onto the courtyard. From the

Konak neighbourhood came the screams of seagulls diving over the fishing boats. A ship was blowing its horn. In one of the nearby rooms someone was cursing someone else – a lazybones who wanted to sleep. Pulling the curtains, he took a deep breath and began his morning exercises in the empty space left by the mattress. His attention, which had been diverted by noises and thoughts, began to settle. His soul filled with breath and contentment.

When he left the inn a half-hour later, his mind, like his breathing, was calm; the morning's distractions had passed. With his five senses, he drew in the world like a sponge. The young man was alert to every sensory impression; he felt things keenly and lived as if each moment were a delicious titbit to be chewed slowly in order to extract its true taste. The wind had picked up. He decided to go down to the docks after his coffee and watch the waves pounding the shore before beginning his duties in the bazaar.

Avinash's primary work in those years was to stroll around the Muslim neighbourhoods and gather information. His day passed wandering through the businesses, baths and bazaars which the Secret Service had identified, following suspicious individuals. His commander mostly wanted information on people with connections to the Young Turks organization in Salonica and Paris, but one ear had to be tuned to the French, who were trying to grab business contracts from British firms and for this reason were playing all kinds of tricks, sending ambassadors and couriers to charm the Sultan with their ostentatious accents. Thus, in the evenings it was necessary that he mingle with Smyrna's Levantines.

At the entrance to the Yemiscizade Bazaar there was an Albanian *sahlep* seller. Avinash drank a cup of the hot, milky, cinnamon-flavoured drink as he stood there and felt warm inside. After filling the cup, Kerim, the *sahlep* seller, squatted down beside his jug and, taking a pinch of tobacco from his pocket, began to roll a cigarette. Kerim was a taciturn man; his face was sharp and hard, his lips always puckered and sulky, as if an unpleasant thought had just come to him. In the mornings one couldn't get a word out of him; not even pliers would have done it. Though Avinash drank *sahlep* every day throughout the winter, he'd not been able to find out anything about the man except that he was from Albania. He appeared to have nothing to do with politics, but one had to be particularly careful about such seemingly indifferent types. He could be an informer for Sultan Hamid, or for the Committee of Union and Progress, or a militant supporter of Greek independence.

Next to the jug was a covered basket containing Damascus doughnuts. While handing back the cup, Avinash took one. The doughnuts were as big as his palm, and he'd been addicted to them since the day he'd eaten his first one. When the *sahlep* seller's cart disappeared in summer, it was mostly the lack of Damascus doughnuts that bothered Avinash. Munching on the doughnut, he headed down the bazaar's long, dark passageway and out into its spacious courtyard. Two workers in leather boots pulled up to their knees entered the courtyard from the Carsi Mescidi side at the same moment as Avinash. They were arguing about something in low voices, but when they saw the Indian man, they stopped talking. A sleepy young fellow with drooping eyelids – the Armenian jeweller's apprentice – was sweeping in front of the workshop.

Under the arbour of the coffeehouse on the Street of the Goldsmiths side of the courtyard, several early risers like himself were seated on stools with their waterpipes already bubbling. Passing by them, Avinash placed his right hand over his heart in greeting. The men responded with only a nod of their turbaned or fez-covered heads. Avinash was aware that his presence in this neighbourhood created confusion. The coffeehouses of Smyrna were accustomed to spice merchants from the Orient, to travellers, acrobats, magicians and herbalists, but they somehow couldn't find a place for Avinash, a well-dressed gentleman from the East. Thus they were uncomfortable with him. His grandfather used to say that 'the mind forever desires to classify the world; it tends to reject what it cannot categorize'.

Inside, the coffeehouse smelled of cloves, plums, apples and freshly ground coffee. It was empty. A fair-haired boy was murmuring a sad song in a language Avinash didn't recognize as he swept the floor. When the coffeehouse owner saw him, he raised his head from his waterpipe and roared, 'Hizir, where in hell are you, boy? Quick! Run and prepare Mr Avinash's waterpipe.'

Avinash settled himself on the couch next to the coffeehouse's cat, Pamuk.

The cat, entirely unconcerned, continued to lick herself. The colourful rays of light beaming in through the stained glass played on her white fur in vain; she was busy cleaning herself.

With a coffee pot in his hand, Hasan approached the couch where Avinash was sitting. Directly behind him, the blonde-haired boy who'd been sweeping the floor now stood waiting with a brass tray bearing a cup and a plate. He set these on the low table in front of the couch and withdrew. Without taking his grey eyes off the coffee pot, Hasan slowly filled the cup. A delicious smell of mastic filled the air.

The coffeehouse owner settled down on the couch next to the cat and signalled with a tiny gesture which only the boys could understand that they were to dust the tables. Avinash took an ivory mouthpiece from under his sash and attached it to the rubber tube of the waterpipe. Pamuk had buried her head in the palm of Hasan's hand.

'Look at that rascal. How well she knows you!'

'And how could she not, Mr Avinash? She was born right here in the back courtyard. You know, it is considered a good deed to care for a cat. Our Prophet loved cats very much. They say that during the Battle of Uhud a nursing cat appeared in front of his army in the desert. A guard was placed at the animal's side and the entire army was ordered to encircle it. When the battle was done, our Prophet took the cat with him, brought it home and named it Muezza. Muezza was a black and white Abyssinian cat, not white like our Pamuk. A traveller once told me that white cats like Pamuk come from Angora; Pamuk had a mother, but she ran away. People say cats are selfish, opportunists, things like that, but I love them anyway.'

Avinash had discovered this coffeehouse the morning after his first night in the inn. He had immediately warmed to the calm, grey gaze of the elderly, white-bearded owner. The coffee-maker talked a great deal, but he was also a secret sage. By asking clever questions of his regular young customers, he managed to expertly encourage them to find their own way. He was a stout man, with a bushy moustache, and before opening the coffeehouse he'd been a night watchman in the Iki Chesmelik neighbourhood. He still kept a cudgel from those days hidden under his couch and if ever there was a problem in the bazaar or the courtyard of the inn, he would take up his cudgel and confront the troublemakers. When he conversed inside the coffeehouse, his voice was low, but when he was angry, the sound rising from his chest was full and strong, loud enough to be heard at the far end of the fleamarket.

With skilful fingers he arranged the Persian tobacco in the pipe and lit the coals. It did not escape Avinash's eyes, trained to see the invisible, that he added some green paste to the tobacco. When the smoke was drawn, the plums and cherries in the water of the pipe danced spiritedly.

'Sir, I have driven you crazy by talking too much.'

Avinash had lost himself in the dance of the cherries and plums in the waterpipe. He straightened up. 'Not at all, Hasan Usta. Your conversation is even sweeter than your coffee. However, I have business I must see to in the city. Then I shall go to our trading house. My boy Selim is probably there already. I will stop by again tomorrow morning, and we will continue then.'

'What's happened? Are you not coming this evening, sir?'

'No, this evening I have business in the Bournabat district.'

'Good fortune, God willing.'

'It is good fortune, Hasan. Good fortune indeed. The Levantine ladies have heard about my precious jewels and have invited me to tea. I will take them some samples.'

Hasan smiled. 'You do well, sir. If word of your gemstones spreads around the Bournabat ladies, you will open a shop on Madama Street and forget all about us.'

'Could your waterpipes ever be forgotten, Hasan Usta?'

Hearing this, the giant man smiled like a child, his eyes becoming slits. Then, abruptly, he grew serious. 'Sir,' he whispered, 'I heard they are going to overthrow the Sultan. Have you received that news?'

As he made his way to the door that opened onto the Street of the Goldsmiths, Avinash spread his hands as if to say, 'How should I know?' He was used to Hasan trying to pin him down at the last moment. Anyway, the coffee-seller didn't expect an answer. This parting comment was a way to remind the spy of his political stance. They walked to the street together.

Thunder rumbled in the sky. Hasan frowned as he looked up at the dark clouds louring over the rooftops as they blew in from the sea.

'In the name of liberty,' he grumbled, 'they've set people at one another's throats. I hear that the Bulgarians are wanting independence. Today or tomorrow they'll break from the empire. Take those Cretans... they just have to attach themselves to Greece! They have the British backing them now. If they were still the Sultan's subjects, could they have done that? They wouldn't have had the courage. If those thrill-seeking youngsters come to power, God help us, they'll cause nothing but chaos. And many will suffer in that chaos, my friend; a great many. When the Ottomans were in power, would such things have happened? Definitely not. All of us must work to make the empire strong and worthy of respect once more. Strength comes from unity, not division. We want no such thing as "a Turk", "a Greek" or "a Bulgarian" – if you divide humanity like that, we will be crying tears of blood. The young ones would like to break up this country into nations now. What did we lack when we were all Ottomans, man? We were getting on with our lives perfectly well.'

'May all be well, Hasan Usta. It isn't only here that is afire, but the whole world. Sultans and kings cannot hold onto their positions. The young are discontented everywhere. Without change, fortune's wheel cannot turn. Don't worry your sweet soul about it. There's a time for everything. Now goodbye.'

'Goodbye, Sir.'

It was raining harder now and the ditches at the side of the street were like streams, brimming with water. Avinash took a five-piastre coin from his jacket pocket, pressed it into Hasan's palm and disappeared into the covered bazaar of the new fleamarket, which twisted along between the inns and courtyards.

Confession

From upstairs, Juliette and the two servant girls, Irini and Zoe, heard the library door slam first, followed by footsteps reverberating on the wooden staircase. As if it weren't enough that she was running inside the house, Edith stormed into the bedroom without knocking. Her curly black hair had fallen over her face and down her back like an unruly river, and her eyes shone like a wild animal's. Irini's fingers, which were buttoning the back of Juliette's dress, stopped halfway up, level with her mistress's shoulder blades. Zoe dropped the pillow that she'd been fluffing up for the umpteenth time. Juliette was just about to reprimand Zoe, but her words froze in her mouth.

In two strides Edith stepped into the space between her mother and the full-length mirror. In a voice loud enough to be heard in the cellar, she shouted, 'Explain to me! Immediately! Now! Who is this Nikolas Dimos? What in hell did you do that this scoundrel of a stranger declares that Nikolas Dimos was my father?'

She could have strangled her mother right there. On the one hand she was shaking; on the other, she was thinking how everything was now suddenly clear: her black hair, the neighbours whispering about her when she was a child, the maids, her mother's eyes turning away from her as though they saw something shameful, her sister and brothers teasing her at the dinner table: 'The gypsies brought you, Edith; that's why your eyebrows are so thick.'

Of course!

Thinking such thoughts, anger surged through her like an eruption of hot lava; her eyes, ears and neck were burning. That strange, cold, distant attitude of her mother's towards her was not because of a fault in Edith, but because of Juliette's own shame. For years she had seen her guilt reflected in her daughter. Every time she looked at Edith, she was met with the ghost of her illicit relationship, and she recoiled. Juliette had always placed the blame for the storm in her daughter's soul on Edith, not on herself. 'Edith, dear, *ma chérie*, I beg you not to make your mother angry by being naughty, *d'accord*? Look, you've been running again and dishevelled your hair. Do you do such things just to spite me?'

No, Edith had never done things just to spite her mother, and now, after what had been revealed today, she realized her mother would have been angry no matter what she'd done. Her mere presence upset Juliette. Edith had carried that burden for no reason. She was innocent. And what about her father? Had he known that another man had sired her?

'It's all made up – lies, slander,' Juliette said adamantly. She threw Zoe and Irini out of the room, then sat on the edge of the newly made-up bed. 'You know that your father loved you dearly.'

Edith's heart was broken, not for her mother, sitting there diminished, withdrawn, with her beige dress only half buttoned, but for her father, who had thought she was his. Monsieur Lamarck had not deserved such deception, such a betrayal. He had loved his daughter with all his heart, had been her best friend. Or had he known of his wife's unfaithfulness and wanted to protect the little girl, the fruit of her sin? Big-hearted Charles Lamarck! Everything Edith had known to be true was slipping through her fingers. Her face flushed as waves of anger surged through her.

'Tell me everything from the beginning. With all the details, please.'

'There's nothing to tell. These are all old slanders. That merchant, Nikolas Dimos, was madly in love with me. He would come and go between Athens and Smyrna, importing your grandfather's grapes for winemaking, and would stay at our house. When I paid him no attention, he was all over me. I rejected him; he got angry, threatened me, and then he left. However, we see that before he died, he planned one last act of revenge. He sent that would-be attorney all the way here to give you this news. Ah, what an unhappy woman I am! Even my own daughter is deceived by the slander.'

Edith was pacing up and down between the door and the window, her arms folded across her chest. An electric current coursed through her. Each strand of her hair – hair whose provenance was no longer a mystery – was alive with electricity; her head was encircled by a black halo.

'I demand the truth, *Maman*. You can deceive your friends with your melodramatic stories, but not me. Why would a strange man leave his entire fortune to me in order to get revenge on you? And why do you suppose the attorney came? There is also a house! I am sure you know which one it is. If I say Vasili Street, would that help you remember?'

Juliette's hand flew to her mouth. She had not expected this much. She had entered a blind alley. Reaching out, she opened the drawer of her bedside table, took a cigarette from the stash she had hidden there, set it in an ivory holder, and waited. Remembering that there was no one to light her cigarette, she leaned towards the wooden lighter on her dressing table. When she began to speak, her voice had dropped to a deep bass tone like her daughter's.

'I was young, Edith. I had been married off to an old man. Your father didn't even stop by the house during that time. If his children had seen him on the street, they wouldn't have recognized him. It was that bad. You want the truth? I'll give you the truth, daughter. Our guests used to spend far longer sitting around our dinner table than your father did; it was they who soothed my young heart with words which weren't even in his repertoire. As for him, if he wasn't on a business trip, he was with his male friends somewhere – at the Cercle Européen or at the New Club. Or he was in the library with the door closed, writing that damn never-ending book of his. If you intend to make out that the deceased was the victim here, do not ignore the fact that he himself committed many sins.'

Edith was standing in front of the window, biting her fingernails. So, this was the story the neighbours had whispered to each other as they reclined on their verandas on long, hot afternoons. With a child's sensitivity, she had always known that behind their fans they were gossiping about something that concerned her. As she and her friends raced from one green, luxurious garden to another, Edith would hover near the women, pretending to be tying her shoelaces, storing away in her memory the words she overheard as if filling her pocket with precious stones she'd found on the beach.

'And then, my dear, Monsieur Lamarck lifted this Athenian man up by the collar...'

'Oh, *mon Dieu*, what are you saying?'

'But, darling, he was such a fool!'

'Ah, *oui*. He went and bought a house. He even got porters to carry a piano in on their backs because Lady You Know Who likes to play the piano.'

'Ah, but *ti romantiko*, how romantic! Monsieur Lamarck beat him up badly, huh? And then what happened?'

'Don't even ask! That two-bit young merchant escaped by the skin of his teeth, found himself on the street with his clothes in tatters.'

'You don't say!'

'Then he jumped aboard the first ship and fled back to his country.'

Speaking thus, the women would bury themselves in silence when they noticed Edith still busy tying her laces. Or, thinking the little girl couldn't see them, they would gesture towards her with an inclination of the head. 'And what about the child?'

Edith remembered how anxious she'd felt as she waited in the silence that followed. Now, however, a surprising calm enveloped her. The news that the attorney had brought was balm for a wound she hadn't even known existed. She felt a twinge of emotions she hadn't experienced in a long time. Relief, happiness, excitement... or was it that she felt victorious?

She looked at her mother. Juliette's face wore none of the expressions she practised in front of the mirror. She was smoking her cigarette and staring blankly at the door. It was the first time Edith had seen her mother this honest, this naked. After her initial panic at the exposing of the secret she had carried inside her all these years, Juliette now appeared relieved. The confession had allowed her to relax, and with that she had became sincere, turning into the mother that

Edith used to long for. Was the wall between them finally crumbling? This wasn't the time for that! Edith didn't want to soften towards her mother just when she had the right to hate her. In an icy voice, she asked, 'And the house on Vasili Street?'

'At first he wanted me to leave your father and run away with him to Athens. Impossible! What impertinence! I refused, of course. He wouldn't leave me alone. He went and bought that house just to be near me. It seemed he would move to Smyrna! Until your father got rid of him for good, he furnished that house as if I lived there – he was a dreamer!'

Edith walked to the centre of the room, then stopped suddenly. She had remembered something. An incident she'd not thought about for years came bit by bit to mind, like a long-forgotten dream.

In the visitors room at the convent school in Paris, a strange foreigner had come to see her. Pointed beard, face like a goat's, sad eyes...

'*Salut*, Edith. I have brought you some rose-flavoured Turkish delight. I hope you like it. I thought you might be missing it.'

He wore an elegant frock coat over a carefully starched white shirt with a collar like a swallow's wings, and a gold chain hung from his waistcoat pocket. His deep-set eyes were as black as Ayvalik olives, with black rings around them.

There was giggling from outside the room. The other girls. The girls who teased little Edith about her Levantine French accent, the girls who took advantage of her being small and pushed her around. The strange-looking foreigner had a pointed beard and a head of hair like a bird's nest. Her own hair escaped from its plait and fell across her face. Her visitor wore an expression that spoke of either pain or pleasure, she couldn't decide. 'I heard you were from Smyrna. I lived there myself years ago. It is the most beautiful city in the world, if you ask me. They call it the Pearl of the East.'

It was uncomfortable, awkward. Her glance slid to the visitor's hands. She was relieved to hear the bell for evening study. '*Kali tihi kori mou, omorfia mou.*' His thick, purplish lips opened as if to say something more, and then immediately closed. His bowler hat disappeared from sight down the school's endless marble staircase.

'May good fortune be yours, beautiful daughter.'

Suddenly she felt dizzy. Stumbling, she sat down on the stool in front of the dressing table. She could no longer follow the progress of her emotions. Anger gave way to sadness. An inappropriate joy bounced in her heart like a rubber ball.

Perhaps Nikolas Dimos had dreamed of his daughter across the sea so intensely that a gossamer bridge had formed between their two consciousnesses. Edith had long sensed this connection. She had always known deep in her heart that there was something linking her to a distant place. Her father's love had been like a lighthouse sending messages into space from the middle of the sea. Through all those years, it had blinked its lights with patience and perseverance, waiting for Edith to take notice.

Now she was discovering Nikolas Dimos's feelings in her own heart. The pain that had consumed her since childhood was not her pain but that of her olive-eyed father. That burning emptiness inside her was only the faraway echo of Nikolas Dimos's lovelorn melancholy. He had truly loved Juliette. Because of the terrible hurt he'd suffered, he had never married, though he was young. He had traced the steps of his black-eyed, black-haired daughter growing up in Bournabat, and, finally, in the throes of pneumonia, he had bequeathed to her all of his fortune and the house he had bought with who knew what dreams.

The sadness that had weighed on Edith's soul, like her mother's shame, that had alienated her from people, was not her own; it was Nikolas Dimos's. Could the half-realized dreams, the sorrows and hurts, the losses of a mother, a father, ancestors, invade one's heart? If so, if she could weed out from it those feelings which were not hers, she could begin life anew, with a fresh breath of air. What was more, there was now a house in which she could live all alone, with no need to speak to anyone until noon!

When joy leapt in her heart once again, Edith surrendered herself to it.

Love

That evening Edith appeared in society for the first time in many years. In the glow of the discoveries concerning her inner world, she felt as light as a feather, and she sparkled with excitement at the vision of the brand-new life that now awaited her. She glided into the reception room of the mansion. So beautiful and so elegant was she that Avinash, who at that moment was showing his emeralds and sapphires to Juliette's guests, knew at first glance that he would love her without cease to the end of his life.

When Avinash had begun receiving invitations to the Levantine mansions, there were many rumours circulating about Monsieur Lamarck's younger daughter, who had not been seen in society for quite a while. A group known to be close friends of Juliette whispered that the young woman was ill and had remained at a sanatorium in Germany. Others agreed that after finishing her schooling she had settled in Paris. Everyone, from ladies reclining on their chaises longues beside ornamental fountains to businessmen sucking on their pipes, had a theory about where Edith had vanished to, and it seemed as if Bournabat Levantine society as a whole had made up its mind to disabuse Avinash of his ignorance about this matter.

'Unfortunately, Edith has been stricken with a most pernicious illness. The disease has spread to her lungs. For this reason, Juliette has taken her to Germany, where she remains, poor girl.'

'Yes, I have heard the same. Apparently, she is in a sanatorium in Switzerland.'

'I heard it was Baden-Baden.'

'Nonsense! Edith wanted to stay in Paris for a time to mingle in its literary circles. I heard this from Edith herself.'

'Just between us, Monsieur Pillai, the truth is that Edith has become the mistress of a poet. She lives in a penthouse flat in Montparnasse.'

'You have the wrong information, sweetie. Edith has joined an organization of women writers. They've come up with something called Women's Rights.'

'They make love with women, not with men!'

'Ah, it is hard to imagine – that tiny little Edith with women, eh?'

'Don't believe a word of it. The truth is that she is the mistress of a poet. She also poses nude for an artist in order to earn money.'

'But, *mon cher*, Edith has no need to earn money! What? Or…?'

'Don't even ask. Before Charles died, his business was about to go bankrupt. The son-in-law Philippe Cantebury saved the sons. Or, and you didn't hear this from me, their situation was hopeless and Philippe bought the business. Pay no attention to those words implying partnership – Lamarck and Sons has passed entirely into Cantebury's hands.'

Amid the buzz of the salon, which was now full of guests, Avinash did not immediately realize that the bright-eyed young woman in the wine-coloured dress was the daughter of the charming Madame Lamarck, who was herself kissing everyone's cheeks in turn and talking vivaciously. How could he have known? In contrast to the daughter's modest entrance, Juliette had blown into the room like a gust of wind, causing a stir among her guests, who were sipping wine that had just been served on silver platters and conversing in soft voices. Opening both her arms wide as if to embrace everyone there, Juliette had shouted, 'My dear guests, welcome! What a pleasure it is to have you here. I must apologize for my tardiness. *Excusez-moi s'il vous plaît*. It was necessary that I inspect the kitchen at the last moment. You all know me – I just had to check that the cheeses, the caviar and the herring were properly aligned on the platters. As I predicted, they were in need of my magical touch. Please forgive me.'

She was wearing a green silk dress that showed off her peach-like décolletage, and the red and yellow of the firelight in the grand fireplace glinted so enticingly in her hair, it made you want to touch it. Juliette Lamarck was a pretty woman. Her features were perhaps a little too sharp for Avinash's taste, but she was definitely attractive. And powerful. The sober atmosphere of the salon had lifted the moment she made her spectacular entrance. Like a butterfly, Juliette passed from one guest to the next, connecting one to the other.

'Good evening, Peter, *mon cher*. How lovely that you came! We are neighbours in name but never see each other. How is your mother? I wish she could have come too; I will visit soon. Is that sweet rascal Edward ever going to return from New York? This summer, God willing – is that correct? *Très bien*. Good! You've not met Dr Arnott, have you? He himself came from New York last year. He works in Paradiso, but I hear that he will join us during the summer. Isn't that right, Doctor? Let me introduce you to my most esteemed neighbour, Helene Thomas-Cook's elder son, Peter. He is a true Bournabat prince, born and raised right here. And he has a great interest in antiques. With your permission, let him describe the neighbourhood for you. Perhaps one day he will even take you to Vourla in his sailing boat.

'Lady Dulcinea! How lovely that dress looks on you! On anyone else it would definitely not be the same. You are so elegant, whatever you wear becomes you, but this is magnificent! You had it made by Dimitrula, did you not? I am sure of it. The tailors in Paris are no match for Dimitrula's hands. She came all the way from Smyrna to sew new uniforms for my maids, bless her heart. My youngest daughter-in-law had a lavender silk evening gown sewn by her recently. It is a fabulous piece. Oh, look, I speak of her, and she appears. Marie, darling, Lady Dulcinea and I were just talking of you. Do join us.

'This cheese is not bad, is it, Monsieur Dumont? I sent our butler to Fasoula specially to buy us some camembert. There is nothing you cannot find at Yorgo's Delicatessen. Have a cracker. What is this – your glass is empty! Sotiraki, would you look here, *se parakalo*? Bring Monsieur Dumont a gin cocktail. *Grigora!* Quick! Or would you prefer red wine, Monsieur Dumont?'

Avinash understood as soon as he first saw her that, in spite of the merry laughter, Juliette was wearing her ebullience like a mask. Anxiety shone out from behind her blue-green eyes like the blinking lights of a fishing boat. If you looked above the smiling mouth and into the eyes, you met with a nervous, even very frightened woman. On the rare occasions when she took a break from talking, for example when she was listening politely to one of her guests, her hennaed eyebrows had a tendency to frown. With the expertise of his profession, the Indian spy registered all the signs of the anxiety that was eating away at her soul and made a note of them in a corner of his mind.

'Ah, Monsieur Pillai, I am so pleased to see you. What an honour! Thank you for accepting my invitation and not disappointing me. I hope you have brought one or two examples of your magnificent gems. Ah, *très bien*, you have already begun to exhibit them. The humble ladies of Bournabat couldn't wait, of course. But they are quite right. What splendid stones they are! You will stay for dinner, *n'est-ce pas*? Wait, let me introduce you to Madame Dumont right away. In a word, she has a superb jewellery coll—'

When the hostess's gaze slid across to where her guest was staring, she stopped mid-sentence. As soon as she ceased talking, the salon chatter quieted too. All the guests turned to look at the door. Noting the silence, which cut through the air like a knife, and the roomful of eyes directed at her, Edith smiled. With one hand on the doorknob and the other lifting a glass of wine which she had plucked from a passing tray, she said, 'Good evening.'

Everyone stared at her, curious and impressed. Avinash felt his ears heating up. How was it possible that such a deep voice could emerge from such a slender, swanlike neck? He swallowed. Her eyes, meeting his for a second, were as warm as embers; her silky lips were a dark pink, like the rose petals from which Yakoumi extracted his oil. His gaze followed this mysterious daughter of the Lamarcks, whose name he had heard countless times, to the centre of the room. There was something about the way Edith spoke, something about the way she comported herself, the way she carried her head, that revealed her to be not the naive younger daughter of a mansion but an already mature woman. She was not coquettish like her mother, but there was a spark in her black eyes that flashed on and off, signalling that her body had tasted secret passions and found unashamed satisfaction therein. And there was more.

Avinash realized with a pain in his heart like the prick of a thorn that this woman would never, under any circumstances, play second fiddle to anyone, to any man; she would never find with a man the peace and pleasure that she found in solitude. Conversely, he, Avinash knew immediately that the emptiness in his heart could be filled only by the touch of those rosebud lips. The yearning that had ravaged his inner being for as long as he could remember could only be assuaged in her arms. From that first night, the desperation and jealousy that Edith's self-sufficiency aroused in him seeped into his blood like a poison.

Just as his lips were about to graze her tiny, lavender-scented hand, Edith's old friends surrounded her and in the excitement of seeing her at a party began screaming, 'Edith *mou*, what a surprise! Have you been in Smyrna?'

They dragged her over to a pink satin sofa in a far corner.

'Wherever have you been, darling? No one has seen your face in two years. Frankly, we were offended.'

'Come, we've so much to tell you. You won't believe your ears.'

In the later hours of the evening, the tea party turned into a grand dinner. Avinash tried in vain to get near Edith. A French attaché had seated himself next to her and was chatting away. When she smiled from diagonally across the table as if to apologize, Avinash noticed the gap between her two front teeth. This gap inflamed his desire still more. For a moment, one brief moment, their eyes met. Beneath the curl of her lashes, her black eyes glistened like cinders, and a tacit acknowledgement passed between the two of them. At least that was how it appeared to Avinash in the intoxication of first love.

The French attaché was calling out with a lisp to Juliette, seated at the head of the table. 'My honourable lady, Madame Juliette, if your daughter had been born a boy, I would have immediately enlisted her to be trained as a spy. One never hears such a pure Istanbul accent around here, not even from the Turkish girls. Bravo, little lady.'

It was clear that the man had drunk too freely of the wine, which was being passed around like water. Juliette nodded coldly, wearing the sort of expression she used when speaking to the servants. Some of the other guests cast furtive glances at Avinash.

Edith joined the conversation. 'Actually, I don't know very much Turkish. I learned a little from our butler Mustafa and his wife Sidika when I was a child. Then at school in Paris my best friend was a girl from a wealthy Istanbul family. When we wanted to say something secretly, we would switch to Turkish so that the other girls couldn't understand. Because of that I can speak three or four words in an Istanbul accent.'

Juliette's face was drawn. It was obvious that her daughter's knowledge of Turkish bothered her. Avinash made a mental note of this detail.

'Such delicious soup – the fish melts in your mouth! In a word, it is perfect,' said the plump woman sitting beside Avinash. She was one of the friends who had pulled Edith over to the far sofa. Good health burst from her pink cheeks;

78

it was obvious she'd grown up on steak and truffles. She began her sentences in French and completed them in Greek, and no one at the table seemed to find this odd. The other heads around the table nodded in confirmation.

The food was indeed marvellous, but Avinash was, as always, having difficulty maintaining his vegetarian diet without being disrespectful to his hostess. 'Never refuse food that is offered; take it onto your plate. If you cannot eat it, leave it there.' This was the advice his grandfather had given when he spoke to him on the subject before going to England.

'Would you like some quiche, Monsieur Pillai? Our head chef works wonders with pumpkin, cheese and cream. Please try some.'

These words uttered by Edith from across the table were not extraordinary, but Avinash perceived every one of them, every twitch of her lips, every tiny movement of her slender white wrist with its emerald bracelet, as a coded message, like those he had learned in his Secret Service training. The glances they exchanged over the china dishes and silver knives and forks were loaded with many emotions. They held understanding and respect. Edith had recognized his dilemma, understood and respected his choice. She hadn't shouted with fake concern, 'Oh, Monsieur Avinash, sweetie, didn't you like the soup?' as the other women at the table had done upon seeing the pieces of fish swimming in his bowl. Edith had spoken in a low voice, as if she were stroking his soul. Maybe, as she looked at him across the quiche platter, there was even in those coal-black eyes promise, hope, and – yes, why not? – love.

Someone was shouting, 'Look, I'm writing it down here and now: they will overthrow the Sultan within a year.' It was the French attaché next to Edith again. 'I know, because I have friends in Paris. You think the revolt will be organized from Paris, do you not? Or from Salonica, ha, ha, ha. Goodness, Doctor, it is so obvious you have only just arrived from Europe. No, my dear fellow, you are wrong. The revolution will be organized from Germany. You will see. If what I say doesn't happen within a year...'

Swallowing down his glass of wine, he wondered briefly what he would do if what he had said did not take place. He did not have to think about it for too long, for by the time he set the empty glass back down, everyone's attention had turned to the head of the table.

Juliette Lamarck, tapping her crystal glass with a knife, rose to her feet.

'Dear friends, today we are joined by a very esteemed new guest. He has been living in Smyrna for more than a year, but it is only now that we have the pleasure of meeting him. He comes from a prominent family in Bombay and was one of the first Indian students to graduate from Oxford University. With your permission, I would like to raise a toast to our new friend. To Avinash Pillai!'

During the rest of the evening, who did Avinash meet and what did he talk about? He remembered nothing. The next morning, as he lay on his straw mattress at the Menzilhane Inn, trying to understand the storm that had broken inside him at his first glimpse of Edith, he went over the events of the evening and even recalled the anxiety on Juliette's face, apparent only for a few seconds, when her daughter appeared at the door of the salon. When the young woman had lifted her emerald-ringed fingers to his lips, something had jumped in Avinash's stomach.

Muezzin Nuri's velvet voice filled his room at the inn. As he lay on his back on the mattress, Avinash allowed the same scene to play over and over in his mind. Every time those slender white fingers touched his lips, his stomach tingled and his heart beat as if it would burst.

Avinash Pillai had fallen in love for the first time in his life.

Gypsy Yasemin's Web of Secrets

'And from then on, my dears, every afternoon, in that house with a garden at the end of Vasili Street, those two – you know who – would, beneath a blanket of smoke from the hashish in the waterpipe... What acrobatics! What tricks! Don't ask me about the rest.'

By the time I heard this story, neither Edith, nor Avinash, nor Vasili Street where the house in which they met and made love every afternoon was located, remained. But Gypsy Yasemin still walked the streets, going door to door, enthralling women with her tales of the rich Europeans.

Much time had passed since they'd found me, just before dawn, in the garden of the house on Bulbul Street, unconscious. Maybe one year, maybe two; I don't know. Time had lost its significance. I didn't venture out into the streets of my ruined city, but in spite of all the suffering I'd endured, in spite of my losses, I was young, and with the fierce strength of the young I kept going. Under a new name, and from within the warm embrace of the Turkish family who had taken me in with no questions asked, I adjusted to my new life.

I had become silent Scheherazade, with no past, no people, no speech.

The power of speech, which I lost on the morning they found me, had still not returned. It was never going to return. In a way, this was a good thing because people who spoke my language were being hounded out of the villages in which they had lived for a thousand years and sent to a faraway shore. I didn't want to ever be separated from cinnamon-scented Sumbul, who had restored me to life, or from other things in that house.

Gypsy Yasemin would lay out the items she had unpacked from her bundle on the large decorative wrought-iron table left over from the time of the Europeans. As soon as she began telling the love story of Edith and Avinash from twenty years back, all the women would gather in the kitchen to listen to her, their mouths hanging open: Sumbul, her widowed sister-in-law Mujgan, Makbule Hanim, Nanny Dilber from Ethiopia, and myself, alias Scheherazade. The kitchen smelled of bergamot and the onions which Gulfidan, a refugee from Lesbos, was forever slicing. Nanny Dilber, black-skinned and quite as massive as Gypsy Yasemin herself, would pack wood into the huge oven, another relic from the Europeans, and fry red mullet in olive oil. I would prepare a salad with mustard greens and endives that I had gathered from the garden as well as poppies and hackberries Yasemin had brought down from the mountains.

We had all moved to the house known as the Mansion with the Tower, which was bigger. It had been given to Sumbul's husband, Colonel Hilmi Rahmi, as a reward for his successes during the war. Only Hilmi Rahmi's father, the grumpy Mustafa Efendi, remained in the old house on Bulbul Street at the top of the Muslim neighbourhood.

'Our boy Avinash had not had much experience with women before, but he was a good student. In Edith's arms, he quickly became an expert. How do I know this? Let's just say I heard it from the cats on Vasili Street, okay?'

Next to me, Sumbul – still sane at that point – leaned her elbows on the table, settled her blonde head and plump cheeks between her palms like a child, and listened to the story she had already heard countless times from the bundle peddler. Her green eyes grew wide and she even set down her peacock-feather fan, laying it on top of the earthenware wheat jar. She was intrigued by the adventures of the Europeans. They had given Smyrna its colour, its sounds, its distinctive flavour, until they were lost to the city in that one night. She latched onto Yasemin's tales of the old days as if clutching a lifebelt.

The contents of the gypsy's bundle lay on the table: lengths of linen, silk, lace…

It was said that the gypsy went into the chalets, villas and mansions of Bournabat, Boudja and Paradiso that had been abandoned by the Greeks and Armenians fleeing for their lives and took dresses, jewellery, hats, whatever. It was true that on occasion a very fashionable linen dress would emerge from her bag, its armpits bearing the scent of distant places, its collar, lace and underskirt of the highest quality, obviously cut by expert scissors.

'A place has ears. When those two, Avinash and Edith, slid beneath the mosquito netting of an afternoon, the house servants weren't sleeping, were they? When I read their fortunes from the coffee grounds later, they couldn't stop talking. Speaking of fortunes, fill up a coffee cup and let me read the fortune of this silent Scheherazade. Why is she so sad? What has caused her to be tongue-tied? Let us find a cure for her troubles.'

From time immemorial, Gypsy Yasemin had been going

in and out of the houses of Smyrna with her bundle. No one knew how old she was. Sumbul swore that back when she'd run away from Plovdiv and had come to Smyrna as a bride, Yasemin was still the same age as she was now. The wrinkles on her face had not deepened one bit. Even the ancient women living over at Iki Chesmelik remembered the bundle peddler from their youth. According to one story, she had discovered the secret of immortality while roaming around India before the Christian Era and had remained the same age ever since. So as not to arouse suspicion, she relocated frequently, but when she arrived in Smyrna, she fell so in love with the Pearl of the East that she settled down there, willing to risk the inevitable gossip.

Another rumour had it that, like all gypsies, Yasemin practised witchcraft and drank the blood of uncircumcised boys. When I was a child, in the Christian neighbourhoods, angry people would accuse the Jews of kidnapping their children and throwing them into spiked barrels. From time to time they would attack the Jewish *kortejo* on Havralar Street, where the town's Sephardic Jews lived together in small tenement rooms around a dirty courtyard. The witchcraft stories about Gypsy Yasemin could have been a hangover from those old legends.

Witch or not, since olden times Yasemin had woven a net – invisible as a spider's web, very thin, very taut – around the women of the city. She'd become famous not only in the poorer neighbourhoods but also in Bella Vista, in Punta, even in Bournabat and the European mansions of Boudja. Wearing high-heeled clogs on her feet, her belly hanging down over her baggy trousers, which jingled with coins, she wandered from street to street. She would call out in a clear voice, 'The peddler has come, ladies! Open your doors and view her delights,' and doors around the edges of that intricate net would open, allowing the huge woman to slip inside.

Gypsy Yasemin would entertain the poor with the love stories of the rich, like that of Edith Lamarck, and she would provide the rich with the magic potions of Old Aybatan the herbalist or the healing oils of pharmacists like Yakoumi. In the old days, when Avinash used to bring precious gems from Bombay, Yasemin was one of the sorcerers who waited in Smyrna harbour in water up to their waists for the arrival of his servant Ravi. She could also perform lead-pouring rituals to cleanse a space of evil spirits, do epilations with wax, read fortunes from coffee grounds, and procure opium or hashish for those who craved it. It was also said that she carried letters between young lovers. Although she would swear on three holy books that she understood neither the Greek nor the Arabic nor the European alphabet, the women knew that the source of her never-ending supply of gossip were the letters she tucked between her enormous breasts.

Even if her oaths were genuine and she really didn't know how to read or write, her tongue was as nimble as an acrobat and she could warble off all the languages of the old city like a nightingale. Her name, like her language, would change as she passed from one neighbourhood to another. From Yasemin to Yasemi, from Yasmin to Jasmine.

'That Edith, you know, was a hashish addict, a dope fiend. How can I be sure? Don't even ask, dearie. The purple-green weed she inhaled was the most superior, the most magical. She knew the good stuff, I'll say that much. You'll have to figure out the rest for yourselves. Do you imagine that without getting high, she could she have gone to bed with that Indian? But then her flesh would get so carried away...

The sounds she came out with would make even the cats on Vasili Street go on heat. Ha, ha, ha! If I'm lying, God strike me dead!'

The laughter that rang out from Yasemin's vast chest bounced off the marble walls of the kitchen like a bomb exploding, making all of us who were sitting around the table jump. Sumbul tried to signal to Yasemin with her eyes and eyebrows that Aunt Makbule was among us. Makbule Hanim was the older sister of Sumbul's father-in-law, Mustafa Efendi. I was afraid of her. I had never seen a smile on her face. She hid herself behind a black veil and spent all day with her prayer beads.

'With her head full of the smoke from such pure weed, the flesh beneath her fingertips would turn to feathers, and syrup rather than blood would flow through her veins, my dears. The Indian had skin like velvet; on my oath, like milk-chocolate. Edith wouldn't agree to marriage, but she couldn't do without that Indian in her bed, the tart. How do you think she preserved that baby-doll beauty? When a man becomes a husband, he sucks out a woman's soul. Children too. Miss Edith knew this very well.'

As Yasemin rubbed at her blotchy face, recalling former passions of her own, Sumbul bent her head over the embroidery she was working on. Her sister-in-law, Mujgan, was more relaxed, having sent her adolescent daughters out to the garden to keep an eye on Sumbul's sons. Disregarding the blush that had by now reached Sumbul's ears – 'For goodness' sake, sister, Aunt Makbule can't hear a thing anyway' – Mujgan insisted that the bundle peddler go into the details of their lovemaking.

For example, how did Edith manage not to get pregnant? Was she sterile? Was it true that Avinash did exercises like a

Hindu fakir in his room at the inn every morning? Maybe one of the functions of those exercises was to hold back his semen. Was it true that he had an emerald earring on his penis? How could he operate with that earring there?

Didn't they understand that it was *my* embarrassment, not Aunt Makbule's, that Sumbul was wary of?

'I swear to you, dearies, I don't know if it was the earring or the hashish, but Edith never once asked me for the herb that draws babies from the womb. Whereas in those days that was mostly what the other European sluts like her requested. How many times was I called to their houses as if it was an emergency! They had no shame. They'd pull their skirts up to their groins and moan and groan in their high-pitched voices. "Help me, Mother Yasemin, for the love of God. Bring me some of that magic potion. Two full moons have passed, and no visitor has come." I'm not talking about Edith but the other sluts. Edith's voice, praise God, was as deep as a drum at Ramadan. I have not had the fortune to hear another voice like it.'

From above her crow-like nose, her green, feline eyes were fixed on me. With her chin she gestured to the sapphire ring on my finger.

'Why are you staring at me as if you've been attacked by an evil spirit? What has happened to those Europeans you all loved so much? Edith ran off to Paris with nothing but a single suitcase in her hand. That no-good brother-in-law got his hands on the girl's entire fortune. The businesses, the bonds all burned up. The mother too – she ran to her own death. Her son couldn't even find her ashes. Such were the wages of her sins. Good God Almighty! I'm telling you, all those disasters that destroyed the Lamarck woman's soul were set in motion way back when she pretended the baby in her womb was her husband's. She brought it all on herself. Those who know, know. You understand what I'm saying?'

No, I did not understand anything. Listening to the stories about those rich people was like listening to fairy tales. I could not imagine what they could have to do with me. My mind went to other things, to my own secrets. When Yasemin said, 'Let me read your fortune; let us find a cure for your troubles, you understand, eh?', and her eyes stared at the ring my dear mama had placed on my finger at our last embrace, fear spread through me. Did this gypsy recognize me from the time before I became Scheherazade? Did she know what had happened to my mother? My father? Did they know that I was alive – were they looking for me?

I would not know the answers to these questions until years later when Yasemin brought to me an elderly person whose hair and beard were all tangled together. Avinash Pillai. The Indian spy retained not the slightest remnant of his former charm. He had been wandering the streets of the new city called Izmir, where people spoke only one language, a place whose past, like the names of its streets, had been erased. These streets smelled now of rotten eggs rather than jasmine.

Yasemin had run into him in an obscure passageway in Tilkilik. This was a half-century after the events I am relating. The crazy old man had still not given up on Edith, even at that age. It was only then, the last time that I saw Avinash, that I would be able to put together the pieces of the Levantine story that the gypsy had told and understand how the end of the story related to me. The story that Sumbul's annoying ghost told over and over like a stuck record was not, as the doctor maintained, a paranoid delusion but the truth itself.

However, by the time I understood this, it was too late.

By the time Avinash told this story to me, a half-century had passed since the morning we found Sumbul's naked, white, cinnamon-scented body hanging from the ceiling. Apartment buildings had replaced the villas and their gardens, and the wind wafting in through the windows carried the smell not of jasmine but of coal. Even the nights when I used to sneak out of my room and creep beneath the mosquito netting of another room at the end of the corridor, those dark nights in a gilded bed, were now but memories from a distant past.

By the time Avinash brought me this story, the mute concubine Scheherazade had long been abandoned to one hundred years of solitude in the Mansion with the Tower.

I will tell all,
Everything,
That death may find me
In the tower of this wreck of a mansion.

Part II

FROG RAIN

Psomalani 1919

'They're coming! They're coming! The British Consulate is spreading the news! The shops on the quay have started closing – ask the folks down there, if you don't believe us. Fishermen coming from over by Lesbos saw their ships. People have even begun setting up camp on sacks and bales. They'll be in the harbour by daybreak tomorrow. This time it's for real.'

When Stavros and the other neighbourhood boys reached Psomalani, Bread-Baker's Square, Panagiota was playing skipping ropes with the girls in front of the low wall on the police station side. It was obvious that the boys had run all the way up from the docks. Their tongues were hanging out, their faces were red and their eyes were lit up like maniacs. Turning the rope with one hand, she glanced at Stavros out of the corner of her eye. His cheeks were flushed and sweat was coursing down them.

In his newly broken voice he shouted, 'Did you hear, gentlemen? They're coming!'

Like parrots, the boys behind him repeated his words. 'They're coming! They're coming! Did you hear, gentlemen? They're coming, as sure as honey.'

They said 'as sure as honey' in Turkish, and then began reciting like a nursery rhyme the names of the Greek battleships they had known by heart since childhood. '*Patris, Themistoklis, Atromitos, Syria*... They're already at Lesbos!'

Stavros and his gang walked towards the middle of the square. The sun had set and only the meadows alongside the railway tracks were still lit up. The men throwing dice in the coffeehouse took no notice of the boys shouting across the square in their croaky voices. The mothers chatting out of their windows didn't stop their conversations. Only the toothless old women picking over the lentils as they sat in chairs they'd brought out in front of their houses smacked their lips and shook their heads. Everywhere was dusty, but the lemon trees were in bloom and the neighbourhood was suffused with a fresh green smell. Niko's mother set down the guts of the fish she'd just cleaned in front of her door and suddenly the roofs got lively. Cats that had been stretched out on the tiles since noon, preening themselves, now converged en masse on Menekse Street.

Even from a distance, Panagiota could smell the sharp tang of salt and sweat on Stavros's skin. It was as if a kitten was turning a somersault in her stomach. It was only May, but the skin of his arms extending from his light blue, short-sleeved shirt were already dark. The roots of his hair were white, probably from sea salt, which meant that he must have been at the beach today, swimming like a fish. Panagiota longed to be able to do the same, but, being female, she'd probably never get the chance. How much fun it would be to just jump on a tram and go anywhere you wanted, to leap into the sea from some random beach, to swim towards the horizon without getting tired. Girls could only go into the water when they were picnicking at the Diana Baths, and that wasn't the sort of place where you could stretch out your arms and take long strokes in full view of everybody. They could only stand in the shallows and throw water at each other.

These picnics, one of Panagiota's favourite summer entertainments, had become more fun since Kyra Eftalia had bought a portable Primus stove from Frank Street. Now the women could bring coffee, sugar, a coffee pot, spoons and cups in their baskets, as well as their umbrellas and tablecloths when they went on a picnic. The coffee-making was most beneficial to the girls. While their mothers were seated around the little stove, stirring their coffeepot, the girls would quickly shove each other and sink down into the water with their dresses on. The mothers, at first anxious for the girls not to get their clothes or heads wet, stopped caring once they were wet anyway, and then they were able to splash about as they pleased. That said, at the end of last summer, Panagiota's mother had admonished, 'There'll be no more jumping in and out of the water after this year. From next spring, you'll sit with us like a lady.' Panagiota had rolled her eyes. Just a little further on, at the cape, the boys were diving off the rocks into the sea.

Last summer seemed a long time ago to Panagiota. So many things had changed in the autumn and through the winter, both in the world and in her own soul. The world war had come to an end and the Ottoman Empire had been defeated. While some of the uncles in the neighbourhood had got really excited about that, Panagiota's father, Grocer Akis, had responded by pulling worriedly at his moustache.

At any rate, defeat had come much earlier to their house. At Christmas in 1915, her two older brothers, who'd been sent to join a labour battalion, both died. The loss of the boys was so devastating that it no longer mattered to them who went on to win the war and who lost. While Smyrna's Europeans and Christians were celebrating the arrival of British soldiers in the city, Akis and Katina ate cauliflower by the light of their kerosene lamp and went to bed early. Let whoever desired it rule Smyrna. There was no news in the world that could make Panagiota's mother and father smile again. Four years had passed since that dire news and Katina had still not taken off her black mourning clothes. She had no intention of ever doing so. The mirrors in the house were still covered with black cloth.

While Akis and Katina spent their days feeling numb and detached, as if cast in perpetual shadow, Panagiota was rushing into adolescence on the back of a crazy horse, with hormones tugging at the reins. Last summer a German family had gone into the sea at the Diana Baths bare-legged, where even the boys could see them. Everyone there – the girls, pushing and shoving each other in the water; the young men on the rocks; and even the mothers – had stared in wonder at the long, white legs of the women who raced into the sea as if they were swimming off their own private beach. It was on that day that Panagiota realized that Stavros, from the other end of the beach, was staring not at the half-naked women but at her. He was sitting high up on a rock, his eyes fixed on Panagiota's suntanned shoulders and the black curls that had sprung free of her plaits. He had taken off his shirt like fishermen did, and his chest was bare. His gaze could have just been wandering, of course, but if that were so, why did he turn away so quickly when their eyes met? When he did that, Panagiota felt as if she'd inadvertently glimpsed something shameful.

Since that day her heart had been besieged by emotions she'd never experienced before. Whenever she ran into

Stavros, she felt as if she was being observed. Her own eyes searched for him everywhere – at the end of the school day, at the square in the evening, at church on Sunday mornings, at the bakery, at the ice-cream shop on the quay. On some made-up pretext, she would routinely extend her walk home from school and divert through Kerasohori where Stavros's father had his butcher's shop. Sometimes, very rarely, he helped his father in the shop or delivered meat to well-off customers in his bicycle basket.

In spite of all this effort, if Panagiota did happen to encounter him, she would turn her head and pretend she hadn't seen him. Of course, her friends Elpiniki and Adriana were aware of the situation. If kids who'd grown up together in the same neighbourhood stopped greeting each other on the street, this was either because they'd taken offence at something or because they'd fallen in love – or both. Since Panagiota kept admiring her reflection in shop windows, this was clearly a case of the latter and not the former. For a while now, Elpiniki had set her heart on the fisherman's son, Niko. Minas the Flea was courting Adriana. Now that Panagiota was besotted with Stavros, the team was complete.

'The fleet set out from Kavala yesterday. Tonight it'll pass by Lesbos, they say. Tomorrow morning before dawn it'll be in Smyrna. They're coming to save us! They're bringing us our freedom! Don't say you haven't heard?'

Panagiota kept on turning the rope as if she were paying no attention. Again, she felt like she was standing in the centre of the world with everybody's eyes upon her. Flames crept through her, from her heart to her temples. She held her head high, raised her chin. People seeing Panagiota that spring were surprised at how she had shot up so quickly. Even her legs, fingers and toes had got longer. Suddenly she didn't know where to put her hands and feet, whose existence she had never previously considered. The sudden changes in her body were uncomfortable, but when old women like Auntie Rozi looked at her face and spat three times in the air – puh, puh, puh; when her mother attached Mother Mary brooches and evil eye pins inside her dresses; and, of course, when she registered Stavros's glances, she realized it wasn't only her height but other things also which had changed.

'Oh, come on!' shouted one of the wrinkled uncles sitting in the coffeehouse, rolling his prayer beads. 'For months now they've been coming to save us and nobody's seen their faces yet.'

'What months are you talking about, *vre*? We've been waiting for them for over a century. Ha, ha, ha!'

'I swear to you, they're coming! We heard it from the British. Down on the docks everybody is talking about it. Fishermen have even seen the ships. Isn't that right, boys?'

The boys stood in the centre of the square and looked around. They were confused. They'd thought the news would be a cause for celebration. Why wasn't everybody on their feet and hugging each other with tears of joy?

'Stavraki, my treasure,' shouted his mother from over where she was watering the red rose in her tiny garden from the jug in her hand. The soil had been baking all day. As the water was absorbed, it turned to steam and smelled like rosemary after rain. Red and purple flowers had opened on the bougainvillea that covered the whitewashed walls of the single-storeyed houses overlooking the square. '*Ela*. Come, change your shirt. You're soaked with sweat.'

Stavros glanced furiously in his mother's direction. Was this the time to be worrying about changing one's shirt?

Panagiota bit her lower lip to keep from laughing. Minas, not having drawn the attention he'd expected, came to the front of the group, and, without taking his eyes off Adriana, who was still skipping, began to shout in a reedy voice. In one hand he was ringing a bell, like a town crier.

'*Foustanella* soon in Smyrna,
After that, Agia Sofia
Back to Red Apple goes Turkos
Zito zito zito Venizelos!'

The other boys joined in the marching song. The toothless old women nodded as if they were listening to a pleasant folksong. The girls playing skipping ropes in front of the wall beside the police station poked each other and giggled. Adriana's feet got tangled up and she almost fell over.

'Sister, you're out!' yelled Tasoula, who was sitting on the wall. 'You're out. So out!' She was the next youngest sister after Adriana. Then she started singing a folksong. Elpiniki's younger sister Afroula, sitting next to her, quickly joined in.

'*Aman, aman, yaniyorum ben*
Aman, aman, seviyorum sen
Tsifteteli yalelleli.

'Oh, oh, burning, I am
Oh, oh, it's loving you, I am
Tsifteteli yalelleli.'

Elpiniki threw the rope to the ground and stalked over to the wall. Angrily, she pinched her sister's calf. 'Shut up or you'll be sorry!'

'*Kita, kita!* Look! Your fat one is over there, sister! I am burning for you, my Niko. Ah, ah, ah. Okay, I'll shut up. You've made my legs go purple, *mari*! Just you wait till I show Mama this evening, then we'll see who's sorry.'

Panagiota felt very fragile and alone in this new life dominated by her emotions. Sometimes girls could be more merciless than boys. What was happening to her? That morning, when she'd woken up, she'd realized that the melodramatic *amanedes* songs she'd always made fun of now burned her heart. Sometimes she couldn't even tell whether what she was feeling was happiness or sorrow; sometimes when she was laughing with Elpiniki and Adriana she would suddenly feel like crying. And in the mornings before school she felt an unbearable urge to go down to the quay and just gaze at the blue of the sea for a long, long time.

The rope began to turn again. The boys lined up like soldiers and, swinging their arms, paraded from one end of the square to the other. Dust swirled in their wake. Without stopping their marching song, they passed the men in front of the coffeehouse, who sat there watching them, some with indifference, some with smiles on their faces. Then they marched around the bakery, with its smell of fresh warm bread, and reached the opposite side of the square, where the halva vendor was sitting idly beside the fountain. The coffee-seller's apprentice was emptying water from a pail in front of the arbour. Stavros wasn't at the head of the line, but he was among those singing the marching song. Just as they entered Menekse Street, a roar was heard.

'What the hell is this commotion?'

The cracked voices of the boys stopped as if severed by a knife. Only the fisherman's son, Niko – Elpiniki's chosen one – continued to chant from the back, '*Zito, zito, zito…*'. But soon his voice faded too, melting into the air. Panagiota let the skipping rope fall to the ground, almost causing Elpiniki, who was jumping, to stumble. From the top of the wall Tasoula and Afroula giggled. The old women nodded.

Panagiota noticed none of this. She was watching her long-legged father striding over to the boys. Grocer Akis's thick black eyebrows, which came all the way down to his eyes, were knitted, his fleshy cheeks were swollen, and his lips, hidden beneath his moustache, were drawn down like a distressed child's. He cornered the retreating boys by the fountain. Catching hold of Minas, who was leading the pack, he bellowed once more.

'Shut up this racket, you unruly brats!'

Panagiota wished there was a hole she could crawl into. Abandoning the skipping rope, she dashed as far away from her father as possible, to the other end of the coffeehouse, where the black-gowned old women were sitting on chairs out on the street or on pillows spread out on their front steps. One of them – old Auntie Rozi – called out to her as she approached, looking embarrassed.

'*Ela, ela, koritsi mou.* Come, darling girl. Sit beside me. Would you like a tangerine?'

Just then, Stavros pushed the other boys aside and stood in front of the grocer. He was as tall as Akis and his tanned, muscular limbs were stronger than the other boys', but he was slender and half as wide as Akis. Akis was both tall and stout. He'd been quite a wrestler in his youth, and one of his arms was equal to two of Stavros's. Although he was past fifty, he didn't have a single strand of white in his hair; the bushy eyebrows, the hair and the curly moustache were as black and glossy as the coat of an Afghan horse.

'Kyr Akis, the Greek soldiers are on their way. This time

the information comes from a reliable source. We heard it a little while ago from the British in front of the Sporting Club. Fishermen passing by Lesbos saw the ships with their own eyes.'

A strong wind had picked up and the square filled with the scent of jasmine from Bournabat, mixing with the aroma of freshly baked bread from the bakery. The old women closed their eyes as if they were praying. Auntie Rozi raised her nose to the air and murmured, 'Rain is on the way. See, cool air from the sea is striking my hand, my face.' Panagiota's stomach hurt the way it did whenever she ate raw dough from her mother's rolling pin. Lowering her head, she looked down at the pink satin shoes they'd bought from Xenopoulo's shop on Frank Street on the first of the month because her feet had grown so much. The shoes were sparklingly clean, with black ribbons and little high heels. But what good were they now? She was most distressed. She inhaled heavily. Auntie Rozi had peeled one of the last tangerines of the season and was handing it to her. Without a word, she took it, peeled off the white pith with her slender fingers, and began slowly chewing.

Everyone in the square held their breath, waiting to hear what Grocer Akis would say. It seemed that if the grocer believed it, the ships really would come. The men playing backgammon in the coffeehouse held the dice in their hands and looked over to where the boys were standing. Afroula and Tasoula stopped making daisy chains; waterpipes stopped bubbling, prayer beads stopped turning. Even the peddlers who had wandered into the square left their trays and kettles beside the fountain and turned their ears towards Akis and the boys.

'If they're coming, they're coming. What's it to you? What

are you making all this noise for – do you think they're coming to die for you?'

Suddenly the square began humming like a beehive. Since Akis didn't deny it, maybe they really were coming. Minas elbowed Stavros aside and came to the front. He was a small, naughty boy. For some reason he hadn't grown tall yet, and nor had his voice broken. Although they were the same age, he looked like Stavros's little brother. The boys called him 'the Flea', and because he was so energetic, so little and so nimble, he was the star of the neighbourhood football games. Last month they'd beaten the Armenian High School thanks to him. Next week they were due to play the English School at Bournabat. Because everybody depended on Minas, he'd acquired a certain attitude; he even openly flirted with the beautiful Adriana, who looked like a big sister beside him.

'Not for us. They're coming to die for Greater Greece.'

In the rosy hue of evening, even from the other side of the square Panagiota could see that the blood had rushed to her father's face. His cheeks were crimson with rage. When her father was really, really angry, a very pale green ring of smoke encircled his dark head. Only Panagiota and Katina could see this smoke. Her mother had placed a mat on the sill of the bay window of their house above the grocery shop. Having shaken the breadcrumbs from the tablecloth, she was now leaning on the sill and watching the argument below, like everybody else. There was a mischievous gleam in her eyes in place of the usual vacant expression. At first Panagiota was furious; then she turned and looked at the old woman beside her as if asking for help. Auntie Rozi smiled a toothless grin and offered her another tangerine. The tension in the neighbourhood meant nothing to her.

'Fools!' roared Akis. 'Fools! What "Greater Greece", *vre*?

Do your ears hear the words coming out of your mouth? What liberty? If they're coming, they're coming to bring disaster upon us!'

'Kyr Akis, don't say that. We are of the same blood,' Stavros said.

'Distant relatives, more like! You know, the ones you don't want to see very often,' called out someone from the coffeehouse. Everyone laughed at this. Evening shadows fell over Stavros's face, and Panagiota's stomach cramped. Curious about the continuing argument, the men from the coffeehouse moved to the other side of the square, taking their dice with them. The circle around Akis and the boys was growing larger.

Akis looked into the face of each boy in turn. 'My sons,' he said quietly, 'you must keep your wits about you. Don't get tricked by this Greater Greece game; don't get yourselves into trouble. Big guys play their games, but they always choose young men like you as pawns. You live in the most beautiful city in the world, one of your hands in butter, the other in honey. Does it matter who rules us? Do you think we'd see this abundance if we were foisted off on Greece? If you don't believe me, go to Athens. Go and see if there's one single part of it that can compare to our bountiful Smyrna. Then come back to your homes and give thanks.'

The expression on Stavros's bony face hardened. His green eyes were blinking like a cat's in the dusk light. Panagiota's insides were humming like an engine.

Although his blood was boiling, Stavros managed to speak in a gentle, respectful tone. 'Kyr Akis, how can you talk like this – have you forgotten what happened in 1914? Don't you remember what tortures our people endured? Are we supposed to close our eyes to the fate of our people – for our own comfort? You yourself know that if we don't do something now, it will happen to us one day. Even your own sons—'

Seeing Akis's face freeze in pain, he stopped. One of Panagiota's hands went instinctively to her mouth. She turned anxiously towards the bay window of their house. Her mother had a sweet smile on her face and was looking at the moon rising like a brass tray behind the hilltop castle of Kadife Kale. Thank goodness she hadn't heard Stavros's last words.

Realizing that he'd hit below the belt, Stavros changed tack. 'Times are changing, Kyr Akis. There is no Ottoman Empire any more, as you know. The Committee of Union and Progress has dissolved itself and the Sultan has become a puppet of the British. This land will most certainly be parcelled out. Do you want Smyrna to go to the Italians? The freedom we have longed for for centuries is finally at our doorstep, and we Greeks will be in charge at last. The American president himself said so. It makes sense for our Smyrna to become a province of an independent Greece. Is there any other logical solution?'

Akis responded with a bitter smile. They saw that the Sultan had become a puppet of the British, these boys, but they couldn't see who was pulling the strings behind Venizelos. All of a sudden he felt exhausted. Being reminded of his sons, dead in the labour battalion, made him feel guilty, not angry. What if they had hidden their boys in the attic like other families had, or found some way to send them to Greece? If he'd known the goddamned war would end in four years, he could have hidden them for the duration, couldn't he? Stavros's elder brother had lived like a rat in the attic for four whole years, but at least he'd survived. And now he was able to walk the streets, to run down to the docks and greet Venizelos's soldiers, whereas Akis's sons had died in a cell worse than a shithole on the plains of Asia Minor. His insides twisted, like beans passing through a coffee grinder.

At the other end of the square Panagiota swallowed the last segment of her tangerine and took a deep breath. The angry green halo around her father's head had evaporated. Stavros's polite attitude, and the hopes and dreams of the young men, all of whom Akis had known since they were born, must have softened his heart. He wouldn't want to be ruled by the Italians anyway.

Before going for his coffee, Akis gave Stavros's shoulder a gentle pat and murmured, 'Watch out, son. Be careful. Don't believe everything the Europeans say. Don't fall for their tricks. They'll make you their pawns and we'll become the bait for a bigger fish.'

The boys' happiness had dissipated. They headed across the square in the direction of the British Hospital, kicking up stones and dust with the toes of their shoes as they went. The air was beginning to fill with the smell of food being fried in people's homes, and a woman was softly singing the folksong Afroula and Tasoula had chanted earlier.

'Aman, aman, yaniyorum ben
Aman, aman, seviyorum sen.

'Oh, oh, burning, I am
Oh, oh, it's loving you, I am.'

From far away a ferryboat blew its whistle. Men from the municipality came into the square with long tapers in their hands to light the street lamps. Thunder rumbled from beyond the mountains. Panagiota got up. She had promised to help her mother fry the fish that Fisherman Yorgo had brought that morning, and she also had to buy some bread. Kissing Auntie Rozi, she waited while the old woman made the sign of the cross three times over her head for luck. She'd got so tall that she had to lean down almost to the ground for the old woman to reach her.

Stavros, hands in his pockets, was still scuffing up stones and dust over on the British Hospital side of the square. Panagiota slowed her steps. Maybe she could exchange a word or two with him on her way to the bakery. Minas and a couple of the others whistled after her. Stavros didn't join in, but before Panagiota turned into Menekse Street she glanced back into the square and their eyes met. A wave as hot as a desert wind tore through her.

Nibbling on the end of a loaf of hot, fresh bread, her heart brimming – whether with happiness or pain, she couldn't tell – she went in through the blue door next to her father's grocery shop and skipped up the wooden stairs to their home. Joy was spreading through her, rising like a spark from the base of her spine, but she also wanted to cry. Swarthy-faced, tousle-haired, sweaty Stavros had stood there on the British Hospital side of the square and hadn't taken his eyes off her as she made her way from the bakery to the house. Her plaits, the top of her head, her ankles – every single part of her that his eyes had touched was trembling.

By the time she got to the kitchen, where her mother was dipping the fish in flour, her emotions were all over the place. Knowing full well that it would annoy her mother, she began to whistle, even though just a moment ago she'd felt like crying her heart out. She longed for tomorrow, so that she could see Stavros again. But... But if the Greek fleet really did arrive tomorrow, her father would never allow her out. She wouldn't be able to see him for a whole day. The thought made her moan as if she were drowning.

'What happened, *kori mou*? *Kala ise*? Are you okay?'

'The Greek army is coming, *Manoula*. Mama dearest. Did you hear?'

'Let's hope it is for the best, *yavri mou*. My child. Let's hope it's for the best.'

'Our teacher has always said that when that great day comes, the whole class will go down to the quay to greet them. I'm going to wear my white dress tomorrow. We must make a crown of laurel leaves for my hair this evening. Let's get the Greek flag we sewed out of the trunk.'

Katina wiped her floury hands on her apron and turned to her daughter. When she squinted her eyes, which were small anyway, she looked like a Chinese woman. A tiny, red-haired, freckle-faced Chinese woman.

'Your father doesn't want you to go to school tomorrow.'

Panagiota had been expecting this, but she was surprised her father had found the time to speak to her mother already.

'*Manoula!* Have mercy! How could you! The whole class will be there, and I have to stay home? *Eleos!* Mercy! I can't believe it! Oof!'

'It could be dangerous, my child. These are not safe times. The Turks are already organized. They're going to release the prisoners from jail. How could we send you out there all by yourself?'

Panagiota was used to her mother's unfounded anxieties. Since she'd lost her sons, Katina had become even more protective of her daughter, forever apprehensive about things that might, or might not, happen to her.

Panagiota rolled her eyes. 'Where did this "all by yourself" come from? The whole class will go down to the docks together. The girls from Kentrikon School will be there, and so will the girls from Agios Dimitris – Elpiniki, Adriana... Even the younger ones will go. The boys from the Evangelical School. Everyone. We're going to go down to the quay like Ancient Greek goddesses. We'll strew flowers in the soldiers' paths. Mama, please, I beg you. We've been preparing for this day for months – don't make me miss it. Speak to Papa, get him to give me permission. *Se parakalo*. Please, dear Mama, *Manoula mou*.'

Katina gave the dish of floured fish to her daughter and lit the coals under the lower rack of the woodstove with fatwood. '*Ela*. We shall see. You fry the fish, I'll set the table. I made artichokes too. Go and cut some dill and sprinkle it on the artichokes. It looks like rain, so we'll eat inside.'

Just as she was going through the kitchen door into the hallway, Katina turned back. She barely came up to her daughter's shoulder. 'Panagiota *mou*, my dear Panagiota, *se parakalo*, keep a smile on your face until your father comes upstairs, please, my beautiful daughter. You know that we cannot bear to see you unhappy. Come, don't break your dear mother and father's hearts, my child. We have endured enough.'

Alone in the kitchen, Panagiota stamped her clogs on the floor. Her father was probably the only royalist in all of Smyrna. Everyone else was in love with the charismatic prime minister of Greece, Venizelos. Most of all, Stavros. Ah, Stavros! She wouldn't see him until tomorrow evening now. Once again, she could hardly breathe. She held one of the mackerels by its tail, dipped it into the frying pan, then quickly took it out again. The oil was hot, sizzling. Nothing mattered any more, save for those moments when she could breathe

the same air as Stavros. As she fried the fish one by one, she muttered to herself, even though she knew this would make Stavros sad, 'I hope they don't come and disturb our peace.'

She was already jealous of Stavros's dream of a Greater Greece; this *Megali Idea*.

Home Alone

In the early hours of 15 May, as Grocer Akis was going off for his coffee, having left his tearful daughter and desperate wife locked up in the house, Edith opened her eyes in fear from beneath her white mosquito netting. She'd had a nightmare. In it, she was running away. She had killed someone, and for the rest of her life she would be a fugitive, on the run from the law. She was at a station, trying to catch a train that would take her far away. Ottoman soldiers, wearing aubergine-coloured fezzes with gold trim, were chasing her.

Trains featured frequently in Edith's dreams, for the house she had inherited from her father, Nikolas Dimos, was right next to the Aydin Railway track. Most mornings she woke to the whistle of the Boudja train arriving at the station. The old machinist, Tall Kozmas, sounded the whistle on approach, and the mournful noise didn't let up until the train had come to a standstill and he had jumped down. On some nights, the rumble of the freight train bringing goods from Asia Minor to the docks at Smyrna would keep Edith from sleeping all night long, shaking the windows of Number 7, Vasili Street like an earthquake. In the daytime the rails leading to the quay were used by the horse-drawn trams.

But this morning it wasn't Machinist Kozmas's train or the quivering windowpanes that had woken Edith. Wrapping herself in her lavender-scented sheets, she tried to recall the dream. She felt cold. Who had she killed, she wondered? These escape–pursuit dreams were becoming more common. Since the Boudja train hadn't come into the station yet, it had to be earlier than eight o'clock; maybe she could sleep a bit longer. Why was it so cold though? Why wasn't the stove alight and where was Zoe? She should have been there a long time ago and lit the stove and heated the water for the bath as well.

Zoe, who'd been a young girl when she worked for Juliette Lamarck, was a married woman now. She lived nearby in the Kerasohori neighbourhood with her husband, an immigrant from Chios, and their small daughter. She came early every morning, lit the stoves, heated the bath water and prepared Edith's breakfast. Edith had never once known her to be late. What could have happened this morning?

She had just reached for the bell beside her bed when a great noise rattled the windows. A big explosion. A bomb? Something had exploded… What? She came to her senses as if she'd been hit on the head. Sitting up in the middle of the bed, she hugged herself for warmth. More explosions followed, one after the other; the noise was coming from the harbour. People were screaming for help – were they at the docks?

The city was being bombarded!

She put her hands over her mouth, trying to stifle her own cries. Bombarded by who? The British? No, impossible. The German fleet that had been waiting out in the gulf had left a while ago. Then who? The Italians? She leaped out of bed and threw a robe around her shoulders. The explosions hadn't stopped; the windows were shaking as if they would break. Turks? Greeks?

Just then, the Boudja train came into the station, blowing its whistle for a long, long time. Pulling her robe tight around her, Edith went out into the corridor in her bare feet. For a moment she felt as if it were the corridor of a different house, and she looked around in surprise. In spite of the rattling windowpanes and the heavy gunfire from the port, the house was unusually silent; instead of the little sounds, whisperings and low laughter of the servants, there was total quiet.

Even though the servants tried to carry out their morning routines without bothering their mistress, they made quite a racket in comparison to this eerie, mysterious silence. In the eleven years she'd lived there, she'd become accustomed to lying inside her netting with her eyes closed, listening to the lively sounds of the house. The opening and closing of doors, Butler Christo's footsteps echoing on the veranda, the whispered giggling of the girls sweeping in the library, Zoe scolding them through the low curtain, the muffled laughter in the kitchen in response to Mehmet the cook's jokes, which he delivered in a voice that carried from the kitchen to the bedrooms, the squeak of the wooden stairs – this morning there was none of that. Instead, there was the boom of gunfire.

When the explosions ceased, a ship's whistle sounded and was met by screams for help from the wharf. Now the ringing of church bells was added to the sounds from the city. Edith had learned from Avinash that the insistent ringing of church bells was a means of attracting the attention of foreign warships waiting in the harbour. It was a coded call for assistance in an emergency, a sign between the city's Christian populace and their allies. Without a doubt, something awful was happening.

Barefoot, she tiptoed along the dark brown wooden floor of the corridor, opening each door in turn: the library, the guest room, another guest room. The rooms Edith didn't use were fully furnished, but this morning they all looked empty and abandoned. Nothing moved except for the dust dancing in the light streaming through the windows. She went into the bathroom at the end of the corridor and closed the door. The water in the basin was icy. She washed her face and sat on the toilet's cold porcelain.

Her breathing was rapid and her underarms were wet in spite of the chill. A strange smell was coming off her skin; the smell of fear.

Although Edith had shown courage as a woman living on her own in Smyrna, she had never once in her thirty years of life opened her eyes to an empty house. She may have woken up alone, but she had never been on her own in a house. In her father's mansion, she had lived with three generations of the family and an army of servants. In France at the convent school she had shared a dormitory with twenty girls. Since she had moved to this house that she'd inherited from Nikolas Dimos, there'd always been someone in the servants' room on the ground floor. And both Butler Christo and Zoe, who was now her housekeeper, always arrived at the house before she woke.

This was the first time she'd ever been in a place devoid of the sound or breath of another person.

More than the bombardment outside, the situation inside the house frightened her, but because she didn't consider fear an appropriate sentiment, she neither recognized nor felt it, even though the smell of fear was coming off her skin. Just as Juliette masked her sorrow and desperation with anger, Edith met fear with ridicule and biting sarcasm, having long since banished it to somewhere deep inside her.

Coming out of the bathroom, she glanced warily over the

rooms of the empty house, which looked as if they belonged to a different era. The wooden floor beneath her feet was like ice. She wrapped her arms around herself. Maybe she'd entered another dimension, as with the space–time theories her father, Monsieur Lamarck, had loved explaining to her while they'd wandered arm in arm around the Bournabat garden at twilight. She had travelled through time while she was asleep and woken to find herself at a different point in history. Or in a different world, like in the Jules Verne novel that she and Edward had read together, lying side by side. The house was the same house, Edith was the same person, but everything else had vanished. If she looked out the window, maybe she would see a scene from a century in the future. Squinting, she looked up to the ceiling.

Gypsy Yasemin hadn't been making it up or exaggerating: Edith was indeed a hashish addict. Without getting high, she couldn't make love; without the pipe's touch on her lips, she couldn't sleep; she couldn't even join a social gathering without taking a few puffs. She justified her addiction by saying, 'People are so stupid, Avinash, that it is the only way I can endure their boring conversation.' More often than not, she was high, and now, wandering around the empty rooms of her house like an anxious stranger and thinking about time travel, she couldn't make up her mind whether this was reality or an illusion. Whatever Yasemin was mixing with the weed in her bundle affected Edith even in her daydreams, even when she was not under the influence. She saw everything from behind a curtain of fog.

Rather than go near the windows with their rattling panes, she started down the stairs, trying not to make them squeak. The noise of the guns was not so frequent now, but her ears picked up other sounds. Was music being played somewhere?

And what about those screams? They were not screams of fear, but they were... Suddenly she saw something that made her heart jump. Down there, on the other side of the door, a silhouette was visible through the colourful stained glass – a man! A man was forcing the door open! She almost lost her balance and fell down the stairs. Grabbing the bannister with one hand, she stopped herself.

An image that had been coming in and out of her subconscious since she'd woken up gained clarity. Of course! It was the Greek landing. She felt relief. The world remained in its place. Neither reality nor time had changed.

Last night before dinner Avinash had stopped by and said that it was now official: the Greek fleet was going to enter Smyrna. The British general had informed Smyrna's Turkish governor, Izzet Pasha, that the Ottoman administration was to have its soldiers wait at the governor's building ready to transfer power over to the Greeks.

At that point, Edith's servant girls, who had their ears pressed to the dining room door so as to hear what the Indian spy was saying, forgot themselves in their excitement and began to squeal with delight. When Edith went out into the hall to scold them, she found them all hugging each other and crying tears of joy.

Still... Still, she hadn't expected it would happen so soon – the very next day. Quite honestly, she hadn't taken Avinash's agitation seriously; after all, rumours of the Greek landing had been circulating ever since the war had ended. Her anxious spy lover hadn't stayed for dinner as he needed to work through the night at the consulate. Kissing Edith hurriedly, he'd been oddly imperious with his instructions.

'Close all the doors, windows and shutters,' he ordered, 'and don't send the butler back to his home tonight. Mehmet and Zoe should leave right now; give them permission to go, and tell them not to come tomorrow. And do not go out of the house until I return.'

Hating to be dictated to by anyone, Edith had immediately sent Butler Christo off to his home, and then ate her dinner at the huge table all by herself, served by the girls, who were chattering in the kitchen like birds. Mehmet the cook and Zoe went to their homes in the city right after sunset, as they did every evening. It had begun to rain, but she still didn't close the shutters.

The dong of the front doorbell reverberated around the high-ceilinged hall like a series of explosions. A jolt of electricity raced down Edith's spine as the scenario she had long feared but had never acknowledged came into her head: with the city in chaos, looters were taking advantage of the lack of control and attacking the homes of the wealthy.

Like all Levantine children, Edith had grown up hearing horror stories of bandits coming down from the mountains to rob the mansions and large estates, and pirates from Chios kidnapping babies for ransoms. Her own big brother, Jean-Pierre, had been rescued from a cart when he was little by their butler, Mustafa. Just a few months ago, the son of the former governor had been kidnapped and taken to the mountains by the Circassian bandit Cerkez Ethem. Bournabat's wealthy British residents had paid 53,000 gold coins to secure his release.

And now, proving both her mother and Avinash, who'd been insisting for years that she employ an armed guard, correct, marauders had come to her door first.

Mon Dieu!

She ran down the stairs. Breathing deeply, she opened the cupboard beside the front door and grabbed the hunting rifle left from the time of Nikolas Dimos. She didn't know whether there were shells in it, but she had learned to shoot a gun on hunting expeditions with her father and their Bournabat neighbours. Without waiting for the bell to ring a second time, she opened the door and aimed the shotgun between the looter's eyebrows.

Once he'd got over the surprise, Avinash Pillai began to laugh. His lover was standing there in front of him in her white silk dressing gown, barefoot and with her wild hair, which she'd not had time to gather up, forming a halo around her head, alive with static. In her slender arms she held the hunting rifle as if it were a machine gun. Lowering the shotgun, Edith took two steps back, raised her head with difficulty, and looked at Avinash, her black eyes magnified beneath her thick lashes, the pink of her rosy lips set off by the paleness of her face.

Avinash waited for Edith to realize the absurdity of the situation and join in with his laughter, but instead she unexpectedly threw herself into his arms. She was shaking like a leaf.

'Oh, Avinash, is it you? Thank God! Thank God! What is happening, for God's sake?'

Avinash caught the rifle before it fell to the ground. It was the first time he'd ever seen his lover of eleven years afraid. Edith was always calm and courageous. During the Great War, when the British were prepared to bomb Smyrna, all the neighbours left the city; only Edith stayed in a by-then deserted Vasili Street. She slept alone in the house with her maidservants every night. With the exception of a few times when they'd come back tipsy from some summer excursion, she never allowed Avinash to spend the night at her home. She was one of those women who would not permit any man to be her protector. At first Avinash had been attracted by this peculiarity, but over time it became a flaw in their relationship, which he felt keenly. This was the first time Edith had ever thrown herself into his arms, and it reminded him of Juliette Lamarck's hysterical episodes.

There was another explosion down at the harbour. Edith pressed herself even more tightly against Avinash. The stained glass of the door rattled and something shattered upstairs. With Edith's arms still around his waist, Avinash nudged her back indoors, closed the door behind them and leaned the rifle against the wall. She was still trembling. He rested her back against the door so that she wouldn't fall and looked around for one of the servants to request a glass of water.

Butler Christo, who still smiled under his moustache at Avinash's visits and never, ever left the young servant girls or the hallway unattended, was nowhere to be seen. Was Edith alone in the house? He took her hands in his. 'The Greek fleet has arrived. The soldiers are landing.'

Edith hid her head in Avinash's shoulder. She'd stopped shaking. 'So who are they attacking?' she asked, her voice muffled. 'Why is the city being bombarded? Is it the Italians? Are the Turks fighting back?'

'No, darling. Nobody is attacking anybody. Those guns are celebrating the fleet entering the harbour. Ah, you thought...'

Avinash enfolded her delicate body in his dark arms, in the way he might hold a child. Part of him was thinking about making love to Edith in the rooms where they'd never yet made love – the kitchen, the pantry, or right there in the hall, where, normally, Christo kept watch.

'Is everything all right? I mean, has public order been maintained?'

'Yes, everywhere appears calm. There are soldiers in some

of the districts and, for now, public order is excellent. If you wish, we can go out together. I'll accompany you as far as the quay. The wharf is thronging with Christians; they've gone wild with joy and it's like a holiday atmosphere down there.'

'So you mean one is free to go out on the streets now, my master?'

Avinash realized that she was referring to his imperiousness of the night before. He pulled himself together. She must have sent Butler Christo home immediately after he'd left last night. Before detaching her arms from around his waist, he tried to catch her eye, but she still had her head on his shoulder.

'You know, some of the Greek soldiers weren't even aware where they were going. They'd been told they were going to a port in Ukraine to fight the Bolsheviks. They only realized that they'd come to Smyrna when they sailed into the harbour this morning.'

'Even the deaf Sultan had heard about the occupation, but they hadn't?'

Avinash was surprised at his lover's choice of words but said nothing. Despite her sarcastic tone, she still hadn't extricated herself from his arms, as much to her own surprise as his. His hands instinctively moved inside her robe, finding her small breasts under the silk fabric. Edith made a sound, whether as invitation or rejection it was hard to say.

'Where are Christo, the servant girls, Zoe...? Where are they all?'

'I don't know. When I woke up, there was nobody in the house.'

'They're probably all down at the quay too,' murmured the Indian, without giving a thought to what that must have meant for his lover, having to wake up alone in an empty house; his lover of so many years, whose caprices he had submitted to and no longer tried to counter, and whom he now believed he knew to an exceptional degree.

The relationship between Avinash and Edith had been going on for eleven years. There were still times – in the wavering light of a kerosene lamp dimmed low on winter evenings, when darkness fell early; stretched out on Edith's bed, smoking hashish from a waterpipe; on spring afternoons with the seashell-smelling wind cooling their sweaty skin – when they made love with pleasure, but they no longer felt the same desire for each other that they once had. Right now, however, they were both hungry for each other, just as they'd been in the early years; they both felt the same urge and wanted to take advantage of the moment, but, fearing that one of the maids or the butler might return to the house at any moment, they instead continued to stand by the door, pressed up against each other, speaking of the outside world.

'What are the Muslims doing? What's the situation like where you are?'

'For now they're in shock. As you know, the news that the Greek army would land was given to the governor yesterday evening. Last night, in spite of the rain, a large group from the Muslim districts assembled at the Jewish Cemetery up in Bahri Baba, overlooking the port. Shots were fired in protest. I went to have a look, but it was more like a fairground than a protest. Rich, poor, women, children – all sorts were there; thousands of people from the Muslim neighbourhoods. There was a lot of beating of drums, but for what? This morning they're all hiding behind closed doors. What else can they do?'

'Is something going to happen?' Edith asked, her voice momentarily not hoarse with desire but deep and serious.

'The soldiers are landing in an orderly fashion, but it seems to me that they aren't quite certain what to do. The atmosphere is very highly charged, and there may well be security lapses during the changeover from the Turkish administration to the Greek one. There will be incidents, for sure. Hopefully no one will get hurt.'

This time his hands went lower, slipping between the folds of her nightgown. His experienced fingers, knowing all the pleasure points, moved between her legs. Yielding to Avinash's expert touch, Edith turned the lock in the door with one hand. Her lover was someone who always paid great attention to his appearance; he bought the finest quality British cloth, had his suits made by the best tailors in Smyrna, and walked around dressed to the nines. But this morning, because he'd been at the consulate all night, his trousers were wrinkled and the underarms of his shirt were stained with that spicy sweat that always embarrassed him so. He had never before come to Vasili Street without having first visited a bathhouse.

Drunk with strange emotions, Edith realized that, on this day when such important work awaited him, he'd come not to make love to her but to check on her. The Greek landing would be considered a victory for the British; in the coming days, Avinash would certainly be very busy. In order to have him all to herself for a short while, to place herself, even at such a critical time, above the demands of politics, the Secret Service and all those other manly preoccupations that lay ahead, the hand that had turned the lock now moved to undo the buttons of his trousers.

Avinash placed the hat that he'd taken off when Edith

pointed the gun barrel between his eyebrows gently down on the floor and pressed her between his body and the joyfully coloured stained glass of the front door. And on the very spot where, thirty years before, Monsieur Lamarck had lifted Nikolas Dimos by the collar and shaken him, Avinash entered Edith hungrily and with deep longing.

Frog Rain

'Mama, Mama, come here! It's raining frogs! I swear, Mama, it's raining frogs. Oh my God! Run, Mama!'

Katina was slicing onions in the kitchen. Wiping away her tears with the back of her hand, she came out into the hallway and strode swiftly to the front window. Panagiota, dressed in her white dress that reached down to the floor, was kneeling on the mat set inside the bay window, her hands and nose stuck to the glass.

'*Kori mou*,' Katina shouted, 'didn't I tell you not to stay in front of the window today! Eh? Why are you still there?'

'*Kita*, look, Mama. Come and look at the street from here.'

Straightening her black headscarf, Katina approached the mat. Her forehead was beaded with sweat. 'Your father has always said that stones will rain down on our heads. And it has started already, even before the sun has set, with this gunfire from the Greek evzones. So where are the frogs? The crickets are everywhere again. What you call frogs—'

'Look at the ground – it's covered in frogs. Have you ever seen anything like this?'

Katina murmured a prayer from between her pursed lips and quickly made the sign of the cross. Frogs truly were raining from the sky and falling – pat, pat – onto the cobblestones in front of Akis's grocery. Some died as they hit the ground, some hopped off into the square after the initial shock. Shadows hovered like ghosts over the ones that had died, making them look double the size.

'*Manoula mou*, may I run down and collect some frogs, please? I'll take a bucket with me so that they can fall into it. *Se parakalo!*'

'Ah, *Thee mou*, dear God, what a thing to ask, daughter! Do you see a single soul on the street? Why would you want to go out there? The gunfire has not stopped since this morning. What a foolish child you are, *vre yavri mou*! Is this the time to be collecting frogs in the street, darling girl?'

'What is there to be afraid of? Everybody's out in the streets. The whole neighbourhood rushed down to the quay carrying Greek flags and flowers in their hands. We're the only ones staying at home like prisoners.' Panagiota's eyes were full of tears as she turned from the window to face her mother. Like a festering wound, her resentment, finding no outlet, had swelled inside her. 'Everybody went, and did anything happen to any of them? They came pitter-pattering back to their homes. Just listen – Elpiniki and Afroula are singing songs next door. Everyone got to see the evzones in their traditional white skirts and pointy shoes and all. It was only me who stayed home. This evening when we go out, they'll all make fun of me.'

'Nobody will be going out onto the streets tonight.'

'Really?' Panagiota's voice was louder now. Her black curls had come loose from her plaits, and her eyes and cheeks were blazing.

She'd been up since daybreak. Knowing full well that her father wouldn't let her go down to the docks, she woke before the sun, dressed in white as her teacher had instructed, and put a crown of laurel leaves on her head. If she couldn't go down to the wharf, she would celebrate the soldiers landing in Smyrna by herself at home. Her father couldn't stop her doing that!

Akis had woken up grumbling as the fleet entering the harbour began to fire their guns. After forbidding the women to leave the house, he went off to the coffeehouse. Which meant that if looters came and ransacked the house, he wouldn't hear them. Katina had tried to comfort Panagiota. 'Is that likely, *yavri mou*? Your dear father isn't far away; he would hear a scream for help from the window and would run over.' As it was, as soon it became clear that the gunfire was coming from the shore rather than out in the harbour, Akis returned home and stayed until everything had quietened down.

Panagiota had been furious ever since, sitting in the window in her white dress, with the crown on her head. The only thing that had taken her mind off her anger was the sudden downpour of frogs.

'I'm a disgrace. The whole school went – everybody except me. Nobody in the neighbourhood except you supports the Greek king anyway. I don't support him either. This evening I'm going to shout, "*Zito, zito!*" at Father. Just wait and see. *Zito o Venizelos!* Long live Venizelos! *Zito, zito, zito!*'

Katina took a step towards the window and slapped her daughter, drunk with her own anger, in the face. 'Watch your mouth, little lady. As long as you are living under your father's roof, you will not behave like that. Come to your senses, *mari*!'

With jaws clenched, mother and daughter glared at each other. Outside, the storm intensified. The lemon tree in front of the window was so confused, it didn't know which way to turn; like a fragile, multi-armed child, it was tossing its branches from left to right and beating at the glass.

When several more frogs fell onto the roof of the house, both mother and daughter burst out laughing. Katina regretted having slapped her daughter, and Panagiota regretted having upset her mother by shouting, '*Zito, zito*'. With the tension now gone, Katina sat down beside Panagiota on the mat in the window and wrapped her arms around her slender form.

'Ah, my beautiful daughter, my darling child, how could I send you out into those crowds? They even sent word to your father not to open the shop. You were here when Uncle Christo stopped by yesterday evening; you heard him yourself. That Indian jewel merchant said shops should stay closed today so as to avoid tradesmen getting hurt or goods being damaged. So how could we let you, our only child, go out by yourself. Huh? Tell me, Panagiota *mou*.'

Panagiota leaned her head on her mother's breast as she used to when she was little, crushing the leaves of her crown. She was fourteen years old and a head taller than Katina, but at times like this she felt like a tiny child. Her ear found her mother's heartbeat. Closing her eyes, she listened to the sound of frogs striking the cobblestones. Her mother's skin was soft and warm. Guilt welled up inside her.

It was always the same! She said things she knew would make her mother blow her top. She would be asking for a slap and then would feel sorry for having upset Katina. But what could she do? She was fed up with all the melodrama. Yes, her brothers had died. But life went on. Panagiota was alive, and so was Katina. During the funeral rites at the church, her father had stood guard on their doorstep so that her brothers' souls couldn't come in, but what good had that done? The ghosts of Kosta and Manoli had continued to haunt every nook and cranny of the house for three and a half years. At Panagiota's age, a year felt as long as a century and death a distant concept. As the memory of her brothers gradually faded, thinking about them no longer brought Panagiota pain, though there remained a residue of sadness around her soul.

Inside their house, there were reminders of them everywhere: in the black cloth covering the mirrors; in the evening meals eaten in silence by the light of the kerosene lamp; in the endless hours her mother spent praying in front of the icon; in the *koliva* dessert made for the souls of the dead and blessed by the priests; in Akis's sighs and in the tears of Katina, who never took off her mourning black. No matter how much her mother loved her, Katina always seemed resentful when Panagiota burst into genuine laughter. It was out of the question that Katina and Akis could ever laugh together. At such times Panagiota would feel very small and insignificant. She missed Adriana and Elpiniki and felt guilty.

When the Ottoman Empire entered the Great War on the side of the Germans, Christian boys were ordered to join the labour battalions. Akis tried to pay in order to have his sons exempted from military service. The amount he paid to the first policeman wasn't enough, so later a gendarme came by. Then a sergeant knocked on their door.

This sergeant was an insolent man. In addition to cash, Akis gave him enough sugar and flour to last an entire village many months. He arranged for a cart to take the provisions to Bergama. But the sergeant was never satisfied. Maybe he was aware that the grocer had a volcanic temper and was just waiting for him to erupt. Sure enough, on seeing the sergeant grinning in his shop doorway yet again one day, Akis lost his rag and strode over to the weasel, ready to punch him out. The sergeant would definitely have had him prosecuted, but that evening Kosta and Manoli announced that they were giving themselves up. They didn't want their father to get into any more trouble.

The image of the twins and the fresh smiles on their faces as they boarded the train at Basmane Station had never left Katina. 'There's nothing to worry about, Mama,' they'd said. 'We'll make some roads, dig a few tunnels. How long can this so-called war last? You should put aside some money for Panagiota's dowry, and send her to Homerion High School.'

At first Katina had been happy that her sons wouldn't be fighting at the front. A childhood friend of Akis's, Ismail from Chesme, even though he was over forty years old, had been called up to the army because he'd done a month less than he should have. He was sent off to the front in the Allahuekber Mountains. His wife Saadet and his children were only able to survive thanks to the sacks of flour and tins of oil that Akis sent to their home. That Ismail managed to return safely from Enver Pasha's unimaginable ordeal was a miracle. At least Katina's twins wouldn't be fighting in battles like that, wouldn't be lice fodder on a snow-covered mountain.

Even though it was a war waged by infidels against infidels, the Sultan had joined it on the side of the Germans and had called his people to a Holy War. Since non-Muslims could not fight in a Holy War, the Christian boys were drafted in to work in labour battalions, building infrastructure.

When he first heard about this, Akis had said, 'The Sultan

would never have thought of doing that; it must be the members of the Committee of Union and Progress, those Unionists, who dreamed up this business of having labour battalions.' But many years later, at the end of another world war, when he saw photographs of the death camps Hitler had sent the Jews to, he was to say to his empty walls, 'It wasn't the Unionists who came up with the idea for those labour battalions that took our sons' lives; it was the Germans.' For one brief moment, Grocer Akis had forgotten that his wife was not with him in the squatter's house with the corrugated iron roof and closed curtains in the New Smyrna neighbourhood of Athens. She couldn't argue with him about his theory about the labour battalions, for Katina had not managed to pass from the old Smyrna to the new one.

Their sons never came home again.

Katina closed her eyes and buried her nose in her daughter's hair, between the laurel leaves of the makeshift crown. Panagiota's neck was wet with her mother's tears.

The letters stopped coming. And then in the spring the neighbour's son, Yanni, brought the bleak news. The labour battalions were essentially prison camps, and the Christian boys were starving and utterly destitute; when any of them fell seriously ill, they were left to die in their own filth. Yanni managed to stay alive despite being at death's door with typhus only because a kind doctor had happened to visit the battalion. He was even given four weeks' leave to recuperate and sent home. Katina and Akis learned the truth from Yanni, himself just skin and bone and prone to talking in his sleep about the camps; he spoke of the living lying with the dead in putrid, windowless ditches, of being left without food for weeks yet forced to continue breaking stones every day.

The loss of her sons left an irreparable hole in Katina's soul and she wasn't sure she could be a strong mother any more with what remained. For the past three and a half years she had carried on mechanically going about her daily tasks. Yes, she filled Panagiota's dowry trunk with care; and when she could catch her daughter, she taught her embroidery and how to roll *dolma* thinly and how to marinate lamb in milk. When chatting with her neighbours at their coffee-scented picnics or in front of the door at dusk, or when reading poems her daughter had written, she sometimes forgot her grief and smiled. But in that still place behind her pupils, the emptiness from where her soul had migrated remained unfilled.

She had become ever more obsessive about Panagiota, increasingly uneasy at how tall her daughter had grown and how much attention she was getting in the neighbourhood on account of her beauty. Her predominant emotion these days was anxiety. Sometimes she spent a whole morning praying in front of the icon of Agia Ekaterini, her namesake and the protector of young girls. Now she was afraid that because of the Greek landing that all the young people were so excited about, she would lose control of her daughter. She couldn't sleep for thinking about how to protect her.

There was a great boom from somewhere in the distance, and Katina jumped up from her seat in the window.

'Get up, Giota *mou*. Get up! I don't know what's happening, but these noises – cannon shots, fighting – do not bode well. Let's not sit in the window. Come, daughter. Your father will have heard it and will come home now.'

Panagiota couldn't take her eyes off the street.

'Giota *mou*, *se parakalo*, please. Come, daughter. Let your father not see you at the window.'

'Aaah! Mama, look. Look! *Ela, ela edo*, come here and look!'

Panagiota was kneeling on the mat, pointing to something under the eaves of the house across the street. Water was pouring from the rooftops in a flood, and rainwater was surging like a raging river from the broken section of the drainage canal in the middle of the street, carrying with it frogs, geranium pots, dead birds, newspapers, handkerchiefs and children's toys in a rush towards the square.

Katina came back to the window. 'I can't see anything, child. Where are you looking?'

'There – over by Fisherman Yorgo's door.'

Katina squinted and saw something moving outside her neighbour's door. The branches of the lemon tree continued to strike the windowpane. 'What is that? Who's over there – is it Niko? Or Muhtar?'

Muhtar was the neighbourhood's short-tailed, yellow street dog.

'Yes, Muhtar is over there. But look carefully – there's a woman there too. Do you see her?'

Kneeling up on the mat like her daughter, Katina saw a fashionably dressed European lady standing under the eaves of the house across the street. She was wearing a dress the colour of a pomegranate flower with a sharp white collar. A small, chic hat sat slightly askew on her head, and a gauze veil covered her face. She was leaning against the wall of the fisherman's house, with the tip of her umbrella, the same tan colour as her cape, resting on the ground.

Panagiota's excitement was not unfounded. One did not

see such beautifully attired European ladies in their poor neighbourhood.

'Mama, look, she's crying, I think. Her shoulders are shaking, and she's sopping wet.'

Mother and daughter pressed their noses against the window, trying to get as good a view as possible. The woman looked like she might fall over.

Katina laughed. 'Look at our Muhtar! He's soaking wet too, but he's still holding his tail high. He's protecting the woman – it's as if he's saying "this will pass", as if he knows a secret we humans don't. Bravo, Muhtar, St Muhtar!'

Panagiota was pleased to hear her mother's laughter. '*Manoula mou*, shall I go down and bring her here? Maybe someone close to her has died. Look, she's crying. She could drink some tea with us and we could heat up yesterday's *kuluraki* bagels in the stove and offer her those. She could warm up and dry off. What do you say? I could speak French with her and you could hear how much I've learned.' Beneath her curly lashes, Panagiota's black eyes began to shine at the thought of a European woman in their house.

'Of course not, daughter! She's just sheltering from the rain. As soon as it stops, she'll get in her motor car and go. Is it up to us to comfort a European woman? You're just looking for an excuse to go outside, *beba mou*, my baby.'

Just then the woman drew a handkerchief from the silk purse hanging from her wrist and with tiny gestures dabbed the raindrops from her nose, face and forehead. Opening her elegant umbrella, she glided down Menekse Street towards the square, as if she were waltzing across a dance floor. She turned the corner and disappeared from sight.

Panagiota watched her leave with a dreamy look in her eyes and murmured, 'How beautiful she is!'

Getting up from the mat, Katina grumbled, 'What could you see that you call her beautiful, you silly girl? Through the rain, and with her face hidden by that veil. She might be quite ugly under there. You are much prettier than her. Come on, get up from the window now – you've turned into a pot plant, sitting on the sill like that.'

Before getting to her feet, Panagiota, dressed like an Ancient Greek virgin in her white smock and laurel-leaf crown, leaned out of the bay window and took one last look at the corner around which the European lady had vanished.

Zito O Venizelos

When Edith reached the little neighbourhood square, she took out her handkerchief and dabbed at her face again. Crying in the middle of the street? What was happening to her today! She had grown up in a family that never showed emotion in public, so this was most unusual and disquieting.

Holding her head high under her umbrella, she continued to the edge of Psomalani. She had come out to look for Butler Mustafa, to ask him to arrange a motor car to take her mother to the train station. She had walked as far as the inner part of the Hadji Frangou neighbourhood, above the French Hospital, but then the rain had caught her. It had to be the extraordinary situation in the city that was making her so emotional; there could be no other reason for this sudden grieving over forgotten losses and crying about them in public.

After she and Avinash had made love in the hallway that morning, he had set out for the British Consulate and she had got dressed by herself, without bathing, for she did not know how to heat water for the basin. She was due to visit her grandmother, who was a patient at the French Hospital, and had arranged to meet Juliette Lamarck there. In the absence of her housekeeper and with no means to reach her mother, Edith had no idea if the plans had changed. Had everyone in Bournabat heard about the arrival of the Greek fleet in Smyrna? The fleet had been expected since the beginning of May, but the actual arrival date had been kept secret until the last moment. As her mother was to have taken the eight o'clock train, most probably she was not yet aware of what had happened and would come to the hospital as agreed. Edith decided to take a quick look at the quay and then continue to the hospital.

The touch of the sun's rays after the rain had released the smell of newly freshened grass and flowers from the well-kept gardens of Vasili Street, and the strong wind blowing in from the docks added a whiff of seaweed and salt to the mix. The little bell on her wrought-iron garden gate jangled as she left and echoed down the empty street. Beneath the deep blue sky, the cobblestones shone as if recently polished. Rays of sunlight beamed down upon the city from behind the clouds. She trod carefully, avoiding any loose stones so as not to muddy the summer shoes she had chosen to wear. Without a maid to help her, she'd been unable to put on a girdle, so she felt naked under her dress the colour of pomegranate flowers and conscious of the sweet imprints of her lover's hands on her body.

Gazing down the silent street ahead of her, the irrational fears of earlier returned. The neighbourhood was always quiet at this hour of the morning, but today it was utterly deserted. Everyone else had obviously locked their doors and closed their shutters, just as Avinash had advised her to do last night, and escaped somewhere. Why hadn't she left the house with Avinash? The hospital was on the way to the British Consulate; they could have walked there together.

Her determination to do everything by herself was sometimes very tiring.

At Aliotti Boulevard, she got a shock. The elegant avenue was strewn with rose petals. The wind coming off the sea was lifting the petals into the air and then whirling them to the ground again, covering the street in a velvety carpet of pink, white and red. The gypsies had left their baskets lined up on the side of the road; they must have run down to the docks or maybe they had fled when they heard that Greek soldiers had come. Edith closed her eyes and inhaled the fragrance of the roses. The father of her Paris schoolfriend Feride used to send his daughter bottles of rose oil every year, to sell if she got stuck for money. French people used to go crazy over it. As did Avinash. Ah, Avinash... Had he too seen these rose petals chasing each other, she wondered.

As she turned into Mesudiye Street, two lines of schoolchildren appeared before her, laughing and singing songs as they headed to the docks; she could hear a band playing down by the sea too. It must have been these sounds that she'd heard from her house, mistaking them for the sounds of Smyrna being bombarded. How easy it was to deceive oneself! The street was becoming more crowded with each step, and unlike in her own silent neighbourhood, the people here had put on their holiday apparel, slicked down their hair and run out onto the street with flags in their hands. As she was about to turn on to Frank Street, she was swept up in the crowd, mingling with young girls dressed in white and carrying daisies, and old women with jars of rose oil in their hands.

The quay was so congested, a dropped needle wouldn't have reached the ground. Everybody from seven to seventy was there, waving blue and white flags at the ships anchored in the harbour and shouting '*Zito o Venizelos!*' in honour of the Greek prime minister, the man behind the plan to have Smyrna given to Greece. Long live Venizelos! The ships sailing into the harbour one after the other were answering the cheers with a continuous blowing of whistles. Church bells added to the racket.

Edith was borne along, past the fancy hotels, fashionable cafés and theatres which lined the street, down towards the quay. She greeted a few acquaintances in front of the Sporting Club, then made her way over to the Pantheon Cinema, from where Zoe was waving to her. Zoe, holding her little daughter by the hand, was shoving people aside as she tried to move forwards. Her curly brown head kept bobbing in and out of view like a cormorant amidst the sea of hats. Finally, she was at Edith's side.

'Mademoiselle Lamarck, they have arrived!' she shouted with childlike excitement. 'Do you see them? Miss Edith *mou*, they have finally come!'

Her cheeks were flushed and her eyes were shining in wonder, as if she had witnessed a miracle. Her daughter repeated her mother's words like a parrot. Edith had known Zoe since she was a girl and had never seen her so happy.

'They arrived early this morning,' she said, swallowing half her words in her haste, as if she'd been starving and was now gulping down her first meal. 'My husband brought me the good news at daybreak. "Get up, Zoe," he said. "*Ela grigora*, come on, be quick." I thought it would be like last Christmas – you remember, when the dock in Kordelio collapsed under the weight of all those crowds who'd gone down to greet the soldiers, and ten people were drowned. I thought it would be chaotic, like then, and that nothing would come of it. But it seems my husband knew beforehand and hadn't said anything. People set up camp here on the docks at midnight, sleeping on bundles and bales. This time the Greeks really did come!'

Edith remembered well what had happened last Christmas. Rumours had spread that the Greek ship *Leon* was on its way to Smyrna. The local Greeks unfurled a giant Greek flag at the entrance of the Church of Agia Photini. People everywhere got very worked up and there was even some singing of the Greek national anthem in bars. But then nothing happened.

Avinash had explained that the Greek forces hadn't been given sufficient support by Britain's Lloyd George or other European countries, so they were obliged to abort the landing. But now, with the Italians having taken over Kusadasi and Antalya without permission from the Allies, Venizelos had hurriedly been given the green light and had despatched the first warships into the harbour.

Zoe, who knew nothing of these powergames and would not have believed them anyway, was warbling like a bird. 'But this time is different. This time the soldiers who landed in Smyrna will not leave. We are saved! We are free, Miss Edith! Freedom has come at last! Look at our evzones! My heroes, my brave lions, how handsome they are in their traditional white uniforms, in their *foustanella*.'

Girded with swords, Greek soldiers in khaki-coloured skirts and with black pompoms on their boots were doing a folkdance around the weapons piled up in front of the Hunting Club. Zoe's little daughter waved to a blue-eyed officer with a proper moustache who was standing near the sea. He smiled back at her.

The place was like a fairground. Peddlers were wandering around carrying sweets, nuts, and halva trays on their heads, occasionally setting down their wares in whatever tiny space they managed to find in order to catch their breath. Edith saw several vegetable sellers entering the merry fray, their donkeys laden with sacks. Her other two maids were over in front of the Café de Paris, holding blue and white flags in their hands. They laughed and nudged each other whenever they happened to catch a soldier's eye. Church bells rang out continually. All of the local Greek women, young and old, showered the passing soldiers with flowers. Zoe, trying to make herself heard above the noise of a marching band that was passing, shouted, 'Ah, Kyra Edith *mou*, I wish you'd been here a little earlier. You should have seen our bishop the Metropolitan Chrysostomos kneeling to kiss the Greek flag. All of us, even the men, were drowning in tears. Then the whole unit got into formation and paraded along the quay. Flowers rained upon them; rose oil was poured on their heads. This is a dream come true!'

As she looked at the crowds, Edith suddenly felt exhausted and very alone. Why did she never feel as if she belonged anywhere? Why couldn't she share in this happiness? Her only desire right then was to get away from all those people milling around, to be by herself, alone with her growing unease.

The French Hospital with its well-kept garden shaded by lofty cypresses would be a refuge from all the noisy confusion, but how could she walk there against the press of all these people? She needed to find a vehicle. While she'd been talking to Zoe, she'd been carried along by the crowd to the Passport Pier. Pushing her way past the adolescent boys yelling at the top of their voices, the Armenian mothers holding their black-plaited daughters tightly by the hand, the peddlers wandering here and there, she managed to get to Frank Street with its row of shuttered shops. There was not a carriage to be seen.

Should she have chosen a different route and gone to the British Consulate to ask Avinash for help?

A vague booming sound came from the direction of the wharf, followed by an explosion. The battleships were presumably firing their cannons. But all at once the cheering ceased, and then there were howls from the streets. Edith saw a young woman running towards her, up Quai Anglais Street, with her son in her arms, screaming, 'They're shooting the soldiers! They're firing on our evzones.'

The soldiers, their bayonets drawn, had dispersed among the panicked flood of humanity. When someone shouted, 'Machine gun!', the crowd surged up from the docks like a giant ocean wave, heading towards Edith. The schoolchildren who'd been marching in pairs just a short while ago were now crying; old women with jars of rose oil in their hands were rushing up to passers-by asking for help, and black-robed priests trying to calm the crowd with their arms opened wide were bumping into women running up the street with their children hugged close.

Edith, squeezing through the crowds in haste, managed, after much bargaining with a coachman waiting under the plane tree at Fasoula Square, to get him to take her to the French Hospital. The closed carriage jolted down the cobbled street, past mothers anxiously pushing their children dressed as Ancient Greeks indoors, past fathers bringing down the shutters of their shops and closing the blinds. In front of Dame de Sion High School an Ottoman gendarme was holding the hand of a boy who was speaking Italian as he cried and asking him in French where he had last seen his grandfather. The crease between Edith's eyebrows was so furrowed now, it was causing her pain. She was still panting and her cheeks burned as if touched by ice. When the carriage slowed down in front of the hospital, she jumped down before the horses had come to a halt and raced past the confused nurses in their long black dresses, who were trying to guard the gate, and into the well-kept courtyard.

From there, the noise from the seafront sounded like distant, surreal howling. The patients sitting on the benches in the shade of the giant trees were conversing in low voices, seemingly unaware of what was happening in the outside world. With its French flag flying from the rooftop, the hospital was a haven, an oasis in the chaos.

Edith ran up the marble staircase. Her grandmother's room was on the second floor and she stopped at the door to catch her breath. Juliette was in front of the window overlooking the courtyard; from her profile, she appeared to be frowning at the piece of paper in her hand. Grandmother Josephine was watching her daughter with a surly look on her face; there were coarse white hairs growing from her chin. She'd had a stroke three months earlier and was no longer able to speak; she could only express herself on paper now, but holding a pen in her right hand was difficult.

'*Maman*, have you heard the news?' Edith's voice came out higher than usual and her grandmother's sour expression became even more puckered.

In exasperation, Juliette handed the note to her daughter as she stood in the doorway. 'I swear, I cannot understand what she wants any more. Her handwriting gets more like chicken scratch every day. Have a look at this. If you can make it out, tell Nurse Liz to bring her what it is she wants. She's been lying there with that sulk on all morning.'

For a moment Edith forgot what was happening outside and looked at the piece of paper. Like all the women in the family, Grandmother Josephine's handwriting was as confusing as

Arabic script; her letters were indecipherable even though written in French. Edith couldn't understand a thing.

'Maybe she wants water.'

'We brought her that. We've brought her everything. Nurse Liz, bless her heart, even brought some sherbet from the maternity ward. She didn't want that either. I don't know what else we can do. Your brother was here – we came in together on the eight o'clock train – and he suggested we hire a nurse and move Grandmother into our house. What nonsense! This hospital is so well equipped, how could we manage with just one nurse at home?'

Then she added in a low voice, 'I think your brother was just being stingy. He really is the limit! He lives like a prince in Bournabat, but when it comes to hospital fees for his grandmother, he gets all miserly. It's all done to please Philippe, that son-in-law of mine, if you ask me. And he—'

'*Maman*, it seems you have not heard the news.' Edith balled up the little piece of paper in her hand and looked into Juliette's face.

'What happened? Did Madame Lupen manage to get her ugly daughter engaged?' Juliette gave one of her vinegar laughs. On seeing Edith's frown darken, she added, 'I heard, darling, I heard. Nurse Liz told me a little while ago. Venizelos has landed his soldiers in Smyrna. Lloyd George has finally got what he wanted, eh? Our people are gathering over at the Sporting Club. When we leave here, let's go there too. We can watch the festivities from there. What do you say? Did Venizelos himself come as well?'

Edith looked at her mother in astonishment as footsteps came echoing down the corridor.

Juliette shrugged. 'Ah, here comes your brother. He went to Kraemer's for lun—'

Before she could finish her sentence, Jean-Pierre burst into the room, shattering her cool detachment, his eyes wide with fear, his cheeks red from running. Taking no account of either his bedridden grandmother nor the quiet of the hospital, he shrieked, 'They killed people right in front of us! In front of our eyes, while we were sitting eating together at Kraemer's, all of us, including the city's most important businessmen – the Whitalls, the Girauds. How could this happen? They killed civilians too. They snatched the fezzes from their heads and tore them to pieces. Unbelievable! *Maman*, are you listening? They took Rauf Bey prisoner. Our neighbour, Rauf Bey – he's an accountant at the bank, for God's sake! We saw him being beaten out in the street and we all ran out. At least he has some loyal friends among the Americans; they pushed the Greek soldiers aside and saved the poor man. Then someone opened fire on the Greek soldiers from the top floor of the hotel and we all ran back inside. Poor Rauf Bey couldn't speak. He happened to have been passing the Turkish barracks just as the fighting began, so he took cover inside. When the Turks waved the flag of surrender out the window, the Greek soldiers rounded up everybody inside the barracks, treated them like prisoners of war and threw them out onto the street. What a disaster! I've never seen such barbarism.'

Covering her mouth with her hand, Juliette turned away from the window. 'What fighting? Did fighting break out? What are you saying, Jean-Pierre? Who shot whom?'

'Somebody opened fire on the Greek soldiers. Witnesses said the shots came from the sea, but the Greek soldiers rushed straight to the Turkish barracks, the Sari Kisla, and opened fire with their machine guns. The Turks responded. They had a good supply of weapons, but finally they ran out of ammunition and surrendered. Meanwhile, anybody, anywhere wearing a fez was arrested and taken away.'

Suddenly he stopped talking and ran to the window. 'Where is Mustafa, *Maman*? Where is Mustafa? Why is he not down there in the courtyard waiting for us? We have to find him – urgently! Something might have happened to him. Someone must go and find Mustafa immediately.'

'Brother, calm down, please. You're frightening Grandmother. Come, sit down for a minute. Nurse Liz, could you please bring a glass of water. I'll go out right now and find Mustafa.'

Juliette let out another scream. 'Edith, you cannot just go running about out there. Say something, Jean-Pierre, for the love of God. Are you both insane? Are you going to send your sister out all alone into the streets on such a day?'

Paying no attention to her mother, Edith sat her brother down at the table in front of the window. A muscle in his right cheek was twitching from nerves. He spilled some of his glass of water on the table.

Juliette, one hand on her forehead, was walking in circles between the window and the door, speaking rapidly. 'What do we do now? Is it safe to stay here? Let's take the first train back to Bournabat. *Mon Dieu*, the station is very near the Turkish district. Or should we go to your sister in Boudja? Edith, what time is the train? No, that's impossible. What can we do? A motor car! Jean-Pierre, I beg you, arrange for a motor car immediately. Quickly, I say. Tell Mustafa to go and find your brother-in-law. Philippe must send the company's private motor car for us. Or should we go to the Sporting Club? We'll be safe there. Here in the hospital we have only women around us. Oh, my God, why did I have to choose today to come to the city!'

Edith shook her head. '*Maman*, I beg you, please calm down. You know no harm will come to us. First of all we must find Mustafa. He will arrange a vehicle to take you to the station and you can catch the first train home. I'll stay with Grandmother. No one will touch this hospital with the French flag flying from its roof. Besides, I'm sure that at the first sign of fighting, Mustafa immediately thought to arrange a vehicle to take you to the station.'

Juliette, cutting her circuit between the door and the window in half, shouted, 'What are you saying, Edith? You're going to stay here by yourself, among these bandits, surrounded only by women? No! I most certainly do not permit this. Enough is enough! Are you not aware, daughter, of how much the local communities here have grown to hate each other over the years? Can you not see that disaster is leaning on our door, that a tragedy is brewing? Absolutely, not! I am not leaving you on your own in Smyrna!'

'We are locals too, *Maman*. We've had no quarrels with anyone. Please do not make such generalizations.'

Edith walked cautiously to her brother's side. Juliette was having another of her hysterical fits. Jean-Pierre was sitting with his elbows on the table, head between his hands. She sighed. Unfortunately, once her mother got herself into a state, there was no getting her out of it. Even so, she said, '*Maman*, trust me, please. Nothing will happen to us in Smyrna. If you'd seen the ships anchored in the harbour, you'd feel comforted. The British fleet is there, along with American and French ships. They're all there, in the harbour. Do you think they would just close their eyes and let us come to harm?'

Jean-Pierre raised his head from between his hands and looked at his sister. His eyes were bloodshot. Juliette's younger son resembled her very closely. They had the same watery, blue-green eyes, the same freckled skin that tanned in the sun, the same sharp features. As he got older, the resemblance became more marked. He spoke softly.

'Edith, I just saw a high-ranking Turkish officer being shot in the back. He was simply strolling by, holding his small son's hand, not doing anything else. One of the Greek soldiers pressed a rifle butt into his back. Blood spurted from his mouth as he fell, and the child was right there, staring at his father. They took the boy to the ship where they're holding all the prisoners. He was ten years old, at most. This happened right in front of all of us. Those European admirals you mentioned who were at the shore watching the fleet arrive were there. We closed the curtains at Kraemer's so that Rauf Bey wouldn't see what was happening. We were trying to soothe him with whisky, and the poor man was crying and saying, "I would never have expected such savagery from a European country." Ah, how the Turks worship Europe. Europe sucks the marrow from their bones and still they cry for Europe. Look at the pitiful state of the great Ottoman Empire. What a shame.'

With a nervous wave of her hand, Juliette interrupted her son's speech. 'Stop talking about such things now, Jean-Pierre. We must leave here immediately. If Mustafa cannot be found, stop a child in the street, write a note and send it to your brother-in-law. He must obtain a motor car for us. Let us get away from this hell.'

Passing behind her brother, Edith looked out of the window into the courtyard, where proud mothers were sitting on benches under the fig trees, showing each other their new babies. It was a scene as far removed from hell as it was possible to be. She worried about Zoe and her daughter

– where had they run to when the bloodshed had started, she wondered. May they not have been trampled by the crowd. Suddenly she was overcome with despair. Maybe her mother wasn't hysterical; maybe a great disaster really was knocking at their door this time. The whole country had been divided up and parcelled out, so what was to stop the same thing happening in Smyrna? She left the room without saying a word, determined to find Mustafa. Juliette's screams echoed down the high-ceilinged corridors.

The streets were empty and the sky had clouded over. Looking neither left nor right, she took short, swift steps and soon found herself at the little square. Her own butler, Christo, lived somewhere around there, she thought. The ominous silence that had descended on her servant-less house that morning came to mind. A group of young boys with knives in their hands shot out of a street and disappeared in the direction of the Church of Agia Ekaterini. The coffeehouse owner was gathering up the tables under his arbour. Could Mustafa be in there, or had something happened to him? Where had those boys been going with knives in their hands?

Jean-Pierre had said that the Greek soldiers were snatching fezzes from the heads of Turks and ripping them to pieces. Mustafa was always very attentive to his appearance. He wore his blood-red fez with its carefully combed tassel proudly. Pressing her hands to the steamy window, she peered inside. There was no one in there except two men playing backgammon in a smoky corner. She heard the sound of gunfire in the distance. The windows of the police station on the southern edge of the square had been broken and the open door was banging.

The wind coming in off the sea suddenly gathered force; leaves swirled in the air and were joined by bits of rubbish.

Edith struggled to stay upright as raindrops began striking her face like a whip.

The rain began to fall in torrents.

Her umbrella blew inside out.

A window opened in the top floor of a house across the street and small white hands quickly gathered clothes from the line. She had to find a place to shelter. In her search for Mustafa, she had come quite a distance from the hospital. The rain was bucketing down with such force that the streets had already become rivers; the water coursing down the middle of them was picking up speed at a tremendous rate.

A milk-seller goading his donkey turned the corner.

Edith was soaked from head to toe. She again cursed the beige summer shoes she'd put on when she left the house that morning.

Following the milk-seller, she wandered into one of the streets that opened off the square and took refuge under an eave, pressing her back against the wall of the house and leaning on her umbrella. The street was so narrow that in some places the eaves of the houses touched, shutting out the sky. Suddenly a confused and sopping wet dog appeared. Seeing Edith, he raced to her side, wagging his short tail. His black lips seemed to be grinning under his yellow fur, as if he'd seen a friend. He came closer, sat up very straight to begin with, and then, sliding slightly, leaned against her leg.

The woman and the dog remained side by side in their waterlogged world.

'You think I'm going to save you, don't you, foolish dog?' Edith said, touching the animal's wet yellow fur with a white-gloved fingertip. 'But I can't even save myself...'

A fiery lump was rising in her throat. Resting one knee against the dog, she closed her eyes. In that lonely corner of a faraway neighbourhood, she allowed the lump to rupture and flow warmly down her cheeks. Like the rubbish floating in the rainwater, her tears brought hidden memories to the surface from the most remote folds of her brain.

Her mind touched on an old wound, a very old wound.

In a dark corner of her heart, the longing for a half-lived love still burned. As tears streamed down her rain-washed cheeks, the crease between her eyebrows, the one that drove Juliette crazy, disappeared momentarily.

The yellow stray lifted his black-rimmed eyes to the sky and glanced suspiciously at the clouds.

Frogs began to rain down into the street.

The Uninvited Guest

The evening when Sumbul saw Edith face to face for the first and only time, things in the house on Bulbul Street (where, three years later, they would find me in their garden) were very confused. The atmosphere was tense, nerves were strained.

It wasn't only because of the Greek landing, the looting of the shops in the Turkish district, the frogs raining from the sky. That day, other things had happened in the house inside which Hilmi Rahmi had not set foot for years. Much later, when Sumbul told me about them, she related them piecemeal, all jumbled up and out of sequence, as if recalling a dream. It was I who put them in order.

As she was telling me the story of the day of the Greek landing in Smyrna, I could feel deep in my bones the turmoil, the fear that came seeping through the doors, the windows. A story is not told with words alone. Dozens, hundreds of minute details complement the words. Only someone like me, who has given up words, can know this. Those who speak are always thinking about what they are going to say next; they forget to listen. The speed with which the speaker talks, their tone of voice, the play of light or shadow on their face, the moments when your presence is forgotten, the moments when your eyes are sought, even the smells that come off their skin, all of these details help you enter the world of the story being told. As you listen, a taste sometimes fills your mouth, independent of the words; in your stomach you feel the storyteller's unease, their hidden passions.

On the evening when Edith came to Bulbul Street in her dress the colour of pomegranate flowers, there was another uninvited guest in the house. A youngish man with cold green eyes, a tall fez and a trim moustache – Tevfik Bey. A perfect Istanbul gentleman. I didn't say a word, but Sumbul added, 'Do not be fooled by his impressive appearance, for there was definitely something strange about him. Everybody has something strange, something off-key about them. Everybody. Who could say what his peculiarity might be?'

On that one night when she slept under the same roof as this young man, was Sumbul yearning to find out what his personal peculiarity was? On that one night out of the dozens that Sumbul spent alone while her faraway husband raced from one war to another, did she dream of climbing into bed beside the stranger whose breathing she could hear from the room downstairs? And why not? Should a young Circassian girl who had not been touched since her son Dogan dropped from her uterus not feel tempted by the prospect of holding a warm body in her arms? What else could explain the way her green eyes lit up with longing as she spoke of this Tevfik Bey?

Or am I making all this up to justify my own sin, to ease my own conscience? Is it only me who creeps into a man's bed at midnight – and into whose bed, of all beds! – to satisfy an unsated appetite? Maybe this hunger is hereditary. One should not forget my own grandmother, Juliette. On a jasmine-scented summer's night painted silver with moonlight she slipped into the room of Nikolas Dimos, who was sleeping under her roof. Let us also remember my mother, Edith, who, although she shunned the idea of marriage, never evicted the dark-skinned foreigner from her bed. Still. Still? Compared to my sin, what the women of my family did – the family I never knew – seems rather innocent, does it not?

At first, Sumbul thought Tevfik was one of her brother-in-law Huseyin's Unionist friends. The man introduced himself as such, did he not? Not as a Unionist, of course, but as Huseyin's friend. At that time, 1919 by the European calendar, no one had the front to say they were a Unionist any more. During the evening meal, which Tevfik had insisted the women also join, Mujgan asked where they had met. To which Tevfik simply replied, 'I am an old friend of the worthy individual.' Then, like a juggler, his stony expression changed into a charming smile, distracting the women's attention.

Much later it was revealed that Tevfik was not an old friend or anything like it. He was a Turkish nationalist who had met Huseyin at the protest meetings in Bahri Baba. Years later, Hilmi Rahmi would blame this handsome Tevfik for his brother Huseyin's death and take every opportunity to berate Sumbul for having welcomed the no-good scoundrel into his home that night. But did this blaming of Tevfik for Huseyin's death on the battlefield, when in fact Hilmi Rahmi's brother had taken himself off to war, actually mask some other doubt that was eating away at him? Did Hilmi Rahmi not suspect, as I did, that the no-good man sleeping under his roof might have created waves in his wife's imagination? Was his anger an expression of the sorrow he felt at the death of his brother or was it an expression of his suspicion and jealousy?

Besides, how was Sumbul to know that Tevfik was a no-good scoundrel? If I could talk, I would like to have asked

Hilmi Rahmi this question. The man presented himself as Huseyin's friend. Huseyin greeted him like a sultan in the men's quarters with its large chestnut table under the colourful crystal chandelier and even agreed to let the women join in the evening meal at his request, treating him like a family member. Who could have guessed that this polite gentleman was a no-good scoundrel whom Huseyin had only met for the first time that evening?

On the evening of 14 May, after the British had informed Smyrna's Turkish governor, Izzet Pasha, that the Greek fleet would be taking over the administration of Smyrna, a huge crowd from the Turkish districts gathered at the hilltop Jewish Cemetery in Bahri Baba to protest the Allies giving Smyrna to the Greeks. As the sun set and the moon rose over the mountains like an orange ball, everyone joined in the protest – young and old, women and children, the educated, the uneducated, the rich and the poor. I myself remember the peddlers who wandered around the different neighbourhoods talking repeatedly about that evening. It was like a fair. Fires were lit, children ate sesame halva, and drums were played through until morning. A resistance organization was formed and plans were made to collect guns, rifles and anything else that could be used as a weapon and smuggle them out of Smyrna and into Anatolia. According to rumour, that same night, under cover of darkness, the members of this newly formed resistance movement went into that terrible jail behind Konak and set all the prisoners free. This Tevfik was one of the ringleaders. Sumbul knew that Huseyin had participated in the Bahri Baba protests, but she did not know that he had gone expressly to meet with Tevfik Bey.

Before dinner that night, Huseyin lit all the lamps; the room shone as if for a holiday celebration. The crystal chandelier glimmered in Tevfik Bey's emerald eyes. His moustache, which he kept twisting, had clearly been rubbed with musk oil. Sumbul appraised the guest from the corner of her eye as she ate the pilaf and lamb prepared by Nanny Dilber. Listening to the rain beating on the windowpanes, inwardly she was cursing Hilmi Rahmi. That day it had been revealed that the telegram she'd received from him the previous week had been a ruse, a lie sent to confuse the British. For a whole week she'd been dancing with bells on her toes, for Hilmi Rahmi's telegram had read: *My most precious wife, Only a few last issues remain to discuss with the officers here in Istanbul. Then immediately to Smyrna, God willing.*

Instead, however, it seemed he had set out for Asia Minor. Neither Sumbul nor their sons were on his mind. He talked of freedom, of liberty, as if such things were to be attained by waging war. Dogan was now five years old and had never once seen his father's face. Hilmi Rahmi was going to be a shepherd for the ragtag army organized under the Ottoman pashas; he was going to save Smyrna from a distance. If you'd asked Sumbul, she would have said that Smyrna should have been left to the Greeks and the family saved. But nobody ever asked a Circassian girl from Plovdiv anything. If they had, she wouldn't have said anything anyway. Being a Circassian was considered morally suspect in those days. No matter how angry she was, she bit her tongue in the presence of her brother-in-law Huseyin, whose veins were swollen with patriotism.

The full moon, shining like a lantern, slipped into the earth's shadow and bit by bit was buried in darkness. A lunar eclipse was a bad omen. From over by the Jewish Cemetery at the end of Bulbul Street, drums were beating to chase away the moonlight-eating shadow. Dogs stretched their necks and howled continuously. Tevfik Bey, unaware of the tension in the family around him, treated Sumbul and Mujgan as 'European women', asking their opinion on works of Russian and French literature, and entertaining them with tales of flirtatious ladies in the mansions of Istanbul. At one point, he turned to Huseyin, who was being made most uncomfortable by his wife Mujgan's careless giggling, and said, 'My dear Huseyin, you still keep the men and women separate in your home. That sort of thing isn't done any more, especially not in a modern city. I really do not find it fitting that you still have the women spend their time upstairs and the men downstairs. Open up the house. Make the downstairs into a library or a sitting room. Move the guest rooms upstairs. Spend your time together.'

Instead of finding an answer for his friend, Huseyin just looked down and mumbled something, which led Sumbul to surmise that Tevfik Bey was not only an old friend but also a person of importance. If the bedrooms were to be moved upstairs, did that mean that the guests and the women would sleep on the same floor? In which case, should their paths happen to cross at, let's say, midnight, what would ensue? Where did the guests of those flirtatious ladies in the Istanbul mansions sleep? Did Tevfik Bey regularly stay in such mansions?

When she looked up and noticed that the young visitor had been appraising her for a while with a teasing expression on his face, the mouthful of food she was eating got stuck in her throat, causing a coughing fit that lasted for several minutes. After drinking the glass of water Ziver filled for her, she glanced across the dining table to find the young man twirling his moustache again.

The real reason for his visit became apparent only after

coffee had been drunk and the women had retired. As soon as Sumbul and Mujgan got upstairs, they knelt down on the step at the edge of the shaft through which the dumb waiter travelled, carrying food from the kitchen in the women's quarters to the dining room downstairs. Nanny Dilber had rolled up her shirtsleeves and with her pudgy hands and pale-skinned palms was kneading bread dough to be sent to the bakery on the corner of the street the next morning. She laughed under her moustache as the two ladies of the house pressed their ears to the wall like little girls.

Though he was trying to speak softly, Tevfik's deep voice was carried up through the emptiness of the shaft as if it were a pipe.

'The British have convinced the Sultan, and a death sentence will now be meted out to anyone involved with the National Struggle for Independence. Papers will be posted to that effect very soon, announcing it to the people.'

'As if our people know how to read and write!' whispered Mujgan.

The women, squeezed together beside the lift shaft, giggled.

'Sister Sumbul, did you see how he twisted his moustache when he looked at you?'

'Shut your mouth, girl! Have you lost your mind, saying crazy things like that? Be quiet and let's listen to what they're saying.' Sumbul turned towards the wall to hide the smile spreading across her face.

Tevfik's voice continued to filter up the shaft. 'After tomorrow, there'll be nothing more for us to do here. The struggle will start in the heartlands, in Asia Minor. The highest-ranking Ottoman officers have already begun to take action. The country is waiting for you, Huseyin Bey; for us. The people are poor and cowardly, and the tribal gangs do whatever blows into their minds. I'm talking about a formal organization. The country has a great need for young men like us – strong and educated. Believe me, this Greek invasion of Smyrna will prove to be to our advantage. You saw the crowd tonight – a common consciousness is growing from our ancient soil. The Greek invasion is the spark that will ignite our gunpowder.'

The women looked at each other in fear. It seemed strange that the two men who had spoken as if they were intimate friends at dinner were now, when left alone, talking so formally. There was a moment of silence. Tevfik was probably lighting one of his thinly rolled cigarettes. The two women sitting on the stone step squirmed as they pictured his long, thin, skilful fingers. An image from earlier came into Sumbul's head, of the smoke from Tevfik's cigarette swirling in the air like a bluish-white cloud as he drank the aromatic coffee Ziver had served on a silver tray after dinner.

When he began to speak again, Tevfik's voice was hoarse. 'I suppose you are wondering how we will finance such an organization's activities. Huseyin Bey, a caravan is created as it travels along the road. Look at what the British have done. Hasn't Lloyd George, fearful after the Italians independently invaded Antalya, sent the Greeks to us? They acted so fast that a part of the Greek fleet still doesn't even know where it is heading. This is inside information I have obtained. They'll wake up tomorrow morning and find themselves in our harbour. We shall do exactly the same thing. First of all, let us set out. People will help us. If we come with a strong enough force that cannot be undermined by the tricks of the great powers, they will support us, of course. Negotiations with the French will begin shortly.'

Makbule Hanim, Huseyin and Hilmi Rahmi's elderly

aunt, appeared at the kitchen door, her face even more sullen than usual. Her black headscarf had fallen to her shoulders, exposing her white roots and strawberry-blonde bun. Prayer beads in hand, she looked in the direction of the dumb waiter. Thank heavens she couldn't see very well. Before she could make out Sumbul and Mujgan in the dim light of the lantern, the two women jumped to their feet and began circling Nanny Dilber, as if inspecting her work. Makbule Hanim had received information that her daughters-in-law had taken their evening meal in the men's quarters in the presence of a strange man. Drily, she said, 'Nanny Dilber, put the boys to bed. It is late. Mujgan, your daughters are still sitting in the garden. Be mindful that they do not walk around in front of the guest. Their heads are not covered. Tell Ziver to repair the garden gate tomorrow. Anyone with a shoulder can push their way in, God forbid. May disaster not befall us on this inauspicious night.'

The women nodded, knowing that she had actually been talking about them. It was not the twelve-year-old girls who had appeared in front of the visitor with uncovered heads but they themselves. The reference to the garden gate was an insinuation that their house had turned into an inn for passers-by. The old aunt's displeasure at Tevfik Bey's presence under their roof was clear.

'And you should waste no time in going to bed immediately. Nowhere is safe. Turn out the light. The house has been lit up like a palace, God be praised. When there is an eclipse of the moon, one should not light so much as a candle; it is bad luck. Nanny Dilber must fill a container with water and place it in front of the window tonight so that the water can absorb the moonlight and the wind. Who knows, we may need that water to break some spell in the future.'

'As you wish, Makbule Hanim.'

'When Nanny Dilber finishes kneading the dough, she will put the boys to bed. She will extinguish all the lamps. We will get the girls from the garden and go straight to bed. Sleep well, Aunt Makbule.'

Though she made it clear by puckering her lips that she did not believe her daughters-in-law, the old woman did not linger in the kitchen. As her footsteps resounded on the marble floor leading to the bathroom, Sumbul and Mujgan ran back to their place beside the wall. Mujgan's face was drained of colour.

Unaware that they were being listened to, the men were continuing to speak softly.

'The Sultan has been turned into a puppet. Look, I'll say it again: very soon a fatwa will be issued by the Sheikh ul-Islam decreeing that it is holy to kill those involved in the National Struggle against the Sultan and the British. These are dangerous times, Huseyin Bey. Are you sure you want to join the forces in Asia Minor and fight for independence?'

No reply came from Huseyin. Mujgan's body was tense, as if she'd had an electric shock.

'The British are putting a great deal of pressure on the Sultan. They know about our resistance movement. They know everything. They've posted the Sultan's men along all the roads, and any vehicle they consider suspicious gets stopped and searched. The first thing the Greeks will do tomorrow will be to make it mandatory to have an official pass if you want to leave Smyrna prefecture. Travelling without those documents will be impossible. God willing, we will still be able to use the Kasaba Railway tomorrow evening. We'll try to make it as far as Afyonkarahisar. After that we will be in God's hands. If luck is with us, we will get the train to Eskisehir, after which we'll continue on foot or by oxcart. The houses where we can take shelter have already been identified. If you are sure about your decision, here's what we will do now.'

The voices had become too low for the women to hear what came next. Mujgan stood up and made her way to the kitchen door as if in a dream. She looked miserable; her shoulders were sagging and her back was bowed. Without saying a word, she took the kerosene lamp and left the room. Sumbul continued to sit beside the dumb waiter as she listened to the sound of her sister-in-law's mules slapping against the floor. So Huseyin was going to run off as well.

Recently, their neighbour Saadet's seventeen-year-old son had run away from Smyrna to join the forces in Asia Minor. At this latest blow, Saadet's hair had turned white; her hands shook continually now. Fourteen years ago, her brother Ali had vanished into thin air, and later her husband had returned like a ghost from the frontline in the Allahuekber Mountains. As if this were not enough, now she had lost the apple of her eye, her son Mehmet. She had not heard a word from the boy since he left. Sumbul couldn't erase from her mind the sight of Saadet on the kitchen floor hitting herself until her clothes were ripped to pieces. Mujgan's elder daughter Munevver had run to fetch Old Aybatan from her shack over by the cemetery, but even her elixir couldn't calm the wretched Saadet.

Perhaps if Mujgan held her husband warmly in bed that night, he would change his mind about this crazy adventure. She was a lively, flirtatious woman; she would know what to do. Furthermore, when Hilmi Rahmi had set off to fight in the world war, he had left his family in the care of Huseyin. Would her brother-in-law break the promise he'd given to his brother and leave the women and children to face the infidels alone?

It's possible that Mujgan's caresses and tears that night might have persuaded Huseyin to give up on his plan, but events the next morning quashed any lingering indecisiveness. The Greek ships entered the harbour, sounding their arrogant whistles. The Turkish barracks known as Sari Kisla were raked with machine-gun fire. Anyone with a fez on his head was taken prisoner. On top of all this, Huseyin's father, Mustafa, was brought home unconscious at around noon. This was the last straw. Huseyin was going. His decision was final.

Upon hearing about his father from Ziver, the servant boy, Huseyin rushed back to Bulbul Street. Greek ships were sailing into the harbour one after the other. The first thing he did was take out the weapons he'd hidden in a sack suspended down the well shaft: the German Mauser, the Russian Nagant revolver and the automatic Parabellum. He put them in a different sack, together with plenty of ammunition. The Greek soldiers had wasted no time in fanning out across the Turkish districts and confiscating every type of weapon they could find in people's houses, including kitchen knives and barbers' razors. Leaving the double-barrelled shotgun and the old Greek Mauser inside, he lowered the sack into the well once more.

Mujgan had never in her life held a gun, but Sumbul was a Circassian girl who knew how to ride a horse and use a rifle. Since the days when she'd gone out hunting with Hilmi Rahmi, the double-barrelled shotgun had been considered hers. She was a good shot, much better than one might have expected from her delicate pink and white complexion, and at least as skilful as Huseyin. If she ever found herself in danger, she would have the courage to protect herself, Mujgan and the children. Huseyin's decision was final. He would leave the women who'd been entrusted to him to fend for themselves, and that night, once darkness had fallen, he would set out on the road to Anatolia to join the National Struggle for Independence.

The Adventure Addict

It was on that same day, with Butler Mustafa lying unconscious in his son's house on Bulbul Street, that Edith rang the bell of their home.

Once the frog rain had let up, she had searched the coffeehouses, alleyways and gardens of the neighbourhood around the French Hospital for Mustafa. Although she knew perfectly well that on such a tense day he would have waited for them in the hospital courtyard, she traipsed down one waterlogged street and into another, peering through the dirty windows of deserted coffeehouses, but did not find her mother's faithful butler anywhere. It was as if the earth had opened up and swallowed the old man.

When she returned anxiously to the hospital, she found Nurse Liz holding cloths soaked in cologne to her mother's forehead and wrists. Juliette had her eyes closed and was moaning as she leaned her head against the brown leather armchair into which she had collapsed.

Edith went over to Jean-Pierre, who was still sitting by the window where she'd left him. 'Brother, I haven't been able to find Mustafa.'

Jean-Pierre raised his head from his palms and looked at

Edith with glassy eyes. In the far corner, Juliette was having trouble breathing, making gasping noises as she fanned herself.

'The best thing would be to telephone Philippe and ask for a motor car.'

'He would bring water from a thousand brooks, but now…'

'Tell him what a state Mother is in. He'll help us if only to avoid Anna's nagging. Go on, run down and telephone him. If I call, it might make things more difficult.'

A short while later, the three of them were in the motor car the ill-tempered Philippe Cantebury had sent to the hospital gates and on their way back to Bournabat. Grandmother Josephine had been left under the protection of the French flag. On the pretext of not leaving the old woman alone, Edith had planned to slip out of the car at the last moment, but Juliette, despite her hysterics, had anticipated that and pulled her daughter into the back seat beside her.

So be it. But could Edith not have returned to Smyrna in the self-same company motor car or have made the chauffeur wait until Dr Arnott, whom they had called, had given Juliette an injection to calm her nerves? No matter how hard Philippe Cantebury had contrived to cancel her partnership in the business – for the past eleven years her brother-in-law had continued to insist that Edith, not even being a real Lamarck, should not receive the annual profit dividend – Edith remained one of the legal partners of Lamarck and Sons Chandlery Business. Thus the motor car could also be considered hers. But, no, Edith Lamarck was an adventurous woman who loved a challenge. Maybe it was not only hashish that she was addicted to but also adventure. The only way she could tolerate her solitary, childless, husbandless life was by fabricating certain excitements. Who knew how long she'd been waiting for an opportunity to go into that Turkish neighbourhood with its connections to old wounds. She knew that this could not be realized in the motor car her brother-in-law had so reluctantly provided, and so, as soon as Juliette had fallen asleep under the effects of the tranquilliser, she slipped out of the mansion into the street, without anyone seeing her, and paused to catch her breath at the gate of the neighbour's estate.

The high gate with the Thomas-Cook monogram – HTC – was locked. Edith rang the bell. Far away a dog barked. After the rain, the air smelled of fresh earth, rosemary and lemon balm. On the other side of the gate, on the white gravel drive leading to the house, two crows had their heads down and were fighting over a dead frog. They paid no attention to Butler Kosta and his dog Chakir as they passed.

Seeing that it was Edith at the gate, Kosta was half running down the drive. Like Mustafa, he was past sixty, an old and faithful servant.

'Don't run, Kyr Kosta *mou*,' Edith shouted through the decorative bars of the rarely locked gate. '*Min anisihite.* There's nothing to worry about. I've just come to visit Edward. Please do not tire yourself.'

Chakir, already at the gate, was wagging his balding black tail. The elderly butler was out of breath. Taking the long, narrow key from around his neck, he unlocked the gate. As a child, Edith had always thought Kosta looked like an owl, and now, in his old age, his close-set eyes had sunk even deeper into their sockets and he had turned into a real owl.

'Welcome, Miss Edith. It is not safe for you to be out alone on the streets on such a day. Not safe at all! Come in immediately, *sas parakalo. Kala iste?* Are you well?'

Edith was accustomed to the butler's anxieties. When she and Edward were children and used to go and hide in a secluded place or play in the poplar forest that formed a natural boundary between the two families' estates, Kosta would invariably appear within the first ten minutes. Opening his owl-like eyes wide, he would say, 'Little master, it is inadvisable for you to wander about here. I entreat you, play within sight of us,' and he'd shepherd them over to where the ladies were having their tea on the veranda or to where he himself could see them. Now, like all anxious people, age had made him even more apprehensive, and his eyesight had weakened.

As they walked towards the mansion beneath an avenue of mulberry trees in new leaf, he whispered, 'They are ransacking the Turkish neighbourhoods, our Greek *palikaria*, our young men. All of the coffeehouses and the barber's shops have lowered their shutters. A messenger has just come from the business office in the city. He saw two bodies floating in the sea near Konak.'

Edith's heart began to beat rapidly. Surely some misfortune had come to Mustafa. She said nothing to Kosta. The two old butlers were very close friends. On Saturday evenings they liked to go together to Yorgi's Tavern at Great Taverns Street, where, to the accompaniment of *raki*, hors d'oeuvres and music, they talked over the lives of their masters and mistresses.

Although the Levantine families had lived in Smyrna for generations, in the butlers' eyes they were still vulnerable foreigners in need of protection. Unbeknown to Edith, Mustafa had been very upset when she left her family home and moved to live all by herself on Vasili Street in Smyrna. 'The little lady is burning down her future with her own hands,' he'd said to Kosta, pouring out his troubles at length to his friend. In Mustafa and Kosta's world, there was nothing more dishonourable than the sharing of secrets beyond the family. Some misdemeanours could be discussed formally within the family as long as secrecy was preserved. Thus Mustafa was perfectly aware of various indiscretions – that on a moonlit night a long time ago a merchant from Athens had shared his bed with the lady of the house; that a baby had been born in the turret one September evening not so long ago; and who knew what else – but it was a butler's duty to ensure that such things never slipped beyond the mansion gates.

What Edith did – moving into a house left to her by the man who had fathered her out of wedlock, thus letting the whole world know of her mother's sin – was not something he could understand. The little lady had both shamed her family's honour and also closed the door to a favourable future for herself. Kosta completely understood his friend Mustafa's troubles but knew of no remedy. The family secret had escaped out the door before Mustafa had had the chance to contain it; a crushing situation for a butler.

Edith followed Butler Kosta into the Thomas-Cooks' high-ceilinged mansion, which was always cool, even on the hottest of summer days. With its chandeliers of Bohemian crystal, silk carpets, marble columns and doorknobs of silver-lined crystal, their magnificent estate made Edith's family home seem like a shack. In the past the differences between her house and the houses of the British families had upset Juliette no end. But now that her elder daughter had married a British man, she was mollified to some degree. Still, when the opportunity arose – at a social gathering where Anna and Philippe were not present, for example – she couldn't resist pointing out 'their' British vulgarity as compared with 'our' French good taste.

Edward was seated at the wide rectangular table in the salon, putting together a miniature train set. All of his attention was focused on gluing the front wheels of the engine; his shoulders were hunched to his ears with the mental effort. At first he didn't notice Edith standing on the threshold of the double doors. He had gained quite a few pounds, and because of the gin cocktails he had become accustomed to from an early age, his slightly flaccid cheeks were streaked with thin red lines. Edith tried to recall when she had last seen him. Since she'd moved to the house on Vasili Street, the two old friends had gone their separate ways. Because of the infrequency of social events during the war years, as well as Edith's having isolated herself, they sometimes didn't see each other from one New Year's ball to the next.

Suddenly the wheel of the toy train jumped out of Edward's fingers and rolled over to beside the toe of Edith's satin slipper.

'Fuck!'

Edith laughed in spite of herself.

Raising his head and seeing his childhood friend standing there, Edward at first appeared angry at having been spied on. Then he too began to laugh.

'*Touché!* You caught me! Please do not tell Mother I cursed like a cart driver.'

Edith leaned down, picked up the little wheel and put it on the table. Edward rose and gave her a big hug. They were too close for such formalities as hand kissing.

'Edith *mou*, what a surprise! You look beautiful. Red is so becoming on you. I thought you never came to Bournabat, finding us too provincial.'

'How ridiculous, Edward.'

'I don't know – you never even come to the van Dijks' Sunday breakfasts any more.'

Edward pouted, the way he used to as a child. According to the rumours, the reason why Helene Thomas-Cook's younger son was not interested in marriage, not even to one of the most beautiful, cultured girls in Bournabat or Boudja, lay in his undying love for Edith. Furthermore, as if the woman's living alone was not enough, the fact that she openly had a man in her bed, a dark-skinned, second-class Hindu man, had caused Edward bitter disappointment, causing him to drown his sorrows in gin cocktails and various other shameless addictions. On the other hand, the fact that Edith after all these years had still not married Avinash kept Edward's hopes alive, giving him reason not to give up on his childhood friend.

'I did not have the opportunity, Edward *mou*. And you? You never come to Smyrna! Let us have tea together one day at Café Zapion. What do you say? Once things have quietened down…'

Edward's eyes, which had been shining with excitement, went blank.

Edith switched from French to Greek. 'I'm talking about Venizelos and his soldiers. You've heard about the Greek invasion, haven't you?'

'Oh, that? *Ne, ne vevea.* Yes, of course. But why should that interfere with our plans? Quite the opposite. Under the Greek administration there will be more parties, you wait and see. Pretty soon the whole city will turn into a giant ballroom. The Greeks are a fun-loving people. Let's go to Zapion at the first opportunity – whenever you like.'

For a moment Edith looked at Edward in astonishment.

'I'm joking, Edith *mou*. Why so serious? I did hear about the landing, but it is not such important news. My brother went to work as usual this morning and just a while ago sent a boy with some papers for me to sign. He said work was going on as normal. For example, a tobacco ship of ours has set out for Alexandria. Please, have a seat. Kosta will have informed the kitchen and our coffee will be here in a moment. *Oriste*, please sit down.'

He indicated the table where his train set was. Wheelless wagons with glass windows, Edward's first accomplishments, were lying on the tracks as if they'd had an accident. As she sat down, Edith glanced at the bronze tan of his arms visible beneath the rolled-up sleeves of his sharp-collared white shirt. Edward's greatest passion was to go out on the open sea in his beloved yacht, whatever the season.

'Edward, the Turkish district has been ransacked. They've even raided the houses of our Turkish neighbours here in Bournabat. The servants told us about it when I brought my mother home just now. They turned Rauf Bey's villa upside down, taking everything of value, smashing up everything else. The poor man hasn't received the news yet. In the morning they almost took him prisoner, almost locked him up in the ship *Patris*. Fortunately, influential friends of his were sitting in Kraemer's and saved him. Jean-Pierre witnessed all this himself.'

A shadow passed over Edward's face. He picked up the tiny metal wheel that had fallen to the floor and began turning it around in his fingers.

'That's awful.'

They sat without speaking for a while.

The sun had come out; the raindrops on the leaves of the trees in front of the dining room shone like silver.

Edith switched to English. 'Edward, I came to ask you a favour.'

Edward raised his head in surprise. He had never heard his childhood friend asking anyone for help. 'Of course. Whatever you want.'

Edith briefly noted the hope rising in his face like the sun, but, as was her wont, immediately forgot about it. 'I wish to return to Smyrna on the four o'clock train, but Mustafa is nowhere to be found. He accompanied my mother and Jean-Pierre to Smyrna on their visit to my grandmother this morning, but while we were at the hospital he vanished into thin air. I searched nearby but couldn't find him. There was the rioting down at the docks and I wonder if Mustafa hid somewhere or, I don't know, maybe went to his son's house. Could he have been taken prisoner, God forbid? Without Mustafa, it is unwise for me to travel by train, especially today, so I thought maybe... um... maybe if I were to borrow one of your cars, for example the Wilson-Pilcher, to return to the city – if you'll let me, I mean. Only for today. I'd bring it back tomorrow.'

She moved her chair nearer to Edward's. The servant girl had brought their coffees. Throwing a pistachio *lokum* into her mouth, she chewed for a long time. It was a gamble. She knew Edward would never allow her to go on her own. But perhaps with Kosta... Her heart was beating fast.

Edward tugged at his russet moustache. 'Things are more serious than I imagined, it seems. In the circumstances, I think it would not be clever for you to return to Smyrna and spend the night there. Why don't you stay here tonight?'

He laughed when he saw the stubborn expression on Edith's face, so familiar from childhood. When Edith got an idea in her head, she would always find a way to make it happen. It would be safer to help the crazy girl rather than risk her courting danger.

'All right. You know I can never refuse you, Edith *mou*. But I tell you: it is not a good idea. Leave aside the chaos in the city, the Wilson-Pilcher is very old. But if I gave you one of the new cars, neither you nor Kosta could drive it. Are you aware of how much the car industry has advanced? They're not making motor cars that look like horse-driven carts any longer. I've ordered a new four-cylinder Essex, due to arrive in the middle of June. It's magnificent – fifty horsepower, automatic transmission, three gears. According to the literature, it will run even more smoothly than my yacht.'

Edith set down her coffee cup noisily in its saucer. Edward had forgotten how impatient his friend was. He continued in French.

'But that would not suit you, *ma chérie*. If I said that I myself would drive you in a different motor car, Mother and Mary, who will be returning from a tea party quite soon, would be frightened at being left here on their own. I promised them that I would remain at home. However, if you could wait for a few hours, we can go to the city together. Perhaps we could even have dinner at Zapion. Ha, *ti les*, what do you say?'

'Thank you, Edward, you are very thoughtful, but I need to go before the evening. Let's have our dinner one day next week, when things are calmer. The Wilson-Pilcher will be fine for today. I beg you, don't worry. Um... if you don't need Kosta for anything urgent, could I ask for one more favour?'

'Whatever you want.'

'I am really worried about Mustafa, Edward. I wonder if, once we're in the city and in a motor car, would you permit us to stop by his son's house to ask about him?'

'You want to go to the Turkish district? Up that serpentine hill and along those narrow, dead-end streets – on a day like this? Edith, do your ears hear the words coming out of your mouth?'

His voice came out louder than intended. Edward only ever went to the Turkish district as a sightseer, to show it to the girls his mother invited over from London as potential brides. The girls would peer through the tightly closed curtains of the two-horse carriage (Edward would never drive his valuable motor cars on such narrow, winding roads) and gaze at the men smoking their waterpipes in front of the coffeehouses, dressed in baggy trousers and with turbans wrapped around their heads, and would imagine themselves princesses in *The Arabian Nights*. This gave Edward indescribable pleasure. For him, the Turkish district was an exotic museum, and for a foreign woman like Edith to venture into it not as a tourist but to make a house visit was inconceivable. Furthermore, he would not allow his Wilson-Pilcher, no matter how old and out-of-date it was, to enter those alleyways.

But… But how many times in her life had Edith asked him for a favour? The last time was when she'd wanted to learn how to drive, and Edward had arranged both a motor car and an instructor. When was that – ten years ago, or fifteen? Why hadn't he gone with Edith then, instead of sending her off with the mechanic Ali for driving lessons? Ah, the carefreeness of youth… Back then, he'd been sure that he and Edith would be married. If he'd had the sense he had now, would he have let those afternoons they could have spent together in the meadows slip away? How could he refuse Edith now, the first time in fifteen years she had come to his door to ask a favour? There was also the invitation to tea at Café Zapion, and plans for an evening dinner. Maybe her heart was slowly turning towards him. How much longer could she amuse herself with that Hindu man?

'Look, here's what I propose,' he said, removing his hand from his moustache. 'Kosta can leave you at your house. Then he can park in the garage at the Sporting Club, jump on a tram car, go to Mustafa's son's house and check on Mustafa. What do you say? That way, you won't have to go to the Turkish district, and Kosta and Mustafa... Well, you know they're very close. It will be easier for Kosta to go to that house than for you to do so. Turks don't readily admit women into their homes, *kseris*, you know.'

Edith, who did not agree with any of this, nodded. She had won the argument for once! Once they'd got going, she would take over the driving from Kosta, and then she'd convince him to accompany her to the Iki Chesmelik neighbourhood.

And that was how adventure-addict Edith and owl-faced Kosta came to take the midnight-blue, four-cylinder Wilson-Pilcher, close witness of that still-aching wound in the darkest corner of Edith's heart, out of the garage and set off down the road.

The Wilson-Pilcher

In those days, it was impossible for a motor vehicle to pass through the Iki Chesmelik neighbourhood where Sumbul and Hilmi Rahmi lived. You had to use a carriage, a cart for heavy loads, a donkey or a bicycle. In some places the streets were so narrow that two neighbours could get stuck if they opened their doors at the same time. If two vehicles met head on, one of them would have to reverse all the way back to the end of the road and any pedestrians would have to throw themselves into the nearest shop – or garden, if the gate happened to be open – for fear of getting run over. While the pedestrians were fleeing, the drivers would be arguing about who should reverse. Occasionally a camel train laden with bundles would pass that way, carrying goods from the local warehouses down to the ships in the harbour, descending the hill behind a donkey, bells jangling; when this happened, all traffic was obliged to come to a standstill.

It was along such roads that Miss Edith drove the car. She crossed the Caravan Bridge, came through the Chorakkapi Gate, then continued from there down to Basmane and along Iki Chesmelik Street until she got to the Jewish Cemetery at the top of the hill. Kosta sat perched on the raised seat in the back as Edith drove them all the way from Bournabat to the Caravan Bridge, taking an hour to travel the one-parasang-long road, past vineyards, olive groves and melon fields and then into the narrow streets of the city itself.

When the men in the coffeehouse at the foot of the bridge saw her approaching, they jumped off their stools in surprise. Within moments they were chasing after the car, racing through the picnic area shaded by dark green cypresses next to the cemetery and leaping over the swings the children had made from the branches of plum and pomegranate trees. The nomad women stared in amazement at the woman driver passing through their encampment. They too followed after her, leaving their babies asleep in the cradles they'd hung from lines rigged up between the pine trees and their tents.

At this point I stopped and imagined the beautiful Edith – I didn't know she was my mother at that time – driving a car. Sumbul saw the dreamy look in my eyes and, being an expert at reading my mind, yelled, 'What children? What coffeehouse? For God's sake, Scheherazade, who was brave enough to venture out into the streets that day? The soldiers were drawing their bayonets on any man wearing a fez, no matter who it was, and *palikaria*, local Greek gangs, were tearing through our neighbourhood with knives, smashing windows, hurling everything out onto the street. When our former street guard, the coffeehouse owner Hasan, refused to give them his watch, they pushed him around. Hasan came at them with a pole, and the Greek soldier who'd joined them pulled out his gun and shot the poor man. We had closed the doors and windows and all of us were hiding on the top floors.'

Okay, the situation is clear. Nobody chased after Edith as she drove the midnight-blue motor car from Chorakkapi into the city. The women in the women's quarters of the house on Bulbul Street had taken up their needlework to distract themselves. The hall door on the second floor and the windows facing the street were fastened tight, the shutters closed. Prayer beads were turning, tick, tick. The maidservant kept refilling the tea glasses. There were no men in the house except for the Ethiopian boy, Ziver, who was still a child. As if it wasn't enough that he was planning to run off that night, Huseyin had left before dawn with Tevfik on some business or other. Great-Aunt Makbule had temporarily dropped her usual grave expression and was looking into Sumbul's eyes, pleading for help. The looters had taken a break when it had started to rain, but they would surely resume their pillaging as soon as the storm abated.

'Don't worry,' said Sumbul, without raising her head from her lacework. 'What business would they have with us? Besides, our neighbourhood is so high up, they won't come all the way up here.'

Even so, she wondered whether they had put ammunition in with the weapons in the sack in the well shaft. Through the slats of the shutters she saw that the neighbours across the street had hung a Greek flag from their window. When had they got that? She wished she'd sewn a blue and white flag and kept it secret from Huseyin. They could have draped it from the window and rested easier. The important thing was not saving your country but saving your children's lives. Being terrified was a thousand times worse than death itself.

Just then the door knocker for the men's quarters was struck hard three times. All at once the fingers holding the embroidery needles, counting the prayer beads and pouring the tea froze.

'They've come into the garden, Sumbul, sister!' Mujgan

screamed. She had sprung up from her place and was standing barefooted in the centre of the room on the rug with the bird and fish design.

Mujgan's daughters, sitting on the couch, drew near Sumbul.

'What should we do, sister? Let's hide the girls in the attic right away. Oh, my God, they're going to tear us all to pieces.'

Without saying a word, Sumbul laid her lacework on the couch, ran to the bedroom and took Hilmi Rahmi's sword bayonet from the bottom of the dowry trunk where they had hidden it. Trying not to make any creaking sounds, she descended the stairs. Ziver had gone into the entrance hall and was waiting at the door, his eyes wide and white with fear. The two of them backed themselves against the wall behind the door.

From outside, a polite, high-pitched voice called out, 'Gentlemen, open the door. Huseyin Bey, it's me, Mimiko, from Yorgi's Tavern. I bring your father, Mustafa Efendi.'

Hearing her father-in-law's name, Sumbul put all her suspicions aside and opened the door wide. On the top step stood a thin, pale-faced man, his capped head hanging low as if in shame. In his weak arms, he was holding, with difficulty, Mustafa Bey, whose fezless head was shaking like a bird with a broken wing. What was this? Oh, my God! Was he dead? Unconsciously, Sumbul took a step back into the entrance hall.

Mimiko rushed into the men's quarters and laid old Mustafa on the couch in the front room as if he were dropping him. Throwing a cloak over her shoulders, Sumbul followed.

'Kyra *mou*, my lady, forgive me, I enter uninvited, but Huseyin Bey, he know me. I play the *baglama*, my name Mimiko. They say "Gypsy Mimiko" because I play music.

I find Mustafa Efendi near the Church of Agia Ekaterini. He fallen in old mansion garden. No one see him because it raining. His head, it hit, I think. I ask coachmen. One of them know. "He Huseyin Bey father," he say. God bless him, he bring us here, not take money. No blood, but will be good if doctor come, yes?'

Sumbul was beside herself. Not with sorrow or worry, but with rage. Because that scoundrel master of the house had fallen in with the National Struggle troublemakers, he had left them with no protection on a day like this. She pulled the fez off the servant boy Ziver's head, and, with no regard for the consequences, replaced it with Mimiko's cap, then sent him out into the street. 'Run fast,' she yelled after him. Her throat, as white as milk pudding, had swelled, the veins on her neck were raised, her green eyes shone like fire. 'Go wherever you need to; go as far as Manisa or Aydin or Chios, but don't you dare return to this house without Huseyin. Do you understand? Hurry! Find whichever hole they're meeting in. Ask, inquire. If you come back empty-handed, you'll answer to me!

'Mimiko, I know it's a lot to ask, but would you go to Reshidiye Street and find Dr Agop. He works at the Armenian Hospital. Tell him Major Hilmi Rahmi's wife sent you and asks that he come urgently.'

Left alone in the big room, she wiped her father-in-law's forehead and held cologne compresses to his limp wrists. The old man's face was drained of blood, his lips as white as paper. What could have happened to him? Had someone attacked him or did he faint? Was Gypsy Mimiko telling the truth? May God protect them! The anger she felt towards her husband for having left them to fend for themselves against the infidels had long been a glowing coal; now it burst into flames. No matter how often she said to those who asked, 'It's all fine. I've learned how to look after the whole house by myself. I got used to packing figs in a factory and rolling cigarettes in tobacco workshops – I'm tough,' tears of injustice fluttered inside her, like a bird caught in her throat.

A while later, Huseyin's footsteps were heard on the steps. He must have been out of his mind with anger, for he was cursing as never before. Thank goodness Tevfik Bey was not with him or Sumbul would not have been able to look him in the face for embarrassment. She quickly closed the door to the room where Dr Agop was examining Mustafa Efendi.

'May they all burn in hell. God damn Greece and the British sons of whores, the bastard *palikaria*. All these years we've harboured snakes. The treacherous sons of infidels, they've shown us what putrid dough they're made of. Where is he? Where's my father?'

Shoving aside Mimiko, who was waiting in the entrance, he stormed into the large room.

Sumbul shouted behind him, 'Huseyin, have some sense, I beg you! Mimiko Bey brought your father all the way from Agia Katerina by cart. Dr Agop is examining him in there. Calm down, please. Thank God, there is no significant damage. Hopefully, he will regain consciousness soon. I'll tell Mujgan to bring you a glass of tea.'

Huseyin turned in anger. With one hand on the door into the men's quarters, he had opened his mouth to curse his sister-in-law when the bell on the garden gate rang. Sumbul pushed him aside, slipped into the salon, grabbed the bayonet she had left under the couch, and was all set to run into the garden. But Huseyin had got there first and was already standing in the hall with the Greek Mauser under his arm, taking aim at the door. As if his running off that morning and leaving them with only the Ethiopian servant boy Ziver for protection was not enough, he must have also removed the weapons from the well – God forbid! – ready to take with him.

When he saw how Sumbul was staring at the Mauser, he growled, 'Woman, when I am here, why are you running to the door?'

'Huseyin, I am aware that you are planning to leave us women here by ourselves. At least allow us to protect our home.' How calm her voice sounded, despite all the anger inside! If she'd been a man, she would have fought Huseyin right there. Fury was boiling inside her. Worse still, under his moustache he was muttering something like, 'I left you the double-barrelled shotgun.' He needed to speak up, make himself clear.

Just at that moment a hoarse and familiar voice came from the street side of the wooden gate.

'Huseyin, my son, we are worried about Mustafa. Is he all right? Is he here? Look, the lady has come from Bournabat to pay him a visit.'

When they opened the door, Huseyin in front, Sumbul behind, whom should they see on the threshold but Kosta, out of breath, and beside him in a red dress, standing as straight as a soldier, Edith Lamarck. Sumbul pinched herself. Was this a dream? What was Lady Edith doing at a poor house like theirs? Great God Almighty! Immediately she began calculating in her head: at the full moon they had wiped the staircase and all the furniture, the wood had just been polished with beeswax, and just yesterday they'd beaten the rugs. She could welcome Lady Edith into the women's quarters without worrying. She stepped back.

Coming into the garden, Edith tried to greet Huseyin, whom she had known since childhood, but Huseyin, with the Mauser still under his arm, didn't look her way. He was almost not going to allow his father's old friend Kosta inside, he being an infidel, but Sumbul's last words must have affected him, for when he heard his sister-in-law saying to Ziver, 'Son, take Mr Kosta to my father-in-law, then bring him a coffee,' he didn't contradict her.

Kosta followed Ziver into the men's quarters with his cap in his hands and his head lowered, as if the attacks by the local Greek gangs were his fault. Sumbul, bursting with excitement at this extraordinary turn of events, took Edith Lamarck, star of so many of Gypsy Yasemin's stories, up to the women's quarters. Uncertain as to whether to speak in Turkish or French, she was stammering.

'How kind of you, Lady Edith, to think of us on such a day and put yourself in danger by coming all this way. We are humbled.' Seeing Edith's questioning eyes – were they also a bit nervous? – she explained hurriedly. 'When my father-in-law was brought here, we should have sent word to your lady mother with our boy. We did not think of it and brought you all the way here. We are very grateful.'

The European woman waved her hand dismissively in the air. Perhaps the natural set of her face was somewhat pouty, but, still, her not smiling made Sumbul think she had done something wrong. She must not let silence descend.

'My father-in-law, Mustafa Efendi, was brought in a short while ago, Lady Edith. Unfortunately, he is unconscious. It is impossible to know what happened to him, of course. Mimiko, a musician at the tavern, found him near the Church of Agia Ekaterini. I know, you are going to say, "How did he come to be there?" Believe me, we haven't the slightest idea. Thank goodness he has no knife or bullet wounds on his body, but his head has been hit. That is the reason he is unconscious. Mimiko – God bless him – ran and brought a doctor from Haynots, the Armenian neighbourhood, and he is now examining my father-in-law. In a short while we will send my elder son downstairs to learn the result of the examination.'

The floors of the women's quarters of the house on Bulbul Street were covered with soft carpets. As soon as you climbed the stairs, the deep reds and purples caught the eye. Multicoloured flowers bloomed under your feet, and fish, deer and galloping horses were woven into the design. Edith stared in wonder at the magnificent scenes beneath her slippers.

Without pausing for breath, Sumbul kept on talking. 'The first things the looters take when they raid a house are the rugs. They haven't come up this far yet, thank goodness, but the neighbourhood below us was ransacked. Don't even ask, Miss Edith. Since morning our hearts have been in our mouths. What will become of us?'

Edith nodded. She had seen it on the roads. Smashed, mud-splattered fezzes on the ground, broken glass, shops turned upside down, their furniture thrown out and splintered into pieces. Hasan's coffeehouse was a bloodbath. She had seen it all, but she didn't share the details for she didn't want to frighten the women even more. She couldn't describe the image of Avinash's barber, Hamid, standing there by himself amid the scattered remains of the lemon-scented hair oil which he used to rush to get from Frank Street at the beginning of each month. Or the refugee child sitting against the wall of Hasan's coffeehouse, holding his master's purple fez in his arms and weeping.

She was exhausted. Why in the world had she made so much effort to get here? Sometimes she got so stubborn, and for nothing. When she was focused on something, struggling to achieve it gave her pleasure in the short term, but once she'd reached the goal, that familiar unhappiness would begin gnawing at her soul again. She was fed up with herself. She looked around the room for a cigarette.

'Sister Sumbul, ask the lady to elaborate a little,' begged Mujgan, somewhat comforted by the fact that there were so many men downstairs. Now, especially with a European woman under their roof, they would be completely safe. The *palikaria* would definitely not touch a house with Europeans in it. Furthermore, Gypsy Mimiko, Dr Agop, Mustafa Efendi, even though he was unconscious, and Huseyin, who wouldn't put the Mauser down, were all downstairs. In addition, last night while he was lying in her arms, Huseyin had promised he would not leave them; he would stay to protect them all. Maybe they would even have a son.

Half in Turkish, half in French, Edith told them about her journey there. The women turned their attention from their needlework to their uninvited guest's story. No one could take their eyes off Edith; not Sumbul, or Mujgan, or Mujgan's daughters, Munevver and Neriman, or little Dogan, or even Aunt Makbule. They gazed at the way her prematurely grey hair contrasted with her rose-petal-soft skin, at the tiny pearl buttons that ran all the way down her silk dress, and at her white hands that fluttered like a dove's wings as she talked. What a beautiful, noble lady she was! On seeing the attractive guest, the servant who'd brought the coffee, rose-hip jam and *lokum* on a silver tray forgot to return to the kitchen and instead squeezed into a corner of the couch. She didn't even notice Aunt Makbule indicating with her eyebrows and eyes that she should pour the tea from the samovar.

'We have British neighbours in Bournabat. Perhaps you know of them. Kosta is their butler.'

The women nodded. They knew of the Thomas-Cook family.

'Their son Edward is my childhood friend. Our gardens adjoin and our families are friends. Edward is very keen on cars—'

She stopped mid-sentence. She wasn't sure how much she should say. Edward and his elder brother, Peter, had five motor cars in their garage, each brought from America or England. They liked to take parts out and put other parts in at whim, even attaching old engines from yachts in their attempts to try and build a car.

The women saw a shadow pass over her face but didn't know the reason. Sumbul became anxious. Had they done something wrong? Had they pushed their guest into talking too much? She motioned to the servant to bring more of Nanny Dilber's jams, to refresh the spoons. Let the lady taste each one. Whatever was bothering her could be dispersed with sugar. With her eyes she made a sign to Mujgan, who was leaning forward slightly as if she'd been struck by lightning. She shouldn't sit like that, she'd fall into the lady's mouth. Unconcerned about being tactless, Mujgan was saying, 'Sumbul, sister, ask Lady Edith how she learned to drive a motor car.'

Edith understood the question without Sumbul's translation. Her face darkened. Aunt Makbule laid her prayer beads down on the side table with a clink, her hawk-like eyes trained on Mujgan's face. The servant brought jams of various colours lined up on a tray. Edith raised her slender white hand in refusal, and Sumbul's face fell. Mujgan, oblivious, kept insisting, 'Ask her, sister.' Edith's eyes had shifted to the flowers, birds and horses of the carpet. She was remembering.

Many years ago, again in that dark corner of her heart... A midnight-blue motor car parked off the meadow road flanked by pomegranate trees; she in a shimmering silk dress, the same blue as the car, and Ali in a starched white shirt, black sash and aubergine-coloured fez. His thick, fleshy lips were shy. Their fingers met on the walnut steering wheel. Because Edward was unable to say no to anyone, particularly to Edith, he had lent her the Wilson-Pilcher for driving lessons. On the black leather seat, legs exchanged warmth; on the steering wheel, arms intertwined. 'Get our Ali to teach you to drive, Edith *mou*. Take the car to the meadows, to Narlikoy or as far as Kokluca. The crankshaft has just been repaired. Drive as much as you want – learn! Women are even piloting aeroplanes now, so how can you not learn to drive a car?'

Poplars, pomegranates, melon fields, olive groves... Two hearts beating as if they would burst their chests to reach each other. A body leaning gracefully over hers, like a deer, not like a person. The hands that she so enjoyed watching while Ali mended the crankshaft – those hands were now making her skin feel like honey. They were dancing almost without movement on the Wilson-Pilcher's black leather seat. The engine was humming; the birds were silent on the bare branches. The starched white shirt dropped, mingling with the shimmering silk dress. The deer was running – quick! quicker! – as if the end of the world was coming. Inside, she felt as warm as a loaf just out of the oven, as sweet as halva. Above, bare branches and a grey sky. From every cell of her body, sherbet fizzed and foamed. Was it her screams that rose from the vineyards and orchards, that beat upon the bell tower of the church and returned?

Edith squirmed. Silence hovered over the women's quarters of the house on Bulbul Street like a cloud in the sky. Seeing the trace of a smile on her visitor's face, Sumbul took a deep breath.

Just then, her elder son, Cengiz, burst in. 'Mother! Mother! Granddad has woken up!'

His shaven blonde head was huge, his eyes as round as Muscat grapes.

In the room there was a flurry of activity. Mujgan and her daughters embraced. Aunt Makbule grasped her beads and murmured a prayer. Edith stood up, then sat down again.

Sumbul pulled Cengiz to her breast and kissed him. Her son was enjoying being able to move comfortably between the two parts of the house. 'I've come from downstairs,' he bragged. 'Great-Aunt, Grandfather has woken up.'

'Why are you shouting so much, son? I am not deaf. I am able to hear, thank the good Lord. Stand up properly when you're speaking.'

Keeping one hand on Sumbul's purple velvet skirt, Cengiz directed his grape-like eyes at each woman in turn.

'The infidel doctor came with a great big black bag full of instruments and tools. There was a knife, a saw... I even spotted a razor blade. Then there were some things made out of beeswax. And brown bottles like Auntie Aybatan's. The doctor drew out some elixir with an injector and a needle. Then he stuck the needle into Granddad's arm and injected all the elixir into his skin. The needle was this big' – he demonstrated with his fingers – 'but Granddad didn't make a single sound.'

Little Dogan raced over from the edge of the room and

jumped onto Sumbul's lap. Munevver and Neriman, sitting on cushions beside the samovar in order to see Edith more clearly, laughed.

'There was this big tool like a hammer. He hit Granddad's knees with that. Then he took out something else and listened to his lungs and heart with that. He raised his eyelids, opened his mouth. I held the torch when he looked down his throat. Then he—'

Suddenly, as if he'd forgotten what he wanted to say, he stopped and looked at Edith.

'Cengiz, what happened? For God's sake, speak up,' Mujgan said.

'Cengiz, son, Dr Agop gave your grandfather an injection. Then what happened?'

'Nothing,' the boy said absently. But it was unclear to what he was referring. He pulled on Sumbul's purple skirt. 'Mummy?'

'Son, do not stare at our guest like that. You are behaving rudely. Look, if you won't speak, we'll send Dogan downstairs, get him to tell us what's happening.'

Cengiz looked worriedly at his mother.

'What did Dr Agop do to your grandfather?'

'He did... uh... He hit him really hard.'

'The devil!'

Mujgan took off her slipper and waved it at Dogan.

'The infidel doctor slapped Granddad a few times. Granddad's cheeks turned the colour of a rosebud. We all saw it. The he woke up. At first he said something confusing. Dr Agop explained that it was normal for him to sound like he was talking in his sleep. He was just waking up, he said. But he said... uh...'

'What did he say?'

Cengiz was enjoying knowing that all the women's eyes were on him. Keeping his silence, he made the most of his newly discovered power. In the meantime, he gave Edith an appraising look.

'This son of yours tests a person's soul, Sumbul! Speak up, boy!'

'He said... uh... that Granddad might not be able to remember certain things.'

'What kind of things would that be?'

Edith spoke for the first time. '*Hafiza kaybi?* Memory loss?'

They all turned and looked at her, as if her knowing such terminology in Turkish was a cause for worry. What should she have done?

'I've heard that being struck on the head can lead to partial memory loss,' she murmured.

'Yeah, the infidel doctor said it could be that,' said Cengiz. 'Mummy, who is this European woman?'

'Shhh. Hold your tongue.'

A short while later, Ziver's curly black head appeared at the bottom of the stairs. He still wasn't wearing his fez. Kosta was waiting for Edith in the hall downstairs. As it was inappropriate for a woman to enter the men's quarters, Edith was not able to see Mustafa, but she met Dr Agop at the door. The doctor was a small man with a large nose and a bald head. When he saw Edith, he bowed and kissed her hand.

'Mademoiselle Lamarck, for a lady like you to venture all the way here on such a day requires true courage. I will definitely not allow you to return home by yourself. I will accompany you there.'

It was obvious that he didn't know about the motor car, but if they walked together to where she had parked it, Edith would be able to gather detailed information about Mustafa's condition. She had taken Dr Agop's arm and was going into the garden when Sumbul ran downstairs with Dogan in her arms and the purple cloak that was so becoming on her swirling behind her. Reaching their sides, she said, 'Lady, Edith, you are so kind, so thoughtful. To come all the way here, especially on such a day, shows great courtesy, and courage too, of course. Certainly, when my father-in-law hears of it, he will be most grateful. As a family we are all very thankful to you.'

Edith mumbled some words, then leaned into Kosta's ear and requested that he run down to Ali's sister's house on one of the lower streets to check that they were safe and ask if they were in need of anything. Years before, she had once knocked on Saadet's door to ask about Ali, who had vanished into thin air. Saadet had shouted at her, 'You infidels made my brother a plaything then threw him away!', and chased her all the way to the cemetery. For hours afterwards, tears had streamed down young Edith's cheeks. It was on that day, as she cried there beside a mossy tombstone, that she realized that her mother had had a hand in Ali's disappearance.

Sumbul looked deeply into Edith's eyes, hoping in vain to be invited to the house on Vasili Street for tea or coffee. But the Levantine woman seemed distracted. Sumbul was only able to hear her say in the butler's ear, 'Be sure to tell her Edward sent you.' Then she stroked Dogan's chin, took Dr Agop's arm as far as the bakery on the corner, left him, and walked towards her motor car, vanishing from sight. She didn't notice Sumbul's downcast face, as she watched Edith from behind, in her purple cloak.

This was the first and last time that Sumbul saw Edith.

And then she went and hanged herself, my darling Sumbul, before she could learn that for years she had nourished under

her roof the true daughter of this Levantine woman, the star
of Gypsy Yasemin's stories, whom she had so adored.

What a shame.

Such a great shame.

Part III

BORROWED TIME

Insistence

'Dear Mama, look, this is where we'll be getting the boat from – right here. It's not some stranger's boat, it's Niko's father's. And I swear I'll be back before midnight. You won't have to worry about me the tiniest bit. All my friends from the neighbourhood are going. If you want, you can ask Uncle Christo – his grandchildren are going. We'll all go together and come back together. Okay? *Manoula mou*, dear Mama, please, I beg you. *Se parakalo*. Please!'

'We've arrived now. Let's get down,' said Katina in answer. The horse tram had stopped in front of the Sporting Club. With baskets on their arms, mother and daughter got off. Panagiota's face was tanned from the sun, her lips were burned and her long black hair was white with salt.

'Let's go over there and drink a lemonade – what do you say, my beautiful daughter?'

'I'm not interested in doing anything until you say you'll give me permission.'

For almost two weeks, Panagiota had been trying to convince Katina to let her go with her friends to the fairgrounds at Agia Triada. First she had shouted and stomped. When that didn't work, she tried reasoning. When that didn't work

195

either, she shut herself in her room and declared she would eat nothing all day long. Today she had left the house for the first time, but she still hadn't given up.

'Daughter, where did the idea to get in a rowing boat and go to Agia Triada come from? You're only children. From the dock, it would take an hour of rowing to get there. At your age, how can you think of going on a moonlit outing without having an adult along?'

Panagiota rolled her eyes. She would soon be entering her fifteenth year. Some of the friends going to the fair, for example Stavros, were seventeen already. But reminding her mother at this critical moment that Stavros would be coming with them could be dangerous. Her eyes filled with tears. Adriana's mother and Elpiniki's mother had both given permission, and they were the same age as Panagiota, but there was no point reminding Katina of this, for her answer was always the same. Those mothers had many other children to busy themselves with, whereas Panagiota was the only one, her mother's treasure, her soul, her heart. If something should happen to her, what would her dear mother and her elderly father do?

'If you don't want a lemonade, carry the basket and walk in front.'

'What? We're going to walk home from here? It's so hot. Why did we get off the tram so far away?'

'We'll stop at the pharmacy first. Your neck and face are bright red. We'll get Fotini to prepare some cream for you. Ah, *paidi mou*, my child! You're a big girl, *vre*, but your head is still in the clouds. You don't even know how to protect yourself from the sun and you up and ask to go on a moonlight outing!'

Dragging her feet behind her mother, Panagiota and Katina turned into Alambra Street, known to everyone as Limanaki, the little port. The schools had just closed and the sunbathing season had begun, but the heat was driving people crazy.

'At least after the pharmacy let's get a carriage.'

'Aah, what a lot of bargaining, Panagiota. We don't have the means to take a carriage for a fifteen-minute walk. The breeze will pick up soon and we'll be able to enjoy the cool evening air. I must buy some pickling salt from Marko. When we get home, you can pour cool water over yourself – you're covered in sea salt. This year it ends, daughter – this dipping in and out of the sea. When we go to the beach, you must wear your hat and sit with us on the terrace. You're old enough to be a bride.'

'Old enough to be a bride but not old enough to go to the fair with my friends, is that right?'

Katina hurried forwards on her short legs, looking at the ground as she spoke. 'Daughter, the issue is not the fair. If you wish to go to the fair, let us take you there and leave you. You can wander around with your friends, we can enjoy the fresh air, and then we can return home together. But you are saying you must go by rowing boat; these are the habits of a big spender.'

As they reached the old plane tree in Fasoula Square, the rising wind interrupted their conversation for a moment and dried the sweat on Panagiota's forehead. One of the butchers was leaning over the chopping board in front of him, beating meat for stew. An old uncle sitting at a coffeehouse table under the plane tree tipped his hat to them in greeting. This was the pharmacist Yakoumi. He was wearing a dark green suit with beige stripes and had a straw hat on his head. He had hung his jacket and his walking cane over the back of his chair and was sitting by himself.

Slipping between the horses and carts, Katina pulled

Panagiota over to his table. '*Kalispera*, good afternoon, Kyr Yakoumi. How are you?'

'*Kalispera*, daughter Katina. Thank you, I am well. And you? How is your husband, Prodromakis? I see our little lady has grown tall, praise God.'

'Thank you, Kyr Yakoumi.'

Katina glared at Panagiota. The stubborn little donkey had her head down and was staring at her sandy shoes out of the corner of her eye.

'We are getting by, thank goodness. We're on our way to your shop actually. "Let's go and see Fotini," we said.'

'Of course. Fotini is at the shop. She'll be happy to see you.' Picking up the folded newspaper on the table, he began to fan his wrinkled face. 'The heat has begun early this year. We'll be boiling in the summer.'

'It seems so.'

Panagiota shifted her weight from one foot to the other. What empty talk! The elderly pharmacist opened the newspaper he'd been fanning himself with and pointed to a news item on the front page. 'The army is again calling for volunteers. They're going to end up taking all the boys.'

Panagiota felt herself grow tense. She was always nervous when the subject of war, the army or military service was brought up in her mother's presence. As if she herself were responsible for Katina's emotional state and should prevent any subject that might upset her from being mentioned.

Katina, oblivious of the storm about to burst inside her daughter, smiled as if to calm the old man. 'I do not think so, Kyr Yakoumi. There are so many volunteering to go. Particularly after Metropolitan Bishop Chrysostomos made that speech in the spring, thousands of young men went and volunteered for the army. Won't that be enough?'

'It might not be enough, my daughter. Fotini's son will turn eighteen next year. If this situation continues, God help us, we will look into taking Italian citizenship. May God prevent it from turning into a serious war.'

Katina was confused. 'Are you afraid that those with Ottoman citizenship will be forced to join the Greek army? Is such a thing possible?'

The old man took a handkerchief from the pocket of his waistcoat and wiped away the sweat that had gathered under his hat. 'We are in such times, Katina *mou*, that anything is possible. Those who lead us are saying that all men between the ages of eighteen and fifty should undergo military training in the mornings and evenings. If this situation continues, they will even send me to the front, regardless of my age and white hair.'

There was silence. All around them, people were anxiously rushing by. Panagiota breathed in. Everywhere you heard talk of politics, of Venizelos, of the Paris peace talks, of whether or not Smyrna would be annexed to Greece. It had been a year since the Greek army had taken over the administration of the city and life had still not become properly settled again. Now they were rounding up soldiers from among the Ottoman Greeks of Asia Minor in order to protect the borders. She thought of Stavros and her mouth went dry. How many days was it since he'd disappeared from sight?

'Please, let me not delay you further, Katina *mou*. I see the little lady has become bored.'

Katina turned and looked crossly at Panagiota. Bidding the old man goodbye, they set off for the pharmacy. Just as they were about to enter the shop, a breeze blew Panagiota's skirt up. Without taking their lips off their hookah pipes, the men in the coffeehouse looked sideways at the girl's exposed calves. Katina grabbed her daughter's arm and pushed her into the shop.

The white curtains of the pharmacy windows overlooking the square were drawn to keep out the sun; inside, they were greeted with scented coolness. Since her childhood, old Yakoumi's shop had aroused a mixture of fear and pleasure in Panagiota. The aromas emanating from the brown bottles lined up behind the counter – lavender, lemon, coconut oil, alcohol – were like doors into a mysterious universe. For a moment she forgot the struggle for the fair and approached the counter with curiosity. Fotini was about the same age as her mother, beautiful, with pale skin, honey-coloured eyes, and hair the colour of polished brass. She smiled as mother and daughter entered the shop.

'*Geia sas*, ladies. Greetings! I see the sunbathing season has begun. Where have you come from – the Eden Baths in Punta?'

'*Geia sou*, Fotini. Of course, we've not come from Punta. What business would we have there? We went to Karatash. They've refurnished the terrace, put out more chaises longues. It's not bad. Next time you should come with us.'

'Hopefully, Katina *mou*. *Makari*.'

'Yes, that's where we've been, and look how sunburned this daughter is! While I was sitting on the terrace, she dived into the open sea and swam all the way over to the men's side. I swear, even I was barely able to save her from that fat-assed baths manager, Nesibe. Because of her so brazenly showing herself to the boys, they were almost going to ban us from the Karatash Baths. Meanwhile, of course, her neck and face are all burned.'

Fotini looked lovingly at Panagiota's sweaty pink cheeks and sparkling black eyes. She spent all day in the back room of the pharmacy she ran with her father preparing creams, elixirs and oils to beautify women. The dream of the women who came to her was to regain the radiance of a fifteen-year-old. Seeing the source of that radiance that no cream could produce right in front of her always gave Fotini joy. Pretending to scold, she said, 'Ah Panagiota *mou*, what did you do, my beauty? Why didn't you sit under your parasol? If that beautiful skin turns brown, no one will want you, darling.'

Then, seeing Panagiota's face fall, she added, 'I'm just joking, dear. You don't seem very happy today – you're pouting.'

Panagiota's eyes filled with tears. Someone else recognizing her sadness made her feel her mother's insensitivity even more. In a voice that was almost inaudible, she answered, 'It's nothing.'

Katina made a dismissive gesture with her hand to the pharmacist. While waiting for the cream to be prepared in a glass mortar, they drank the cherry sherbet Fotini had offered them in the cool, dimly lit pharmacy. Neither of them said a word.

Panagiota was sick and tired of hearing the same thing! She was a miracle, God's blessing, her mother's treasure. She wished she weren't. If only she could have been like Adriana, the fifth child of eight. If only her father went from tavern to tavern playing the *baglama*, the traditional stringed musical instrument, and her mother was a washerwoman. If only no one cared about her and there was no 'miracle' burden on her shoulders. If only... If only, instead of a mother who was so afraid of losing her, she had a mother who got her name mixed up in a crowd of children.

When they were out in the square again, she erupted like a volcano. 'If I can't go on a moonlight outing at this age, when am I supposed to go, Mama? After I'm married with a bunch of children? I am so fed up with your cautiousness – I want to live my life!'

Even before she'd finished speaking, she regretted her words. Her mother would be very upset. What's more, other things would come to her mind. Without raising her head from the ground, she looked at Katina from the corner of her eye. But what was this? A smile had spread across Katina's freckled face. Unbelievable!

They walked in silence past the shops with white awnings on Frank Street. Panagiota didn't even dawdle in front of the windows. Any other time, she would have dragged her mother inside to look at the dresses and handbags from Paris and London. Near the French Hospital, the vegetable seller from Crete passed them, doubled over under his large basket. Katina bought five fresh courgettes and some tomatoes from him, throwing them into the beach basket Panagiota was carrying without saying a word. If it had been a different day Katina wouldn't have been able to restrain herself from mentioning that most difficult birth as they passed by the hospital where her daughter had been born. She would point out the window of the room where she had first held Panagiota in her arms. Panagiota knew by heart the story of the European nurse who appeared behind the curtain with the baby her mother believed had died.

That day they walked past the hospital's yellow walls in silence.

In their own neighbourhood, the old women were taking advantage of the evening cool and had brought chairs out in front of their houses and settled down to wait for the young people to come back from the sea. Children were already racing around outside, raising clouds of dust. Katina waved to Auntie Rozi. Panagiota looked for Elpiniki and Adriana. In a little while they would wash the salt and sweat from their skins, put on something nice for the evening and maybe all go down to the quay together for ice cream. She was still thinking about the lemonade she had refused out of stubbornness. But first she had to settle this fair business. While she was considering how to broach the subject, her mother spoke up.

'*Kori mou*, tell me, who else is going to this fair?'

In truth, Katina was not sure what to do about her daughter's persistent nagging of the past two weeks. It was all right if she went to the quay for ice cream, but to row over to Agia Triada at night? Katina just couldn't get her tongue to say yes. Although the neighbourhood children had known each other since the day they were born, she knew how unreliable young men could be at that age. What if one of them should put a hand on Panagiota... and the girl, drunk on moonlight, let herself be taken... God forbid!

Katina had had four miscarriages between the twins and Panagiota. Because of this, from the moment the baby dropped into her womb, Katina had been afraid of losing her. When the two of them had come back from the dead during that difficult birth, Katina's fear had intensified. For years she had gone to see all sorts of people noted for breaking magical spells, from a priest in their neighbourhood to a powerful *hodja*, one of the best-known Muslim spiritual guides who lived behind Basmane train station. She had made offerings, lit candles, left holy water on the windowsill on moonlit nights. Though Panagiota was a perfect child – healthy, smart, beautiful – that initial fear of imminent misfortune had not passed. 'Had not passed' is not the correct expression. Her fear, like the white in her hair, multiplied day by day.

To make matters worse, the girl had grown so beautiful

of late that ever since the lemon trees had blossomed, all the boys from the neighbourhood had been taking up their fiddles, dulcimers and tambourines and singing love songs under her window. Actually, it was not clear whether the serenades were for the blonde beauty Elpiniki, who lived next door, or for Panagiota. But every night the boys, like faithful lovers, made the whole street moan. It perplexed Katina that Akis didn't take this carousing seriously. Even if it was Elpiniki they came for, she thought Akis should go out and do something. Elpiniki's father, their neighbour, Kyr Iraklis, had been in hospital with tuberculosis for several months, and since Elpiniki's brother had not returned from Athens, it was Akis's duty to his sick neighbour to let everyone know that Elpiniki was not alone in the world. And most important of all, he had to protect Panagiota.

Whenever the scratchy sounds of a fiddle and dulcimer along with the cracked voice of a boy under the bay window rent the midnight silence, Akis would tease Katina, saying, 'What were you expecting, Katina *mou*? Or did you forget the young man who used to read poetry to you under your own window?'

Katina would toss and turn in the bed. Then, distressed by the knowledge that she was contradicting herself, she would say, 'Kyr Prodromakis, was I a child at the time of those serenades? I was at the marrying age, whereas Panagiota is still playing skipping ropes in the square. Also, times have changed. Our daughter is a pupil at Homerion High School.'

Turning and embracing his distressed wife, Akis would reply, 'But I remember when you also used to play skipping ropes. I would come and undo your sash, then run away. You would race after me until you caught me in some hidden corner. You weren't even fifteen years old then, *vre* Katina.'

Katina's heart would soften with the sweet memories of her youth in Chesme. But the croaky voice of the boy reciting poetry under her bay window would ignite her anger once more.

'Kyr Akis, you must put an end to this! It's as if we've placed a bottle on our roof to announce that we have a daughter of marriageable age, like the villagers do. How shameful this is! If you don't care about your own daughter, give a thought to our neighbour, Rea. The woman's husband has tuberculosis, and her son crossed to Chios to escape the labour battalion and then went on to Athens and started his own family. These clowns have their eyes on your daughter, and I'm sure it's because these two, Panagiota and Elpiniki, are the only ones who go to Homerion High School. I swear, if you hadn't insisted and we'd sent the girl to the church school, there would be none of these disgraceful goings-on. It's rubbing elbows with those snobbish girls that's brought our daughter to this.'

Most nights, Akis, unable to endure his wife's nagging, would get up, lean out the window and shoo the boys away. But they always came back again the following night. Maybe if he aimed a gun at them, shouted, 'Get away, you scoundrels,' and fired a few shots into the air, they wouldn't dare serenade in the same place again, but when Akis saw them he couldn't stop a smile from spreading across his face. Everyone was familiar with the grocer's temper, so if he were to pretend to be furious, no one would be fooled. When he stuck his head out of the window in his hooded white nightshirt and smiled from beneath his bushy moustache, the boys could tell that he didn't really mind, so they happily made themselves scarce, until the next night...

While all this was happening, Panagiota would gaze down

with sadness at the crowd of boys from behind the tulle curtain of the window she had tiptoed over to in her bare feet. Stavros was never among them. He had not once joined in with the serenading on Menekse Street; all his friends from the neighbourhood gathered under her window, but Stavros stayed away. Hopefully he hadn't fallen for some rich girl and was not at the quay feeding her ice cream – one of those girls who got all dressed up and went down to the quay to attract the attention of the officers who spent the whole day trotting round in circles on horseback. Thoughts like that hurt, as if her heart were being clamped.

Katina repeated her question. 'Daughter, who is going on this rowing boat excursion? Who will pull the oars? What if the boat capsizes, God forbid?'

They'd reached the centre of their little square. Panagiota came to an abrupt stop and put down her basket. Something had changed in her mother's voice. She pivoted round and looked at Katina, whom she towered over, these days. Yes, her mother's eyes had turned the colour of hazelnut shells. Could it be…? A smile spread like sunshine across Panagiota's face, revealing the evenly spaced teeth, like pomegranate seeds, in her small red mouth.

Seeing her daughter looking so fresh and innocent, Katina's heart melted. Panagiota was her diamond. A miracle. God's blessing. As beautiful and pure as a droplet of water.

'Ohooo,' boomed Panagiota in a deep voice quite at odds with her mother's image of a water droplet, 'everyone you can think of is going! All the boys and girls from the neighbourhood. They'll be coming out into the square soon and you can ask them. Elpiniki and Adriana. And from the boys, there's Minas, Pandelis, the fisherman's son, Niko…'

She hesitated briefly, then added, 'And Stavros.' She hoped her tone of voice hadn't changed when she'd said his name.

'Oh, so Stavros is going too?' Katina puckered her lips as she always did when she was displeased.

Panagiota's cheeks felt hot. She was surely blushing. Hoping that the sunburn would hide her embarrassment, she picked up the basket again and began to head towards home. She'd had to think fast and come up with something quick, and eventually she'd blurted it out. In truth, she wasn't even sure that Stavros was coming. Why had she brought up his name? Did she hope, like an idiot, that if she said it forty times, it would happen? She'd heard from Adriana that Stavros was coming – maybe. Adriana had heard it from Minas. Stavros and Pandelis would row, that's what Minas had told Adriana, leaving the two of them to sit at the bow under the stars and... whatever.

Panagiota didn't even dream of sitting side by side in the bow of the boat with Stavros. They weren't a couple like Adriana and Minas. Everybody considered those two to be engaged; when the families had completed the dowry talks, they would exchange rings. Feeling sorry for herself, she moaned silently, 'No one would even call us a couple.' The boy was like a thorn, appearing and disappearing. Could a fiancé behave like that? But his hands... his huge hands were like fire... How many days had it been since she'd seen him, since his hands had touched her body?

'Panagiota *mou*? Where are you running to, *vre* daughter? Wait for your poor mama. I swear, I'm out of breath.'

Panagiota slowed down when she got to the entrance of Menekse Street. Since last summer they had been meeting at the far end of the square, beside the cold stone wall of the British Hospital, to embrace and kiss amid the smell of fresh grass, tobacco and fried fish carried on the wind from their neighbourhood. The boy would take hold of Panagiota's shoulders with his huge hands, put his tongue – which tasted sour, of the cigarette smoke that also infused his hair and skin – in her mouth for several minutes, and bite her lips until they turned purple, sucking on her as if he wanted to drain her of water. Panagiota, drunk from his hands moving over her body, from the hardness of his groin pressed against her, tried to reciprocate as much as she could.

They hadn't gone further than kissing, and the whole kissing scenario never lasted longer than five minutes. Panagiota always had to get back to the square before Katina noticed her absence. Even though their encounters were brief, Panagiota was conflicted. One part of her would tell herself that something was lacking, that she wasn't doing it right, that Stavros would prefer a girl who could kiss better than she did. And the other part worried that she shouldn't be giving her precious body into his huge hands and that Stavros would prefer a girl who sold herself less cheaply.

Anyway, these love scenes – was it love? – beside the hospital wall did not happen every evening. If they had, Panagiota's emotions and confusion could not have endured the storm in her soul.

Katina caught up with her daughter in front of their house. Akis had lowered his shutters halfway and gone to the coffeehouse to play backgammon.

'What is it – you don't talk to Stavros any more?'

To herself, Panagiota replied, 'What do you mean by "talk," Mama? When he's with the other boys, he doesn't even acknowledge me. He never once looks me in the eye or turns to say a word to me. Whenever it suits him, he sends me a signal, and I run to the hospital wall like a lamb – what lamb? I run like a rearing horse – to be crushed between his body and the wall.'

Katina, noting her daughter's silence, stopped in front of the blue wooden door with the key in her hand. The street was in shadow now. Panagiota wrapped her arms around herself.

'*Yavri mou*, what's the matter? Did Stavros break your heart?'

'No, why should he, *kale*?'

She turned her head towards the British Hospital, where she and Stavros had kissed, in order to hide the tears welling in her eyes, then added hurriedly, 'There's nothing between us.'

Katina was aware that Stavros had not been seen around for quite some time. He wasn't among those boys who hung around under the window in the evenings. He was a quiet, self-contained boy who never said much, just walked around with a sullen face. Akis had mentioned that some of the neighbourhood boys had joined one or other of the various underground movements – what if Stavros had got mixed up in all that? He was the tough, silent type; why had Panagiota set her heart on him? Had she fallen in love with those hard, green eyes? Oh, dear. The tight-lipped girl wasn't telling her anything.

'*Kala*, okay. Let's see what happens.'

They went through the blue door. Inside, it was dim and cool. A muted yellow-green light seeped in through the colourful stained glass above the door as Katina walked down the corridor. The clothes she'd hung out in the back courtyard were flapping in the wind.

'*Ela*, come, pump some water. Let's wash the pebbles and sand from our feet before we go upstairs.'

The water was as cold as ice, for the tank from which it was drawn kept it chilled even in the burning heat. When she was a child, Panagiota used to think djinns would jump out of that tank when the water was pumped. As she washed her feet, hands and face with particles of crumbling soap, the coolness spread from her toes into her bones and throughout her body.

'Take off your clothes and get in the bath if you wish. The water in the basin is hot. You're as wet as a duck anyway.'

'You will give your permission, won't you, dear Mama? I really want to go. I want to very, very, very much. Please, *se parakalo, gia to hatiri mou*. Please, for me. We'll all go together and come back together, *ma to Theo*. I swear to God.'

The girl's eyes had filled with tears again. Katina sighed.

'Wait until the evening when your father comes home. I'll talk to him.'

Panagiota ran barefooted to her mother and wound her arms, dripping with water, around her neck. It was up to her father now. When Stavros saw Minas and Adriana cuddling in the boat on the night of the fair, he would relax and treat her like a real fiancée. Then when they were ashore, they'd buy a cone of hot peanuts and walk along the streets of Agia Triada, chatting like two lovers, like a real couple. That night would be a turning point in their love.

Rejoicing in her dreams, she turned to her mother. 'Come, *Manoula*, let's get dressed up and go out to the square. The sun has set and everybody is out on the streets. There's a full moon tonight – let's go down to the quay together.'

'Well, thank goodness you've come to your senses. *Doksa to Theo*. Thanks be to God. As if I've not been saying this all along, Panagiota *mou*. Go and change your clothes and then we'll go, my little crazy, *kori mou*. You've made yourself miserable for so many days. And me too.'

Pushing and shoving each other like children, they climbed the narrow staircase to their home.

Serenade

That evening, Lieutenant Pavlo Paraskis saw Panagiota for the first time, sitting with the other girls lined up like birds on the wall in front of the police station. With her eyes shining like embers, her red cheeks and cherry lips, the girl was a perfect sun goddess.

Her hair was pinned back with enamel combs above her small white ears. From time to time her dreamy eyes gazed at the green spaces beyond the railway tracks. She gestured extravagantly with one hand as she laughed at something her friend was saying. Her calves, exposed beneath the loose white dress she was wearing, were strong, her ankles slender. Her curly hair tumbled down to her waist, dancing in the rosy evening light.

Pavlo stopped walking and stared at Panagiota, radiant in the twilight. Was this a simple trick of the light or was it a sign sent from Almighty God? It was as if the girl were encircled by a glow that only he could see.

When Adriana noticed the lieutenant standing across from them, she stopped talking and prodded the others. They all turned at once and eyed Pavlo fearlessly. The young lieutenant took off his cap and greeted them, causing them to cover their mouths with their hands and giggle. Panagiota smiled shyly, filling Pavlo's heart with happiness, like sunshine after rain. The girl's teeth were a little strange, but there was something about her face that made him want to look at it over and over again. Her long, slender nose gave her an air of nobility. Though her cheekbones had a slightly masculine hardness, one could lose oneself in the black of her almond-shaped eyes shadowed by long, thick lashes. For certain, Almighty God was sending him a sign. Thank you, Holy Panagia!

Just a short while earlier he had felt crushed by the weight of his troubles and his homesickness for Ioannina. The gendarme had arrived late for night-guard duty; the man was a low-ranking member of the paramilitary police and yet apparently he did not take Pavlo seriously. The gendarmes were all from Crete anyway; they looked out for each other, talked behind his back. He really should not have to put up with this, being assigned to a neighbourhood police station with soldiers from Crete; if only his position at Stergiadis's office had not been terminated because of a stupid accusation. And what was that anyway? Listening at doors!

Anger had settled in his stomach like a hard, hot fist, but now his heart was rejoicing like blossom trees in spring. He understood all at once why he had come into this world. Lieutenant Pavlo Paraskis had somehow failed to bond with the people of Smyrna, with their passionate devotion to the wind and the water, to taking their pleasures and having fun where they could. Since setting foot in the city, he'd seen many beauties, had even chatted with a few at their garden gates, but he had never come across a scene that had made his heart race like this. For example, before he'd been assigned to Stergiadis's office, when he was still Commander Zafiro's orderly in Bournabat, he had fallen for a servant girl at the next-door mansion. He had somehow never learned this beauty's name. When evening fell, she would take her place behind the wrought-iron garden gate and, choosing from a basketful of rose petals, would flirt with the soldiers passing by. Appraising them with her black eyes, she would ask, 'Tell me, are you for Venizelos or are you a royalist?' Her voice was so sweet that even those soldiers who weren't taken in would change their route just to catch sight of her.

Pavlo knew that the soldiers trying to win the girl's heart could never give the correct answer. If one of the innocent boys should say, 'I'm for Venizelos,' the flirtatious beauty would answer, 'Ah, too bad. I'm a royalist.' If he should say, 'I support King Constantine,' she would bow her white-bonneted head over her basket and say, 'Forgive me, soldier, *zito o* Venizelos.' From the next-door garden Pavlo would see that as she lowered her face she was biting her lip to keep from laughing. She was quite aware that the lieutenant in the neighbouring mansion was watching her tricks, but not once did she turn and look in the direction of Commander Zafiro's headquarters.

Before he saw Panagiota that summer evening sitting with the other girls like birds lined up on a telegraph wire, Pavlo had thought the servant girl with the white cap was the prettiest girl in the world. If Commander Zafiro had not been sent to the front, and if his posting in Bournabat had therefore not come to an end, he would have proposed to her. Afterwards, he considered finding a reason to return there. The only thing holding him back was that the girl would ask why he hadn't gone to the front as well; why he, a great lieutenant, had been left at a police station in a poor neighbourhood. 'We have stayed here to protect you, little lady,' he could perhaps have said, but he had never spoken with that sort of bravado in his life and wasn't sure he could now, particularly to her. Now, however, the storm in his heart brought about by this cherry-lipped angel had erased in a single swipe the meaningful words he'd planned to say to the Bournabat servant girl. The owner of those appraising eyes that had once haunted his dreams and the puckered mouth that used to say, 'Tell me, are you for Venizelos or are you a royalist?' was now no more significant to him than the ordinary village girls of Ioannina.

Panagiota, leaving her shouting friends, jumped down from the wall. There'd been some bad cheating in the game and an argument had broken out. No one noticed her slipping away. Except Pavlo. Glancing up shyly through her long lashes, the girl walked towards one of the streets that opened off the square, went into a grocery shop and disappeared. Her shoes were too tight and she was perhaps a little skinny, but Pavlo's doting mother would feed her on lamb shank marinated in milk, buttery pilaf and fig marmalade. With these pleasures in mind, he bought a cone of dried chickpeas from the nut seller who had set his tray down in the middle of the square and leaned against the wall in a spot where he could see the door of the grocery shop. Though he knew he should appear serious, he couldn't keep the smile from his face. Nearby, the girls were shouting, 'You're out, you're out!', as they crossed and uncrossed their fingers. From one of the houses, a French melody came wafting over the street. Either someone was having a music lesson or there was a gramophone.

For the first time since Pavlo had set foot in Smyrna last May, he thought it would be possible to establish a life there. If that goddess accepted his marriage proposal – and why wouldn't she? – he could build a house there, he could embrace those slender white arms. He got dizzy just thinking about the nights when he would have her in his bed. He had to go and talk to her father as soon as possible.

The first serenade that made Akis furious took place that night.

Pavlo left Great Taverns Street after a few hours and headed back to his officer's lodgings behind the police station. It was a warm night and moonlight was painting the city silver. The young lieutenant was half drunk. He considered going to one of the 'houses' of the girls who worked in the Hiotika neighbourhood, but, as usual, he couldn't summon the courage. Anyway, he had again got upset in the tavern. The reluctance of these men of Smyrna to enlist in the Greek army offended him. He and his fellow soldiers had left their homeland and come all the way there to save these people, and yet, like whining children, they routinely came up with a thousand excuses for not going to war. And this at a time when the army needed them more than ever.

What had happened to that crowd that had greeted them with such joy a year ago? Rich families were sending their sons to Europe, even to America, to avoid military service. Meanwhile, men like him, soldiers of mainland Greece who had no connection to this land, were being mown down in the fight against bandits and armed gangs on the arid plains and mountainsides of Asia Minor. All to safeguard the lives of the Christians of Asia Minor, to rescue them from five hundred years of tyranny. How to explain all this?

That evening the whole tavern had with one voice expressed the view that the Greek army should not advance beyond the province of Aydin. At any rate, the peace treaty with the Allies, which was expected to be signed soon, would formally turn the administration of Smyrna over to Greece, and in a few years Smyrna would surely be annexed to Greece. In which case, was not the decision to advance to Bursa based purely on greed? Pavlo argued that to ensure the security of Smyrna province, all the land to the west of the Eskisehir–Afyonkarahisar line needed to be under the control of the Greek army and that even the Ottoman sultan's signing of the peace treaty was connected to the victory of the Greek forces. But somehow he wasn't able to get a handful of drunk Ottoman Greeks to understand this.

'What are you going to do after you take Eskisehir – go on to Ankara and fight Kemal?' they said, then laughed and toasted each other with their glasses of wine. The more they drank, the more they talked. They cursed Stergiadis, the Greek High Commissioner; the commander-in-chief of the Greek army, General Paraskevopoulos; the general of the newly formed Turkish military forces, Mustafa Kemal; and the British prime minister Lloyd George, who was using Greece to further his own ambitions.

There were as many Turks drinking there as there were Ottoman Greeks. When they were drunk, just like the Greeks, they would swear in a strange mixture of Turkish and Greek. If war broke out, the economy would be in tatters, and it was this that really concerned them. Which made Pavlo even more unhappy. Pavlo and his fellow soldiers were putting their lives in danger, they'd come all the way there, and all these people could think about was filling their moneybags. Where was the great Hellenistic soul?

'If there's war, the caravan won't come next January.'

'Do we use caravans now, Kyr Kosta? You are living in the past. Our goods all come by train now.'

'Yeah, these railways took all the bread from the camel drivers' hands.'

'Caravan or train, the harvest won't come, I say. On the other side of the mountains, they're laying waste to the land. My beloved Aydin was reduced to ashes in a week. There will be nothing but chaos from now on; only the gangs will thrive.'

'Yes, there are bandits every step of the way.'

'If the trains stop, even the Europeans won't be able to work.'

'Whoa, not so fast. Those people can make money out of anything, war or peace.'

'It seems to be different this time. Their businesses have slowed down already. My son-in-law is a waiter at Panellinion – you know, that restaurant that used to be Kraemer's – and he says they've taken to making their midday meals last a really long time, ordering wine and not whisky. Instead of going back to their offices, they stay at the bar drinking until their cheeks turn red. Even the Europeans have become lethargic.'

'Even them, eh?'

'I'll drink to that, then! Come on. *Gia mas!* To our health!'

Everybody laughed and clinked glasses of wine or *raki*. A breeze brought the smell of jasmine in through the open window. The tavern owner Yorgi got up and refilled the glasses.

'They're going to hang lanterns in front of our houses,' someone said. At first nobody understood what he was talking about. It was an old man who spoke in a low voice. His Greek sounded like the Greek spoken by the Muslims of Ioannina. He had white hair, a white beard, and wore a fez proudly on his head, with the tassel carefully combed and hanging from the left side.

'The Greek Administrative Committee is going to decree that all Turks have to hang lanterns in front of their houses. That's what I heard, but...'

Everybody shook their heads as if to say, 'Such a thing is not possible.' Some of them couldn't look the old man in the eye. Several of them turned and stared at Pavlo sitting by himself at one end of the table, as if he himself had told the Turks to hang lanterns in front of their houses.

'It will all pass, Mustafa,' said a small man sitting beside him with deep-set eyes like an owl. 'Public order will be maintained. Maybe the army will just stay where it is and not go any further. Anyway, Kemal is having his own struggles with the Ottoman forces. He's proceeding in an orderly way, with steady steps. He's a clever man. He won't come as far as Smyrna.'

'If he got the Bolsheviks behind him, he could go as far as Athens. He wants to take back Salonica anyway.'

At these last words from a red-cheeked Greek, an uncomfortable atmosphere settled over the tavern. A fat middle-aged man sitting on his own at the other end of the long table from Pavlo said comfortingly to the Turk, 'Our Smyrna will be like it was in the past. Look at Stergiadis. We say a lot of stuff about him, but the man has a strong sense of fairness. He treats all Turks, Greeks and Armenians the same, and that's how it will be in the future. There's no other way.'

Mustafa shook his head sadly. The drinkers in the tavern remembered with shame that the year before the old man had been beaten and left for dead in the garden of an abandoned mansion. To mask their shame, they again turned their eyes on Pavlo, as if he were the enemy.

Without saying anything, Pavlo left two drahoma beside his *raki* glass, got up, left the tavern and began to walk along the quay, which was brightly lit by the hotels. To his left, the dark water swelled like the pointed tops of miniature tents. A bit further out, beyond the harbour area, three fishing-boat lanterns were sparkling. Street dogs passed him, and children riding donkeys, and whispering couples. The moonlight was making the bay glitter like a diamond. Songs spilled out from the bars, some sad, some happy, mixed with drunken laughter.

He rolled a cigarette and lit it. He felt confused. The *raki* and the moonlight were making him burn with homesickness for his country. It seemed that all the things which gave meaning to his life were slipping from his hands, one by one. Living among these bad-tempered old men, his excitement about the *Megali Idea*, the dream of a Greater Greece, was fading. Let the army take Akhisar, then Bursa, then Canakkale, then Thrace, even Istanbul. Then he would go to Yorgi's Tavern and order *raki* for everyone – even the Turkos – to celebrate the victory! He threw his cigarette to the ground, crushed it with his boot, and turned off Bella Vista.

The neighbourhood coffeehouse was closed, the chairs under the arbour upturned. There was nobody around except a few young men having a drunken chat in front of the fountain under the plane tree. The gas lamps which lent a greenish hue to the streets hadn't been lit for some time, but the full moon was lighting up the city as if it were daytime. He stopped suddenly, thinking of the Hiotika women. There was music coming from somewhere. A mandolin, a drum, jangling tambourines, even a ukulele. Laughter and croaky voices singing love songs.

Curiosity sent him in the direction of the music. A crowd had gathered on one of the streets that opened off the square near the police station, and a group of five serenaders were standing under a bay window, trying, by turns seriously and then lackadaisically, to sing a song. In the windows of the nearby houses, women and children with sleep dripping from their faces were leaning with their elbows on the sills, watching the merrymaking as if it were a theatre performance. It was only in the house of the girl being serenaded that there was no movement. All of a sudden, Pavlo realized that this was the second floor of the grocery shop into which the angel he'd seen earlier had disappeared.

Which meant that these brats were serenading the girl he loved! Damn their shamelessness! Damn their impudence! Insolent rascals!

The military position he held and the *raki* he had drunk gave him the courage to walk into the middle of the street and shout. The boys scattered in every direction. Looking up, he seemed to see in the girl's window a twitch of the tulle curtain which was shining like silver in the moonlight. Immediately, he grabbed two of the boys who were hiding round the corner and dragged them in front of the shop.

'Play, you brats – the most colourful of *amanedes* among your soulful Smyrna songs.'

Without wasting any time, Minas the Flea and the fisherman's son Niko began to play a song Pavlo had learned as a child from a Tunisian friend he used to play with in the street. The boys didn't know the song but had no trouble improvising. A little later, Pandelis emerged from his hiding place and joined in with his tambourine.

Entering into the spirit, Pavlo took off his jacket, slung it over his shoulder, unbuttoned his shirt to expose his chest, got down on one knee and began a dance resembling the *zeibekiko*. At the same time as he was belting out the song that began with the words '*Aman, aman*' and continued in a language the boys didn't know, he was also continually squatting down and standing up again beneath the lightless street lamp. He had taken off his cap and placed it on the head of Minas, whose fingers were flying over the mandolin.

It was this scene that met Akis when he went to the window to perform his nightly duty of shooing away the boys. An officer with a bare head and bare chest was down on his knees under the window shouting out a song in Arabic at the top of his voice. The neighbourhood boys had come out from their hiding places and were clapping their hands and beating their drums, egging on his strange dance.

Akis immediately headed to his bedroom, grabbed the gun he had hidden in the drawer of his bedside table, ran down the steep stairs in his white nightshirt and slippered feet, and stormed out of the blue door. At the sight of Akis having come all the way down to the street with a gun in his hand, the boys got lost in a trice. Pavlo was so caught up in his dance that until the grocer fired his six-shooter in the air, he noticed neither that the music had ceased nor that the street was now deserted.

Revolver still in hand, Akis stood looming over the lieutenant, who was jumping around on his knees. Before beginning his dance, Pavlo had put his own gun on the doorstep of the house across the street. He now straightened up and took a step towards it, but he was too slow. Akis grabbed him by the open collar of his shirt and with the strength of his onetime wrestler's arms hoisted him into the air. Pavlo's uniform jacket, which he had so pretentiously thrown over his shoulder, fell to the ground.

The street, which had grown accustomed to the wailing sound of the fiddle, banjo, drum and breaking voices singing 'Aman, aman' was now utterly silent, the quiet broken only by the screams of seagulls diving in the bay. And Akis's voice.

'Have you no shame? You, a great officer, making a mockery of the honour of the neighbourhood?'

The whole neighbourhood knew how Akis roared when he was angry. A few more shutters creaked open. An apprentice at the grocery shop had once accused a refugee child recently arrived from Bulgaria of taking some sweets that he had in fact pocketed himself. When Akis found the sweets, he beat the apprentice in the middle of the street. 'You insolent, immoral dog! Son of a donkey! Did I teach you these kinds of manners? Get away from here, and let my eyes not see you again, you scoundrel, you *malaka*!' He had roared so loudly that the cats waiting to steal some cheese from the outside counter had gone into hiding beneath it.

'I hope Akis beats this idiot up,' whispered Minas with an uneasy expression on his face. 'I don't like foreigners like him wandering around our neighbourhood. They make passes at our girls.'

'Our girls are not innocent either... It's obvious that Panagiota has looked sideways at this fellow, otherwise, where would he have found the courage? Our girls are really off track, my friend; they're all set on becoming an officer's girlfriend. Somebody saw Elpiniki with an officer – a high-ranking officer, too. They were sitting together at the bar next to Messageries Maritimes – you know, that Anglo-American bar – and we know what that means. Nobody goes to that bar who hasn't first been to the hotel upstairs.'

Minas mumbled something unintelligible.

When the boys returned to Menekse Street from their hiding places, Pavlo was walking towards his lodgings behind the police station. His head was bowed, his clothes dishevelled. Akis waited by the grocery door until Pavlo had turned into the square and disappeared from sight. Then he picked up the gun left on the fisherman's doorstep and examined it. His hood had slipped from his head and fallen to his shoulders; his hair, which he slicked down with British pomade every morning, was sticking up on end, like thorns, but he was pleased with himself. After this, his wife couldn't accuse him of behaving too leniently regarding his daughter's honour. He had thoroughly frightened that poor excuse for an officer. It remained to be seen whether he would dare come for his weapon in the morning.

If he had glanced up and seen the bay window's tulle curtains moving, he would have put it down to the wind. He went back inside, mumbling to himself, 'If only this war would come to a good conclusion and we could have some peace.' Rearranging his hood over his head, he dropped into a deep, self-satisfied sleep full of manly pride at having pleased his wife.

Panagiota sat wrapped in the tulle curtains of the bay window for a while longer, listening as her father's breathing deepened. The display on the street had frightened her. Was the victory she had finally achieved on the subject of the fair at Agia Triada going to go down the drain at this last minute because of that stupid soldier? In the far distance a train whistle blew. A *hamal* freight train from Aydin was coming into the station. She stuck her head out the window and looked up at the sky. The moon had travelled towards the bay, turning yellow as it prepared to set. Taking advantage of its dimming light, the stars shone like diamonds over the top of Kadife Castle.

Panagiota raised her chin and sniffed the air. She filled her lungs with the smell of salt and seaweed coming off the bay. It was as if she was drunk on the lovesickness in her heart. Just the thought of a night at Agia Triada was so sweet that she almost wished the night would not come for a long time, so as to prolong the dream. Sitting with her feet tucked under her, she rubbed the white tulle against her face, inhaling the aroma of mastic and lavender and licking the remnants of sugary halva from the corners of her mouth. Her heart was beating to a harmonious rhythm. She wanted to hold this moment in her mind, for there in her mind was a place made beautiful even by the absence of Stavros. Opening her nostrils, she breathed in. The light breeze was carrying the scent of Bournabat's jasmine flowers.

But, ah, why couldn't this boy come to her window and play the fiddle or the dulcimer like Minas and Pandelis did? If he did come, would she love him as much? She had never thought about that. Could it be Stavros's absence that was causing such exhilaration in her heart – like her dreams about the fair? As if she were shooing away a fly, she pushed this thought from her mind. If Stavros were to appear under her window right then, he wouldn't have to do anything. Not sing or recite a poem. His coming would be enough. When she thought of what she was willing to do to gain his love, she was afraid of her own courage; her cheeks burned like fire.

The stray yellow dog Muhtar was walking slowly towards the grocery shop with a huge bone in his mouth, who knew from where. The cats who saw him interrupted their racing over the rooftops and paid attention. When Muhtar took his place in front of the grocery door and began to chew his bone, everything was silent, even the turtledoves. Panagiota, hanging out of the window, took one last hopeless look at Menekse Street, abandoned even by the moonlight, before tiptoeing back to her bed, where, unlike her father, she drifted into a restless sleep until morning.

The Ghost

It was a very beautiful day when we first heard the voice of the ghost coming from Sumbul's mouth. Cold but fresh. A perfect day for doing the laundry. The earth in the mansion's garden was sleeping; the fruit trees had shed their leaves, and their twisting branches were naked, reaching for the sky. It had been exactly three months, three weeks and three days since we'd moved to the Mansion with the Tower.

Aunt Makbule believed that this mansion, given to Hilmi Rahmi as a reward for his success in the war with Greece, was cursed. Considering what happened to us later, she might not have been wrong. Even Sumbul cried when we entered the house and saw the half-finished lacework with the needle still in it. How frightened the woman must have been to leave her needlework like that and run away in such a hurry.

All around us were the burned ruins of the Great Fire. Even Nanny Dilber didn't go out onto the streets. The ruins were full of crazy people sleeping on the verandas and digging through the possessions of those who had died or run away. The ground was covered with shards of glass, nails, razor-edged pieces of metal. Here and there were piano keys, scorched books, bags of dried figs, bones, teeth...

Not a sound came from the city now. Even the cats were silent.

Before dawn, Nanny Dilber had heaved the trough out in front of the laundry room. On the steps exposed to the sun we were rubbing, scrubbing, rinsing, wringing and hanging out the linen, sheets and cloths that had been soaked in bluing. 'Before spring come, dis place need hoe to it,' she said, beating the clothes in the trough with her powerful black arms.

We raised our heads from the trough and looked at the garden. A very thin layer of frost covered the weeds. On windless days the sea also had a thin layer over it in the early morning, like milk, like tulle. The water would be like a lake then. My eyes filled with tears. It was clear that I would never be able to go anywhere now. My mother, my father, everything had vanished. I would be a prisoner in that cursed Mansion with the Tower for the rest of my life.

At that time, I was not yet aware just how cursed it was, but...

I was up to my elbows in the lavender-scented water.

'That's enough, girl,' said Nanny Dilber. How high her voice was! Quite comically shrill, coming from such a heavyset woman. 'You going to tear it. That pillow all clean now. What stain you trying to rub out?'

I gave it to her to rinse in her own basin, got up, went into the laundry room and took another piece of clothing from the pot where the whites were soaking. A gauzy shirt. The light travelled right through it. It was Hilmi Rahmi's nightshirt. I put my hand over the left side of the chest where the pocket was. A trace of my hand, like a ghost, appeared through the back. Nanny Dilber was standing at the door, watching me, the whites of her eyes shining like flint in the darkness. She had a bucket in her hand and was on her way to the kitchen to fill it with water. I threw the nightshirt back in the pot as if I had touched fire.

'Must be careful. That in your hand is sensitive garment.'

I nodded. Her kidneys must have been hurting her. It was obvious from the way she walked, waddling, with one hand on her waist. Inside, she must have been thinking, 'If only Mrs Sumbul would call in a washerwoman from de street...' If we'd asked her, Sumbul would surely have done so, but we never once raised it. Nanny Dilber wanted Sumbul to understand that without her having to say anything. She also wanted a seamstress, a girl to sew on missing buttons, mend the tears under the armpits of the clothes we put aside while ironing, and repair holes in socks. Ever since we'd moved into a mansion that had been home to a rich family before they'd abandoned it, she'd been set on living as they had. She'd clearly forgotten that just three months ago we'd been living on crooked Bulbul Street in a dark, draughty house that let the moaning wind inside.

Sumbul's sudden scream rent the silence that had settled on the city, and then passed.

Just before the scream, taking advantage of Nanny Dilber's absence, I had again pulled Hilmi Rahmi's nightshirt from the pot. When the scream reached the laundry room, I dropped the shirt right there and raced outside, into the cold, in bare feet and with my legs wet to my knees, and ran across the sleeping earth.

Where was I running? I did not know.

Not to save Sumbul, that was for sure. If they'd come to ransack the house, they were not the ones I was running from. I was running to throw myself into the sea.

It was then that I understood. I had unfinished work to do. I was running away from that deafening scream. I was running to the silent kingdom of seaweed and starfish, a kingdom that was already full of corpses. I would sink along with them. Boys with knives in their hands would jump into the water, as they had that evening. They would tear the necklace from my throat; they would sever my finger at the root in order to pocket the sapphire ring that my dear mama had tremblingly placed on it as we held each other for the last time on that railway track.

I had made my decision long ago.

It was as if I had been waiting for a scream.

I was running to the sea.

Sumbul and I crashed into each other, chest to chest, on the white-gravelled road on the other side of the mansion. She was wearing a thin, pale blue nightgown that revealed her fleshy, ivory-white arms and the shape of her mature, full breasts with their nipples half exposed. Instead of her usual scent of cinnamon and honeysuckle, she had taken on a sharp animal smell. Her curly blonde hair fell over her shoulders as if she'd just got out of bed. Her eyes were so huge, it was as if half her face was a pool of green light. I immediately turned my face away, not from her nakedness, but from some secret fragility.

She fell into my arms, sobbing, as if I'd been running towards her, as if I'd been running to save her. What would such heroism have had to do with me?

'It was good you were there that morning, Scheherazade. If you hadn't been, I would have lost my mind, by God,' she used to say later, unaware of the irony of her words.

She was shaking all over. I held her plump shoulders and led her away from the laundry room to a far corner of the garden, over by the marble stairway. I didn't want Nanny Dilber to see us walking arm in arm like that. Her green winter cloak was hanging behind the door inside. I grabbed it, wrapped it around her shoulders and sat down beside her. Broken light from the bay was shining right in our eyes and the steps were slightly warm from the winter sun. Sumbul was sobbing; a sound like a ferryboat's foghorn was coming from her stomach, and she was panting.

Had a thief or a bandit got into the mansion? Would those crazy-headed people digging through the rubble from the fires dare to come and loot a great colonel's house? I glanced at the garden gate; the lock was securely in place. In the kitchen, Gulfidan was humming a folksong; over in the flower garden the gardener and Hilmi Rahmi's orderly, Selim, were sitting on the ground smoking cigarettes. Everything was as normal. Maybe she'd just had a nightmare.

While I was thinking of what I could do to calm her – should I boil up some chamomile tea or light the water heater and splash water over her head? – the atmosphere suddenly changed. An indescribable current of emotion passed between us. Sounds and colours took on new shapes, as if we had dived into the depths of the sea. When I turned and looked, Sumbul's face had become that of a stranger. Her cheeks were sunken, her chin distorted, and an angry shadow had fallen over her usual gentle expression. Narrowing her eyes, she examined me from head to toe. The animal smell that I'd noticed earlier had become sharper and her lips were protruding.

'There are things I need to tell you.'

My hands went to my mouth in fear. I had forgotten that I was unable to speak. The voice was not Sumbul's voice. The eyes were not Sumbul's eyes. It was then that I understood: the woman sitting beside me was not Sumbul. I wanted to jump up and run away and hide, but I stayed there as if nailed to the spot, on the warmish marble steps.

'There are things I need to tell you.'

She was speaking in French.

I shook her shoulders. I shook her to make her come to herself. What kind of voice was that? What kind of look in her eyes? Where had the French come from? Her cloak had slid from her shoulders, her blue nightgown was open to her stomach, exposing her nipples, which looked like ripe grapes on a vine. I was filled with anger. Forget the nipples; if she had fallen down the marble stairs at that moment, hit her head and died, I wouldn't have cared. I couldn't bear hearing that voice. I was violently shaking the woman who had taken me under her wing. I was intentionally hurting the one who had protected, supported and nourished me; I was treating her as if she were a doll stuffed with straw. I was struggling to silence that voice forever as if my life depended on it.

I don't know how long this scene lasted. Her breathing eventually slowed, the gentle light in her eyes that I was accustomed to returned, and I stopped.

'There is a ghost in this house, Scheherazade,' she whispered.

She had reverted to Turkish. She turned and looked into my face to see if I'd understood. She was unaware that she was naked from the waist up. I straightened her blue nightgown, settled it on her shoulders and covered her with the cloak that had fallen to the ground. The gardener and the orderly, Selim, seeing us in that state must have run off to the back garden. We were alone on the mansion steps.

'She spoke to me a while ago. The ghost. She was looking for someone; that's what she said. Now she's found the one she was looking for.'

She looked pleadingly into my eyes.

I heated the bath water, took off her clothes and washed her all over with hot water and foaming, fresh-smelling soap. I boiled hibiscus flowers and washed her hair with them, and I massaged sesame oil infused with rose petals into her skin until it turned pink from the rubbing of the bath glove. I did whatever I could to make whatever was haunting her spirit come out of her flesh.

I was unsuccessful, however.

Much later, in the abundance of time which my seemingly never-ending lifespan afforded me, I did some research and learned that the dead who have not been able to complete their business in this world before passing to the other side – or, more correctly, in order that they can pass over to the other side – will 'invade' a highly sensitive individual. In the mansion's magnificent library there were many books on the subject of mediums, as there were on every subject. I read that some mediums can assist souls who have become stuck between two worlds to complete their earthly affairs, and I also read that some souls use people like Sumbul as a channel for their unfinished business on earth. At that time we did not know this, of course. If we treated Sumbul as if she was crazy, it was out of ignorance. May God forgive us.

When the ghost first appeared, the sky above Smyrna was so jam-packed with souls that they greatly outnumbered those of us on earth. When Avinash visited years later, he told me that in the September of 1922 Smyrna's dead numbered approximately one hundred thousand. One hundred thousand souls hovering above the city. The bottom of the sea had been their grave and some of them did not even realize that they had died. They wandered crazily among the ruins. Before they could rest in peace, they had accounts to settle, secrets to reveal and treasures to hide; there were also children who'd been left in enemy hands. All of them were struggling to find someone sensitive like Sumbul whom they could use as a channel in order to return to earth to complete their half-finished business.

When the ghost had command of Sumbul, she spoke perfect French. Not only I but everyone in the house heard that oriental-accented French. When the nerve doctor that Hilmi Rahmi brought all the way from Vienna to Smyrna learned that Sumbul had taken lessons from a private woman teacher in Plovdiv, where she was born and raised, he decided that her warbling perfect French like a nightingale was nothing but a minor detail. Wait a minute – what exactly did he say? That when a patient lost their healthy brain function, languages they had learned previously might come to the surface, like subconscious memories. For example, a senile, elderly person might begin to speak the language of the country in which they had lived as a child.

When I heard this, I bit my tongue. Hilmi Rahmi, in his sadness at being told of this new proof that his wife had gone crazy, was pacing up and down in the library where he had welcomed the doctor with a mint liqueur, a cigarette hanging from the corner of his mouth.

There were questions in my mind. If I could have spoken, I would have asked the nerve doctor if the lady teacher in Plovdiv could have taught Sumbul to speak in that lilting Levantine French spoken only by the Catholics who lived in Smyrna and by no one else in the whole world. The worst part of being mute is not being able to get answers to the questions that are making your brain itch. It's like reaching out to kiss someone's lips and their lips not responding. However, whatever the cost, it was absolutely imperative that I did not attract the attention of the nerve doctor. He kept asking Hilmi Rahmi questions about me, as if it was because of the mystery surrounding me, rather than Sumbul's situation, that he had been called to Smyrna.

Had the little lady been mute since birth or was it some sudden shock that had made her lose her ability to speak? Did she have trouble hearing? Had her tongue been cut or otherwise injured? Was her ability to comprehend intact? Did Hilmi Rahmi know what her native language was? When he realized that I understood the French they were speaking, he became even more interested and wanted to know at what age I had learned this language. He found it extremely interesting that I was able to learn a language without a brain function for speaking.

If I could have spoken, I would have reminded him that babies begin to understand a language long before they say their first words. However, at that time, people whose only crime was that their names were foreign – people who often couldn't even speak the language whence that name originated – were being forced from the homes they had lived in for two thousand years, from their villages, their animals, the graves of their ancestors, and exiled from the country. I again bit my normal, healthy tongue and remained silent.

The ghost kept telling the same story. Since the emphases and pauses delivered in its shrill voice never changed, after a while when Sumbul began to speak French it came to seem as if someone was turning the handle on the gramophone.

'*Le jour où la fille est descendue du bateau, il y avait tant de monde au port que des mats on ne voyait même pas le bleu de la mer.*' The day the girl disembarked from the ship, the harbour was so crowded that one could not see the blue of the sea for the masts of so many sailing boats. Those coming into port kept complaining that from the deck one could see nothing but sailing boat masts and ferryboat funnels. What a shame to have to grope one's way like a blind person when arriving at such a beautiful city. *Quel dommage!*

Nanny Dilber would ask, 'What she saying, Scheherazade, my little lamb? For God sake, speak to us. Why she going so crazy?'

I would open my hands wide. How should I know?

Maybe if we had alerted Hilmi Rahmi in time, he would not have been so terrified when he saw how his sweet, sociable wife had transformed into an angry-faced Levantine woman, and maybe he wouldn't have taken such a cruel step as to lock her up in the tower.

We did not think of it.

Months passed.

When it got to the point where Sumbul began speaking in the voice of the ghost while in the presence of Hilmi Rahmi's guests, the issue became serious. At that time there were a lot of comings and goings in the house. Hilmi Rahmi would meet with various men in the library. The shutters would be closed and there'd be much whispering and rustling of paper. They would argue for hours on end; perhaps they were making secret plans.

'These important peoples,' murmured Nanny Dilber as she rolled *boreks* in the kitchen. 'Members of parliament among them, you know. Look at they heads, all wearing hats. Whatever our gentleman up to, may God protect him.'

It had become obligatory for members of parliament to wear hats.

It was about this time that the nerve doctor from Vienna arrived at the Mansion with the Tower. Sumbul had wandered into the library busy with working, whispering men with hats on their heads. She was wearing a purple silk evening dress and was laughing, with a glass of sherry in her hand. Speaking perfect French, she approached the frowning men to have her hand kissed.

After this incident – this scandal – Hilmi Rahmi had the tower that gave the mansion its name remodelled after the rooms at the spa hotels he had seen in Germany, with a Western toilet and all. He had pipes installed to carry water from the well to the attic. The water didn't rise that far, of course, the pressure not being sufficient, so he brought a battalion of soldiers from the barracks and had two huge tanks carried up there. We filled the tanks and covered them with wooden planks. He had iron bars put on the windows. He gathered up all the knives, matches, scissors, poison, kerosene, whatever Sumbul could use as a weapon against herself or anyone else. The nerve doctor said that as the paranoid delusions advanced, she might become dangerous. She might set fire to the house, or kill herself or one of us. As he said this, he peered over the rimless eyeglasses that sat almost at the very end of his nose, and looked straight at me. Later, whenever he went up to the tower to examine Sumbul, he would not let me leave his side.

When all these preparations had been completed, Hilmi Rahmi picked up his wife as if she were a cut-crystal bell jar and carried her with care to the tower. At the bottom of the steep, winding staircase there was a door hidden beneath the wallpaper and he had a lock set into it. He put the extra key on a chain and gave it to me. It still hangs around my neck. From then on I was to take care of his wife. I was to bring her food, sit with her to keep her cheerful, clean the room, and take her to the bath downstairs to be washed once a week. If Sumbul were to be seen in the house or in the garden, I would be held responsible, and I probably knew what that meant. It was the first time he had spoken to me so harshly. My eyes filled with tears.

I needed him to love me so much!

That night for the first time I visited the bed vacated by his wife.

Shutting Sumbul up in the tower was of great benefit to the ghost. She started talking non-stop. Whenever I went up with pails of water and emptied them into the tanks, whenever I was up there picking up off the floor the records that had been taken out of their leather bag and scattered about, she would be telling her story, at top speed. I pretended not to listen. If I showed the slightest interest, she would take that as validation and assume complete control of Sumbul. No matter where I happened to focus my attention, no matter what I was concerned with, she would branch out, send out shoots. But my presence alone was enough to make her joyful, it seemed, for as soon as the European ghost heard my footsteps on the stairs, the shrill voice would get louder. It was then that I learned the rest of her terrifying story. It made my flesh crawl.

'I slapped her in the face. She was beating on the door, shouting and cursing in the worst way. As if her whoring wasn't enough, her mouth was as dirty as a street-woman's. Blood attracts blood – she was just like her father. Let the summer heat come, and let her suffer, shut up in that glass jar of a tower.'

When she said that, a curtain fell and she began asking questions, pleading for answers.

'Was there anything else I could have done? Huh? Any other thing? She forced me into it. She started it. I had no choice.'

At that point she got angry again. Sumbul's soft hands clenched like claws, her nails piercing the flesh of her palms.

'For three months I took care of her like a princess. She swelled and swelled like a balloon. I made lemonade for her to drink, I fanned her with a large peacock feather like a sultan in his harem. What more could I have done? Should she have stayed out there on the street with her bastard and become a whore? I saved her life. Do you hear me? I saved her life. Hers and this one's!'

She waved her hand towards me.

At this point the ghost stopped talking. Holding her breath and staring ahead with glassy eyes, Sumbul would return to herself within a few minutes. Worn out by the invasion of her body, she would lay her head on my knees and cry. Her face was becoming more translucent by the day. In truth, the Sumbul who came back after the ghost departed was not the Sumbul of old. Like the pregnant girl in that cursed story, her eyes were encircled with purple shadows; her dull, silvery face had taken on the desperate expression of a lion cub caught in a trap.

The nerve doctor, who visited the tower every day at nine o'clock sharp, did not believe in the ghost's story. That pleasant old man with a goatee did not believe in the ghost. He would shine a light into Sumbul's pupils, listen to her heart, measure her pulse, and record all this in his notebook with meticulous handwriting. But he was not at all interested in whether the pregnant girl in the story lived or died, what happened to her baby, and so on. According to him, the birth, blood and midwife were all symbols of trauma in Sumbul's subconscious.

Furthermore, he learned that in her childhood Sumbul had escaped from her family home in Plovdiv after it was burned down by Bulgarian armed gangs and that she had come all the way to Konya on foot. After prodding Hilmi Rahmi, he also discovered that Sumbul's mother had lost her mind and died in the mountains while they were escaping. Near the end of their journey from Plovdiv to Konya, she had abandoned her child, Sumbul, while she was asleep in an inn. She ran away, never to return. A Skopje family travelling with them from Plovdiv took Sumbul to Konya and handed her over to a distant relative. A year later, a gendarme brought the mother's body to their doorstep. For months she had lived like a wild animal in the mountains, biting anyone who approached her. When a gang of men tied her hands and arms and tried to rape her, she bit the neck of the brute on top of her, severing his carotid artery.

When Sumbul saw her mother at the place where the dead were washed, she couldn't recognize her. Her full breasts were empty, her soft belly sunken, her hair stuck to her skull in patches. But the main reason the twelve-year-old girl couldn't recognize her mother was the mouth. The woman's white lips were wrinkled, her mouth twisted inwards. Villagers, afraid that she would bite them, had pulled her teeth, one by one.

The nerve doctor listened with surprise and undisguised happiness on his face to what Hilmi Rahmi was relating about his wife's past. He took copious notes in his leather-bound notebook. Later, when he was listening to Sumbul – to the ghost – he would look through his notes, shake his head and mumble some things to himself. '*Aber ja, natürlich, sehr interessant.*' He couldn't have cared less about the baby or its mother or even the prisoner in the tower, Sumbul herself, who was foaming at the mouth like someone having an epileptic seizure as she spoke.

When I took up the breakfast tray or washed her in the

bath, I couldn't look into Sumbul's face any more. Every night, as soon as darkness fell, I would rise from my bed, walk like one afflicted with sleepwalking to the door at the end of the corridor, open the white mosquito netting and slip between the lavender-scented sheets and into the arms of the grieving husband. There, in the light of the moon seeping between the shutters, the silk nightshirt embracing my naked skin would come alive, would burn like fire. Our connection was as old as history. I wrapped my arms around his waist as I had done on that fateful night. We were riding a galloping horse. Only he heard my voice.

In the light of day, life continued as if the night had never been.

Sumbul asked me for some clothesline rope.

Not the ghost. Sumbul herself. She was begging.

'I implore you, Scheherazade, bring me a strong piece of rope from the laundry room.'

I kept on with what I was doing, as if I hadn't heard her. Sumbul's voice, as if the station on a radio had been changed, moved to a different wavelength. Holding her head, she repeated, '*Le jour où la fille est descendue du bateau...*' The day the girl disembarked from the ship, the harbour was so crowded that one could not see the blue...

The Love-of-Small-Touches

'*Vre* kids, don't thrash around so much, you'll capsize the boat – this thing is like a hazelnut shell anyway,' yelled Minas, who was sitting on a kilim in the pointed bow. He was surrounded by baskets and bags, and under his arm was Adriana, looking like his big sister.

'Oh, shut up, *malaka*! Instead of sitting there lecturing us, come and row for a bit and let us have a smoke.'

Stavros and Pandelis, stuck on the oars, were out of breath. Minas pretended not to hear. He had brought his mandolin and was playing while Adriana sang. 'With seven of us packed into such a tiny boat, it's obviously going to sink,' muttered Niko, squashed among the fishing nets in the bottom of the boat.

A little while earlier, the full moon had risen like a cannonball from behind Mount Nif at the stern of the boat. Elpiniki, snuggled in beside Panagiota like a princess, got confused and shouted, 'Look at the sun – what a beautiful sunset!', whereupon the boys teased the poor girl until she turned as red as the rising moon in her embarrassment. They were still laughing.

'Tell us, Elpiniki *mou*, if the sun rises behind that mountain, will it set in the same place? What do they teach you at Homerion, *yavri mou*, eh, babe? About the fairies of Mount Nif?'

'Elpiniki, look! There's another sun over here. It's setting on this side. Ha, ha, ha.'

'You guys are all so mean. I'm never coming out to watch the moon with you again.'

'Is there a moon? I only see two suns.'

Panagiota gave her friend's arm a gentle squeeze. Elpiniki was blonde and as beautiful as the legendary fairies of Mount Nif, which was why they were having a go at her for having said something stupid. Because the two of them were the only ones in the neighbourhood to go to Homerion School for Girls, they were the butt of lots of jokes. Homerion was a school for rich girls, girls from families living in mansions in Punta and Kordelio. The other kids in the neighbourhood were all at the church school and took every opportunity to make fun of Elpiniki and Panagiota.

A British cruiser passed them at full speed. In the darkness it slid across the sea like oil, as if it wasn't even touching the water. The girls, chewing on their lower lips, turned to look at the captain, who touched the brim of his cap in greeting. He was a handsome man, about the age of their fathers. Elpiniki read out the name of the boat, written in Latin letters on the side: '*Silver Light*'.

'Is he an American, do you think, Giota? Did you see how he looked at us? He's a sexy one. Shhh, listen to me. There are men who go around picking up girls in our neighbourhoods for the officers from Greece. Have you heard about them? They have the most expensive silk dresses sewn for the girls and they rent rooms for them at Kraemer's.'

'Shhh, *vre* Elpiniki. Don't say crazy things, *yia to Theo*, for God's sake. And that place has changed its name now. It's called Splendid. You have no idea.'

The long, slender muscles in Stavros's back kept appearing and disappearing as he pulled on the oars and the wet sand splashed over him. The boys had taken off their shirts and were rowing like fishermen, with bare backs. Stavros's shoulders, broad from swimming, were set off by the puny white body of Pandelis sitting beside him. He looked exactly like the Ancient Greek statues Panagiota had seen in the museum at the Evangelical School.

This time it was Elpiniki's turn to nudge her friend. 'Girl, you're going to fall into that boy. Don't sell yourself so cheap or he won't pay you any attention.'

As if he paid her any attention anyway! Without saying anything, Panagiota turned her face towards the dark water. When they had gathered in the square before going down to the wharf, Stavros had greeted her with a vague nod. That was all. Even though they hadn't seen each other for weeks. Recalling his indifferent, even bored, attitude, her heart tightened. She tried not to look at Minas and Adriana fooling around in the front of the boat. In the silver moonlight, the sea was filled with sharp-nosed gondolas, called *kurit* in Smyrna. From all of them came laughter, songs and mandolin melodies.

Elpiniki, still staring at the British cruiser, said in a voice loud enough for Niko, sitting on the fishing nets, to hear, 'I'm going to get a European man like that, you wait and see.'

Niko took his harmonica from his pocket and joined in the song that Minas was playing and Adriana was singing. Its penetrating notes rang out sharply in the darkness.

'Heya mola, heya lesa,
Heya mola, heya lesa...'

Elpiniki was frowning. Panagiota took her friend's hand to comfort her. Recently, word had gone around that Niko had fallen in love with a Turkish girl living in Karantina. It was said that the girl's family had connections to the Sultan's palace and that her father was so rich, he was buying up the hotels on the quay from the Europeans, one by one. Was such a thing possible – could a Muslim ever run a hotel on the quay? And what would a girl raised in a mansion in Karantina be doing with Fisherman Yorgi's son Niko? Anyway, if Niko married a Turkish girl, his father would disown him. This was all just empty gossip. Elpiniki was worried for nothing.

'I will kiss your freckle, my love,
Just please don't cry
Aman, aman.'

That rascal Minas could play any instrument he took in his hands like a professional. The strings of the mandolin were really coming to life under his small, swift fingers, and Adriana's voice was like velvet. Panagiota could tell from the contractions of Stavros's naked stomach that he was laughing silently. She burned inside. She hung her arm down from the boat and trailed her hand in the sea. Water passed through her fingers like silk.

When they landed at Agia Triada, they made their way to the crowded courtyard of a house. It was a windless night and cigarette smoke hovered like a cloud over the tables. The musicians were playing a village greeting song and a few people were dancing in the space in the middle. Those sitting at the tables were raising their glasses to the musicians, calling out their names and sticking money on their foreheads. Everyone there, men and women alike, clearly knew how to behave at a dance. Adriana wanted to leave immediately and so did the others; but then Minas saw that wine was being served and insisted that they stay for a while. They sat at a table. Niko perched on the edge of his chair and swung his amber prayer beads in the air. Elpiniki was supposedly talking to Pandelis, but her eyes were on Niko.

Everyone was casting sidelong glances at them, as if making fun of their inexperience, their youth. Panagiota was upset. What in the world were they doing there among the adults? She and Stavros had still not said a word to each other. She was tired of waiting, tired of figuring out how to reel him in. She drank down the wine that had been placed in front of her in one gulp.

When the folksong ended, the musicians were joined by two girls with tambourines, a dulcimer player and a *baglama* player, and together they began a merry piece that made fun of the Greek king and praised Venizelos to the skies. The girls went round encouraging everyone at the tables to sing along, shaking their tambourines and making the gold discs on their headdresses quiver. It was a comical piece. Minas began to clap in time to the music and the others joined him. Even Stavros was smiling. Panagiota was suddenly filled with happiness. All by itself, her leg reached out and rested on Stavros's knee; the heat passing between their two legs was like warm, sweet sherbet flowing from the heart. Out of the corner of her eye she examined his profile, strong and flawless, as if carved by a fine knife. Their shy, trembling elbows touched on the table.

After the Venizelos piece, when the musicians struck up a polka, Stavros jumped from his seat as if he'd sat on a pin.

Knees and elbows separated. Minas drank down his wine, stubbed out his cigarette in an ashtray, took hold of Adriana's arm, and pulled her onto the dance platform in the centre of the courtyard. Neither of them knew how to dance the polka, but it wasn't long before they'd picked up one or two steps by looking at other couples. While the others were applauding them, Stavros grabbed Panagiota's hand and led her away – unfortunately not to the dance floor but in the opposite direction, towards the door.

Unlike Adriana, Panagiota did know how to dance the polka. During break times at the Homerion School, their snobbish friends had shown Elpiniki and Panagiota the steps they'd learned in dance lessons, and when they returned home in the evening, the two girls practised together on their shared terrace. So she was cross when she and Stavros ended up out on the street. The wine was burning her stomach. But when she realized that her hand was clasped in Stavros's huge palm, her disappointment turned to joy. They mingled with the crowds thronging the narrow streets around the church.

While they'd been sitting in the courtyard, the streets had filled with hordes of people who'd come from Kordelio or Bournabat by sea or overland to enjoy the first fair of the summer. Officers in uniform, stylishly dressed ladies and rich merchant families were alighting from their carriages. Itinerant peddlers had hung lanterns above their carts to show off their goods, and because this little village did not have gas lamps to light the streets, the lanterns swaying on the boats out at sea shone more brightly than usual.

Small, shaven-headed village boys were shouting, 'Over here!', as they jumped off the axles of the carriages. They were covered in dust from head to toe from wrestling each other in the heat. Some of them were barefoot. Suddenly they all raced off in the direction of a barker's voice, to the square in front of the church. Little girls with blue ribbons who had all got down from the same carriage were pulling their father by the hand.

Seeing the children scattered across the street like grouse, the barker raised his voice. 'Hello, hello, hello! The Wonder of Wonders acrobatics show will begin at exactly nine o'clock European time. Children, grown-ups, don't tell me you haven't heard about this? Come, ladies and gentlemen, come and see! See who has come to liven up our beautiful Smyrna – the world's most famous tightrope walker, Kerim the Arab! He walks the rope with his hands held high, does somersaults in the air, and climbs down like a cat. Children, grown-ups, ladies and gentlemen, Kozmas the Crier does not lie. *Oriste*. Come see with your own eyes. Alongside him will be the famous hypnotist Dudu Sultan, and Chios's velvet-voiced eunuch-boy Yellow Haralambis. Tonight, it is for you that we make beautiful Agia Triada merry. Gentlemen! Ladies! *Gia sas! Gia sas!* Welcome! Welcome! You bring delight with you. The performance begins at nine o'clock. Don't say you didn't know!'

With her hand in Stavros's and her heart fluttering like a little bird, Panagiota stood on tiptoe to try to see the stage where the acrobats would perform through the crowd that was filling up the square in front of the church. The flames of the candles which had been placed along the wall encircling the church flickered in the wind, their shadows licking at her face. Inside, the priests walked among the wooden benches, sending out a cloud of scented ambergris and sandalwood which mixed with the street smells of burned sugar, *lokum* and salty crackers.

'Stavraki, come,' said Panagiota, tugging at him, 'let's buy some halva.'

Wow, had she just called him Stavraki? Up until now she'd only called him that in her dreams. Maybe now that she was getting more relaxed in his company, she could begin to act more like herself. Maybe it was the effect of the wine. She really wanted to dance.

Without answering, Stavros followed her. Was he a little withdrawn? Had she done something wrong? Maybe he considered her rude for childishly running after halva. Maybe he would prefer a mature woman, one of those European girls in Bella Vista who knew how to sit and stand properly even before they were thirteen. The melody being played on a passing barrel organ depressed her spirits.

'What is your name, pretty girl?' the halva seller asked, handing them slices of sesame-paste halva wrapped in paper.

'Panagiota, sir.'

'*Poli orea. Bravo su*, Panagiota, my child. May your life, like your name, be filled with light like that of the Holy Mother Mary. Young man, how lucky you are to have a fiancée so beautiful inside and out.'

A burst of happiness shot up Panagiota's spine like a firecracker. If she hadn't been wary of giving herself too cheaply, she would have hugged Stavros and kissed his cheeks right there.

'*Hronia polla*, best wishes, children.'

'*Hronia polla, kyr!*'

'Come on, let's walk along the beach,' said Stavros.

The joy that had been rising in Panagiota landed – bam! – in her stomach. Were they going to end up kissing in a dark corner again? This was supposed to be a night when they would mingle with the crowd, behave like a real couple. The only thing she wanted to do was walk hand in hand, eating halva. But, afraid that he would withdraw his hand from hers, she said nothing. Without speaking, they headed for the beach where they'd pulled Niko's father's boat up on the sand. The sound of the barrel organ faded into the distance.

Stavros helped Panagiota climb up onto a rock behind the boats, then followed her and sat down beside her. Their hands had come unclasped. Rowing boats filled with young people kept approaching the shore. Some couples didn't even make it as far as the crowded streets but hurried straight for the darkness of the beach. Panagiota kept her hands on her lap, on top of the frothy skirt of her pink dress, where Stavros could see them. Her knee touched his knee again.

For a while they stared out at the sea, lit up with the blinking of countless carbide lamps. Then Stavros began to speak.

'Giota *mou*,' he said, his voice muffled, 'there's something I need to tell you.'

Panagiota closed her eyes. Her head was spinning. She breathed in deeply to take in the night, the moonlight, the stars, the cool wind smelling of jasmine, burned sugar and seaweed, the laughter of women, the music wafting from the houses. Stavros had called her 'Giota *mou*'. My Panagiota! He'd never done that before. All those times they'd kissed in the darkness beside the wall of the British Hospital, he had never called her by name or whispered words of love in her ear.

When she opened her eyes again, she saw that her lover had taken a tobacco pouch from his pocket. Once he'd finished rolling and lighting his cigarette, he would surely take her hand in his free hand. She leaned her knee against his knee.

A new boat was approaching the shore, the lamp at its bow glittering. A middle-aged man with a thick moustache quickly jumped out, pulled the boat up the beach and then began to help the women to disembark, one at a time. When he made as if to embrace several of them, the women pretended to object. All of them had make-up on their faces and were wearing very showy hats. Their tight skirts fitted their slender waists perfectly, and their breasts almost jumped out of their frilly, low-cut blouses. These were the women Elpiniki had been talking about. People said they were gathered from various different neighbourhoods, even from as far afield as Aydin and Manisa, for the pleasure of the Greek and British soldiers. Generally, they rode around in motor cars parading up and down the quay in front of the grand hotels, but they must have wanted to come to the fair tonight like everybody else. Panagiota could not imagine these women praying to the Holy Spirit. What would the priest say if they went into the church?

Stavros waited until the women had dispersed into the village streets. His cigarette was half smoked and he had still not reached out to take Panagiota's hand, which was lying patiently in her lap.

'I haven't told anyone else except you and I'm not going to.'

Panagiota's heart again began to beat wildly. So, the moment had finally come; the moment she had dreamed of during all those nights spent tossing and turning in bed like a fish caught in a net. So, Stavros loved her. That air of indifference when he saw her in the square the day after he had stuck her on the hospital wall and kissed her, those bored expressions were because he was shy, nothing more. She breathed rapidly, licked her lips, rubbed her palms together, and checked one by one the pink ribbons her mother had tied in her hair.

She was so engrossed in her dreams that when she heard

Stavros's words, she almost fell off the rock on which they were sitting side by side. He reached out and grabbed her arm just in time. When he'd pulled her back up, he didn't let go but wrapped his arm around her waist. Panagiota moaned softly, as if warm, sweet sherbet were pouring down her throat. She was just going to rest her head on his shoulder when she registered what he'd said.

'You what? What did you say you'd done?'

'I signed up for the army as a volunteer.'

From far away came the sound of the barrel organ again. Panagiota started trembling. The clock in the churchyard gonged nine o'clock.

'Are you cold? Here, wear my jacket.'

Stavros took off his jacket and placed it over Panagiota's frilly pink shoulders.

He was perplexed. He'd thought Panagiota would be thrilled by his news, would be proud of him. He again put his arm around her waist and tried to draw her towards him. She was as immovable and heavy as the rock beneath them. Her head was bowed and she was examining her white shoelaces intently. Finally she opened her mouth and spoke, as if in a whisper.

'When?'

'We're setting off tomorrow. To Manisa first.'

He ran his fingers through his hair, which he'd rubbed with musk oil, pulled at the braces he was wearing over his shirt, and then, to fill the silence, said, 'We'll take Constantinople soon, *makari*, God willing. Then all of Thrace... We'll bring liberty to our people.'

'But you're not old enough,' Panagiota said, as if she hadn't heard him.

Stavros smiled proudly. 'I told them I'd be turning eighteen at the end of the summer. Also, for two months now I've been attending drill twice a day, with other volunteers. The officer said he was very pleased with me.'

Turning, he looked into Panagiota's eyes. His frowning eyebrows had relaxed, his hard face had become sweet, like a child's. As he leaned forward to place a kiss on her cheek, she slipped from under his arm like a fish and jumped down onto the sand.

'What liberty, *vre* Stavraki? Aren't Smyrna and Aydin enough? Aren't we liberated enough? What more does this Venizelos want?'

Stavros shook his head in amazement. All of their friends were talking about how the dream of a Greater Greece was finally going to be realized. What was wrong with Panagiota now? Ah, but, of course. She was Grocer Akis's daughter. Stavros had not forgotten how the grocer had told him and the other boys off in the middle of the square that time they brought the good news that the Greek army was about to land in Smyrna. There was also a rumour that Grocer Akis's father, Panagiota's grandfather, hadn't been able to speak a word of Greek when he'd emigrated from Kayseri to Chesme. It was even said that Akis himself only learned Greek when he started school in Chesme. Akis's family were Karamanlis, Ottoman Greeks who spoke Turkish even in their homes. It would be no surprise if they were against the liberation.

'How far is this war "to liberate our people" going to go? If they, say, go to Ankara, would you go too?'

He bowed his head and considered this, as if such a possibility had never occurred to him before. 'I would do whatever is needed for Greater Greece.'

'Oh really?'

Panagiota was standing on the beach, her hands on her

waist, looking at him as if she was mocking him. In spite of the anger burning in his face, he managed to speak calmly.

'Panagiota, you don't understand. We must secure our borders.'

Stavros, all gangly arms and long legs, was stuck on the rock like a lobster. He clenched his fists. What a disaster this was! He had wanted to snatch a farewell kiss from Panagiota, a sweet memory to dream about while he was at the front, and perhaps even steal a touch of her soft flesh as well, if he was lucky, enough to linger on his palm. If not, the taste of her cherry lips would have to last until they returned home victorious. But the beautiful night had taken a turn he'd neither expected nor wanted. It was clear there would be no breasts, no lips. He would go to the front empty-handed. He looked around in desperation. The beach was empty.

When no further words came from Stavros, Panagiota raised her own voice.

'What's the Greek army to us – did we ask them to come? We were living peacefully. Did we lack for anything? And then they liberated us and now look at us: no street lamps lighted, no garbage collected – the city's gone to shit. They're hiring women now to collect the garbage. The streets are filled with refugees, gypsies, worthless people. Is this what you want?'

It wasn't only Stavros's face and ears that were aflame now, his muscles were also burning. Things were about to go too far. 'Panagiota, *se parakalo*, I beg you – stop.'

Firecrackers were exploding in front of the hotels on the quay down at Smyrna, and floods of blue, red and gold were lighting up the sky above Agia Triada. Floating lanterns with candles inside them, called *klobos*, were bobbing on the surface of the sea. Young girls in white dresses were walking arm in arm with clean, pure-hearted soldiers just arrived from

Greece. Children were competing with each other to see who could swallow a cone full of *lokum* the fastest. That war might break out in Smyrna that summer was a possibility no one gave a thought to.

As for Panagiota, she was not about to stop talking. If these officious Greek soldiers had not come to 'save' them, life in their beautiful neighbourhood would have continued. She would have married Stavros and planted geraniums, roses and bougainvillea in the garden of their home. Like her mother, father, grandmother, grandfather and all those before them, stretching back two thousand years, she would have lived a calm and happy life on that bounteous land. She would have raised children that swam in the turquoise waters like fish. But now a huge injustice had been done. Swallowing the lump in her throat, she began spilling out what she had heard from her father.

'Are you aware of the conditions of the roads in Asia Minor? You won't find a drop of water to drink. By the middle of summer the whole army will be in a state of collapse.'

'That's why I have to go,' Stavros said quietly. 'I am a child of this land. I am strong. When they fall, I shall fight.'

Panagiota stared straight ahead. Now she hated the silk stockings and pink, short-skirted dress she'd put on with such care a few hours ago. She sniffed back her tears.

Stavros jumped down from the rocks, stumbled through the sand and stood in front of her. Putting two fingers under Panagiota's chin, he turned her face towards the moonlight. The wind had tousled her long black hair and her ribbons had slid down to the ends of her curls. She was more sad than angry, but Stavros didn't understand that. He was too busy defending himself.

'Panagiota, do you know what defeat would mean for us?'

'Of course I know. It would mean the end of the Greater Greece dream. We'd be back under Turkish rule. But at least ships would come into the harbour again and men who sit all day in the corners of coffeehouses could get back to work. Everything would be the way it used to be. With the situation as it is, I would one thousand times over prefer to be governed by the Sultan or even Kemal than by bad-tempered Stergiadis's men.'

In the darkness Stavros saw something making an arc in the air, but he didn't realize that thing was his own hand descending with force on Panagiota's cheek. Slapped full in the face, Panagiota sprang backwards, caught her foot on a piece of rock, lost her balance and fell onto the soft sand.

Stavros raced to her side and knelt down. How had he done such a thing? When Panagiota wouldn't take her hands away from her face, he panicked. One of her eyes was closed. Had he hit her in the eye? Oh, God! He would never be able to save himself from Grocer Akis now.

'Giota *mou*, I am so sorry. Sweetheart, please forgive me.'

Panagiota, one hand pressed to her cheek, was biting her cherry lips and staring fixedly at the ground. Her coal-black eyes had grown so large, they seemed to have taken over her entire long, thin face.

'Panagiota, my sweetheart, forgive me. I don't know what came over me. Please let me look and see if you're hurt.'

She slowly removed her hand from her cheek and lifted her head. Nothing was visible in the darkness. Letting out the breath he'd been holding for some time, Stavros touched her cheek; it was burning hot. He leaned down and kissed the place where he'd hit her. Was she angry? Was she crying? Slowly he lowered his right palm, rough from the rowing, to her neck, towards the pink and white ribbons of the collar of her dress. Panagiota had closed her eyes again. She was biting her lips but was not objecting. A while earlier, when he'd thought things were going too far, this had not been in Stavros's mind at all. He would not have even dreamed of doing this before getting married, except with the women in the Hiotika houses. Particularly not with Panagiota. He'd never considered doing anything more than kissing with her – never! But somehow he found himself on top of her.

The lanterns on the rowing boats pulled up on the beach had all gone out, their passengers lost on the streets of Agia Triada. The Wonder of Wonders acrobatics show must have started; they were alone in the darkness behind the rock. And Panagiota, her eyes closed, was lying under him, like a doll stuffed with straw.

'Sweetheart, darling, Giota *mou*...'

Beneath the rough, paper-like taffeta that covered her legs, the skin was like cream. Even the legs of the silk-stockinged women of Hiotika were not as soft and smooth. And she had still not said no. Just then it occurred to Stavros, maybe for the first time, that there was a chance he might die soon, crossing mountains, passing through deserts. A soldier always had death on his mind, of course, but Stavros had never until that moment considered it a real possibility. This thought released hundreds of sparks in his groin. He grasped Panagiota by her shoulders as she lay there on the sand, as if he were gripping onto life itself, and with all his strength he thrust himself deep inside her.

Moonlight was striking the dark waters of the bay. Katina was dozing in the window from where she'd been watching the street for her daughter. It was good she was dozing or she would have seen the diamond she doted on walking up from the square with her legs wide like a little boy who'd just been circumcised. She would have become very agitated. She shouldn't have fallen asleep. The many tiny pink ribbons she herself had tied in Panagiota's wild black hair had come undone, and she would have seen that several of them were torn. She would have realized from the way her daughter was walking that she was naked under the pink taffeta skirt, but it wouldn't have occurred to her that the underclothes stained with blood had been dropped from the rowing boat into the dark waters when no one was looking.

If she had been awake, she would have seen Panagiota turning into Menekse Street without even saying goodbye to Stavros. She would have seen her leaning against the wall of the house across the street, crying, and then smiling through the tears streaming down her face when she caught sight of Muhtar. And maybe she would have noticed the startling resemblance between her daughter and the European woman they'd seen last spring leaning and crying against that same wall.

But Katina Yagcioglu, stretched out on the mat, asleep in the bay window, saw none of this.

The next morning, Katina woke at sunrise. As she was walking to buy *katimer* turnovers for her daughter from Zakas Pastry Shop at the quay, she heard the sad whistle of the Afyonkarahisar train. She didn't know that the train was carrying Stavros away from the rose-scented city, never to return. Gazing at the green hills in the morning light of early summer, she spontaneously offered up a prayer. Golden dust motes poured through the open windows of the train speeding towards the mountains. The boys in the third-class compartment were restless on the wooden seats, their blood fired up with the dream of a Greater Greece.

As for Panagiota, she was tossing and turning on her narrow bed, her nose blocked. There was nothing to wake up for now. At the Agia Triada fair she had lost not only Stavros but also the love-of-small-touches. She closed her eyes and turned her face to the wall.

New Year's Eve

'Is Mademoiselle Edith ready? I won't go in. Would you please let her know I am here, Christo.'

Butler Christo, with his usual unflustered demeanour and inscrutable expression, ushered Avinash into the brightly illuminated hall and disappeared behind the staircase. Hoping to find a clothes brush, Avinash searched to the right and left of the mirror, on the coatrack and umbrella stand behind the door. Although he'd come from the Hatuniye Mosque in a covered carriage, the city's dust had seeped into his clothes, his hair and his felt hat trimmed with satin just out of its box. In desperation he brushed the dust off his shoulders with his hand. Taking out his pocket watch and chain, he checked the time.

Five to seven. They would be late, which upset him.

He had arranged for one of the consulate cars to drive them, but it would take at least an hour to get to Bournabat given the ruinous state of the wintry roads. The guests invited to the New Year's Eve party at the Thomas-Cook residence had been requested to arrive at approximately eight o'clock, with dinner to be served from nine.

Was she doing this on purpose?

In the silver-plated mirror he straightened the lapels of his jacket, the matching velvet bow tie, his hat. Then he turned around and dusted off the tails of his green tuxedo. He pulled at his newly oiled moustache. It was pushing the limits of Avinash's patience to be late to a New Year's Eve ball at which all the Europeans, Levantines, high-ranking officers and wealthy local Smyrna families would be assembled. Edith had somehow not learned to respect his need for promptness.

He left his hat on the console table in the hall and in three strides was at the sitting room door, where he came face to face with the butler.

'Could you tell me what's happening, Christo?'

His voice came out louder than intended. He was more tense than he thought. Covering his mouth, he coughed. The butler held the door open. Avinash hurried through, impatient, after which the door was closed quietly behind him.

The ceiling lamp had not been lit; in the dim light of the wall-mounted night lamps, the room looked gloomy. As always, it was messy. Whenever he went into that room, Avinash couldn't help thinking that Edith was too lenient with her servants. The tea tray had been forgotten on the table in front of the window, biscuit crumbs were scattered about, drips of milk stained the wooden floor. One of the navy-blue armchairs was occupied by a pile of books brought down by Edith from the library upstairs. A crystal ashtray full of half-smoked cigarettes had been pushed under the armchair, and the smell of the cigarette butts mixed with the marijuana smoke and the aroma of old coffee grounds left in a cup in a corner of the room.

Avinash's sensitive nose ached.

Because of the gloom, he was at first unable to make out Edith's form. For a moment he thought the butler had brought him in there to wait for her. But no, unfortunately not. Edith was in the room. Dressed in a sea-green evening dress which came down to her ankles, she was sprawled out on the sheepskin-covered divan, unconcerned about wrinkling her gown. She was smoking a pipe and staring, with half-closed eyes, into the waning fire in the fireplace. She had kicked off her shoes; one lay under the divan, the other was not visible.

Avinash was both surprised and angry. 'Edith, *mon amour*, what are you doing?'

Instead of answering, Edith laid her head back on the gilded pillow behind her and exhaled the smoke she'd been holding in her lungs for who knew how long. As her face disappeared in the blue haze, she wiggled her white-stockinged feet.

'Edith, it has gone seven o'clock. We must leave. The motor car and chauffeur I have arranged are waiting for us at the station. Edward particularly asked that we be there by eight.'

Without opening her eyes, Edith murmured, 'Ah, Edward! Edward and his New Year's Eve party of the century... Ah, these British! One must be on time. They even take pains to add a note to their invitations. "It is requested that guests display sensitivity to the hour of arrival." Ha, ha, ha! And you, Avinash darling, want to be just like them.'

Letting her arm hang down, bare beneath her sea-green evening dress, she dropped the pipe on the floor, then lifted her head with difficulty and looked into Avinash's face.

'How do you like my hairdo? Zoe styled it.'

Avinash approached her. Edith had wound a thick black turban around her head and pinned an emerald brooch right in the middle. Above the turban, her raven-black hair, unchanged from her youth, was gathered in a huge bun on top of her head. The prematurely greying roots were hidden under the turban. With her eyes outlined in kohl, she resembled a Hindu prince. Was this a new fashion or was his lover making fun of him?

'It is very becoming, Edith. Come, please get up.'

Edith sat up a little straighter. She checked her drop earrings with their stones the colour of her dress. The pearl necklace she'd wound three times round her neck was awry.

'Your dress is getting crumpled. Come, Edith.'

He looked at the watch he was holding in his hand. It was seven after seven. Edith, propped up on one elbow, was trying to light the pipe she'd picked up from the floor.

With one step, Avinash grabbed the ivory pipe from her hand. 'Edith, for God's sake, what is going on? Why this devil-may-care attitude on such an important evening?'

Edith watched the opium pipe roll across the antique Usak carpet, spilling ash as it went, before replying.

'And what is so important about this night, Sir Avinash? Or should I say "Sri" Avinash? Sir Sri Avinash! Not very proper? I'm reading a book. The author is really a poet, but this book I'm reading is about spiritual things. You'd like it. He says a person's journey is a journey from rules to love, from discipline to freedom, from morality to spirituality. Wait a minute – what's it called? I learned that "Sri" business from that book. You add it as a prefix to respected people's names. "Sri" instead of "Sir" – ha, ha, ha!'

She laughed at her own joke for a long time. Avinash was frowning. Seeing this, she switched to Greek, as if fooling around with him in bed.

'*Ade vre* Avinash *mou*, come on, are you upset? He's a very good writer. He says… What was it? "For the evil inside a person…" Wait a minute, what was it he said? The book should be around here somewhere.'

Wringing his dark hands helplessly, Avinash sat down on the end of the divan, next to her little feet.

Edith's addiction to hashish had really taken control of her in the last few years. He cursed the day he'd given her a waterpipe full of the stuff as a gift twelve years ago. That waterpipe was still upstairs in the bedroom and Edith was now unable to sleep or make love with pleasure without first smoking hashish. It had become impossible for her to attend a social gathering with a sober head. Everyone agreed that she had become very strange. In conversations she laughed in inappropriate places or walked away without waiting for the person speaking to finish their sentence. Sometimes she would sit in a corner with a mysterious smile on her face. Her old friends, afraid of her ill-judged laughter and the comments she made in her deep voice, were too scared to be with her.

The sheepskin thrown over the divan was as warm and soft as bread just out of the oven. Clearly Zoe had warmed it beforehand with water bottles. To get Edith up from this hot opium bed and out into the winter's night would be harder than he'd thought.

'Let's tell Christo to make you some coffee.'

'Not necessary. I'm fine. My head is as clear as day.' Saying this, she lay back on the gilded pillow and settled her legs on Avinash's lap.

'Then get up and let's go. If we keep on like this, we'll even be late for dinner, which will be a shame.'

'Shame! Shame!' repeated Edith, like a parrot.

Avinash closed his eyes and took a deep breath. The devil was telling him to slap her face, take her by the arm and throw her into the car. Then they'd see whether she would say another word all night long.

'Do you know what the really shameful thing is, Avinash?'

She had stopped laughing and the deep crease between her eyebrows had appeared. 'The really shameful thing is that we are still waltzing at balls, doing the polka.'

'Why do you say that? How many balls have there been since the world war? People have been staying at home for years. Tonight, for the first time, society will come together. Edward has worked very hard, as you know, to have this be the ball of all balls. He's even brought a jazz orchestra over from America for tonight.'

'Should we not take account of the war that's going on now, because it isn't our war? Haven't we lived in this country for centuries? Not you, okay, you've just recently come, I don't dispute that. But my family settled in Smyrna in the 1700s. The only French thing about us is this language we speak. And that's with a strange accent, as you know. Look at our family tree – you can't find a single individual born in France. As for the ones organizing this ball of all balls, the Thomas-Cook family, they've been controlling trade with the Orient for at least three generations. Caravans and the ocean weren't enough for them, so now they've taken over the railways. Insurance companies, mining, banking, import–export – everything is in their hands and the hands of their important friends invited to this ball. There's no end to the bids they've won from the Sultan because of their privileges. It's thanks to their encouragement that Greek soldiers and Turkish armed gangs have destroyed the land beyond these mountains, pitting villager against villager. My beloved country is weeping blood. Given all this, is not these children's war' – she waved her hand towards the kitchen, where her Turkish and Greek servants worked together – 'to be considered our war?'

Avinash was staring at the now extinguished fire. He spoke softly.

'There is always a war going on somewhere, Edith. Since the beginning of time, human beings have created with one hand and destroyed with the other. What is yours today was someone else's yesterday and will pass to someone else tomorrow. Birth and death complement each other; good and evil find their own places in the universe. There will never come a time when wars will cease and the world is peaceful. But your numbered days will come to an end; the day you leave the world will arrive. To spend the happy life God has blessed you with in displeasure is the greatest sin of all. You, like everybody else, have a duty in this life. Please, let us go.'

'For me the happiest life is right here,' Edith said, like a spoiled child. Extending her leg, she tried to roll the pipe back towards her. Seeing that her lover meant to prevent this, she pulled his hand to her and placed it between her legs. 'Or here.'

'Edith, I beg you, stop. High-ranking officers, generals and top officials from the consulate will be at the ball. Being late will put me in a very difficult position.'

Edith pouted sulkily. Looking at her from close up, Avinash realized that behind the kohl, her eyes were small and bloodshot because of the hashish. He stood up.

Edith yawned. 'Go. Go. You go by yourself. Much better. I do not wish to be in the same place as those snobs.'

'Don't be funny, I beg you. Of course, we shall go together. Come.' Grasping her by the shoulder, he tried to raise her from her opium bed.

'Oh, ho, ho! Sir *Sri* Avinash, take it easy! May I remind you that I am not your wife. You can very well attend a gathering without me. Out of interest, why didn't you make a date with another woman? I am sure there are throngs of young women who would love to go to this ball on your arm.

The neighbouring houses are filled to bursting with girls from Paris and London who chase after officers. You don't even have to go out onto the street, just standing on my balcony will be sufficient. They are all surely dying to attend the ball of all balls. Please, go ahead. *Oriste.* I probably don't need to show you the way to the balcony.'

Jerking her arm from Avinash's grasp, she rose, picked up the pipe, took a pinch of hashish from the silver box on the side table beside the divan and packed it into the bowl of the pipe. Standing in her stockinged feet on the orange, red and green antique rug, and without taking her almond-shaped eyes off Avinash's face, she lit the pipe with Monsieur Lamarck's lighter.

Even in the dim light the shadow that fell across Avinash's face was obvious. Of late, Edith had reminded him many times that they were not married. The old wound continued to burn.

Years earlier, in the first twelve months of their relationship, Avinash had stuffed into his pocket the diamond ring he'd had Manuel Usta make, rung Edith's doorbell, and asked her to be his wife. Coincidentally, on that beautiful April day, Edith happened to be wearing a long, layered, white dress like a bridal gown, with skirts that swept the ground; she looked precisely as Avinash had imagined she would. On her head was a straw hat decorated with cherries the same colour as her lips. Those were the years when her spirits were light with the freedom afforded her by her new home, when her coal-black eyes were sweet with happiness. They were sitting in the garden of the house on Vasili Street, beside the ornamental pool. (Avinash had planned the scene exactly this way.) The cool spring day refreshed their skin; the almond and plum blossom that had fallen from the trees was like a pink and white rug beneath their feet. It was as if everything had come together on this happy day, ready for a diamond ring to seal their love.

But, unluckily, just as he was concluding the speech that he had written and rewritten over the course of many weeks, had pondered on, had practised time after time as he walked along the quay, had corrected and revised, a mischievous breeze gathered strength and blew Avinash's hat off his head, exactly as it had done on the day he first came to Smyrna. Edith giggled like a little girl. That the most important moment of his life should be interrupted by the wind was enough to make him angry, but what really upset Avinash was that instead of being captivated by the magic of his words, Edith was amused by the tricks of the wind.

However, that little burst of laughter was quite innocent and unimportant compared to the sight that met him when he returned with his hat restored to his head. Sitting beside the stone pool, her feet covered with almond blossom, the young Edith was twirling the huge diamond ring rapidly in her white-gloved fingers. Then she put it into its box decorated with gold-embossed flowers and handed it back to him.

The young spy, who had run from success to success, had never known defeat in his life and did not recognize it. Thus it took a while for him to realize the significance of the box in Edith's hand. It was a day when even the sea, sparkling like a porcelain pool, had seemed to be supporting his plans. It was the day before Easter, the whole city was got up like a bride. Tablecloths had been starched, balloons were hung in front of shops, multi-coloured lamps lit up the doors of taverns. Avinash had arranged an elegant, highly polished, victoria-style carriage in which to parade his fiancée up and down the quay after he'd given her the ring. Now, confronted with this unexpected hitch, he raised his eyebrows. Disbelief spread across his face.

Edith, on the other hand, was smiling, with a teasing sparkle in her black eyes. Avinash looked in vain for traces of shame or regret in her fine, delicate features, but all that he saw, thanks to the light shining through the holes in her straw hat, was a dance of dots on her pink and white face. He returned the box in his palm to his jacket pocket and managed to walk to the black iron garden gate. The carriage he had arranged was waiting at the corner of the street for the engaged young couple. Its handmade brass lanterns shone joyfully in the sun. Without even greeting the coachman, he sat down on the leather back seat, all alone, and departed.

Edith had refused him because he was from India. He was not French or British; he was nothing. The white woman had simply used the black man for a short while for her own pleasure. Most certainly she was saving herself for someone else – one of those Levantine high-society snobs she danced with at the balls at the Sporting Club. What other explanation could there be for that self-confident smile he'd just seen on her face, that expression devoid of guilt?

All of the young spy's doubts had come to the surface and salt had been poured upon the wounds opened by those doubts. Avinash was an insignificant, worthless, second- or even third-class human being. His being an Oxford graduate and working for the British did not change this fact. It was as it was. In her letters, his mother had for a long time now been saying that she had found him a wife-to-be. She kept writing that the wedding would take place on Avinash's first visit to Bombay. In his replies, which were never lacking in words of love and respect, Avinash determinedly avoided the subject. He was sure that when he informed his mother that he had married Edith, the Bombay bride issue would be closed. She might be angry at first, but eventually she would be pleased at the idea of him having a 'French bride'. At any rate, her son was not a traditional Indian; he was a modern man who had studied in Europe. His family would understand.

Now, though, everything had changed. Avinash had been defeated. In the back seat of the carriage going clickity-clack over the stones of the quay, he put his hand in the pocket of his jacket and took out the box decorated with embossed gold flowers. Manuel Usta had worked on the box as much as he had the ring, attaching miniature feet underneath it. How fine, how elegant it was. The workmanship, the beauty, the value. It was a symbol of his love. What could spoiled Edith understand of this? At the first opportunity he should go and put this ring on the finger of the girl his mother had chosen, then return with her to Smyrna. Edith and her snobbish Levantines could go to hell. He would have built a mansion fit for a Turkish pasha at Kordelio, with its own dock, its own boat, his children swimming like fish in their private sea bath.

Yes, listen to the drums; they say find a mate who is your equal...

If his grandfather had been in his place, he would probably have spent the next few days in meditation at Smyrna's Sufi Dervish lodge, but Avinash preferred to spend them holding on to his waterpipe at Hasan's coffeehouse, the plums and cherries bouncing around in the water, his emotions numbed. Hasan's hashish was truly healing. While he was sitting on the couch with Pamuk the cat stretched out beside him, hookah tube in hand, Avinash felt light-spirited and clear-headed, the troubles of what his grandfather called his 'small mind' diminished. It became difficult to believe that he had woken that morning with a heavy heart. So, this was how it felt when a person freed himself from the vicissitudes of the mind. Light, sweet, carefree... However, when the effects of the hashish faded, the heavy weight in his heart returned in full force.

Then, one night in May when the moon had reached its zenith in the sky, he somehow found himself on Vasili Street. He had gone out with a group of Unionists, first to Café Klonarides, then to Kraemer's Brewery, then to Aristidis's Tavern on Great Taverns Street. At the end of this drinking party, he separated from his Unionist friends and decided to get some air by walking along the quay for a while, nothing more; he had absolutely no other intention in mind. Later he would jump in a carriage and return to the Menzilhane Inn in Tilkilik, to his mattress on the floor.

It was a little before midnight and the tram was still running at the quay. Countless gangs of young people were hanging around in front of the cafés. Rather than focusing on the families stuffing themselves with halva and nuts they'd bought from peddlers, Avinash kept noticing the lovers hiding in the many dark corners. The quay – called *ke* by the local people – was full of couples, from the harbour all the way up to Punta; on the moonlit rocks were the sailors who'd given their lives there, now in the embrace of fiery mermaids; and the gods who'd been seduced by the fairies of Mount Nif were busy clasping them tight. Out in the water he could make out the hem of a beribboned skirt, a cigarette ember, hoarse laughter.

After he'd walked all the way to the wooded dock at the end and reached the cape, he didn't know what to do. If it had been daytime, the terrace and shallow pools of the Eden Baths would have been packed with people, but at this time of night the facility was deserted. Although the café across the street was open, it was empty. Up ahead, the rowing boats carrying passengers to Agia Triada had quit for the night; tied to the dock with thick ropes, they were rocking gently. Beyond them, a sailing boat with its sails curled high up was at anchor. He turned and, unnecessarily, began to walk towards the station to find a carriage.

He only realized that he'd veered into Vasili Street when he saw Edith's house from a distance. All the houses were buried in silence under the greenish light of the gas lamps. His feet had acted instinctively and carried him there. With his head as confused as his heart, he continued along the street.

Suddenly he stopped.

From the top balcony of Number 7, which Nikolas Dimos had purposely chosen for its seclusion from prying eyes, a pale yellow light was seeping onto the dark street. He walked towards it as if drawn by a magnet. In his benumbed brain only one thought was blinking like a lighthouse: Lady Edith had lost no time in finding someone to share her bed. She was with another man inside that lavender-scented, white silk mosquito netting – a German officer or one of those Armenian intellectuals whose random conversation at a garden party she had not got enough of. Moaning and groaning, they were making love. Or perhaps it was another dark-skinned, second-class citizen or a dashing young Turk whom she had taken to her bed this time. She obviously had a special interest in exotic men.

While he had avoided making love to the girls of those famous houses, the girls whom his Unionist friends couldn't stop talking about – 'You must come with us and taste them, my friend' – Mademoiselle Edith had been opening up her bed to another man!

All right, then!

Wrapped in the only emotion he could feel in his drunken confusion – anger – he bounded up the marble steps, two, three at a time, and began pounding on the door of the stone building with all his strength. He vowed to break it down if no one answered, but it opened much sooner than he anticipated, before the third blow. Avinash had expected to see one of the servant girls who slept in, either Vasiliki or Stavroula, both of whom used to smile secretly whenever he visited Edith; he planned to smash whichever one it was against the wall like a fly with a single shove and run upstairs to the bedroom where Edith and her paramour were making love. When he saw before him not the maid but Edith herself, his feet got tangled together and he almost rolled down the marble steps into the street.

In spite of his drunken state, he noticed that underneath the beige cloak which she had quickly taken from the hanger behind the door and thrown over her shoulders, Edith had nothing on except a white nightgown with thin straps. Her hair hung in ringlets from her shoulders to the base of her spine, and the shadows on her face danced in the light of the lantern she had grabbed from the top of the stairs. She was so beautiful. Anger swelled like a red wave inside him.

Edith reached out and took Avinash, who was swaying in the doorway, by the arm. Without saying a word, she led him to the sitting room, where a fire was still burning in the fireplace, sat him down on the divan with a sheepskin coverlet and told the servant girl, who'd been woken by the noise, to prepare tea.

On that moonlit May night in Edith's sitting room in front of the fireplace, Avinash understood two things clearly.

First, for the rest of his life he would never give up on Edith. He would do whatever was necessary to keep her in his life; he was prepared to play by her rules. If she didn't want to get married, they would not get married; if she wanted to move to another country, he would go with her. Knowing full well that his family in Bombay would grieve deeply, he was prepared to accept a childless life with Edith. (Avinash assumed that a woman who was averse to marriage would have no interest in motherhood.) Secondly, as long as he loved Edith, he would always feel this jealousy, like poison in his blood, and he would never be free from the feeling that there was something missing in their relationship.

There was no other man in Edith's bed and there never had been. That night while they were making love, more with nostalgia and love than with passion, Avinash realized that this woman who had refused to be his wife would remain faithful to him all her life. His main rival was not a German officer, an Armenian intellectual or a dashing young Turk, but her desire for solitude.

Avinash came to himself when he felt Edith's hand on his cheek. Shaking off all those memories that were pressing on his head, he stood up. It was almost seven thirty. This was no time to be raking over the past. If Edith wasn't coming, he would have to go to the Thomas-Cook's New Year's Eve ball by himself. But to his great surprise, Edith had already put her shoes on and was standing waiting for him with a sweet smile on her face.

Christo held the door as they went out into the night. It was so cold, it was as if the starlight was ice striking the earth. Fireworks were already being set off at the quay to celebrate the new year. The Milky Way and myriad other stars were scattered in all their glory across the moonless sky, winking at the people below. Edith hugged her fur coat around her, took Avinash's arm and leaned her body against his. Her turbaned head was lowered meekly. Not a leaf moved, causing a strange tranquillity to spread across the city that even the exploding fireworks couldn't disturb. Colourful *klobos* balloons hung in the sky. Soon the bell of the Anglican church would begin to ring out its greeting to the new year.

Without speaking at all, Avinash and Edith walked along the cobbled street that led from Vasili Street to the station square, like an old married couple who had run out of words.

Suicide

It was I who found Sumbul swinging from the end of the silk sash she had tied around her neck. She had hanged herself from one of the beams in the tower. Her blonde head had fallen on her chest at a strange angle, like the recently executed Smyrna assassins whose photographs had been all over the newspapers. Her naked white body swayed in the air, keeping time with the breeze blowing through the room. Her white feet were hitting against each other. Dust danced joyfully in a ray of sunshine streaming through the barred window, as if challenging death's dominion.

'By God! Where did she find that sash?'

Thus moaned Hilmi Rahmi a short while later as he knelt among the pile of thick books that Sumbul had knocked over with one kick of her foot in the tower in which he had locked her.

He was right to be confused. The two of us had cleared the room together before he shut her up there. We had collected anything she might use to harm herself or us, should she fall for the ghost's tricks: knives, cutting utensils, rope; we didn't even leave a matchstick in the tower. He had nailed boards over the tops of the water tanks with little brass faucets at

275

their base so that she couldn't plunge her head into them. He had even taken away her silk scarves so that she couldn't tie three together and hang herself. For the same reason, Sumbul slept in her pink bed on a mattress with no sheets. At evening time it was I who went up to the tower with a long taper to light the lamp hanging from the ceiling, set high so that Sumbul could not reach it. Actually, by piling books one on top of the other she could have reached it. Unlike the nerve doctor, I did not think the poor wretch had any intention of burning down the house.

'By God! Where did she find that sash?'

Straining my ears, I listened carefully to the tone of his voice for any indication that he was suspicious of me. There was none. Compared with us women, men can be as naive as lambs sometimes. That being said, all the atrocities I have endured in my life have been instigated by men. How is it that men can be as innocent as children when it comes to women's tricks, yet be responsible for all the violence in the world?

'We must have neglected to check the pocket of her dressing gown.'

I looked up at the scrap of cloth still knotted around the beam from after we'd cut the silk sash and taken her dead body in our arms. How had such a delicate thing taken the soul of a fleshy woman like Sumbul? I found it hard to believe. A person is so fragile, death so easy.

Not everybody's heart was as pure as Hilmi Rahmi's, of course. Even before Sumbul's funeral, gossip about me was spreading. The trouble-making whispers of the crowds who filled the mansion rose up to the tower where I had hidden myself. Yes, it was true, Sumbul's husband and I made love every night. At my current advanced age, there is no reason to hide how I anticipated with all my heart those nights when my lover's fine long fingers moved over my flesh, when repressed human emotions were poured into my body and his soul whispered into my ear.

While we made love, an aromatic cloud of roses and incense hung over us, the unique chemistry of our mingled sweat. Buried in silence, our words, our moans, our screams exploded within us like fireworks. Hilmi Rahmi was not able to restrain himself at his climax; as his tobacco-scented head lay on my neck, he would whisper words of love into my ear from his *raki*-sweet lips. Whether for me, for Sumbul or for some other woman, I never knew, but hearing those words was even more beautiful to me than the river of lust hidden deep in my body that I had never known before.

This is not to say, however, as certain sharp-tongued people claimed, that it was I who was responsible for the death of Sumbul, whom I loved like an older sister.

On the morning that I found her dead body hanging from the ceiling, my face in the mirror had been pale and thin, my eyes disproportionally large and bright, with purple circles beneath them. My body was still tingling delightfully from the raptures of the night before. I spread my hair, which reached to the base of my spine, like a black curtain over my face and smelled it. I sighed at the memory of Hilmi Rahmi's three-day beard tickling my neck. I couldn't stay still. Excitement and pleasure erased guilt and shame, and I felt an uneasy happiness. Was this what they called love?

While I was preparing Sumbul's breakfast tray of honey, clotted cream and olives marinated in grape vinegar, I kept forgetting things and went back and forth to the pantry six times.

It was such a strange feeling. I even thought that my excitement might make sad Sumbul happy. I had forgotten that the man into whose arms I slipped secretly every night was her husband. If I ever happened to run into Hilmi Rahmi by chance in the daytime, he was always the distant, frowning, handsome colonel, an entirely different person to the one whose long fingers touched my deepest parts and who breathed into my ear at dawn, 'You are the only one, my most treasured, my sole reality.'

I was drowning in the whirlpool of a familiar duplicity and I wanted Sumbul to feel it with me, to rejoice with me in the wonderful emotions that were filling my heart and soul. The thrills would be amplified when shared with someone else; they would intensify when I repeated the story so that I would experience them not only when I was in the arms of the man I loved but also in the presence of everyone to whom I'd told my love story. For the first time since that horrible September night, I felt a crazy desire to speak.

At the risk of spilling the tea on the tray, I climbed the stairs to the tower two at a time. Outside, sparrows were chirping as they picked at the fruit on the heavily laden branches of the mulberry tree in front of the window, singing together with their tiny, honeyed beaks. Downstairs, someone – probably Hilmi Rahmi; who else would it have been? – had put a record left by the former owners of the mansion on the gramophone. An American song about having fun that I had known in my old life was playing.

Looking back now at my century-long life, I understand this: since he had put this happy American tune on the gramophone the morning I found Sumbul hanging in the tower, Hilmi Rahmi must have been feeling as exuberant as I was. Maybe he too felt the need to speak, to explain, to swim in the pleasure of words. Perhaps he was murmuring the words of the song with a joy that overflowed from his chest

278

or tapping his fingers in time to the music on the wooden table in the dining room.

I was looking at Sumbul's sweet white body swinging in the empty air.

Nanny Dilber said later that she heard me screaming. I do not remember. I only remember the music that had drifted out through the dining room window, into the garden, up two floors, through the branches of the mulberry tree and into the tower where we were. That's all. And the sun with its merciless beauty playing games with her hair that had fallen into her face, and her pure white breasts with their erect pink nipples pointing to the sky, defying death. The pale hairs on the poor woman's arms and stomach were standing on end, as if she were frightened by her own demise.

One morning after the funeral, when I was sure that every last visitor was gone, I came down to the kitchen from the tower where I had been silently hiding myself. It was getting light outside, but the mansion had not yet awoken. Sumbul's absence was everywhere. Wherever I looked, there was a jar her hand had touched, a stain she had given orders to be wiped clean. The laughter she hadn't been able to hold in while listening to Gypsy Yasemin's naughty jokes echoed from the tiles.

Hilmi Rahmi and I came face to face at the door to the pantry. He was wearing a beige linen suit I guessed he'd also worn the day before. It was wrinkled. His grey hair had gone completely white. His beard, which he'd not shaved in days, had grown and had also turned white. His cheeks were sunken, his skin was the colour of olives. The hazel eyes which I was accustomed to seeing shining like flint in the darkness had faded.

My God! Could a person age so much in a week?

Both my hands were full of coffee beans I had taken to grind. I did not know what to do. He, too, was surprised. He rubbed at his beard. He looked extremely miserable. He moved to the side so that I could pass but did not leave the kitchen. It seemed strange to see the great Hilmi Rahmi in the kitchen.

I ground the coffee beans, lit the stove, brewed the coffee, filled our cups. He motioned to the garden with his head. The garden of the Mansion with the Tower was very pleasant on summer mornings in the early hours before the fiery heat took hold. We walked towards the arbour, he in front, me behind, carrying a silver tray. The red earth was soft under our feet. Mulberries had fallen to the ground and bees were hovering over them, moving from one to the next. As the breeze blew, the scent of the lavender that Sumbul had planted alongside the road rose fresh and cool.

I brushed the fallen leaves off the cushions of the decorative wrought-iron chairs under the arbour and we sat down across from each other. My nose filled with the smell of salt and seaweed, and the pain of all the people I had lost became a burning lump in my throat. I brought the cup to my lips. The ferry for Karsiyaka was lazily sounding its whistle. Was today Sunday? Because the bells had been silenced on the same date as I had, I could not know. I had a vision of the ferry as it used to be, when Karsiyaka was known as Kordelio and its ferry overflowed with engaged couples, officers, groups of young people showing off.

Hilmi Rahmi had drunk his coffee in one gulp and was smoking a cigarette. Thinking my eyes were glistening because of the smoke, he switched the cigarette to his other hand and held it near his cheekbone so that the smoke was carried away on the breeze. He was muttering as if talking to himself.

'The first time I saw Sumbul, all I could see of her was her hands, nothing more. She was selecting potatoes at the market in Konya, and the hands peeping out of her purple robe were like doves. It was those nervous white hands that I went to ask for, taking the *muhtar* with me. When the robe came off, a young blonde girl appeared. Her eyes were as clear as the waters of Lake Aci. I snatched her up and came straight to Smyrna. Her relatives were so wretchedly poor, they were ready to get rid of her yesterday, but Sumbul was apprehensive. She had only ever known Plovdiv and the road to Konya. Even so, she grew to love Smyrna very much. When I took her to the hotels on the quay for a beer, she'd sit shyly in a corner. She wanted me to shield her, didn't want to be seen by people passing by. Gradually she got used to it and began to remember how to laugh again. But then came the children, war, separation, the fire... And then this... this disaster. Oh my God.'

His exhausted face seemed on the verge of tears. He looked beyond the rose garden in the direction of the invisible sea. I tried to imagine the man I loved at a young age, bringing his new bride to Smyrna for the first time.

I saw him standing at the door to the entrance hall of the house on Bulbul Street in Iki Chesmelik, a cigarette again dangling from the corner of his mouth, watching the setting sun paint the clouds pink and purple. With his tall boots made in Crete pulled up to the knees of his navy-blue trousers, two guns stuck in his leather belt, and an aubergine fez just out of its mould on his head, he was most handsome. Before coming home, he would have stopped by the barber's shop for a shave and to have his moustache oiled and lemon cologne splashed on his cheeks.

There was movement over by the kitchen door that opened

onto the garden. Gulfidan had got up and was drawing water from the well, looking at us from the corner of her eye. To show that I was not simply a concubine but the lady of the house in Sumbul's absence, I pointed to the coffee cups. Five minutes later she reappeared, her face expressionless, and served us our second cup of coffee.

Oblivious of the tension between us two women, Hilmi Rahmi rolled another cigarette and stuck the paper together with his pale, dry lips. The sun had risen behind us and the smell of dry grass was beginning to drift over the garden. At that moment I felt Sumbul enter the arbour, in the elegant manner of her pre-ghost days, and sit on the edge of the empty third chair. Hilmi Rahmi must have sensed the same thing, for he opened his eyes, having had them closed for some time, and stared at the heavy white-painted iron chair between us. He coughed, then suddenly stood up.

'Get up and dress. I'm going to take you somewhere.'

I involuntarily held tight to the arms of the iron chair. He leaned down, took my chin between his hands and turned my face to his. In spite of all my sorrow, my fear, I shivered inside. I turned away, as if my eyes were dazzled by the sun, and gazed at the roses.

'I beg you, do not be afraid. This is just a brief outing. *Mia volta!* Please do not hurt me by refusing.'

I looked with disquiet at his face, his disproportionately large ears. Were those tears in his lustreless hazel eyes?

It was the first time I had been out on the streets since we'd moved into the Mansion with the Tower. The European houses in the neighbourhood had filled up again. Tow-headed little boys sat on the walls surrounding the mansions like birds, and little girls with big white ribbons in their hair raced from house to house. Some of the Europeans who had fled at the time of the Great Fire had returned from Malta or Europe, where they'd stayed for two or three years. Turkish officers like Hilmi Rahmi had moved with their families into the homes of those who had not come back.

The Mansion with the Tower was very near the Aydin train station, which we used to call Punta Station. We were there in five minutes. Walking side by side, we passed through the square in the shade of giant plane trees. Because the fire didn't get that far, the houses overlooking the square stood as they had in the past, faced with green stone or marble. I was relieved. I wasn't going to have to confront the ghost of the lost city as I had on the day we'd driven from Bulbul Street to the Mansion with the Tower in an open-topped motor car. I cried so much that day that Sumbul had closed my eyes with her hands – the same hands that reminded him of doves.

Hilmi Rahmi was looking about him in surprise, as if he were in a dream.

'This square is like a painting, isn't it, Scheherazade? Just look at the British perfection of the paving stones, for God's sake. Despite all the looting, fighting and disasters, not one stone is out of place. And they're sparkling clean. No dust, no mud. When it rains, they gleam. Truly, this place is like a picture postcard.'

With Hilmi Rahmi in the lead and me following, we passed the vehicles waiting outside and went into the station building, through its wide door. The orderliness and tranquillity of the square continued inside. Beams of red, blue and green light from the coloured glass of the windows set high up near the ceiling played on the mirrors of the walnut console tables. Passengers were waiting in grave silence on the wooden benches that lined the walls. Hilmi Rahmi joined them and I sat beside him, holding my hands in my lap. If it hadn't been for the huge round-faced clocks, I would have thought I was in a church, not a station.

'Everything changed so suddenly. The city's main arteries were severed and this became a silent, lifeless, lost land. Whereas when Sumbul and I first came here, everywhere was full of life and excitement. Beautiful, stylish ladies, immaculate gentlemen, bright-eyed children twirling whirligigs…'

Hilmi Rahmi had placed his elbows on the knees of his creased trousers and his face between his palms. He spoke in a whisper in order not to disturb the reverent atmosphere. I leaned forward to hear him.

'There was a stationmaster, Giannakos Efendi. You should have seen his uniform – so fancy! He had learned from the British to speak in a low voice. He was a heavyset fellow with a bushy moustache and eyebrows that were equally thick and black. Even his giant hands, when he held the door, were covered with black hairs. He must have been two metres tall.'

He raised his head, looked up at the ceiling with its crystal chandelier, and smiled, showing his orderly teeth. The conductor was calling from the platform. The train to Boudja was about to depart. There were no passengers to be seen.

'He was a poet. One of the local newspapers had published his poems. When Sumbul heard this, she burst out laughing. She was a child then, of course, but even Giannakos Efendi himself found it hard to believe, so he carried a copy of the newspaper folded in quarters in the pocket of his uniform. He took it out and showed it to us – not that we understood anything; the newspaper was in Greek – but, anyway, little Sumbul turned as red as a beet. Those first years she got embarrassed a lot and would blush frequently, poor thing. It passed after Cengiz was born; she relaxed, got used to things. Then... Oh, God, why have you deemed me worthy of such sorrow?'

He lowered his gaze from the ceiling. The floor was decorated in an elegant mosaic of purple and white stars, circles and flowers. It was becoming harder and harder to hear his whispering.

'They took Giannakos Efendi as a prisoner of war. We were picking up everyone then; all the male infidels who remained in the city. They were marched through Smyrna in a group with their hands tied, as a lesson to everyone. Then over at Degirmendag they were executed by our soldiers, all of them. I learned too late that they had taken Giannakos Efendi. The poor man hadn't even been to the war. He had stayed here, working for the British officials, with his fancy uniform and his poems in his pocket. The soldiers got him and took him away. But even if I had known in time, could I have saved him? So many people died. Some pleaded, 'I am not Orthodox, I am a Catholic, please don't shoot me,' but our soldiers would just laugh, saying, 'An infidel is an infidel,' and pull the trigger. War, Scheherazade, is not what you know. It's awful, a calamity that makes a man ashamed to be human. May God not wish it on anyone, not even an enemy.'

Lost in the nightmare of his dark past, a tulle curtain had lowered over Hilmi Rahmi's face. He didn't notice that I had begun to tremble like a leaf. The blood drained from my hands and feet, I was sweating beads of perspiration. I struggled to open the pin of Sumbul's old cape the colour of pomegranate flowers that I had foolishly thrown around my shoulders despite the summer heat. I couldn't get it open. I reached out my hand and put it in his lap, as if begging for help, then tried to stand up, but it was as if my legs were made of clay; I couldn't straighten my knees. The wall clocks were whirling, mixing with the stars and squares of the floor mosaic. Just as I was falling to the ground, Hilmi Rahmi's arm caught me, like in an old dream. My legs left the floor.

When I woke up, I found myself in the mansion, in my room. After that day, I swore an oath. I would never again set foot outside the Mansion with the Tower.

Borrowed Time

'How have we sunk so low, Sumbul, sister?' grumbled Mujgan.

Side by side, she and Sumbul were rolling out dough in the spacious kitchen of the Thomas-Cook residence. The kitchen was like a beehive. Women in colourful headscarves were leaning over counters, working non-stop, their skilful fingers shaping dough, meat, vine leaves. The Italian head cook was strolling among them, inspecting their work. Instructions were being called out in all the languages spoken in Smyrna. Young men were carrying trays laden with hors d'oeuvres and canapés to the ballroom packed with guests.

'Don't complain, Mujgan,' whispered Sumbul, wiping flour off her forehead with her arm. 'Where else can we earn this kind of money these days? We get five times more here than we make packing figs.'

'For God's sake, stop, sister! Are we the kind of women to work as maids for foreigners?'

'We've been here for two days, making savoury pies and baklava, and we haven't even seen a foreigner!' said Sumbul. Mujgan had touched on a sensitive subject. 'We've rolled out this much dough, made so many pies, we should at least get to catch a glimpse of the ball.'

'If Hilmi Rahmi were here, you could have been one of the ladies invited to the ball, sister. Don't you ever think about that? But instead, we're making baklava and pies for the European guests.'

'Hold on a minute, Mujgan. Hilmi Rahmi is not a pasha; he's just a colonel. And even if he was a pasha in Mustafa Kemal's new army, what difference would that make – the foreigners don't recognize this new Ankara government anyway.'

'They might not recognize it today, but they will soon, and then they'll kneel down in front of it,' grumbled Mujgan. Taking out her rancour on the dough, she was extra forceful with her rolling pin.

Since Huseyin had left to join the nationalists, Mujgan had grown increasingly fanatical in her support for them. Sumbul was accustomed to this now. Without saying anything, she arranged her dough in the pan. 'Don't roll it out so thin, Mujgan. It will tear when they fill it.'

'Oof, Sumbul, sister, you always know best.'

'I am trying to be extra careful so we don't embarrass our father-in-law, Mustafa Efendi. Don't misunderstand me, please.'

Mustafa had arranged for his daughters-in-law to work in the kitchen for this New Year's Eve ball given at the Thomas-Cook residence for the wealthiest and most influential people of Smyrna, Bournabat, Boudja and Kordelio. Multitudes of assistant cooks, servants and valets had been hired for the evening.

'They've filled the kitchen with the whole city, sister. Just look at all these people working here!'

Sumbul glanced around the kitchen. It occupied the whole basement floor of the Thomas-Cook residence and could not be described simply as a kitchen; it was a series of kitchens, a place with connecting zones, pantries like an aircraft hangar, multiple ovens, and separate counters dedicated to slicing onions or rolling out pastry dough. Implements that Sumbul had never seen in her life hung from nails along the wall. Some were powered by electricity and caused Sumbul and Mujgan to jump at the noise they made when they were turned on. Only the Thomas-Cooks' servants themselves were allowed to use these machines, and even among them there was a hierarchy. A little earlier the head cook had caught a woman using the electric mixer who did not have the authority to do so, and he had raised the roof.

'Since Mr Edward brought this machine back from America, many fingers have been chopped off, so naturally the head cook is very particular. It would be a huge disaster if there were an accident on a day like this,' explained a young girl sitting beside Sumbul. She wore a pale blue headscarf and she had a sweet face, like a squirrel's, and a soft voice. As she spoke, she was shelling the pistachio nuts piled in front of her with great dexterity. After they'd been shelled, the nuts would be ground in a mortar and sprinkled on the baklava.

Mujgan glared at the girl. Since Huseyin left, she had stopped talking to Christians or buying from their shops.

'He's a little upset anyway because they hired two extra chefs for this ball.'

'You mean three different chefs are working in the kitchen?'

'Yes. The one who just walked past us is the Italian chef. He's the real head cook of the house. Madame Helene hired two more chefs just for tonight. One is here only to cook the fish, and I don't know about the other. And of course there's Hayguhi Hanim. She makes the desserts. Hayguhi Hanim taught all of us how to make desserts for parties in the past – profiteroles, crèmes caramel, croquembouches... She's the wife of the famous baker, Berberian, who has a shop on the quay. You know it? Anyway, they're the only Armenians in the pastry business.'

While the squirrel-faced girl was talking, Sumbul looked at the balls of dough the stout woman across from her was making. After she shaped the balls, she injected something into them with a needle. Was this what they called 'croquembouche', she wondered?

'Once those balls have been baked in the oven, they'll be filled with sweetened whipped cream. Then we'll pile them one on top of the other until they are two metres high.'

'How tall is two metres?'

'I don't really know either, but it's as tall as I am. We'll all be called to squirt cream into them.'

Sumbul leaned towards the squirrel-faced girl's ear and whispered, 'Have you been upstairs at all? Have you seen the guests?'

Without raising her head from the mountain of shells in front of her, the girl whispered her reply. Her Turkish wasn't bad. 'I have. I went all the way up stairs a little while ago to hand over a tray to one of the waiters. The tables are lined up end to end, like a railway track. They stretch as far as the eye can see. There are plates and plates of food I've never seen in my life on the tables. It's the apprentices in the kitchen over there who made those dishes; they trained in France. Our people are doing the caviar, squid, octopus, fish in mayonnaise... Bottles of champagne...'

Sumbul didn't know what mayonnaise was and had never

seen champagne. She stopped talking so that her ignorance wouldn't become obvious.

'After I'd handed over the tray to the waiter, I waited a while at the top of the stairs to see the ladies. Oh, my God, *hanim mou*, what gowns, what jewellery! Their necks shone brighter than the lamps. Every single one was like a movie star in the films shown at the Pantheon Cinema. They were so beautiful, so magnificent! Layered evening gowns with long trains; emeralds, rubies and sapphires around their necks and hanging from their ears. Some were wearing diamond tiaras; they must have been princesses. I can't describe it – you've got to see it for yourself.'

The fat woman making dough balls across from them joined the conversation. 'Did you hear? They invited High Commissioner Stergiadis to the ball.'

With the Greek she'd picked up, Sumbul understood what the woman had said. She asked in Turkish, 'Do you think he'll come?'

'I doubt it. He refuses all invitations. A very bad-tempered man. None of us like him. They say he even shows favouritism to Turks.'

The squirrel-faced girl gave Mujgan a nasty look. Mujgan continued to roll out her dough as if the girl wasn't there.

'The man is trying to be fair,' said Sumbul.

As soon as Stergiadis had taken control of Smyrna, he'd pushed to punish the men who'd looted the Turkish neighbourhoods on the day of the Greek landing, including the men who'd killed the coffeehouse owner, Hasan. All the civilians and soldiers who'd supported them were also called to account.

'But it's become so impossible to make everyone happy now that whatever he does ends up benefiting no one.'

'What good is fairness to infidels who have set their eyes on other people's homes and country,' grumbled Mujgan.

As if she'd not heard her, Sumbul turned to the girl beside her. 'My name is Sumbul. Do you know Mustafa Efendi, the butler of the house next door? We're his daughters-in-law. This is my sister-in-law, Mujgan. Our father-in-law, God bless him, always looks out for of us, especially now, during these difficult times. He got this work for us.'

Upon hearing Mustafa's name, a light passed across the girl's sweet face. Mujgan angrily slapped a new ball of dough she'd grabbed from the bowl onto the counter.

'Oh, I am so pleased to meet you, Lady Sumbul. *Harika poli.* Butler Mustafa is a very honourable gentleman. All of us have great respect for him.'

Just as Sumbul was about to open her mouth, Mujgan interrupted. 'Wait a minute. Let me guess...' She'd put her dough and rolling pin down and was leaning her bare arms, covered in flour up to the elbows, on the counter, looking at the squirrel-faced girl and Sumbul with a challenging expression on her face. 'At the time when that Mustafa gentleman whom you so respect was being assaulted, beaten unconscious and then left for dead in an abandoned mansion, you were waving flags and strewing flowers in the paths of your Greek evzones, were you not?'

The voices in the kitchen that until then had been buzzing like a beehive suddenly fell silent.

Sumbul felt herself blushing up to her ears. 'Mujgan, please, we are in the house of foreigners.'

The squirrel-faced girl was looking at Mujgan with her mouth open. Sumbul reached out and touched Mujgan's arm. Mujgan shook her hand away, as if a fly had landed on her arm.

'Is what I said a lie?'

Silence. After a moment of confusion, everyone decided the best thing to do was to get back to work. Half the people in the kitchen were refugees from Chios and didn't understand what was being said anyway; the other half pretended that they'd didn't understand. The head cook, who'd come into the kitchen just at that moment was surprised by the quiet. He was a cheerful, amiable man who always had a glass of wine with him as he worked. If he had been upset by the hiring of additional cooks for the ball, he wasn't showing it.

'Come, ladies, *signore*, the filling for the pies has been prepared. Bring your pans of dough over here.'

It was a cold and crystal-clear night in Bournabat. The Thomas-Cook mansion was lit up from top to bottom. Thanks to the generators which Edward had bought in emulation of the grand hotels on the quay, the ballroom was as bright as day, dazzling the eyes of the guests coming in from the velvet darkness of the night. Everyone was talking about the flood of light cast by the chandeliers across the ballroom. Even those guests who were accustomed to attending balls at the grand hotels could not resist praising the electric lighting at the mansion. Edward rejoiced in their compliments like a little boy, swaggering as if he had indeed accomplished a great job.

Pink, yellow and purple lanterns had been hung in all the trees between the garden gate and the mansion to light the road for the guests. A stream of carriages rolled through the heavy iron gate with its HTC monogram, all of them drawn by glossy and immaculately groomed horses. At the clean, white-gravelled entrance to the marble-columned residence, with light streaming from the windows, valets assisted the guests to alight from their carriages and ascend the stairs. The women, their bosoms revealed in low-cut gowns, their arms wrapped in furs, knew how to appear reluctant to leave their carriages and go up the marble stairs. From the opened door of the carriage, first the toe of a high-heeled slipper would appear, followed by a leg escaped from chiffon and silk, then a gloved hand adorned with a mischievously winking diamond ring. It was only when the tuxedoed gentlemen smoking their pipes beside the marble columns had turned their attention to the carriage door, held open by the valet, that the lady would display herself fully in her many-layered ball gown.

Seeing Avinash and Edith at the ballroom door, Edward came to their side in a few strides of his long legs. He wore the overly wide smile that appeared whenever he saw Avinash.

'Welcome, my dear Edith *mou*. Monsieur Pillai. What an honour to see you here.' Reaching out, he kissed Edith's sparkling hand.

'We're pleased to be here, Edward. You look very handsome.'

'It is I who should be saying that. Dear Edith, you get more beautiful as the years pass. Are you stealing the elixir of youth from witches, or what?' He turned and flashed Avinash a theatrical smile.

Edith looked around the ballroom filled with deliciously scented women wearing gowns with colourful trains and officers with multiple epaulettes. Edward's mother, Helene Thomas-Cook, had settled herself like a queen in an armchair on a raised platform at the furthest corner of the room. If with her hawk eyes she recognized Edith, she pretended not to have seen her. She held this spoiled daughter of the neighbours responsible for her son's demise.

'Joking aside, how do you like my new style? Did I tell you I just returned from America last month?'

'You must have brought your hairstyle from there.'

With the tips of his fingers Edward touched his hair, which had been slicked back and polished with lemon-scented pomade. Leaning towards Edith, he whispered, as if imparting a secret, 'It's a Valentino cut.'

'Very impressive.'

'But see here,' he said, waving a hand. 'Let me show you something even more impressive.'

A girl with a tray hung around her neck containing different brands of cigarettes appeared beside them. She was wearing a black satin dress with a skirt that barely reached her knees and was clearly ashamed to be showing her bare legs. So as not to embarrass the girl even more, Avinash turned towards the dance floor, where the orchestra was situated.

Edward plucked a packet of cigarettes from the girl's tray and offered them to his guests, grinning like a naughty child. 'How do you like that? Mother was very resistant to my cigarette girl idea, but it's not so bad, is it? It introduces a bit of American atmosphere to this antiquated mansion. We cut the girls' hair too, as you can see. Would you believe it, Edith *mou*, there's not a head in America now with long hair. Our girls are keeping up with the fashion, which is good. It's better, isn't it, Riri *mou*?'

The girl raised her hand self-consciously to the back of her neck, seemingly as ashamed of her exposed neck as she was of her bare legs. She was clearly keen to disappear as quickly as she could; when Edward gestured that she could go, she hurried to the stair landing where the other servants were standing.

After lighting Avinash's cigarette, Edward pointed out two

black musicians in the orchestra. 'I met them in a speakeasy in Charleston. Next year our ships will come from Virginia, it's all settled. These men play fantastic music – unbelievable. When you hear them, you'll see what I mean. I put them on a ship and brought them here just for this ball. The real show will begin after Mother dear goes to bed. Wait and see.'

Edward was in fine form tonight, as he was at every ball. He wore a grey-striped suit over his white shirt and starched collar, with a silk handkerchief the same burgundy colour as his cravat in the pocket of his jacket. His copper-coloured moustache shone like a narrow bow above his thin lips and from his immaculately shaved skin rose the scent of top-quality lavender and lemon. His cheeks, which had begun to look slightly drawn, were flushed as red as apples and his small blue eyes were starting to sting and go red from all the gin cocktails he'd drunk.

'With your permission, Edward, we will go and greet your mother,' said Avinash.

Edith and Edward looked at each other and rolled their eyes like two disobedient children. If Edith had come there alone, she would have spent the entire night avoiding Helene Thomas-Cook, but Avinash did not appreciate the spoiled-little-girl attitude she adopted among these people in whose neighbourhood she had been born and raised. Arm in arm, they passed through the ballroom until they reached the throne on which their hostess had established herself.

Helene Thomas-Cook had been the matriarch of the family for almost thirty years. Her husband had died at a young age of a shameful illness no one wanted to mention. No doubt he'd caught it at one of the Greek taverns that Edward now frequented. Fortunately, following the birth of her youngest daughter, who was disabled, Helene had moved into a bedroom separate from that of her husband, which was why she'd lived to the age she was now. Two of her three sons had married and brought their wives to live in the mansion, but for some reason neither of the daughters-in-law had produced grandchildren. Her youngest son, Edward, who was leaning on the ladder of thirty-five, was still only interested in debauchery, sailing boat races, and socializing with every class of women in the city, from the most noble to the cheapest. All of this had turned Helene Thomas-Cook into a grumpy old woman.

Avinash bowed to their hostess and kissed her hand, its white skin speckled with brown age spots. Edith immediately understood, from the fleeting expression of disgust on her face, that she wasn't at all pleased to have an Indian man as a guest at her ball. Although it was no longer a secret that Avinash worked for the British Empire, in the eyes of Helene Thomas-Cook he was still an Indian man and a simple gemstone merchant. Sensing that she was being observed, she turned her eyes on Edith.

Edith, biting her lip to stop herself from laughing, was about to greet the old woman with a nod of her head when a voice in her ear hissed, 'Go and shake the hand of your hostess and thank her for inviting you to such a delightful ball.'

Edith would have recognized that cinnamon-scented breath on her neck anywhere. Without giving her a chance to speak, Juliette Lamarck caught her daughter by the arm and sashayed up to Helene Thomas-Cook as if she were presenting her twelve-year-old girl to the queen. Taking the hand which Avinash had kissed moments earlier into her own palms, Juliette spoke in exaggerated English.

'Lady Thomas-Cook, how lovely you look, my dear. And

what a splendid ball! Definitely equal in elegance and service to last year's. In one word, it is perfect! *Magnifique!* As you see, Edith is also here. This year she has decided to leave aside her solitude and honour us with her presence. Furthermore, she has promised to help us with the charity event we are planning on Sunday for the Bayrakli Orphanage. Isn't that right, darling?'

Edith glared at her mother. Juliette was an expert at pressing people into service, giving them no choice. With a fake smile showing all her pearly teeth, Juliette turned and inclined her head towards their hostess. Edith murmured, 'How are you, Mrs Thomas-Cook? Thank you for the invitation.'

Although her mother had released her arm, Edith still felt Juliette's fingernails in her flesh. She hadn't even heard of the charity event for the orphanage. It infuriated her when her mother made decisions in her name, without even asking if she was available; she acted as if Edith was either incapable of managing her own life, even though she had lived alone for years, or lived a life that was insignificant and worthless. Turning, Edith glanced over at the rooms in the back, screened off behind purple velvet curtains. It was in those dimly lit rooms that guests from London were usually invited by specially employed Levantine girls to partake of a pipe for the 'complete oriental experience'. She decided to seek them out herself as soon as she could.

The orchestra began to play a waltz. After kissing Juliette's hand, Avinash put his arm around Edith's waist and led her to the dance platform, which was shining in the pool of light from three giant crystal chandeliers. Heads swivelled in their direction. Although they had been appearing at gatherings together for many years now, Edith and Avinash were still a gossip-worthy couple.

Helene Thomas-Cook smiled triumphantly from her throne. Juliette, pressing her thin lips together, took leave of her hostess and walked away. She did not get as much pleasure from this kind of society entertainment as she once did. Her elder son, Charles, had taken his family and moved to his wife's country, Holland. Her elder daughter, Anna, thanks to the children she'd had one after the other, had turned into a brood cow. Although she lived in a residence in Boudja that was like a small palace, she looked after her children herself, like a village woman, and also took on the cooking. Edith, graced with beauty and elegance, could have been the child who stayed by her side at parties, but she veered from one scandal to another.

All at once Juliette felt very tired. She looked around for Jean-Pierre and Marie. Her younger son and his wife always took her under their wing at parties like this. Unable to spot them, she gathered up the skirts of the red silk gown she'd worn in defiance of her years and made her way over to Edward's side. Party boy Edward would find a way to include her in a group of his guests.

Edward had loosened his collar studs. His shining eyes were following the van Dijk daughter, Anika, who had recently returned from Amsterdam where she was studying. There it was. Edward was no less mired in scandal than Edith, but people had stopped gossiping about him years ago, even though he was a grown man, and, unlike his brothers, had not even deigned to try and get involved in the family business. He loved to take young girls on his lap in the Greek taverns. He also frequented the Hiotika houses, and every time he went to the Hiotika district he brought necklaces and bracelets for a tiny little girl there with almond-shaped eyes and white skin. The girl even had crooked teeth. And yet this was not discussed at every opportunity, unlike Edith's love life, which from the beginning had been a topic of mystified fascination.

Juliette took a deep breath, straightened her shoulders, stuck a smile on her face and lifted a glass of champagne from the silver tray being proffered by a waiter wearing a red uniform with gilded epaulettes. She could still feel the hostess's hawk-like eyes upon her. If only, at this advanced age, they could stop competing with each other over their children and instead have sincere chats befitting their status as next-door neighbours of forty years' standing.

As soon as Helene Thomas-Cook had taken leave of her guests and retired to her rooms after the meal, Edward gave the orchestra he'd brought over from America a sign. Edith had given Avinash the slip and disappeared into one of the dimly lit back rooms. As the clock neared midnight, the orchestra really warmed up. The American girls from Paradiso began a dance the like of which no one had even seen before. Paying no attention to the bewildered crowd gathered around the dance platform, they were shaking their milk-white legs out from beneath their short skirts.

'Is this a dance?' Juliette muttered. 'They're just showing off their legs, like cheap nightclub girls in Paris.'

To one side of her was Edward, and on her other side was Avinash, busy scanning the ballroom for Edith. Edward was in high spirits. What a good idea it had been to bring the two musicians over from America. They were the only ones able to hold that rhythm. This ball would definitely be talked about for years to come.

He threw his champagne back in one gulp and shook his head. 'I think it's marvellous! Just look, Madame Lamarck, how freely they are enjoying themselves. I wish I knew a few steps – I'd jump in with no hesitation.'

He had begun his sentence in English, finished it in Greek. Juliette grumbled her reply in French. 'There are no steps to learn, Edward, *mon cher*. You just shake your leg like a kicking horse. They must have shortened their skirts for this dance – and no hint of an underskirt. What do you say, Monsieur Pillai?'

While Avinash was thinking of an appropriate reply, the deep purple curtain behind the orchestra opened slightly and Edith appeared. Her pearl necklace was awry and she had a hand over her face as if shielding her swollen eyes from the glare of the chandeliers. She looked like a lost child. Avinash, weary of the people around him jumping from one language to another in the middle of a sentence, quickly crossed the dance platform, took her arm, and led her to the corner where her mother and Edward were.

'Edith, are you all right, dear? *Kala ise?*'

Edith escaped from Avinash's arm and stood swaying in front of Edward. Juliette was watching her daughter anxiously. She turned to Avinash as if asking him for help. She did not approve of her daughter's scandalous relationship with this exotic spy, of course, but if one fell into the sea, one would embrace a snake. Avinash opened his arms wide in helplessness.

'Edward,' Edith shouted, trying to make herself heard above the orchestra, 'where did you find such men, able to play like this? Bravo!'

Edward was drunk. Without taking his eyes off Edith's face, he grabbed her arm. 'Come on, Edith *mou*. Let's try it!'

Edith's face lit up like a child's. She drank down the champagne she'd snatched from a tray as she'd passed through the room on Avinash's arm and thrust the empty glass into Avinash's hand.

'Edith, darling, how many glasses have you had already?'

'*Maman*, you may ask Monsieur Pillai, if you wish. Undoubtedly he, like you, has been keeping count. Edward, darling, shall we?'

'But of course, Madame Lamarck! We are still young,' shouted Edward with his mouth to her ear. 'Also, it is shameful to leave these girlies alone on the platform like circus animals. As their host, it is my duty to make them feel at ease.'

Saying this, he smiled at one of the girls whose hair was cut as short as a boy's. When the girl came over and without hesitation pulled Edward up onto the platform, Juliette breathed a sigh of relief. Meanwhile Avinash had seated Edith on one of the velvet sofas in the back. What was wrong with those children?

Ten minutes later, the dance platform was filled with young people shaking their legs like kicking horses. Edward was throwing the American girls into the air and catching them. At five minutes to midnight, without letting go of the waist of the short-haired brunette, he grabbed another glass of champagne, pointedly avoided looking over at Edith, asleep in Avinash's arms in a dark corner, and gulped it down. Keeping time with the wild rhythm of the orchestra, the guests began counting down.

On the sofa in the corner, Avinash had his arm around Edith's waist and was stroking her back while keeping his eye on a group of men whose faces were flushed with alcohol. The group included some of Smyrna's top businessmen, high-ranking officers of the British army and British Consulate officials.

A group of former Ottoman officers had organized an army made up of armed gangs from Asia Minor, and under the command of Colonel Ismet they were preparing for their first battle. With Venizelos's defeat in the Greek election the previous month, plans were now in disarray. Avinash knew for a fact that in the absence of Venizelos, pawn of Lloyd George, and the architect and leader of the Greater Greece *Megali Idea*, Britain's support for Greece would dwindle and perhaps one day cease altogether.

News had spread that Mustafa Kemal had come to an agreement with the Bolsheviks, who would supply him with arms. The Italians had declared that they would support Turkey in revenge for Smyrna having been given to Greece despite having been promised to them. The Allied Powers were to meet in Paris at the end of the month to re-evaluate their plans and perhaps prepare for a conference which the rival governments of Ankara and Istanbul as well as representatives from Greece would attend. The possibility of making amendments to the Treaty of Sèvres that would be beneficial to Turkey was under consideration.

When the clock struck midnight, Edward, still not letting go of the short-haired brunette he was pressing to his chest, popped the cork of a bottle of champagne with his free hand. As high-spirited shouts rose from the ballroom, the crowd clustered around him, filled their elegant glasses with bubbling champagne, lifted them in unison towards the crystal chandelier, and clinked them merrily in the air. The American girls, champagne dripping from their hair, hugged each other, screaming and laughing. The carefree crowd in the Thomas-Cook ballroom embraced one another with cheerful abandon.

Edith, stretched out on the red sofa with her head on Avinash's knees, had dozed off. She did not hear the countdown fanfare. A slither of a moon was about to top the mountains that were visible between the purple curtains framing the windows behind them. As he ran his fingers through the curls that had escaped Edith's undone turban and were spread over his knees, Avinash's heart was heavy with what he knew to be true. Closing his eyes, he thought of the two armies camped on the other side of the mountains, of the soldiers who had grown up together and were now lying under the same sky, dreaming the same dream. While they lay in their tents, the people in the floodlit ballroom of the Thomas-Cook residence were embracing each other amid laughter and mad music and greeting the new year in all the different languages spoken in their paradisal city. *Hronia Polla! Bonne année! Buon anno! Hayirli seneler olsun! Pari gağant yev amanor! Happy New Year!*

Knowing full well that he would not be heard above all the commotion, Avinash whispered, 'We are all living on borrowed time, my love. And not one of us is aware that the day of reckoning is swiftly approaching. Happy New Year!'

Edith's beautiful lips, which he never tired of kissing, were parted and she was snoring softly in his lap.

Part IV

COINCIDENCES

First Encounter

When she went down to the quay that Wednesday morning, marriage was the last thing on Panagiota's mind. If anyone had told her that before the weekend was over she would be engaged to Lieutenant Pavlo Paraskis, she would have made a sour face as if she'd heard an unpleasant joke.

On her way to Fasoula she ran into Elpiniki's younger sister, Afroula, in front of the new building being constructed at the Evangelical School. 'Wow, so Pavlo has his eye on you,' said Afroula playfully. 'He says he's going to take you to Ioannina and treat you like a princess. Congratulations!'

Panagiota whacked Afroula with her umbrella and then ran nearly the whole way from Agia Katerina to Fasoula. She was going to tell this Pavlo off! He'd put on airs just because they'd spoken two words at the meadow in Kordelio – and that was only because she'd had to. As if stopping her on the street and inviting her to the cinema was not enough, he had shamelessly begun to spread baseless rumours.

After she'd crossed Fasoula Street, turned onto Poyraz Street and was walking towards the sea, she began hurrying even faster. She grasped her umbrella tightly and held her chin high as she made her way through the twisting colonnades between the buildings used as warehouses. Whistles and ribald laughter from the drivers waiting at the head of the road followed her as she went. You had to remain strong in the face of such remarks from those good-for-nothing bums in the coffeehouses. Just as the gentlemen on the quay were notably modern and polite, so these men in the back alleys around Parallel Street were notably crude. Most of them were Maltese sailors who worked on the merchant ships, or seasonal fig pickers and packers from the islands. Ne'er-do-wells who, whenever they saw a young woman walking alone, felt they had a duty to make a comment and then laugh and brag among themselves.

'Po po po… *Principesa*, look over here! Did your mummy feed you honey, *yavri mou*? What is your name, princess? Hello! *Ciao*, baby!'

She took a deep breath when she got to the quay. On this winter's day the sea was shining like glass; the red, yellow and white fishing boats tied up ashore swayed in counterpoint to the porcelain-blue calm of the water. The front of the Sporting Club was still wet from the wild wind's waves that had pounded the shore through the night. If only the rest of the city were as clean and orderly as the quay. Here, there were none of those swaggering catcalls from clay-faced bums; instead, gentlemen greeted ladies by touching the tips of their fingers to their hats.

More than a year had passed since Stavros had volunteered for the army. And now everybody else had gone to the war too. Last summer they'd rounded up all the boys and herded them out to the plains of Asia Minor. Only the fisherman's son, Niko, remained in the neighbourhood. Stavros had never been an enthusiastic letter writer, not even at the beginning, and after the twenty-one-day Battle of Sakarya his letters had stopped altogether. If it hadn't been for Minas's letters to Adriana, Panagiota wouldn't even have known if Stavros was alive or not.

Thank goodness, the letters Minas wrote without fail to his fiancée gave news of all the neighbourhood boys. Stavros had proved a tough nut, but Pandelis had come down with tuberculosis. The boys were in a dire situation, marooned in an arid region with no water and barely any food. The supply routes had all been attacked. Even before the battle had begun, most of them were worn down with illness and hunger. Communication had become more and more difficult as railways and telegraph lines were blown up. Minas begged Adriana not to stop writing. *Tell all the girls they should write*, he urged in one of his letters. *Even if they don't have a sweetheart in the army, they should reach out to their brothers. My Adriana, we are desperate for encouragement from the people we are fighting for. The Turks have a goal that inspires them to carry on fighting. As for us, we are losing faith from one day to the next.*

Fighting back the tears welling in her eyes, Panagiota hugged the purple velvet coat with the astrakhan collar which she was wearing over her navy-blue school uniform. She had stuffed her hair inside her wide-brimmed hat, leaving a few strands that she'd secretly cut to just below her ears curled over her cheeks to give the impression of short hair. The light velvet coat had been a birthday present from her Aunt Lili, a seamstress. A European lady had had the coat sewn for her daughter who was studying in Paris, but the girl hadn't liked the colour, so the coat had been returned to Aunt Lili. They didn't even ask for any money back. Her mother had bought the broad-rimmed black hat with peacock feathers from Bon

Marché. When Panagiota posed with the hat and coat like the girls on the pages of *La Mode Illustrée*, the women had looked around hurriedly for wood to knock on, she looked so stunning.

That morning the quay, with its grand coffeehouses, theatres, bars and wealthy homes stretching all the way to Punta, was empty and relatively quiet. Panagiota, breathing in the sea air, walked towards the north end of the quay. In the sleepy morning the restaurants and beer houses had not yet opened their doors. There was not a soul in front of the Lux, which was always packed full to bursting in the evenings. In front of the Pantheon Cinema an Englishman getting his shoes shined touched his fingers to his fedora in greeting to her. A horse-drawn tram was coming, and as it passed, its driver gave a light ring of the bell. Trying to put Pavlo's invitation to the cinema out of her mind, she speeded up.

In the summer months, the quay was always very lively and a holiday atmosphere prevailed. Over the last three summers in particular, since the Greek administration had taken over the city and the male population had doubled, things had really hotted up; the girls positively smouldered, drunk on their newfound freedom. On every corner, they flirted merrily, indifferent to public opinion, competing with each other to get a front-row table at the cafés so that the wind could ruffle their hair and lift their skirts. They treated every passing officer and soldier to warm glances, smiling at them through thick lashes. The men were so overwhelmed by the girls' beauty and friendliness, they didn't know which way to look.

The neighbourhood boys thoroughly resented their girls ignoring them and focusing all their attention on the Greek soldiers. They said everything there was to say to the soldiers and to the infatuated girls.

Elpiniki had found herself an Athens lieutenant, in one night forgetting Niko, for whom she had burned a year ago. When she grabbed Panagiota and dragged her to the rural tea-house in Kordelio, she was all over the lieutenant from Athens, practically crawling into his lap. And what a coincidence: Elpiniki's lieutenant had brought Pavlo with him. Panagiota had been forced to chat with the soldier who'd danced under her window last summer.

Compared to Stavros, Pavlo was rather naive and boring, but he was actually a well-mannered and educated young man. With his unexceptional clear brown eyes, his face couldn't be called handsome, but his features were regular; he had thick, bony arms. One evening when Panagiota was sitting with her friends at the Café de Paris at one of the tables near the street, she saw him strolling around with a group of soldiers. She might have grinned too much, but she didn't pull up her skirt or do anything ill-mannered like other girls did.

She decided to wait until she got home to think about his invitation to the cinema. The French version of *The Three Musketeers* was playing at the Lux, *The Unseen Hand* at the Pantheon. They were both cowboy films. Where was *Red Love* being shown? Elpiniki had raved about it. Out of curiosity, she walked to the Ciné de Paris. She would need to see if her father would permit her to go anyway. What was more, they didn't show these films in their entirety; if she enjoyed the first half, she'd have to get permission all over again if she wanted to see the rest of the film the next day.

She walked back, bought a biscuit from Zakas Pastry Shop below the Hotel d'Alexandria, then leaned against a lamppost so she could spy on the Kraemer Palace. Seagulls were spreading their wings in the cloudless sky, ready to dive into the sea. In spite of the cool weather, Café Zapion had set up its tables outside and at one of them two European ladies were drinking tea and eating lemon cakes.

The hotel's young doorman was pretending not to see Panagiota. He was dressed in a very showy black, red and yellow uniform, with a bowler hat on his head, like the British wore. Panagiota spent a while trying to catch his eye. Perhaps her beauty would have an effect on him, just as it had on the neighbourhood boys who used to serenade her, and he would let her in. She longed to go inside that magnificent four-storey building with its electric lighting, to walk on its soft carpets, take the lift to the top floor and gaze out at the horizon from its windows, drink tea in its café, sit at a table next to foreign women wearing the most intoxicating perfume, order a slice of torte.

Just at that moment a sharp sea breeze blew her short curls against her face and caused them to stick to the powdered sugar on her cheek. Bringing her hand to her mouth, she anxiously wiped the sugar from the corner of her lips and looked round at the hotel's blue-shuttered windows to be sure no one had seen her.

The 'Kraemer Palace' sign on the front of the building had been taken away and a new sign, 'Splendid Palace', hung in its place. There was a new Muslim owner now. Was it the father of Niko's Turkish girlfriend? The famous Panellinion to the left of the hotel had also changed its name to Ivi last year. She didn't like it when the places she knew changed owners and names. It caused her inexplicable anxiety. She wanted the world to stay the same while she herself changed.

She turned her dreamy eyes to the hotel's spacious balconies. Who knew how many high-ceilinged ballrooms there were inside! She pictured the scratches on the parquet floors made by the shoes of women waltzing or doing the foxtrot or the polka; the grand pianos and vast, gilt-framed mirrors; the lifts that opened directly into rooms, and the soft beds, diamond-beaded curtains and who knew what else in the suites fit for kings.

If only she could see inside!

Two officers in khaki uniforms with red epaulettes were coming out of the hotel. At their sides were a couple of heavily made-up women, the sort Panagiota had seen once or twice in closed-topped motor cars. They were dressed like European women, with skirts that ended just below their knees. The officers kissed the girls' hands with exaggerated flourishes, and the girls continued flirting, right there in front of the door. Their capes, which only just covered their bare, narrow shoulders, looked like genuine rabbit fur. Panagiota had seen such capes at Xenopoulo's shop on Frank Street but hadn't dared ask the price. She'd made do with stroking the fur when the grumpy shopkeeper wasn't looking. Seeing the goose pimples on the girls' bare legs, she hugged her coat a little tighter.

After they had put the girls into a black motor car, the officers, laughing, crossed over to the sea side of the street, where Panagiota was standing. The tall officer with the carefully groomed handlebar moustache was talking nonstop, and the other officer, who looked like a little boy, with no moustache or beard, kept nodding. As if she wanted to crumble up the uneasiness that was troubling her heart, Panagiota began hurriedly chewing her biscuit. Her eyes watered as she tried to swallow the dry mouthfuls.

The tall officer was speaking in a loud, deep voice as if haranguing an audience from a stage. 'I can promise you,

Stefo, not a thing is going to happen.' With one hand he gestured to the European fleet anchored in the harbour. 'They'll get as far as Afyonkarahisar, Aydin, but they won't enter Smyrna. Forget about us, forget about the local Christians – just think of how many Europeans live here. And I mean rich ones! The banks are loaded with their bonds and they have many investments here – factories, agencies, railways, shipping lines. And see the *Iron Duke*, waiting over there like a gatekeeper? It's had our back up to now; it's not going to suddenly leave. And of course there's our fleet. If they get this far, we'll open fire on them.'

He seemed very self-confident as he cast a sidelong glance at Panagiota.

The one with no beard nodded yet again. 'You're right. We've been naval fighters for centuries. If only the war had broken out at sea, it wouldn't have lasted so long. Instead of going to Ankara, we should have concentrated on Constantinople.'

'That too will come, God willing. *Makari*. This Ankara business was a big mistake. They understand that now, but it's too late. We should have sent our army from Thrace; Constantinople would have fallen in two days. As it is, our divisions have been waiting west of Sakarya for months. Hungry, starving. And it's cold. The Turkish gangs control the supply roads, so not even a couple of mouthfuls reaches their bellies. How much longer can they endure?'

Panagiota was all ears. A carriage passed behind them. The coachman was standing upright, whip in hand, as if he were directing the whole world from up there.

'The enemy is in the same situation. Maybe even worse. I wonder why they aren't attacking. They've kept us waiting for months.'

The officer with the waxed moustache frowned. 'I'm not sure. It could be that the Turkos are expecting ammunition from somewhere. I heard they'd reached an agreement with all the Allies.'

'It looks that way. Even the Italians have retreated.' The beardless officer had a high-pitched voice.

'Oh, forget the Italians. Their problem is with us.'

'Sure, but since they've retreated, somebody must have convinced them that this place isn't going to stay in our hands.'

Forgetting even to wipe the powdered sugar from her face, Panagiota looked over at the officers fearfully.

The moustached officer put his hand on the boy-faced officer's shoulder. His frown relaxed. 'No need to be pessimistic, Stefo *mou*. The most powerful empire in the world has our back. Even if we've made a strategic error, I don't think there's any possibility that we'll lose the war after all our victories. Come, let's go inside. A man can't enjoy a smoke in this crazy wind, and look at how rough the sea has become. Some coffee with cognac would go down nicely. What do you say, should we invite those ladies sitting in front of Zapion to join us?'

'Do you know them?'

'I noticed the auburn-haired one at a party in Bournabat. They've come from London – European ladies looking for officer husbands. How can they refuse us!'

Throwing his cigarette into the sea, he crossed the street.

The women drinking tea at Café Zapion examined the officers from beneath their lashes. Words spoken in a foreign language and laughter rang in Panagiota's ears. She was trembling inside. Was it from the cold or something else? When she put her hands in the pockets of her coat, her fingers closed around a pebble she'd picked up last week at the Diana Baths. Although she knew very well that the pebble wouldn't skip across the surface in such choppy water, she flicked it anyway. To hell with the Kraemer Palace, the officers, the stylish European women, the fallen girls with their rabbit fur!

The pinnacle-shaped waves swallowed the pebble. Putting her hand back in her pocket, she chose another. Gripping the smooth white stone between her fingers, she took expert aim, swiftly swinging her elbow to release it backwards.

A hoarse scream went up from behind her. 'Ah! Slow down, little lady! Take it easy! Ah!'

A gentleman wearing a frock coat and a hat was bent double, moaning as if he were choking.

Panagiota covered her mouth with her hand. 'Oh, I am so sorry. *Signomi!* I didn't see you. Please forgive me. *Me singorite*. Mister, are you all right? *Monsieur?*' In her fright she had forgotten the French she normally spoke when strolling along the quay.

The man slowly straightened himself into an upright position. 'I am fine, fine. No need to worry. I hope in the future I shall never have need of entering into a disagreement with you, for you know very well where to strike a blow. Your hand is quite forceful, *mademoiselle.*'

Frightened, Panagiota took her hand from her mouth and hid it behind her back. Hurled with all that anger, she threw her arm backwards and, as she was aiming, had hit the man's testicles. Her face burned.

The man laughed, revealing a set of sparkling white teeth. 'No, no, I was just joking. You see, I am fine. I was not looking where I was going. I was looking at this beautiful scene – the colourful fishing boats rocking in such pleasant harmony with the sea. Look at that yacht over there; it glides like a swan. A magnificent thing.'

Panagiota looked at the sailing boat sliding over the sea. It was flying a British flag. Let a north wind blow and then they'd see if the inexperienced captain could make it to shore!

'*Mademoiselle*, could I have met you somewhere before?'

The foreign man – where could he be from? – was examining Panagiota's face, squinting at her.

'I don't think so. Why do you ask?'

'Your face seems so familiar.'

'No, we haven't met, I am sure of it.'

When he saw the girl raise her chin, a smile spread across the man's face. His Greek was good, but he spoke with a strange accent that Panagiota had never heard before. 'How can you be so sure?'

Panagiota couldn't stop herself from blurting out, 'How could anyone forget having seen you before?' When she realized what she'd said, her cheeks again flushed bright red and she immediately turned her face to the sea. How shameful! Oh, God, what a shameful thing to have said!

The man laughed. 'It should be me saying that, not you.'

Panagiota continued to stare out to sea in embarrassment.

'Not for the same reasons as you, of course. You probably meant that you would remember me because my dark skin seems to be at odds with the way I am dressed and you find my hair strangely long for a man. Whereas I felt the need to say the same because I see before me a rare beauty.'

Curiosity got the better of Panagiota and she turned round to inspect him. Truly, she had never seen such a man. He had dark skin like that of an Arab slave but was dressed like a foreign gentleman in striped trousers with a matching frock coat, a green silk handkerchief in his waistcoat pocket, a cravat of the same colour, and a bowler hat on his head. Under his cravat a thick gold chain glimmered. Rings with large gemstones – a sapphire, a ruby, an emerald – adorned the long fingers of his brown hands. Was this man a prince, or Aladdin or what? She again examined his face, confused. Maybe he was from the palace. With his long thin nose he had the look of a sultan.

'Are you a Turk?'

'No, but we can speak Turkish if you like,' he said, in Turkish that was as perfect as his Greek. 'I am Indian. My name is Avinash Pillai.'

Panagiota knew enough Turkish to understand what the man said. An Indian man, eh? She'd thought Indian people only came to work as servants in the homes of rich Turks. Never in her life had she seen an Indian man dressed like a European. Busy gazing at his smooth round face with its beaklike nose, she didn't notice that the stranger had reached for her wrist.

'Would you honour me by telling me your name, *Mademoiselle*?'

She came to herself when she felt the man's thick, purplish lips on her skin. 'I beg your pardon?'

'Your name?'

'Panagiota. Panagiota Yagcioglu.'

As if tasting a glass of wine, Avinash Pillai rolled the name around in his mouth for a time. 'Panagiota... Panagiota. A marvellous name. It befits an angel-faced lady like you perfectly.'

Not knowing what to do with this compliment, Panagiota took off her hat. Her curls tumbled free, over her shoulders and down her back.

Seeing the girl's bared head, Avinash frowned in consternation. But he did not forget his manners. '*Enchanté*, Mademoiselle Yagcioglu,' he said. 'I am very pleased to make your acquaintance.'

Again, Panagiota did not know how to respond. Not counting the French teacher at school, no one had ever addressed her as Mademoiselle Yagcioglu before. Trying to hide her smile, she asked, 'Are you visiting Smyrna?'

'No, I live here.'

'You must be a merchant then. Do you lodge at the Kraemer Palace?'

As if he had just realized that they were standing in front of the Kraemer Palace, Avinash turned and looked at the hotel's blue-shuttered yellow facade. Panagiota's shoulders dropped a bit.

'No.'

'Then?'

It was clear from her bass voice that under the girl's delicate outward appearance, there was a spirit like a rocket ready to be fired. He took off his hat and scratched his head. Where could he have met this girl? There was a familiar fragrance coming off her hair, her skin, quite separate from the smell of jasmine and lavender.

'I am not a merchant, and nor do I lodge at the Kraemer Palace.' He smiled victoriously, as if he had posed a difficult riddle.

'Ah?'

The girl bit her crimson lips. There was a gap between the two front teeth that was very familiar.

'You are not a merchant. What then is your business in Smyrna?'

After a moment's hesitation, Avinash decided to tell

319

the truth – or something close to the truth. 'I work at the consulate.'

'The Indian Consulate?' She blinked her bright black eyes several times.

Avinash smiled at the girl's innocence. What a beautifully wide white forehead she had. 'No, India does not yet have a consulate anywhere in the world. One day, hopefully. *Makari.*' Seeing her impatience, he added, 'I work at the British Consulate. But why do you laugh?'

'Mister, you look nothing like those British men – that's why! I pass the British Consulate every day on my way here, and the men who go in and out of that building are grumpy and old and look like they've swallowed their walking canes. Their skins are a purplish white. I've never once seen someone like you there.'

This time it was Avinash's turn to laugh. 'I am not British, but I studied at Oxford, which is one of England's most prestigious universities.'

Panagiota lowered her head slightly and appraised his face with narrowed eyes.

All at once Avinash felt that he was about to figure out how he knew her. 'How old are you, Panagiota?'

Panagiota was startled. The man had gone from flirtatious to fatherly. There was no more of that Mademoiselle Yagcioglu business. Why was that? Had she said something inappropriate? Oh, she had certainly asked too many questions. The bad woman inside her had woken up again, it seemed, a woman so cheap, she would do anything to get a man's attention and approval. She remembered the tension in Stavros's face as he'd untied the ribbons of her dress on the warm sand. Staring at Kraemer's windows, she murmured, 'I complete my seventeenth year in September.'

'How wonderful. What a great age! Treasure your youth!'

She nodded. She had heard that kind of thing from the old aunties in the neighbourhood so often that she no longer even bothered to reply. She waited for the man to ask what she was doing in this area so early in the morning, but Avinash Pillai's mind was elsewhere. Panagiota was offended that he had lost interest in her. Putting on her hat, she tried one more move.

'May I ask you something?'

Avinash took out his elegant gold-chained pocket watch and, after glancing at it, turned to the girl. '*Malista*. Of course.'

'I know it is not probable, but if the Turks entered Smyrna, the British would protect us, wouldn't they?'

Avinash had not been expecting this question.

Panagiota had only said it to get the man's attention, but as soon as the words were out of her mouth, she felt her eyes fill with tears, which meant that the possibility that the Turks would take over Smyrna was the reason she was frightened.

Putting his watch back in his pocket, Avinash drew close to Panagiota. His forehead touched her wide-brimmed hat. His skin smelled of something beyond the spices of distant lands.

'Panagiota, tell me, does your family have relatives in Greece?'

Panagiota cocked her head like a dove listening to faraway sounds. 'Why would we have relatives in Greece? Neither my mother, nor my father, nor my grandparents have ever set foot in Greece, not in their whole lives. We are from here. You have come from far away, so maybe you don't know. Our country is here. I mean in Mikrasia. Asia Minor.'

'Okay, what about the islands? Do you have family on Chios? Lesbos?'

Panagiota looked at him as if he'd lost his mind. 'No, sir. Why would we? We're not immigrants from Chios, so we wouldn't have relatives in Greece or on the islands. My grandparents emigrated from Kayseri to Chesme, and when my mother and father got married, they came to Smyrna. My father has a grocery shop. His name is Prodromakis Yagcioglu; everybody in the neighbourhood knows him as Grocer Akis.'

When Avinash made no comment, she added, 'Soon Smyrna will be a part of Greece. That's what the British promised. They signed an agreement in London, isn't that right?'

Avinash felt as close to this young girl as if he saw her every night in his dreams; he was filled with a desire to take her in his arms and protect her. In the distance, bales of tobacco were being loaded onto ships. The Kordelio ferry was entering the inner harbour, heading for the Hamdiye Factory's small wooden dock. Soon the Homerion students would be all around them. When she heard the whistle of the ferry, the anger that had blazed like embers in Panagiota's eyes softened and faded; the mask had dropped and her face was now full of fear. She looked pleadingly at Avinash.

Avinash reached out, took off her hat and put his lips very close to her ear. His hair tickled Panagiota's neck and she smelled that smell of distant lands again. Stavros and Pavlo didn't smell like that. The smell wasn't salt or pine but a cool, hard scent. As soon as she inhaled it, a sweet, warm cloud bloomed between her legs. Ashamed, she tried to draw back, but froze as she heard his whispered words.

'If you want to save yourself and your family, my dear Panagiota, I advise you to escape to Greece as soon as possible, before the Turks enter Smyrna. Get rid of your possessions, take what you can carry, and go. Make a new life in Greece. If you do stay here, all you can do is pray that Almighty God will protect you. Do not expect protection from anyone but God.'

Even as his hot breath blazed through her, from her neck to her stomach, like a ball of fire, Avinash was placing the hat he was holding on Panagiota's head, like a father sending his child off to school. Then he disappeared behind the yellow walls of the Kraemer Palace.

Escape Plan

For a week after that encounter, Panagiota did not go down to the quay. Throwing a knitted shawl around her shoulders, she would hurry to Fasoula to buy the things her mother asked for, then come back home and sit on the mat in the bay window until it was time to go to school. Katina assumed her daughter's apathy was due to an argument she'd had with Pavlo. She sent her to the bazaar for unnecessary things in the hope that the two of them might bump into each other and have the chance to speak and make up. 'While you're in Fasoula, stop at the butcher's and buy an *okka* of liver, enough for at least three days, and remember to have him slice it very thin,' she would say. Or, 'Wait in the square until the fresh bread comes out of the oven at the bakery; let's eat it when it's as hot as can be.' Using such pretexts, she tried to keep her daughter out on the streets for a while longer. But the child had no appetite for anything. Her pink cheeks had faded to an ashen grey.

Katina's hopes came to nothing. By Friday evening, when Panagiota went to the theatre with Pavlo, her mood still hadn't improved. In fact, the poor girl looked even paler and more exhausted the following morning, though she didn't refuse to go to the market. After returning to the house, she once again settled herself on the mat in the window, like a cat curled up in front of a stove. Pulling at her chin, she lost herself in the rooftops in the distance.

'Find a way to escape to Greece. Only Almighty God can protect you. Do not expect protection from anyone else.' For a week, the words of that strange man from India had been going round and round in her head – at home, at school, on the streets, at the theatre she'd gone to with Pavlo. (Her father had not given permission for the film.) His words seemed to imply that if Mustafa Kemal's army entered Smyrna, the British would not protect the city's Christian population.

Was that possible?

No, no. Impossible.

Those officers who'd come out of Kraemer's with the fancy prostitutes had been very confident that the British fleet anchored in the bay would protect the city. 'And if it becomes necessary, we will fire our cannons,' they'd said. Who really knew what lay in store for the city – those officers, or that Indian man, Pillai, who worked at the consulate? Fear and anxiety gnawed at her insides and she'd not been able to sleep for days. She listened intently to every discussion about the war overheard in the coffeehouses, the square, the grocery shop.

She had heard nothing of comfort.

That first encounter between Panagiota and Avinash took place in March 1922, at which time the two armies had withdrawn to opposite edges of the Eskisehir plateau. They were waiting for the Allies in European cities far from the war to make decisions which would determine their fates. After the Italians withdrew their forces from Asia Minor, the French followed suit. The British, who had Constantinople in their hands, had ceased all mention of Smyrna being annexed to Greece. Some of the soldiers from Greece, fed up, had deserted and gone back to their homeland. King Constantine, who'd been ill for some time, had collapsed both physically and spiritually after the Battle of Sakarya and returned to Athens. Rumour had it that Commander Papoulas, who had lost the battle, was to be fired and replaced by Dousmani, head of the armed forces. News coming from the front was relentlessly depressing, relentlessly dire.

On the morning that Avinash met Panagiota by chance in front of Kraemer's, the British Secret Service had been shaken by Churchill's latest telegram. The telegram, relayed from Cairo by the Secretary of State for the Colonies, stated: *The Greeks have got themselves into a geo-political situation where anything short of a decisive victory means defeat, and the Turks are in a position where anything short of a comprehensive defeat means victory.* The government of Lloyd George, which had encouraged Greece for years, was now cutting off its support. The Greek army had been left to fend for itself in the middle of Asia Minor.

Panagiota could not get Minas's bitter letters out of her mind: *My love, I know that we are setting out on a bloody campaign of death.*

'*Kori mou*, take these potatoes and peel them with Auntie Rozi. The poor old woman must be bored and lonely sitting all by herself the whole day on that chair in front of her house. You can keep her company.'

Taking the bowl full of freshly washed potatoes from her mother and tucking it under her arm, Panagiota went down to the street like a ghost. Without even noticing the children playing marbles over by the fountain, she walked slowly across to Auntie Rozi's house and sat down on her doorstep, wrapped in her cardigan. The sky was completely blue and the little square was lit up in the sunlight.

Dressed in black from head to toe, toothless Auntie Rozi was peeling oranges with her wrinkled fingers. She handed a piece to Panagiota. Cats were licking the stomachs they had bared to the sunshine. They sat side by side for a time without speaking. From nearby came the smell of freshly ground coffee, the tinkle of backgammon pieces, and occasionally the raised voices of men sitting under the coffeehouse arbour. The coffeehouse apprentice came out, swinging his tray.

'Coffee? Ladies, would you like some coffee?'

This apprentice had been one of the boys who'd serenaded Panagiota under her window on Menekse Street in the summer. A lewd smile crept across his face when he saw Panagiota sitting on her elderly neighbour's doorstep.

'*Lokum? Lemonada?* Ice cold.'

'Go away. We don't want anything. Get lost.'

She put another piece of orange into her mouth; it tasted like sunshine on her tongue, sharp and refreshing. Biting her bottom lip, she glanced over at the police station. Her lip was crusty from being chewed on.

'You must find a way to escape to Greece.'

Panagiota had not mentioned the fear that was eating away at her to her mother and father. They would have been alarmed that she'd been taken in by the words of an Indian man she'd met on the street, and they wouldn't have taken her concerns seriously anyway. If she'd brought up what Avinash Pillai had said at supper, for example, her father would have shouted angrily, 'For God's sake, that's crazy nonsense!' And her mother would have been sad that Panagiota was sad.

As the only child left in the family, Panagiota felt responsible for the happiness of her mother and father. Once, when she was younger, she'd been caught humming a song in class and had been sent out to stand in the corridor by herself for the rest of lesson. But her real punishment had been anticipating the disappointment on her mother's face when she read the note that the principal would send home. Panagiota was their miracle baby. It was her job to be the source of joy in the house and to never say or do anything that would frighten or upset them.

For days now, she'd been trying to come up with a way to save them all, should danger strike. After school, she'd been coming straight home and settling herself on the mat in the window, spending hours staring at the red tower of the nearby orphanage as she thought of a plan.

They had no relatives in Greece, and nor did they have the money to pay for a boat to take them there in an emergency. If she were to gather up the earrings, bracelets and crucifixes that had accumulated in her dowry trunk and sell them to the jeweller Dimitri in Fasoula, there was no doubt that Grocer Akis would learn of it. And if she took the gold to the Armenian district to sell, she could get cheated. Besides, her own jewellery wouldn't be enough to save them all. What if she were to remove a few pieces from Katina's jewellery box, pieces that her mother never wore, one at a time? No, she would never dare do that.

The Indian man had advised them to get rid of all their possessions and keep only what they could carry. What did that mean – were they supposed to sell the house? Her mother would never leave her home or her father his grocery shop. And when they came back, where would they live? What about their furniture?

It was obvious; there was only one thing to do.

With her face set in an expression like that of a commander going into battle, she stood up from the marble doorstep. Auntie Rozi was choosing a cauliflower and leeks from the bent-over vegetable seller, Mehmet; Panagiota waited patiently for her to finish and make the sign of the cross three times over her head. Then, following the vegetable seller Mehmet with confident steps, she made her way to the southern end of the square. The bowl of unpeeled potatoes remained on Auntie Rozi's doorstep.

In the back room of the two-storey police station building that smelled of toilets, Pavlo Paraskis was sitting at his messy desk with its overflowing ashtrays reading the *Amaltheia* newspaper. On the wall behind him there was a large map showing the district of Aydin under Greek control. Pavlo did not immediately notice Panagiota standing in the doorway, and Panagiota took the opportunity to observe him. He had thrown his cape on the desk. His brown hair was slicked back and carefully waxed. He was giving all his attention to whatever he was reading, like a child struggling with a mathematics problem. His wide, protruding forehead shone in the sunlight striking the room. Why didn't he have a moustache like everyone else? A small beard and moustache would improve that childish appearance. God, what if he was unable to grow a beard?

When he lifted his head and saw Panagiota at the door, the young lieutenant almost fell over in surprise. Leaping from his chair, he stood to attention and from habit almost saluted her. Panagiota put her hand over her mouth to suppress her laughter.

'Welcome, Panagiota *mou*. What a great honour! Such a happy surprise! *Kalos tin!* Wait, tell me... No, don't wait...

I mean, don't stand there, will you not sit down? Come, sit here. Yanni, look here, *ela*, bring the lady a coffee, and some *lokum* with it. Come on, *grigora*, quickly. Run!'

As Panagiota sat down on the worn brown leather armchair he indicated, its straw stuffing rustled beneath her. Pavlo was running around the little room like an ant carrying food to its nest.

'Ah, *signomi*, Panagiota. My room is such a mess. If I had known you were coming... We can go out if you like. Shall we go down to the quay and drink some lemonade? Or what is the name of your fizzy drink – ginger beer?'

He looked with surprise and shame at the disorder of his desk – files piled on top of each other, overflowing ashtrays – as if seeing it for the first time.

'That won't be necessary. I came to speak to you about something.'

Pavlo had stacked the ashtrays one on top of the other and was carrying them out.

'Pavlo, would you sit down, *se parakalo*.'

He took the ashtrays out to the corridor, came back in, pulled the chair that was next to the door in front of Panagiota's armchair and sat down across from her, their knees almost touching. His milk-chocolate eyes with their puppy-dog expression widened in fear.

'Did you enjoy the theatre last night?'

When she didn't answer, the soldier's anxiety increased. Because Grocer Akis had not given his daughter permission to go to the cinema, on Katina's recommendation they had gone to a vaudeville performance by actors from Patra at the Phoenix Theatre. The actors did comic things, sang songs and danced. Pavlo had really wanted to laugh when Nilufer, the Egyptian dancer, sank the ship with her enormous hips, but seeing the serious set of Panagiota's beautiful profile, he had restrained himself.

After the performance, he had taken her home and then gone down to Great Taverns Street, where he met Niko. Only exaggerating a little bit, he had described what had passed between himself and Panagiota. What else could he have done? The fisherman's chubby son had described with such passion, giving unbelievable detail, his love scenes with his Turkish girl. Under the influence of *raki*, Pavlo might have slightly prolonged the kissing scene, added an episode in which he pinched Panagiota's breasts, and put a few passionate words into her mouth.

What if that crazy Niko had gone and made a snide remark to his perfectly innocent sweetheart? In the stuffy police station that smelled of stale cigarettes he anxiously took Panagiota's thin white hands into his thick bony ones. 'I am listening, Panagiota *mou*. What has happened?'

Not knowing how to begin, and just to say something, Panagiota grumbled, 'You've been telling everybody that you're going to marry me and take me to Ioannina to live with your mother! How dare you, *yia to Theo*? Why do you make up these lies?'

The young lieutenant's face darkened. It was as he had feared. Oh, that *raki*, it didn't just stay in the bottle! Why hadn't he kept his mouth shut? At the very first opportunity, he would shake down that idiot Niko. While these thoughts were passing through his mind, without realizing it, he'd been squeezing Panagiota's hands like a giant.

'Ouch, you're hurting me!'

Panagiota pulled back her hands and crossed her arms over her chest. What a peasant he was! One who knew only how to tend the earth and handle a hoe and a rake but not how to touch a lady, how to caress her. She recalled Avinash Pillai's plump purple lips. He had taken her wrist without her even realizing it, and how gently yet confidently his mouth had brushed her skin. His hands were as soft as if they'd come from a tin of butter. She turned her head and looked at the door behind her.

'It is not a lie, it is a dream, *agapi mou*, my love. You will marry me, won't you, *etsi*? Why do you look like that? After what passed between us last night, do not tell me that the possibility has not entered your head?'

To remind her of their kissing under the umbrella, he brought his face close to hers. Panagiota turned her eyes to the floor.

'Ah, what is the matter, Giota *mou*? I beg your pardon. I did not want to hurt you. Won't you just look at me? Are you crying?'

Panagiota shook her head.

Pavlo glanced into the corridor through the open door. There was no one there. He stood up, closed the door, brought his chair very close to the brown leather armchair, and, reaching out, tried ineptly to embrace Panagiota's slender body. Now they were practically sitting in each other's laps. Panagiota had covered her face with her hands, but she still slid forward in her seat and let herself fall into his arms. Although Pavlo didn't want to frighten her by squeezing her too hard, he was very aroused.

'*Agapi mou*, you do love me, do you not? What other reason could there be for your tears? Come, do not be shy. Tell me, *pes mou*.'

She remained motionless in his embrace.

'Panagiota, will you be my wife? Will you spend the rest of your life with me?'

The rigid body in Pavlo's arms suddenly began to shake. Panagiota was sobbing. Pavlo loosened his hands around her as if he was carrying a bell jar. What was he supposed to do now? He stared anxiously at the worn brown leather of the chair.

'Giota *mou*?'

Almost imperceptibly, she nodded her head.

'Do you mean "yes", Panagiota? Just raise your head and look at me. Come on.'

Reluctantly, Panagiota did so. Behind her thick wet lashes, violets were dancing in her tearful black eyes. Pavlo's heart was filled with joy. This most beautiful of all beauties would be his wife, the mother of his children, his mother's daughter-in-law!

'Panagiota, *pes mou*, tell me. Is it yes? *Ha, ne agapi?* Is it yes, my love?'

Panagiota nodded compliantly. Pavlo felt himself swell with pride and power. With this energy he could conquer not only Asia Minor but Constantinople itself, even the whole world! He removed his arms from around Panagiota, sat up straight in his chair and reached once more for her thin, white, long-fingered hands. If they hadn't been in the police station, he would have laughed out loud.

'My love, you have made me the happiest man in the world. I promise I will give you the life you desire. Whatever you desire. I will hire servants so that you never have to work. You will do only the things that you want to do. You will live like a queen, like a sultana... *Sultana mou, vasilisa mou*, my queen. You are my queen. Tell me, when should I speak to your father? Or should I speak to your mother first? Whichever is proper. Anyway, that's not the most important thing right now. Panagiota *mou*, you do love me, don't you?

Let me hear it from your beautiful lips just once. *Se parakalo.* Please.'

Panagiota managed to withdraw her hands from Pavlo's bony palms and wipe away her tears. 'I will marry you, Pavlo, but there is one condition.' Her nose was blocked.

'Of course, *sultana mou.* Ask whatever you wish.'

She sat upright and looked into Pavlo's milky brown eyes; the young lieutenant was jumping around like a colt.

'If the Holy Panagia, Mother Mary, protects us and we win the war – God willing – we will stay in Smyrna. We will live here. This is my country. I will give birth to my children and raise them here. Forget about Ioannina and buy me a house here.'

'If that is what you wish, that is the way it shall be, my Panagiota. From now on, you are my country. Whatever you—'

'I haven't finished what I wish to say.'

'Whatever.'

'However, if... *Theos filaksi*, God forbid...' She reached down and knocked her long fingers on the wooden desk behind Pavlo. 'If Kemal should enter Smyrna...'

'That cannot happen, my Panagiota. We are here for that very reason.' Pavlo stood up, smiled, strode confidently to the desk, selected a cigarette and walked over to the window. Lighting his cigarette, he turned to Panagiota. Under his white shirt, his chest was as strong and wide as that of a knight in armour.

'There is no need to fear, my love. There is not the slightest possibility that we will lose this war. We have many aeroplanes and thousands of machine guns, cannons, rifles and rounds of ammunition.'

Panagiota waved her arm in the air impatiently. 'I know,

I know. Everybody, everywhere – in the coffeehouses, at the bakery, at school – talks about how many weapons we have. We have them, but what are we doing with them? Ever since last August we've been waiting to hear news that we've been victorious, but the only thing we've heard is that we're in retreat.'

Pavlo drew on his cigarette, looked out the window, and spoke in a deep, authoritative voice.

'Retreating is a tactical manoeuvre, *yavri mou*. When we retreat, we do not lower our flag. On the contrary, we are blowing up the railway lines and bridges, and burning the villages that supply the gangs with food. Furthermore, we have succeeded in drawing all the weapons to the west of Sakarya. We haven't left the Turks so much as a sword.'

His sweaty forehead shone like brass in the light coming through the window. While he'd been speaking, Panagiota had come to his side. Not finding an ashtray, Pavlo extinguished his cigarette on the window sill and brought his lips close to her neck. Panagiota continued to look out the window.

'But, Panagiota, please forget about such things. What a happy day this is for us! Today you have become my fiancée – mine! I cannot believe my good fortune. Thank you, God!'

He turned her face towards him to kiss her.

Panagiota clasped her hands behind her like a child. 'Yes, we don't need to talk about the war now. I just want to make one thing clear. If we should lose the war and if the Turks should enter Smyrna...'

Leaving her at the window, Pavlo passed behind his desk, sat in his chair and leaned back, smiling.

'Why are you smiling like that? Am I telling you a fairy tale?'

'No, God forbid. But the situation you mention is so

impossible… Anyway, I'm not smiling at that. I'm smiling at your beauty and my happiness.'

Panagiota walked angrily to the desk, cleared a place for her hands amid the stacks of files and documents and leaned towards Pavlo, who was sprawled in his chair. She had rolled the sleeves of her blue cardigan up to her elbows. Her two thick plaits fell on the desktop like a pair of pendulums. With her eyes on the map on the wall behind him, she murmured, 'If we hear that the Turks are near, let's say…' She continued looking at the map. 'Let's say they get as near as Usak…'

'*Yavri mou*, how could they get to Usak? Usak is within our borders. We have borders that were sketched by a great international treaty. There are soldiers posted all the way along the Eskisehir–Afyonkarahisar line.'

There was no point in revealing to Panagiota that Usak was indeed within the Greek line of control, though in reality it had not been allocated to Greece by the Treaty of Sèvres.

She walked around the desk and came to stand in front of Pavlo. 'Do not go on, please. If the Turks do get to Usak, I want you to immediately send me and my family, along with all our valuable possessions, to Greece. That is all. That is my condition. Do you accept it?'

When Pavlo heard those words, the chair that he'd been rocking back and forth stopped with a thud. Without the squeak of the springs, the room filled with the shouts of children playing ball nearby.

'You want to go to Ioannina?' A grin that made him look quite ridiculous spread across his face. 'But a few minutes ago you said—'

Panagiota made clear her exasperation with a loud 'Oof!' How thick-headed this boy had turned out to be! Quite inappropriately, the image of Stavros's long thin fingers untying the ribbons of her dress came into her head. If they fled from Smyrna, would she ever see him again?

Will we ever be able to return to our homes, Adriana? Will we ever live peaceful lives again, as we did before the war? Will I live to see the beautiful day when I can put a ring on your finger?

Ah, Minas's letters… If only Adriana had never read them to her.

'If the Turks get as far as Usak, is what I said. Did you not hear me?'

'My dear child, I want to take you and your family to Ioannina more than anything. You know that. But you do not need to worry. Even if the Turks reach Usak, they will never enter Smyrna. You understand, right? Such a thing cannot happen.'

He had got up from the rocking chair and now stood directly in front of Panagiota. As they were about the same height, they were looking straight into each other's eyes. Panagiota was the first to glance away.

'Still, promise me, on your honour, that if the situation gets to that point, you will take us immediately to Greece.'

'I swear on my honour and on my land. At the first sign of danger, I will put you and your family on the first ship leaving for Greece and get you away from here. Is that enough? Will you now allow me to embrace you, my love?'

He grasped Panagiota by her shoulders, drew her towards him and wrapped his arms around her waist. The smell of jasmine rising from the neck of his beloved – My fiancée! he thought joyfully – almost caused him to faint. With the confidence of a man who had done his duty, he took her pale face between his palms, pressed his lips to hers and kissed her for a long time. Panagiota closed her eyes and thought of

337

Avinash Pillai's breath, which smelled of the spices of distant lands and of something else also.

'My darling love, my... I am going to make you so happy.'

While Pavlo's tongue was roving around incompetently in her mouth, his bony hands were sliding down from her neck, searching under her cardigan for her breasts. Panagiota was ashamed of her small breasts. She did not have a full bosom like her mother. She'd expected them to have grown by now, but it seemed that God had not treated her as generously as he had her mother when it came to breasts. Anxiously, she pushed Pavlo and moved away.

'What are you doing? We're at the police station and there's a gendarme standing guard at the door. Did you forget?'

As if Pavlo had truly just remembered where they were, he looked around in confusion. 'I beg your pardon. I forgot myself in my happiness. You are so very beautiful.'

Panagiota went round to the front of the desk, buttoned up her cardigan and pressed the short curls that had escaped her plaits behind her ears.

'All right, then. Since you have accepted my conditions, you may come tomorrow evening and ask my father for my hand. I hope you are not expecting much dowry. Around here it is the custom that the man's family buys and furnishes the house.'

Pavlo was so happy that he didn't register Panagiota's cold and calculating comments. The thought of never returning to Ioannina had burned his heart for a moment; he found himself almost wishing that the Turks would enter Smyrna, that being the only way he'd be able to take Panagiota to Ioannina. God forbid! How could he even think that? The love of Greater Greece surpassed all other loves.

He recalled the cherry-sherbet taste of Panagiota's lips.

What difference would it make which corner of the world he lived in as long as he could kiss those lips whenever he desired? And he might even get rich in Smyrna. Just let this war end and he would have the most beautiful wedding celebration. Then he'd earn some money and buy a house. Not in this miserable neighbourhood overlooking the dusty, smoky square but down in Bella Vista. He'd build a two-storey villa with a balcony and huge magnolia trees in the garden. He'd bring his mother and they would all get along together.

He was so lost in his dreams that he didn't even notice that Panagiota had left the police station.

The Last September

Even as the knocking at her door got louder, Midwife Meline remained asleep, immersed in that same familiar dream.

She was sitting on the back of a dun-coloured donkey, travelling along a village road with pomegranate trees and melon fields to either side. An elderly village man was leading her, walking with difficulty, holding the donkey's reins with one hand and leaning on his stick with the other. The stars, seen to their best advantage now that the moon had set, were scattered across the entire sky, from the mountain slopes to the dark sea. The baby in her arms was crying.

'*Daha mi lar bzdi.* Don't cry, little one. The darkness just before dawn is the darkest of the dark. Dawn will break soon and we will find a cart to take us to the city. *Daha mi lar bzdi.*'

From beneath her cloak she stuck her thumb into the tiny mouth. At first, thinking it had found a nipple, the baby was comforted, but when it realized that the skin in its mouth was dry, it again began fussing.

'Lady, we can stop and feed the baby if you like. See how hungry it is. It never stops screaming.'

'That won't be necessary. Keep going.'

The old villager shook his head from side to side and turned to face forward again. It took at least two hours to get from Bournabat to Smyrna by donkey.

When Meline finally opened her eyes and heard the knocking at her door, one hand involuntarily went to her chest in search of the velvet money bag she had hidden there seventeen years ago. Downstairs, someone was pounding on the door in a frenzy. She jumped off the bed, threw a shawl around her shoulders and hurried down the stairs in the pitch black, not even lighting a lamp.

Someone in the neighbourhood must have been having a difficult birth. The young midwives only came knocking at her door if there was an emergency. She had worked for years as the head midwife at the French Hospital and had trained the city's best midwives before retiring two years ago. The young ones were very respectful and would never wake her for a situation they could handle themselves, like a breech birth or the baby having the umbilical cord wrapped around its neck.

With these thoughts in her mind as she descended the stairs, when she opened the door she was stunned to see before her not a young midwife but her daughter, son-in-law and grandchildren. In their hands were suitcases and bundles. One of her hands flew to her mouth in fear. She scanned their faces one by one. Her youngest grandchild, Nishan, was not with them. 'What's happened?' she screamed. 'Where is Nishan?'

'Don't worry, Mama. Calm down. There's nothing to be alarmed about.'

'Nishan? What's happened to my Nishan?'

'Mama, dear, do not shout, please. You'll alert the neighbours. Nishan is with his other grandmother. Nothing has happened. We've come to get you.'

Midwife Meline's daughter interrupted her cool-headed husband. 'Do you know how long we've been knocking? You frightened us to death, Mama! Where were you?'

Meline put her hand on her heart to quieten it. 'I'd fallen asleep, child. Are all of you all right? What's happening?'

'How can you sleep at a time like this? Come, gather up your things – we're leaving. Bring all your valuables.'

Midwife Meline touched her chest again, as she had in her dream, checking on the imaginary money bag. That was where she'd kept the gold coins she had counted out into the hands of Mahmut Aga when she'd gone to see him, all by herself, at his castle-like mansion in Goztepe. A part of her consciousness was still there, on the donkey's back, reliving that morning.

She had gone all that way in order to get a document from the aga, who had set his sights on her daughters' honour because of a gambling debt incurred by her accursed husband. The officially stamped document testified that the debt had been paid in full. The aga's insolent henchmen had shamelessly suggested to Nishan (not her grandson Nishan but her husband) that he use the girls to settle his debt. Fresh young girls were always happily accepted into Mahmut Aga's harem.

Meline had obtained the aga's word that those despicable henchmen who had for months been frequenting her house, sticking their heads round the door and licking their lips as they watched Arpi and Seta doing their homework at the kitchen table, would never bother them again. Thank goodness, Mahmut Aga had shown himself to be an honourable man. Once the paper, which Meline did not understand a word of, had been officially stamped, he had kept his men away. The girls had gone on to make good marriages and have happy families.

By allowing herself to be a tool in Juliette Lamarck's demonic plan, Meline had saved her own daughters' lives.

'Mama, I'm telling you, come on. Are you not hearing me? Kemal's forces have taken Alasehir. Pehlivan's murderous gangs are on the way. We must hide. Come on, hurry! Collect up whatever you have; we're leaving. We're going to hide on the top floor of Hayguhi Hanim's bakery.'

Meline shook herself as if she were waking from a dream. 'Pehlivan's men are coming here? But what about the Greek line of defence?'

'Unfortunately,' her tall, slim son-in-law Arakel said softly, 'the Asia Minor defence line is crumbling. The Turks have taken all of the Menderes Valley. Aydin, Usak and Manisa are burning. As the Greek army retreats, they're setting everywhere on fire. We're afraid that when the Turks arrive here, they'll want to take revenge. As a precaution we've decided to hide in the attic of my mother's bakery. Because it's outside the Armenian district, we're guessing it will be safer. Don't leave anything valuable in the house. Collect all your money and your gold, and sew your jewellery into your dress. Are you able to walk as far as the quay? We may be able to find a carriage much sooner, near the cathedral.'

Meline nodded.

Suyane Street was dark and silent. Wouldn't it have been better to do as their neighbours had and just close the shutters and hide in their house? The bakery run by Hayguhi Hanim, her daughter's mother-in-law, was all the way over on the other side of the city, near the French Hospital. It would be no trouble to walk there – she wasn't that old yet. She was a woman who had walked long distances all her life, and at fifty-seven her legs were still as strong as they had been in her

DEFNE SUMAN

youth. But now, fear, like a wily snake that had been growing fat and strong in her intestines for years, had woken up and cut off her strength.

As they entered the courtyard of the cathedral to cross over to Dilber Street, Meline turned her face towards the dome of St Stepanos and said a prayer. Shadows were wandering about beneath the tall cypresses that filled the wide courtyard, and footsteps hurried in and out of the cathedral; people were carrying things inside. A couple pushing a covered wheelbarrow entered from the Suyane Street side. Seeing Meline and her family, they momentarily froze, until Arakel made a sign with his hand. They nodded and turned back to their work. The oldest grandchild, who was holding Meline's hand, spoke not a word. Arakel was carrying his sleepy younger daughter in one arm. Under his other arm he was carrying Meline's rug, which she couldn't bear to leave behind.

The group crossed the courtyard in silence, went out of the gate opening onto Iman Street, descended to the Agios Yorgis district, and continued from there to Great Taverns. Everywhere was smothered in darkness. Meline felt a current of electricity passing from the sweaty little hand of her granddaughter into her own body.

Further down, the port was buried in a deathly quiet. Seeing the docks so silent was terrifying – docks that were always busy with the chaos and confusion of shouting porters, trunks lined up all the way from the warehouses to the sea, sacks full of figs that stopped you from walking more than two steps, camels with little bells tied around their necks, donkeys, horses, carts, and merchants from every country. The moon had disappeared behind the clouds, and beneath the unlit gas lamps the dark, undulating sea seemed to echo the disquiet which had taken over the city that night. There was not a single carriage in sight.

Suddenly Meline's granddaughter squeezed her hand. 'Grandmamma, look! Look! Over there!'

Everyone turned towards where the little girl was pointing. Up ahead at Passport Pier, on the sea side of the road, there was a great dark mass of something, moving slightly. Meline narrowed her eyes to try and make it out. Arpi, used to taking charge, marched a few steps towards it. Her eyes began to distinguish some shapes – a trunk, a rolled-up carpet, a table, then bags, bundles. And lying down among all those possessions was a river of people.

'Grandmamma, who are they?' Her granddaughter's voice was shaking.

Meline slipped her hand out of the little girl's palm and made the sign of the cross. 'Dear Lord, protect us.'

'Grandmamma, what are all these people doing? Why are they camping on the quay?'

Arpi came over and took her daughter's hand.

'Mama?'

'Don't be afraid, darling. It's nothing. They have come from nearby villages and towns. They are refugees, escaping from the war. They left before the soldiers got to their villages.'

'Where will they go?'

'I don't know.'

It was the first time the little girl had ever seen adults in a desperate state. She began to cry.

Arakel spoke in a low voice so as not to wake the other child sleeping on his shoulder. 'Greece will send a ship for them and they'll get on it and sail to Chios. There's nothing to worry about. By tomorrow they'll all be gone.'

The question on everyone's mind but which no one wanted

to voice hung in the air until finally the little girl asked it. 'What about us?' she said tearfully. 'Will we be able to get on those ships too? Does Greece take Armenians?'

'Mama, if you are tired, shall we rest?' Even in the darkness, Arpi's normally shining face was noticeably pale, and her head was dipped. She tried to smile. 'What do you say, can you walk a little further? Grit your teeth – see, we're almost there.'

Midwife Meline was praying. She just nodded. Bad things, very bad things, were going to happen.

They had reached the dark mass, which swelled like a huge wave to their left. Old people, women, children, men – hundreds of people were sitting, lying down, crying silently, moaning, gnawing on dry crackers with empty eyes, rocking their babies and speaking in low voices. Horses, donkeys, goats, cats and dogs wandered among them. They were all bunched close together, staring at the sea, a mixture of horror, sadness and hope on their faces.

Suddenly something moved in the crowd. In the darkness a young man with a cap on his head and tattered shoes on his feet jumped out into the middle of the road.

'Baby! The baby is coming! Help! My wife's pains have begun. Somebody help!'

Meline automatically jerked her hand from her grand-daughter's tiny warm palm. Arpi and Arakel straightaway moved to block her path. 'Mama, no!'

In one breath Meline shed her exhaustion and became once more the hawk-like midwife of old. She spoke to her daughter in a tone of voice Arpi remembered from her childhood. 'You must all carry on. I will find you at Hayguhi's Bakery.'

Striding towards the dark crowd, she vaguely heard her daughter's protests, her granddaughter's cries. As she walked, she was calculating. The French Hospital was too far away. Grace's Maternity House was even further. The Dutch and Austrian Hospitals and Agios Charalambos were all fairly near; they could reach one of them.

She caught the man with the cap by his arm. 'Young man, you must run and find a cart. I'm a midwife. There are hospitals back over there – hurry and let's get your wife there in time.'

The young man took his cap in his hand and bowed his head. 'Mother, I do not know how to find a cart in the city. Couldn't we put my wife on the donkey we came on from the village?'

'Impossible, son! Go on – run. It's not as if you're in a foreign country. Go and find a driver.'

As he disappeared into the dark streets, hands and arms bundled Meline to the side of the pregnant woman. She was lying on an old rug that had come all the way from her single-windowed village hut to Smyrna's quay. The shoes lined up along the edge of the rug conveyed a feeling of home to the people camped out on the dock. In the centre of the rug a single kerosene lantern was burning.

The pregnant woman was on her hands and knees. Those around her were wiping her forehead and neck with handkerchiefs wetted with sea water. Seeing Meline, they stepped back to the edge of the rug. There was something in the woman's manner, her attitude, that reminded them of the midwives in the village. Meline knelt beside the mother. She was a village girl, with big black eyes and dark skin. Under her dark red shirt with the sleeves rolled up to the elbow her arms were full and strong.

'Be calm, daughter. You are young and sturdy. You will push your infant out in one breath. What is your name?'

'Eleni.' Without wanting to, the poor girl screamed. Ashamed, she turned her head away.

'*Endaksi*, Eleni, my girl. All right. Your husband has gone to find a cart. We will take you to a hospital. Now, tell me, is this your first birth?'

With her head, the woman indicated a boy with huge black eyes sucking his thumb at the far edge of the rug. He was sitting there bare-bottomed. Meline put her hand under the woman's skirt to measure the dilation of the cervix; her fingers touched the hair on the head of the baby. The birthing had begun. She raised her eyes anxiously and looked at the crowd of barefooted women encircling them.

'Ladies, prepare yourselves. The baby is coming! May God help us. She'll have the baby here. Quickly, bring all the lamps, lanterns and candles you can find.'

Within moments, the women had all knelt down in their patched skirts and surrounded Eleni.

Meline took control. 'Hold her behind the knees and pull back hard. Bring the lamp closer; hold it so that there are no shadows. That's good. Eleni, come on, girl, push. Push as hard as you can. You've swum and swum and come to the end.'

The young woman gave a piercing shriek. The crowd undulated with her scream and contracted as everyone moved closer together.

'What's happened? Have they come – the soldiers?'

On the shore of that dark sea, in the midst of thousands of poor people who'd been forced to abandon their towns and their homes, Meline pushed one hand down on the woman's belly and plunged the other between her legs. While her hands worked independently with all the skill which a lifetime of experience had given them, a different scene was playing out in her imagination.

'The baby will be born dead, do you understand me, Midwife Meline?'

It was Juliette Lamarck's shrill, commanding voice.

'Did you hear me? It will be born dead. We will bury it in the church graveyard, and we will never see you again. Do you understand? *Tu comprends?*'

But no. The baby had clung to life. Life wanted to live. The tiny head had opened a way through the mouth of the cervix and pushed forward with all its might. The poor mother, just a child herself, had fainted from the opium and was not pushing her baby out. Meline had pressed on the girl's stomach, then rushed between her legs.

On the rug on the quay, a thick, sticky fluid was flowing from between Eleni's legs.

Edith's white sheet had been a lake of blood.

This was not a job that could be done alone. 'Help me, ladies!'

Midwife Meline's consciousness flitted between the present and the past. Images from the past merged with the salt-smelling night.

The village girl's baby had to live.

Edith's baby had to be born dead.

The women on the quay, old and young, rushed to help.

In the Lamarck mansion, she'd been all alone on the top floor. The servants weren't even aware that Edith was living in the turret. Juliette Lamarck had locked her daughter up there. Because she'd spent the last months of her pregnancy lying flat in her bed, young Edith's legs had no strength.

'Oh, my God! They're both going to die!'

The women were shouting.

No, Edith would not die. That was the agreement. The baby would die. The mother would live.

'I want my own daughter safe and sound. Do you understand me, Midwife? Next week she must be back on her feet and mixing with people. This scandal must end here. No one else will know except the two of us. Otherwise...'

Juliette shook the wine-red money bag hanging around her neck. Gold coins rattled inside.

'Otherwise, prepare your daughters for sex with Mahmut Aga's henchmen. They are insatiable, I tell you, Midwife! Why are you staring at me so stupidly? Roll up your sleeves and get to work. You are an experienced midwife. No doubt you know how babies die in a delivery. Find a way. I shall be waiting downstairs.' Meline caught the baby in the air. The women all made the sign of the cross and shouted in unison, '*Ena koritsi, ena koritsi!* A girl child! Eleni, your daughter has been born! Congratulations! Ah, *Panagia mou*, dear Mother Mary, how tiny! *Mikroula*.'

She placed the tiny girl on her mother's bare breast. Young Eleni was smiling as best she could from where she lay. There were no scissors to cut the umbilical cord. It didn't matter. It could wait. The umbilical cord, beating like a heart in between the two beings, lay like a snake from the woman's stomach to her breast. Just long enough to reach the nipple. Almighty God planned everything perfectly; the umbilical cord was exactly long enough to reach the nipple.

The baby's cries brought brief smiles to some of the faces in the crowd. Men, women and children who just yesterday had left their fertile villages and the bones of their ancestors gathered round the rug to see the tiny new arrival. The old women moved their lips; the men craned their necks to observe the intimate scene from a distance as they rolled their cigarettes and exhaled smoke into air that was filled with alien smells.

Hope spread through the quay. *Mana Ellas*, Mother Greece, would send ships tomorrow to save her children!

A young man took the mandolin he'd brought with him out of its black case. The baby, having found her mother's nipple, ceased her crying. With the birth of Eleni's daughter, the crowd had become one family. They embraced each other; they were all victims of the same sad fate. As yet they had no idea that over the coming days their number would swell by three or four times, all of them squeezed between life and death.

Exhausted, Meline collapsed onto the rug. The women ran to bring her water and she closed her eyes. Edith's infant appeared in her mind. Its face was purple and it was making no sound. Had it died? Edith's pulse was very weak. Wrapping the baby in a blanket, she placed it on the bed behind her and sewed up the tears in Edith's flesh. When the beating stopped, she cut the umbilical cord. The girl's lips were parted, her head had fallen to one side, her hair was stuck to her sweaty chest, her breasts, full of milk, spilled over from her nightgown's frilly neckline. The baby's tiny lips were searching in vain for a nipple; she had a bright red mouth and, just like her mother and her grandfather from Athens, she had curly black hair. Juliette Lamarck's sin had produced another fruit. Eh, dear God, what you are capable of!

Juliette Lamarck's footsteps on the stairs.

In her hand a moneybag full of gold coins.

She looked at the baby; looked and in one glance realized it was alive. It was supposed to be born dead. Recalling their agreement...

So be it. She replaced the moneybag around her own neck. Meline threw herself on the floor, covering the woman's feet.

'Madame Lamarck, I beg you! Madame Lamarck, I

kiss your feet. Please have mercy. If I do not pay our debt, tomorrow morning the aga's men will come for my daughters. Look, your daughter is alive. I saved her life. She was weak, I revived her. Madame Lamarck, I beg you, have pity on my children.'

'This was not our agreement.'

A hand on her shoulder. She turned and looked. She was still on the quay. The pregnant woman's husband had come. He kneeled beside her, twisting his cap in his hands.

'Mother, are you okay? Look, I found a carriage, but we don't need it any more. You brought my daughter into the world. May the Lord Jesus bless you. May Panagia the Virgin Mary bless you, your grandchildren and the children of your grandchildren. Come, *pedia*, boys, let's give our mother midwife a hand, let's help her into this carriage.'

Hands from the crowd – hard hands with calluses; rough hands that had known grapes and figs and earth – carried Meline to the carriage and sat her down on its red velvet seat. The coachman urged his horses forwards and their shoes clattered across the cobblestones. In the darkness behind the carriage, hands rose all at the same moment, like birds taking to the air. The village bade farewell to the midwife who had brought them together as a family.

'May Holy Panagia protect you, Midwife Mother. Tomorrow we go to Greece. Stay safe here. May God help you.'

Towards Punta, the quay regained its usual calm, fashionable atmosphere. Fishermen with fishing lines and nets in their hands walked slowly to their colourful boats.

Dawn was about to break.

Behind the fishermen, small groups of villagers who'd been walking all night were making their way down to the docks. Most of them were seeing the sea for the first time in their lives. Placing their suitcases, trunks and bundles on the ground, they stared at the European ships anchored in front of them; this was the image that had filled their imaginations as they'd walked, giving them strength through the torturous journey.

'We are saved,' they were thinking. 'Mother Greece, *Mana Ellas*, will send her ships and tomorrow they will take us away.' For a moment they forgot the horrifying sight of their neighbours' villages being burned to the ground.

'We are saved!'

From within the carriage, Meline watched the scene around her as if it were a silent film. Her heart tightened. What would happen to her and her family, the Armenians of Smyrna? She tried to take comfort from the tiny little lights of the European fleets anchored out beyond the harbour. British, American, French and Italian battleships – Allies waiting to protect their own citizens. Since it was those Europeans who were responsible for the whole catastrophe, it was their duty to protect the city's Christians, was it not? No, nothing bad would happen to them. They'd been living in Smyrna for so many generations. She rested her head on the back of the seat. The horses were breathing heavily. The coachman urged them on.

Everything as it was in the past.

Let the ships come and take those poor, miserable wretches away; then their dear Smyrna would return to its old self again. To the squeaking of the carriage's wooden wheels and the rhythmic tossing from left to right, Meline closed her eyes.

'Madame Juliette, I beg you, listen to me. I know how we can keep our agreement. You will tell Edith, "The baby was born dead." You will say we buried it. I swear to you on my honour, on the souls of my children, that our secret will go with me to my grave. I beg you, Madame Lamarck, do not plunge yourself and me into sin. Do not make me take a life that God has spared. I promise you, you will never again have cause to think of this baby. Trust me. Let me set out now, before daybreak, with the baby. Please allow me to do this. The baby will be dead to you.'

That night, as she travelled to Smyrna on the back of a donkey, the sky was just as it was now, like a purple blanket covering the city. What a hot and humid September night it had been. So hot that even the morning breeze had carried the scent of jasmine from Bournabat to the city.

Meline raised her head from the red velvet seat of the carriage rattling over the cobblestones of the quay and smelled the air.

What day was it today?

Thursday.

What was the date?

All at once she understood why that piece of the past which had burned in her conscience for many years had appeared in her heart tonight of all nights.

This night was that night. The night joining the sixth of September to the seventh.

If by chance the poor thing had lived, Edith's daughter would have been completing her seventeenth year today.

Vasili Street

As the carriage carrying Midwife Meline was slowing to a halt in front of Hayguhi Hanim's bakery, Edith was looking down from the window of her bedroom onto the garden turning pink in the first light of dawn.

That day had come around again. No matter how much hashish she smoked or how many secret ingredients Gypsy Yasemin added to it, whenever this date came around, that long-ago memory returned, like the sun shining through fog. That poor infant. Edith had never even held it in her arms. It didn't have a grave because it was never baptized; it would have been buried anonymously in a mass grave in the churchyard. Edith remembers the difficult birth from behind a curtain of opium. She'd not had another child, and the absence of that child pricked her heart like a thorn every September. It angered her that motherhood had been stolen from her.

She leaned out of the window that overlooked the street. Flocks of families, villagers carrying suitcases, bags and bundles, were still streaming past the house. Some of the women wore trousers, some were wrapped in colourful fabric, and some were enveloped in black robes like Muslim women.

Almost every woman had at least two children hanging onto her skirt. Many had babies tied to their backs.

Some of the villagers, on seeing that other evacuees had set up camp in Edith's garden, shoved open the wrought-iron gate, decorated with a leaf design, that Christo had padlocked the evening before, and tried to enter. There were women, children and old people curled up everywhere in the garden. Many of them were asleep on bedspreads and rugs that they'd carried from their village homes and that were now laid out around Edith's stone pool with its waterspout in the shape of a lion's mouth, under the fruit trees, even in her flowerbeds.

The previous morning, when Edith had woken to this scene beneath her bedroom window, she hadn't been able to believe her eyes.

A column of people was flowing down Vasili Street towards the sea in ghostly silence, listless, endless. At first it was the sight of the soldiers that struck her. Thousands of Greek soldiers, their feet bare, their bodies wounded, heads wrapped in bloody bandages, bent over, their ribs showing beneath torn shirts, their hands and faces black with soot, not even bothering to pick up rifles that had fallen to the ground. They shuffled like sleepwalkers towards the sea, towards ships which would take them away from defeat and disaster and back to their homeland. Some had open wounds soaking the sleeves of their coats red, others could not walk a single step without the support of fellow soldiers. It was clear that on the other side of the mountains, in the barren lands of Asia Minor, the Greek army had suffered a great defeat. Those who had survived had made it this far.

Joining the soldiers on their wretched walk were Greeks and Armenians who'd fled their villages. Hearing that the approaching Turkish army was set on massacring the entire

Christian population of western Asia Minor in revenge, they had set out, fearing for their lives. Children clung to their mothers with eyes wide from the terror they'd witnessed along the way; big strong men sobbed at every step; old women were carried on the backs of boys no taller than them; elderly grandfathers with glassy eyes rode on donkeys. In among them were dogs, goats with bells tied around their necks, dilapidated oxcarts carrying a family's worldly goods. Everything passed under Edith's window in horrifying silence.

How had the powerful Greek army of 200,000 soldiers been reduced to this? Such was the relaxed tempo of life in the city, made even more beautiful in the autumn light, that no one around Edith had given much attention to the war, for it had not been sufficient to distract them from the daily pleasures that gave their lives meaning. As they strolled along the quay at sunset or sat in cafés or beer halls, Smyrna's residents, when discussing the war, never mentioned the possibility of such a monumental, crushing defeat. Even the news that Mustafa Kemal's forces were nearing the Mediterranean was passed over indifferently in the cafés as rumour with no basis in reality, gossip not in harmony with truth.

Furthermore, the Greek newspapers were filled with good news from the front. Retreat was merely a strategic tactic. A great victory had been achieved at Afyonkarahisar. The army would not stop until Constantinople had been taken. No one was aware that the soldiers sent to Constantinople had returned to Smyrna long ago, or that, because they had not wanted to come into Smyrna itself, they were now on ships anchored beyond the harbour, waiting to return to Greece.

There was such an enormous gap between what was whispered from person to person and then forgotten amid the milky tea and biscuit crumbs at the quay and the scene she saw beneath her window that Edith was eager to find out more. With Zoe's help, she dressed quickly and hurried out into the garden. Even at that early hour of the morning, the weather was hellishly hot and extremely humid. Opening her parasol, she walked up to the wrought-iron gate that opened onto the street. Seeing her approach, a group of women began to flow towards the gate, like a river finding a new course.

'Where are you going?'

'We do not know.'

'Where will you stay?'

'We do not know.'

'What happened to your villages?'

Silence. A thick, hot silence full of suppressed tears, ready to burst with a scream.

A young woman with a black headscarf came through the crowd and approached the gate where Edith stood.

'My lady, three days and three nights we've been walking. Look at me – I walked here from Bursa with my babies. Just let us catch our breath in your garden. Take pity on us; let us eat two bites of your bread.'

Her eyes were red from crying. Her children, a boy and a girl, were hiding under the skirt of her torn dress, which was the colour of dust. From under their mother's legs they were eyeing Edith's pink parasol. The woman stuck her hands through the iron bars of the gate – joints swollen, skin blackened – and grabbed hold of Edith's skirt.

'I do not know where my husband is. The Turks captured my brother in Afyonkarahisar. I had to leave my mother and father on the road. Their feet had become open sores, their shoes were torn to pieces and they couldn't endure the thirst. They set me free. "Take your children and go," they said. And I, my lady—'

Edith opened her gate wide. The crowd out on the street responded immediately and within moments was snaking its way into the garden of Number 7, Vasili Street. Edith ordered the servant girls and Butler Christo to give the refugees water, bread, cheese and grapes. She commanded that a pot of rice and beans be cooked and everyone fed.

Seeing the crowd of people pushing and shoving as they struggled to get themselves inside, Christo decided to say something to Edith, even though he knew it would make her angry. 'Mademoiselle Lamarck,' he murmured, 'we must close the gates now. We cannot look after any more people. You know best, of course, but for the safety of ourselves and the people already inside, we must put a lock on the entrance.'

He was right. After just ten minutes there was not even enough space to stand a chair in Edith's garden.

'Very well. You may lock the gate, but if someone comes seeking refuge you must open it and feed them. Are we agreed? Zoe, go to the market. Buy several sacks of flour, wheat, barley, lentils and dried beans. Hire a cart and a porter to carry it all. Then come directly back and get to work in the kitchen. If we do not have enough pots, tell Christo to go to the coppersmith and buy more. If necessary, you can light a fire in the garden. I shall go now and fetch a doctor to care for the sick and the wounded, and to apply ointment. One of you go and tell the midwives at the French Hospital that there are many women here with bellies swollen up to their noses. When I return, I shall help you all. Come, hurry. We have much work to do.'

It was now the following morning, and as she stared down at her garden full of villagers tucked into every nook and cranny, she felt exhausted but happier than she had in her entire life. An old man was leaning over the stone pool to wash his face. She would get a temporary toilet constructed in the back garden, behind the wood and coal shed perhaps. How long would they stay, she wondered. Who would rescue these poor people and how?

She was grateful for having been blessed with the good fortune and affluence that made it possible to help these poor, miserable souls. It was as if, after long years of not even knowing how hungry she was, someone had put a bowl of food in front of her; only now did she understand the real meaning of hunger and satiation. She felt so satisfied inside. It was how she imagined motherhood must feel – tiring but gratifying. When she recalled what date it was, as she somehow did each year like a precision clock, for the first time ever, she did not feel angry.

If the poor thing had lived, it would have completed its seventeenth year today.

When she left the house and turned onto Aliotti Boulevard she saw that not only her own garden but also the courtyards of the churches and hospitals, the bazaars, the inns, the hotels and the stations were filled with refugees. There was no end to the human flood pouring into the city from every direction. Several foreigners had locked their doors and left the city, but there were many families who had done as she had and invited refugees into their gardens.

The boulevard's wealthiest residents had hung British, French, Italian or American flags from the gates of their mansions. She would have to send Christo out to find a French flag as soon as possible. Or Zoe could quickly sew one. If Edith had been on her own, it would never have crossed her mind to be so patriotic, but there were now at least a hundred people whom she was protecting on her property. Looters would never dare break into a residence occupied by French citizens.

Hopefully.

At the corner by the French Hospital a shirtless Greek soldier was carrying a wounded comrade on his back. Although it was not her custom, Edith made the sign of the cross.

She could not believe what she was seeing when she got to the quay. The waterfront, normally impassable because of all the trunks and bundles, and camels foaming at the mouth, was now filled with people from one end to the other. Among the soldiers – barefooted and wounded, some of them armless or legless, most of them with vacant stares – were thousands of women, children and old people lying, sitting, crying silently, rocking their babies, talking. They were all looking out at the sea.

One of the Greek ships that had come to evacuate the luckless soldiers was just departing from the wooden dock at Punta; another was approaching to take its place. Desperate villagers were trying in vain to exchange their most precious possessions, brought with them all the way to Smyrna, for a small corner on one of the ships; they offered their women's jewellery, even the gold in their teeth, but every request was rejected, without exception. The captains of the Greek ships were hitting and kicking the civilians who'd managed to get on board; they pushed the stowaways they found in the engine room back onto shore and threatened to throw those who resisted into the sea. The army had to be demobilized first. Other ships would come for the civilians. Fishermen, not wanting to miss an opportunity, had pulled in close to the shore where the villagers were camped and had already begun bargaining.

Despite the refugees sprawled on the ground, the quay, by contrast, was its usual lively self. Ladies were twirling their colourful parasols and music swelled from the cafés. Young American sailors, who had not the slightest idea why they were there, were sitting on chairs brought outside from the bars and staring in wonder at the women and young girls passing in front of them.

Avinash and Edith had made plans to go to the new film at the Théâtre de Smyrne that night. From the crowd gathered in front of the entrance, it seemed there'd been no change to the programme, but Edith was taking her new responsibilities seriously and felt that she should not attend. She could not desert all those people sheltering in her garden. Her heart again filled with compassion.

Avinash looked exhausted. Edith guessed that he'd had a sleepless night. Things must have been very busy on that top-secret floor at the consulate that had been appropriated by the Allied spies. He was distracted and uneasy. He said nothing as he ate the potato salad served with his beer, pausing a long time between mouthfuls. Even though he was clearly preoccupied, Edith couldn't resist telling him about the thrilling events of the previous day – the refugee camp in her garden, what the villagers had said to each other. She spoke excitedly as she threw the fried sardines, head, tails, bones and all, into her mouth.

'I've held more babies in my arms in one day than I have in my whole life. I wouldn't have believed it, Avinash! Zoe and I even washed their bottoms with water we drew from the well. And that's not all! One poor man had cut his leg with a rusty piece of iron and I helped the doctor treat it. Then do you know what Dr Arnott said to me? He said, "You will manage the rest of them, Mademoiselle Lamarck."

I cleaned and bandaged the wounds of several women and one young boy. You see, *mon cher*, I have become a nurse.'

With a weary smile, Avinash looked into his lover's black eyes. They were burning brightly, reminiscent of her younger years. Her pink cheeks were framed by curls of grey. As if reluctant to dispel her joy, he spoke quietly in reply.

'My dear Edith, the situation is extremely dire.'

'Yes, indeed. That is obvious.' She gestured at the barefooted soldiers limping towards the ships.

They were sitting outside at Café Ivi, taking advantage of the warm and sunny September weather.

'What we are seeing is only the tip of the iceberg. Edith, it is very bad; an enormous catastrophe may be about to engulf us. The information sent to us by our agents in the interior is not promising. The American ambassador in Istanbul thinks that the Turks could wreak havoc in Smyrna as a way of celebrating their victory. He sent a telegram to the consulate saying that the British generals must act immediately to protect the city's Christians.'

'And what do your people say? For example, that old drunk, Maximilian Lloyd?'

Avinash shook his head in displeasure. Edith had never forgotten that the man had made a pass at her, years ago, at Juliette's dinner table.

'Our people don't seem to be listening to Morgenthau's words.'

Edith was surprised. 'But the consulate formally declared that the Christian population of Smyrna would be one hundred per cent safe. One of your admirals – he had a very ostentatious name, which I can't remember now – sent that assurance to all the newspapers, via a British preacher. As

I recall, it was only the American Consulate that made no promises. Or have I remembered this incorrectly? What was that admiral's name?'

Avinash sighed. 'You've remembered correctly. Sir Osmond de Beauvoir Brock declared it. But still—'

'Ha, ha, ha. Just listen to that showy name and then see if you believe his words! Don't worry, my love, I read in the morning paper that Mustafa Kemal has decreed that any soldier who so much as touches a hair on the head of any civilian in Smyrna will be sentenced to death. If you don't believe Brock, believe Kemal Pasha. Not a thing will happen. Look over there.' She waved her fork towards the sea. 'I just counted them. There are nineteen battleships anchored in the bay. All with the Allied forces. And look, there's another one arriving – where's that one from?'

Avinash narrowed his eyes – eyes that Edith likened to those sweets that tasted of milky coffee – and looked at the ship that was coming into the harbour right across from them.

'It's the USS *Litchfield*, I think. American. Bringing Admiral Bristol, perhaps.'

After a short silence, he turned to Edith. 'With the situation as it is, I would advise—'

Edith knew what he was going to say. Because her mouth was full, she could only shake her head. Kraemer's chef, Pavli, had cooked up yet another masterpiece. The sardines melted in her mouth. She waited until she'd swallowed the whole fish before speaking.

'I'm not going anywhere, Avinash. Don't waste your breath. Particularly now, with all those sad unfortunates in my garden. I'm not going to go scurrying here and there. I cannot.'

Avinash wiped his mouth with the linen napkin. He knew

there was no point arguing with Edith. 'I'm not saying that. You should stay here, I agree; and I am here anyway. I was thinking not of you but of your mother.'

Edith raised her eyebrows over the giant beer mug. A moustache of foam had settled above her red lips. 'What were you thinking concerning my mother?'

'I don't know if you are aware, but the British have closed up their houses. Some of them are on the British ship *Thalia*, which is being used both as a refuge and a hospital, and some have moved into their winter homes in Smyrna.'

Edith sensed where Avinash's words were leading, but she continued to listen without speaking.

'Bournabat is deserted. Without your brother Jean-Pierre there, it is not safe for a woman of her age to remain there all alone.'

'What do you mean, Bournabat is deserted? Has everyone left – including the Thomas-Cooks?' Edith laid her fork down beside her plate and turned to Avinash as she challenged him. 'Don't tell me that Edward abandoned his house because he believed some rumours?'

Avinash sat there twisting his moustache and looking at two young girls who were walking past them, happily licking their ice creams. As if he'd just remembered something, he suddenly rose from his chair, but then immediately sat down again.

Edith looked to see what had attracted her lover's attention. 'What's up?' she asked with her customary sarcasm. 'Do you know those girls? They're very young, very pretty in their blues and pinks.'

'No, I do not know them.' In distracted silence he rolled a cigarette and licked the paper. 'Bournabat is not completely empty,' he said, 'but that does not mean that your mother is safe there on her own. True, Edward is still there. His mother and brothers moved to their homes in the city long ago, but he stayed. Because of that, I am obliged to go there in person and speak to him very soon, at the request of our consul general. We are issuing travel passes to all British citizens so that they can leave the country. Edward's is still not completed. If he cannot prove that he is British, he could get stuck here.'

'What does Edward have that is British except his name?' said Edith with a careless smile. 'Ah, of course, he has his latest-model motor cars...' She realized with surprise that this was the first time in years that her heart had not constricted at the thought of Edward's cars.

'We spent the whole of last night printing passports, Edith. There are so many people like Edward in Smyrna, you wouldn't believe it. British citizens who have never in their lives set foot in Britain. Edward is one of them – he's never even been to the consulate. Which is why I have to go to him; not because I adore your childhood friend but because it's an order from the Consul General. Should we need to organise an emergency evacuation of all our citizens, they must all be in possession of the requisite travel documents.'

'The French Consulate hasn't issued any such warning. Nobody has said, "Leave Bournabat," or anything like that. I think your consul general is exaggerating a bit. The only thing I've heard is that Admiral Dumesnil said he would intervene if Greek soldiers tried to burn or loot the city. If that happens, he'll prevent the Greek repatriation ships from leaving the harbour until the Turks arrive. I think your people are just acting like heroes out of spite.'

Then, abruptly, she said, 'Anyway, forget about that for now. I was going to go to Bournabat today, to pay my mother a teatime visit. Let's go together. Seeing as your consul general has given you his motor car, it'll be a breeze. Maybe we could stop for a picnic on the way.'

When she saw how Avinash's face darkened at this, she regretted her flippancy. She wouldn't leave the refugees in her garden anyway, and they'd taken into the house a woman who had just given birth, and her baby. But she couldn't help how she felt. In spite of Avinash's dire predictions and the heartbreaking flood of desperate villagers into the city, she had never felt so strong and content. Was this what it meant to be happy?

Suddenly there was a clamour from the crowds in the port area. Some people were clapping, others were booing.

'What's happening?'

Avinash stood up and, taking a pair of gold-plated opera glasses from his waistcoat pocket, looked towards the port.

'It's Stergiadis. High Commissioner Stergiadis is leaving the city. People are jeering at him. Even from this distance it's obvious how broken he is. He's aged such a lot in the last couple of days – he looks ten years older.'

Lowering his opera glasses, he sat down, his face gloomy. 'What a shame – a great shame.' He sighed. 'Stergiadis was such a fair, honest and highly respected man; he could have been of enormous benefit to Smyrna. He had so many wonderful plans for our city. He was building the world's largest university, a university that was to be open to all nations and races, to women as well as men, and teaching was due to start next month. What a shame!'

He looked as if he might cry if she touched him. Edith knew how important this university project had been to her spy-lover. Last winter he had met with Stergiadis to discuss bringing scholarship students from India to the university.

The meeting had gone well, and Ionia University's first Indian students had been due to arrive in Smyrna in 1923. Now all of those dreams and plans had been shelved. With Stergiadis and his Greek administration withdrawing from the city, the future of the university open to all nations and races, like the future of the refugees camped on the quay, was now in the hands of fate.

'Avinash,' Edith said, reached out to take his hand, 'just now I made a tasteless joke quite inappropriate to the seriousness of the situation. Please forgive me.'

Avinash paused for a moment, trying to remember what they'd been talking about before Stergiadis appeared. Oh, yes. The motor car and the picnic.

'How were you thinking of getting to Bournabat?'

'By commuter train, of course. Why?'

'Darling Edith, you really have no idea, do you? Did you not know that Hadjianestis, nicknamed "Batty"', has been made head of the Greek armed forces and that for a week now trains have been carrying nobody but soldiers and the wounded. Why do you think all these poor wretches have been streaming in on the backs of donkeys, in oxcarts and on foot? All public vehicles have been commandeered to evacuate the Greek army before the Turks reach Smyrna. There's no chance of a place on a train for you or even for those desperate refugees in your garden, my girl. It's time you opened your eyes!'

Edith was just about to tell him that she'd decided not to go to the cinema that evening when something distracted her. An officer was bidding farewell to his young Smyrna sweetheart. With his neatly ironed uniform, polished boots and slicked-back chestnut hair, he stood out from the pitiful soldiers around him. His girl had black curly hair that tumbled down her back and Edith realized that she was one of the blue and pink girls who'd passed them earlier, eating ice cream. She couldn't see the girl's face, but her pink satin shoes with worn toes had caught her attention. The young officer's face, round and sweaty, was turned towards Edith. His forehead shone like a mirror. He'd taken the girl's hands in his palms. It must have been because he was trying to say so much in such a short time that he was speaking so fast, as if there were horses chasing after him. He kept glancing over his shoulder, towards Punta; he could not miss the ship that was to carry him back to his homeland.

From her seat outside Café Ivi, Edith couldn't take her eyes off the touching and rather strange goodbye she was witnessing. Avinash had gone inside to say hello to someone from the consulate.

The young lieutenant took the girl by her shoulders and drew her to him, burying his face in her hair. They stayed like that for a time. In his neatly pressed khaki uniform, he looked strikingly clean, strong and healthy. He had to be one of those lucky officers who'd been left in the city rather than being sent to Asia Minor. As they parted, he wiped the tears, which he hadn't bothered to hide, from his cheeks.

Edith felt an irresistible urge to see the girl's face. She waited for a horse-drawn tram to pass, then stood up and picked up the parasol she'd hung over the back of the chair. She was just taking a step towards the parting couple when all at once the quay began to move.

Another ship was departing. The barefooted soldiers who'd just arrived at the dock dropped their rifles to the ground and with one last spurt of energy rushed ahead, racing towards Punta through the throng of camels, porters, refugees and fashionable ladies. The young officer released the girl's hands, glanced at the disorder around them with a desperate expression on his face, whispered something in his sweetheart's ear and then quickly joined the herd of soldiers flowing forwards. As he was dragged along by the crowd, he turned one last time, jumped up, pointed at something in the sea, waved his cape in the air, and disappeared from sight.

Avinash appeared at Edith's side, his round face full of anxiety.

'Edith *mou*, the gangs congregating in the mountains are taking advantage of the chaos and are about to come down and raid Bournabat. I have this from a reliable source. I will go at once to fetch your mother. Please stay at home tonight – don't go anywhere.'

'But...' Something had stuck in her mind, but as she tried to recall it, it eluded her, like a dream that faded in and out. She couldn't even remember what it concerned. A strange, strange thing, but what was it?

'Edith, listen. When the Greek soldiers here were retreating from Afyonkarahisar, they burned all the villages, looted the houses, raped the women, filled the mosques with men and set fire to them. They nailed girl children to crosses and hung them from trees in the village squares. If Asia Minor wasn't going to be theirs, they vowed to leave only ghosts behind. I don't tell you these details to upset you, but you must know that we are now in real danger. Go immediately to the French Consulate and obtain passports for you and your mother. Then return home, close the doors and padlock them. Do not take new people into your garden. I will bring your mother to your home. Send a telegram to Jean-Pierre. He should bring his family from their summer place in Foca and return immediately. Get in touch with your sister too. It would be better if they came here from Boudja too.'

Avinash's voice was harsher and more authoritative than she'd ever heard it. Without even opening her parasol, she set out for the French Consulate with hurried steps. In disregard of all the fear and agitation below, the sun was caressing the quay and its blue waters with a golden light. The mischievous wind was slipping between her legs and puffing up her chiffon skirt like a balloon. With her free hand, she held on to her hat so that it wouldn't blow away. Her stomach, full of Pavli's sardines, was beginning to ache from within the hooks of her tight corset. A group of young girls in colourful dresses passed her, their gaze distracted. Uneasiness hung in the air. In the seclusion of an empty building, hair and moustache entangled, a young soldier dressed like a vagabond and a curly-haired blonde woman were locked in an embrace, weeping silently.

The gate of the French Consulate on the Limanaki Street side was packed with refugees, shoving, pushing, elbowing and kicking each other, and screaming in broken French that they were French citizens. Edith managed to slip past them, shaking off the children who grabbed at her skirt and the mothers who tried to thrust their swaddled babies into her arms. A uniformed guard opened the door just wide enough for her to enter before closing it in the faces of the shouting, crying, fainting crowd.

Edith paused, blinking, in the coolness of the high-ceilinged hall. She stood for a moment beneath its Bohemian crystal chandeliers. The scenes she'd witnessed outside had shaken her to the core.

A surprising silence filled the consulate. The heels of her shoes echoed on the stone floor as she walked in the direction the guard had indicated to the room where travel documents were being issued. All at once she worked out what had been bothering her. It was something she'd seen in that farewell scene. It wasn't that the officer was crying openly or that the young girl had been laughing with her friend and eating ice cream ten minutes earlier. That wasn't the detail that had escaped her. Something else had happened, something that had slipped from her mind when Avinash came to her side. As soon as the tearful lieutenant had disappeared from sight, his fiancée, the young girl, had pulled the engagement ring from her finger and stuffed it into her pocket.

My God, what a world!

Good News!

Adriana ran from one side of Bread-Baker's Square to the other. She'd gathered up the skirt of her pink-and-white-striped dress and was out of breath. The men sitting under the arbour of the coffeehouse stopped shaking the dice they were about to throw, left their waterpipes and their newspapers, and, as one, stared at the strong white calves showing under the scalloped dress. Adriana's breasts were heaving under her low-cut neckline, and her thick, chestnut-coloured plaits flew out behind her as she ran.

Paying no attention to the eyes staring at her bared flesh, Adriana raced past the coffeehouse, the fountain, and old Auntie Rozi sitting on a wooden bench in the shade of the plane tree, and into Menekse Street. Stopping in front of Grocer Akis's blue door, she began to shout at the top of her voice.

'Giota! Open the door, girl! Hurry! *Ela, ela!* I have good news!'

Panagiota was in the kitchen with her mother. They were making hors d'oeuvres, pies and saffron pilaf to go with the lamb that was to be roasted in the back courtyard for the birthday feast that evening. What with the pots bubbling on the stove and the hot and humid weather, the small kitchen was unbearable. Katina had taken her daughter prisoner for the past two days to prepare this feast, not even allowing her out in the evening to sit in the square. Pavlo would be attending the celebration for the first time, as Panagiota's official fiancé, and Katina, wanting everything to be perfect, was being more meticulous than ever. She was making Panagiota rush from one job to the next as if it were Pavlo's birthday, not hers.

Hearing Adriana screaming from the street, and without taking her eyes off the vine-leaf *dolma* she was wrapping, Katina nodded at the door. Most of the preparations had now been completed: the pie was filled; the lamb, salted and spiced, was marinating in olive oil; and the hors d'oeuvres were cooling. Her daughter could go out now.

Seeing her mother's slight inclination of the head, Panagiota didn't waste a second; she tore off her navy-blue apron, hung it on a hook on the wall, hurled herself out of the hellishly hot kitchen and thundered down the stairs. The clatter of her clogs on the wooden steps caused everything to shake, even more so than Adriana's fists beating on the door. Grocer Akis's apprentice ran out into the street, thinking there was an earthquake.

When her friend finally appeared at the door, Adriana, with tears running down her cheeks, threw herself into her arms. She was laughing and crying at the same time. Panagiota had thought she was coming to wish her a happy birthday, but given the state she was in, she had obviously brought important news. Panagiota's heart began to beat wildly. Had something happened while she'd been shut up with her mother in the kitchen?

'Adriana *mou*, what's going on? What's happened, girl? *Ela*, come on in. Let's go upstairs.'

Adriana didn't have the patience to climb the stairs before sharing her good news. She exploded, as if finally revealing a secret she'd been keeping for a long time.

'He's back, Panagiota! He's come home! *Irthe o* Minas *mou*. Minas has come back!'

Staring at the stunned Panagiota, who was standing in the doorway with a huge smile on her face, Adriana stopped shaking her friend's shoulders and took five steps back to let her digest this wonderful news. Her tearstained cheeks were red from the running and the excitement, and beads of sweat had gathered at her hairline. Unable to stand still, and not caring that the skirt of her dress was flying up, she twirled around in the middle of the street, her long plaits flapping like birds' wings beside her ears.

It was as if Panagiota's brain had stopped. She gazed at Adriana as if she hadn't understood what she'd said. Then, gradually, the pieces began to fit together. Minas had returned. They were sending the soldiers home. The soldiers were returning. Minas... War... Had the war ended?

Because of the birthday feast, Panagiota had not been out of the neighbourhood for two days. She was unaware that villagers were flooding into the city and that desperate soldiers were boarding repatriation ships. Caught up in their feverish preparations, mother and daughter had not heard that the Turks had already crossed the Usak border.

Only Grocer Akis knew of the approaching danger, from conversations in the coffeehouse. He had already taken the gold that Katina kept hidden in a pillowcase, and the credit notes he'd saved, and put them in a biscuit tin which he'd then hidden at the bottom of one of the sacks of wheat in the storeroom at the back of his shop. Because a lot of his business was done with credit notes, he didn't have much cash.

Some of his friends from the coffeehouse were sending their families to stay with relatives who lived outside the city for a few weeks. Akis had arranged with a coachman that if the situation got more tense the man would take Panagiota and Katina to his sister's in Chesme, but he hadn't said anything to his wife and daughter in order not to worry them needlessly and ruin Panagiota's birthday excitement.

Besides, most probably everything would be fine. The British would take over the administration of the city. They wouldn't allow the Turks to enter Smyrna, let alone permit them to wreak havoc. Everybody was saying that. Besides, Akis was sure that the Turks, their former administrators, would not harm the people of Smyrna. Once public order was restored, the Ottoman 'millet' system of semi-autonomous authority, which had run like clockwork for five hundred years, would be reinstated and everyone would be able to breathe easily again.

Adriana raced back to Panagiota, who was still standing in the doorway, and wrapped her arms around her friend's neck. The two girls giggled as they hugged each other and danced round and round until they almost fell over.

'Watch out, girl! *Katse, vre matia mou.* Sit down, stop, my friend. I came out in my clogs – wait here a second.' Panagiota rushed inside and slipped on a pair of old pink satin shoes that were beside the door.

Adriana was a tall, strong, big-boned girl from a large, happy family, natives of Chios who had come to Smyrna in the last century. Grabbing Panagiota by the waist, she began to waltz right there in the middle of Menekse Street, singing while she danced.

'They're coming home, Giota *mou*! Do you hear me? My Minas is already here. They're all coming home and our

Smyrna will be back to its old, joyous self. Bravo! They're coming, coming, coming.'

Breathlessly, they tripped into the square together. Panagiota was finally starting to take in what Adriana was saying. She slipped out of her friend's embrace and, taking her hand, pulled her over to a wooden bench beside the fountain, directly across from the coffeehouse.

'What are you saying, Adriana? *Ti les?* Tell me everything – quick! When did he come? How? Where is he now? What about the war? What's been happening these last two days?'

'Wait... I'll tell you everything. Minas, my Minas, is at his home now, sleeping. He came early this morning. The sun was just rising when I woke to the sound of little pebbles being thrown at my window. That's the way Minas used to wake me up, you know, whenever we met at midnight. I opened my eyes immediately. Could it be...? I'd prayed so much to beloved Panagia, and every day my eyes would stream with tears. I slid out of bed without making a sound. I was so afraid of being disappointed, but I crawled over my sisters' beds and got to the window and looked down at the street through the tulle curtain.'

'Ah, *ti romantiko*! And Minas was standing there, in his uniform, looking so handsome!'

Adriana shook her head. 'It wasn't quite like that.' For the first time a shadow passed over her face.

'How was it not like that? So how was it then? Was it not Minas who was throwing pebbles at your window?'

Adriana tried to turn it into a joke, in the way that people do when they're forcing themselves to be positive. 'Well, it was both him and not him.'

Panagiota was getting impatient now. She shooed away a boy carrying a flagon of water who wandered too near them.

Emotions that she'd thought had been long extinguished had rekindled deep in her stomach, and, like a fire burning on the far side of the mountain, the smoke was filling her heart.

'Don't make me crazy, girl! Tell me!'

They were sitting side by side on the bench. When Adriana turned to face Panagiota, her green eyes were filled with tears. Without saying anything, Panagiota reached for Adriana's clasped hands and took them between her palms.

'When I got to the window, I looked down. As I had feared, disappointment was waiting for me. There was nobody down there but villagers passing by like ghosts.'

Panagiota didn't understand why villagers would be passing along Katipzade Street so early in the morning, but she didn't interrupt her friend to ask.

'Then I heard another "psst" sound. Another pebble hit the windowpane. I looked down and saw a beggar. It was he who was throwing the stones. Just a vagabond. A-ha, it's a Turkos, I thought, because his feet were bare and he was wearing a grey jacket like the Turkish soldiers do.'

'Was it Minas?' Panagiota asked, whispering the question as if she didn't want to hurt her friend.

Adriana nodded, tears rolling like beads down her cheeks and onto her dress and her clenched hands. Panagiota understood that her friend, who'd been dancing with glee just a few minutes ago, had been hiding her sorrow behind a mask of happiness, as she always did. She squeezed her hands again. For some reason Adriana felt she had to act as if she was carefree and happy the whole time, perhaps because she was a big sister to so many little brothers and sisters.

'I didn't recognize him, Panagiota. I didn't recognize Minas! And then his shoulders slumped and he disappeared into the crowd of passing villagers. I was all confused. I got up, made breakfast, and woke, washed and dressed the little ones. As if having eight mouths to feed isn't enough, my dear mama has taken in two women who escaped from Manisa along with their children. I gave each of them a bowl of soup. And so on. But I felt uneasy inside. I was going to come and see you anyway – ah, how could I have forgotten! *Hronia polla*, Panagiota *mou*! Happy birthday! *Signomi*, I'm sorry, I left your present at home. Never mind, I'll bring it this evening.' She smiled at her friend through the tears.

Her birthday was the last thing on Panagiota's mind right then. Stavros was coming back! Stavros! Any minute now, he might come round the corner into the square and see her sitting there on the bench under the plane tree with Adriana! Maybe he'd be riding his dilapidated bicycle, the way he used to on those summer nights when they would kiss beside the wall of the French Hospital, with the smell of frying fish in the air. Could there be a more wonderful present? Her heart felt like it was about to burst out of her chest.

She turned to her friend. 'Forget about all that, *vre* Adriana! So what if you didn't recognize him at first glance. His hair and beard must have got longer. He'll go and get a bath, change his clothes, go to a barber's shop for a haircut and a shave, and turn into Minas the Flea again.'

Pensively, Adriana shook her head.

'He's done all that already. Two hours later he came to our door all cleaned up. I was hanging out the laundry in the courtyard. My darling Minas – when he saw that I hadn't recognized him, he realized what a state he must be in, so he went to a bathhouse and a barber's shop, and he took off his Turkish jacket, went home and got all dressed up. When he appeared at our door, I lost my mind! I realized that the vagabond had been him and I was so ashamed not to have recognized him. I begged his forgiveness. But, Panagiota...'

Adriana stared at the square in desperation, as if she might find there the words she needed to tell the remainder of her story. A clutch of doves were pecking busily at some sesame crumbs that had been shaken out in front of the bakery. Cats had occupied all the shady spots out of the midday heat; they hissed at Muhtar from where they lay, as he wagged his stubby tail and trotted around looking for a place on the marble where he could cool off. Not a leaf on the plane tree above them was moving. The air was as heavy as lead. Adriana's little brothers and some runny-nosed refugee boys were playing one-goal football with a ball of paper in front of the bakery. Adriana's brothers looked like princes next to the village boys, who were running amok with their shaved heads and torn and dirty shirts. A proud smile crept across Adriana's face.

'What? But what happened?' Panagiota pressed. 'Tell me, Adriana, for God's sake.' One part of her mind was wondering where those village boys had come from. Her heart, which earlier had been too big to fit inside her chest, had now contracted in fear. Why was Adriana squirming like that? Was it Stavros...?

'Something's changed, Giota *mou*. Minas is not the old Minas. The way he looked at me, at every woman passing by, at the washing on the line, the pots my mother was boiling on the stove, the hats in the cupboard, at everything, it was as if he was seeing ghosts. It's like he's living in a dream. Or as if everything he sees is a hallucination. He doesn't talk. And this morning... I realized why I hadn't recognized him – it wasn't his hair, or his beard or the Turkish jacket. I would know my Minas under any circumstances. But this man... this man,

Panagiota, has a frown on his face and lips that have forgotten how to smile. Can you imagine a Minas who doesn't smile? I don't know what's happened to him, Panagiota! It's like… It's like he's been shot in the heart and his soul has leaked out, gone, leaving only the shell of his body.'

Adriana withdrew her hands from Panagiota's, covered her face and began to sob. It was clear that she was only now, for the first time, allowing herself to acknowledge the truth of what she had seen.

Panagiota's eyes also filled with tears. The idea that Minas the Flea's warm soul could leak away through a hole in his heart burned her inside. Minas, who could bring a mandolin to life with one touch of his fingers, or a guitar, or an accordion; Minas, whose olive-black eyes twinkled with mischief as he told his funny stories. Ever since they were children, he'd been the sweetheart of the neighbourhood, its rubber ball, its source of joy. It was truly impossible to imagine him with a frowning face and eyes which had lost their sparkle.

'Adriana *mou*, it will pass. Let him get some rest and I'm sure he will be his old self again. He has come back and you are together again – what could be more important! Minas is alive. You'll get married soon. You'll have a beautiful home and a gang of babies. He'll play his mandolin for you at night and you'll wash his feet.'

From behind her hands, Adriana gave a little laugh.

'Ah, that's better. Is it a time for crying, my crazy girlfriend, *filenada*? No, it's a time for celebration! Come on, get up. Let's go down to the quay. Katina Sultan has finally released me. I'll buy you an ice cream. Today's my birthday, it'll be my treat. *Ade!*'

Adriana dropped her hands in her lap and smiled at Panagiota in gratitude. 'He'll be all right, won't he, Giota *mou*? He'll be the familiar old Minas the Flea. He walked all the way here from Afyonkarahisar without sleeping. He hasn't said anything, but he has definitely seen some horrible things. Our soldiers are burning the Turkish villages. Minas has such a sensitive heart; he can't tolerate cruelty. I hope he wasn't forced to do horrendous things...'

'Adriana *mou*, tell me, did Minas mention the other boys? Are they all coming home? Is the war over?'

'Ah, *Thee mou*, my God, Panagiota, my sweet friend, here I am thinking of my own troubles, and I completely forgot you. Forgive me, I beg you. I forgot to give you the news about Stavros. Yes, Stavros is on his way home. Minas last saw him in Afyonkarahisar. He was trying to board a train. He was fine, as strong as ever. He hasn't been wounded at all. Today or tomorrow he'll definitely be here. Ah, Panagia, Mother Mary, thanks be to you, our sweethearts are coming home, one by one.'

Glancing uneasily in the direction of the police station, with one hand Panagiota indicated to Adriana that she should lower her voice. Today, sure enough, she was someone else's fiancée. To impress the groom-to-be, her mother had locked her up in their kitchen for days, to cook. But so what? He wasn't her legal husband! If Stavros were to stroll round that corner, she would immediately take off the ring and throw it away.

The faded memory of her former love, which had been simmering inside her, suddenly flared up into a longing that seared her whole body. Everything was going to turn out fine, even if the Turks took over. When she'd said that to Stavros's face two years ago on the beach at Agia Triada, he'd got so angry! But no, she was never, ever going to make him angry again. She would always go along with whatever he said, be his sweet-talking one and only wife. She removed the engagement ring with her name and Pavlo's engraved on the inside from her finger, then put it back on again.

In her excitement, Adriana had forgotten that her friend was engaged to another man. Seeing her playing with the ring on her finger, she put her hand to her mouth, as if to push back her words.

'It's not important, Adriana *mou*. You are my closest friend, my sister. We have nothing to hide from each other.'

Adriana saw roses bloom in her friend's beautiful face. The dimples either side of her lips deepened and her black eyes widened, the embers in them ignited by the flames of passion. Seeing Panagiota like this, love and happiness filled her own heart once more. A peaceful life awaited them. Stavros would return. She and Minas would have a bundle of babies.

Standing up, she reached out her hand. '*Glassada, mademoiselle?* Ice cream?'

Panagiota, copying the fallen women she'd seen in front of Kraemer's, fluttered her thick lashes. '*Avec plaisir.*'

Captured by the eyes of the men in the coffeehouse with their waterpipes, the girls strolled down the road, arm in arm and laughing, to the quay.

The Exchange

Midwife Meline woke up with a start in a narrow bed on the top floor above Berberian's Bakery. At first she couldn't remember where she was. Blinking her eyes, she looked around. There was no one else in the small room. It was a box-like place, with a low ceiling, one small window and cream wallpaper with a floral design. On the floor near her bed she saw a familiar red wooden horse lying on a circular crimson and blue rug – her grandson's, Nishan's. Oh, of course; she was at Hayguhi Hanim's house, her daughter's mother-in-law. The wooden building was as hot as a Turkish bath; it was as if flames were blazing from the walls.

There was a great racket going on outside, with people loudly booing someone; it was the sort of commotion that happened down at the docks whenever a fight broke out between sailors and porters. What time was it, she wondered? After delivering that young girl's baby on the quay, she'd not been able to get to sleep until the first rays of dawn, and she'd only just now woken up. Where were the others – her daughter, her son-in-law, her grandchildren?

Closing her eyes, she listened to the sounds coming from the docks. When her Smyrna ears heard the familiar chug-chug of a fisherman's engine and the laughter of children, she relaxed. If children were laughing, then life was continuing. A happy song wafted out onto the street from the tavern next door to the bakery. A deep voice ordered some soldiers to hurry up – another ship was departing.

With a moan, she buried herself in her blanket. She was probably too old now to be working all night. She felt exhausted, not at all keen to get up and join in whatever was happening. Furthermore, she'd had that same dream again. Lying back on her pillow, and in the hope that she might at last close her account with the past, she let the events of exactly seventeen years ago unfold in front of her eyes.

They had reached Smyrna before daybreak. The old villager, the owner of the donkey, walked in front, followed by Meline on the donkey with Edith's baby in her arms. At the entrance to the city, by the gasworks, she got off the donkey and pressed some money into his hand. With rapid strides she passed the Greek Cemetery at Daragaci and then the train station before coming to Grace's Maternity House. She could leave the baby there without anyone seeing, ring the bell and run away. Grace was an efficient, angelic woman; she would definitely find the infant a good home. Or should she leave it in the courtyard of the Anglican church next door?

No, it would be best to avoid anywhere with a connection to the Levantine community. Under no circumstances could she allow the relationship between the Lamarcks and this child to be discovered. The Greek Orphanage on the corner of Hadji Frangou was a better option. That would mean forgoing any chance of the baby being given to a good family, but Meline could not put her own daughters' lives at risk.

She passed Agios Ioannis Church and turned left. A sea breeze sprinkled salt on her skin; the humidity was less intense here. Under her cloak the baby was howling and wailing. She stuck her thumb in its mouth.

'God, have mercy on this unfortunate soul. Mother Mary, I pray that this child be found and put into the arms of a wet nurse urgently. Please show me the way and hold us in thy protecting hands.'

Pushing open the iron gate of the orphanage, she slipped inside the dark courtyard like a thief. Dawn was about to break and the sparrows had woken up. Ragged sheets were hung out on washing lines. Behind a broken-down tricycle two cats had set an ambush for a rat. All three were frozen, waiting for one of them to make the first move. The ground under the chestnut tree was soft. That's where she should leave the poor thing. It was right across from the door. Maybe someone would hear the screams and wake up. Could the child live that long? Lowering the yellow blanket to the ground, she made the sign of the cross over the baby's black head.

'Almighty God, forgive this helpless human being. I am a mother protecting her own children. Forgive me my sins and spare this tiny infant. We entrust ourselves to thee.'

Quickly making the sign of the cross three more times, she hurried from the courtyard into the street. Under the chestnut tree, the baby, detached from the midwife's warm breast, began to cry with all its might. Meline took a deep breath. Pulling her cloak over her head, she looked around. No, she had not been seen. She turned the corner. The baby's screams echoed like a bell along the deserted street. What a strong spirit; how she clung to life! Someone in the orphanage would be sure to wake up soon and take her inside. Almighty God protected the innocent, kept them from harm. He would not take that child's soul.

As she passed the French Hospital, where she worked, Meline covered herself carefully. From behind the ramparts of Kadife Kale a purple light was delicately tearing at the darkness. At this deserted hour of the morning, she thought it best to avoid the twisting back streets of Agia Katerina and Agios Dimitris. She would go down to Trassa Street and walk along the wide straight road there. Perhaps she would find an early coachman and get home as the sky lightened. After that, everything would be all right. She would make some coffee, wake the girls, and prepare their breakfast as if the day were just beginning. She touched the money bag hanging round her neck. She would count out her husband's gambling debt into Mahmut Aga's hand herself, one coin at a time.

When she came to the high walls surrounding the courtyard of the French Hospital, she speeded up. There was not a sound on the street. As soon as she turned the next corner, she would leave the hospital behind. It was just then, precisely at that corner, that she came face to face with Midwife Marika. The young midwife let out a scream at the wholly unexpected sight of Meline standing before her in the early morning darkness. It briefly occurred to Meline to keep her head down and simply hurry on past the midwife she herself had trained. How could she explain her presence outside the hospital at that hour? While she was struggling to mutter something in Turkish before slipping away, Marika again screamed out.

'Oh, Midwife Meline! Oh my God, Midwife Meline! You've come at exactly the right time. Oh, Mother Mary, Panagia *mou*, I thank thee. Quick, quick! We're in a really difficult situation, an emergency.'

With no idea what was happening, Meline found herself suddenly in the maternity room in the basement of the hospital. In the dim light, she could see a pregnant woman lying with spread legs raised on the green birthing chair in the centre of the room. The woman was unconscious – or was she dead? Nurse Liz was standing at the woman's head, pressing a cloth soaked in vinegar to her forehead, wrists and ankles. The nurse's tiny lips were moving constantly; she was clearly praying.

When all hope had been lost for the mother and her baby, Midwife Marika had fled the maternity room and run out into the street, perhaps to cry, perhaps to think up some plan to conceal her defeat, or perhaps to escape and never return. At any other time, Midwife Meline would have punished her young colleague most harshly for having left the maternity room while the mother's heart was still beating, but, fortunately for Marika, Meline was in no state that morning to concentrate on anyone but herself.

She hurried over to the mother and grabbed her wrist. The pulse was about to fade.

'Liz, run, light all the lamps and bring one here. Hang it on that hook above us. Hurry, run! Marika, tell me quickly what you have done so far.'

Marika began to cry. 'I went to her house for the delivery. She's from our neighbourhood. She's had twins before, so I thought it would be an easy birth. Her cervix didn't dilate. Hours passed. Ah, Midwife Meline, I should have brought her here straight away. I should have called you. Oh, what have I done? What have I done!'

Meline examined the woman's stomach, the opening of the cervix. Nurse Liz had lit all the lamps and was standing at Meline's side with a carbide lamp that gave off a bright white light. Marika had attached an oxygen mask to the woman's mouth.

'When you say hours, how many exactly? The cervix is

dilated to nine centimetres. Where did the birth begin – at her home or after you brought her here? How many centimetres was the cervix dilated when she came here?'

Marika mumbled something, but Meline was no longer listening.

In her mind a plan was forming. Like fate, that plan had begun to weave a web.

Could she make it happen? Was it possible?

God willing, anything was possible.

She turned to the women standing around her.

'That'll be all, Marika. You've done everything you could. Now go upstairs and get some rest. You too, Nurse Liz. Do not allow anyone to disturb me. Tell the other nurses not to come into this maternity room, not to even come down to this floor. If I hear so much as a footstep or even a whisper, I will have you all fired. That's it. Now go; leave me alone. You've made enough mistakes already. I will work alone and try to save at least one life.'

Meline was the hospital's head midwife and the younger ones were accustomed to taking orders from her. Especially now, with Marika fully aware of what a big mistake she'd made, it was very easy to get rid of her. Once her footsteps and Nurse Liz's had receded down the corridor, Meline rolled up her sleeves.

She had realized a while ago that the baby had died from lack of oxygen. With her skilful hands she drew the dead baby from between the legs of the unconscious mother. Blood flowed from the woman's uterus. Meline held the baby in the air and examined it. It was a girl with red hair and a tiny nose. The purple face and clenched fists made it look as if it was angry at the merciless ways of a world where life ended before it had begun. Its blood-crusted body was still warm and the umbilical cord still pulsed, though weakly. After cutting the cord, Meline slapped the baby on its back, in one last attempt. But its tiny face was already dark purple, and its body, disconnected from its mother, was quickly cooling. Placing the baby on the counter beside her, she rapidly sewed up the woman's torn flesh. The oxygen passing through the tube to the lungs had not been enough to save the baby, but it had kept the mother alive. The gush of blood from the womb was subsiding and the pulse was getting stronger.

After making sure that the mother was alive, she washed the child's corpse. Its face was now very dark. Wrapping it in a clean pink blanket, she hurried out of the maternity room. It was God's gift that there were no other births in progress on that floor just then. Was this not a sign from Almighty God that her plan would be fruitful?

If she was going to save a life, the time to do so was now.

She raced towards the door at the end of the corridor that opened onto a back street and with the dead baby in her arms ran all the way to the orphanage. If Edith's daughter was still there, if Edith's daughter was still alive, that would mean that Almighty God approved of what she was about to do.

She made it to the chestnut tree in the courtyard. And, yes, the tiny one was still there where she'd left her. No one had woken to her screams. Meline knelt down and took the baby in her arms, shaking the dirt from her blanket. Not a sound came from the baby.

Oh God, had she died? Had her lungs collapsed from hunger and the cold? The baby still hadn't made a sound; her face had turned purple. Meline patted her on the back. With the last particle of her strength, the baby let out a noise.

'Oh, thank you, Holy Mary, Almighty God! Thank you! She's alive!'

Time was running out. The darkness was lifting and a pinkish light was filling the courtyard. Opening the blanket, she took Edith's naked daughter in her arms. Keeping one eye on the orphanage windows, she wrapped the lifeless baby in the yellow blanket and placed it under the chestnut tree. Swaddling Edith's daughter in the pink hospital blanket, she hurried back out onto the street. A group of gypsy women had settled cross-legged on the ground. They were sitting around a cloth they'd spread out, passing a marijuana pipe between them and reading each other's fortunes from cards they'd set out in front of them. They didn't notice Meline coming out of the orphanage courtyard and slipping through the back door of the hospital, which she'd left open a crack.

She rushed along the corridor with Edith's baby in her arms, hoping she was still alive, and entered the maternity room. The woman was still unconscious, lying there with an oxygen mask on her mouth. Pushing aside the straps of her white nightgown, Meline exposed the woman's breasts and stuck the baby's half-opened lips onto one of her nipples. In a primal instinct for life, the baby's lips clasped the nipple. When the first drop slipped down her throat, she opened her tiny fists and touched the naked skin of her new mother with the tips of her red fingers.

When Nurse Liz and Marika heard the bell ringing in the waiting room and ran down to the maternity room, they found Meline sitting on a stool with the baby, wrapped in a pink blanket, in her arms. The mother was still unconscious, but her cheeks had some colour now, and her breathing was regular. Nurse Liz screamed; Marika, crossing herself, knelt in front of the baby.

Midwife Meline lifted her head and smiled. She was worn out but not sorry. Almighty God had wished it to be this way.

She had saved a life.

The life of this little child whom she had saved was worth the world.

The women hugged each other. While they were congratulating Meline, the baby began howling at the top of her voice. The midwife said in a tired but calm voice, 'Nurse Liz, let's arrange a room for Kyra Katina upstairs. Take the baby to a wet nurse until the mother wakes up. When she wakes, you may turn the baby over to her.'

While Nurse Liz was putting an identification bracelet on the baby's arm, giving the day and hour of birth, Meline walked to the door.

'With your permission, I shall go home and prepare breakfast for my daughters before school. Midwife Marika, she is in your care now. You did well. *Kalimera sas*. Good day.'

Farewell

Panagiota was taken aback by the crowds at the quay. Adriana, who'd been watching the refugees flowing into the city from the window of her house since yesterday, laughed at her friend's innocence.

'Ah, Panagiota *mou*, what universe are you living in? While you've been rolling out pastry for your *spanakopita* these last two days, everything's changed; the mountains have come to the sea. *Ela*, here, meet your new neighbours, the city's new residents. That ship over there is ours too. It's full. Apparently, it set out to conquer Constantinople, then came back. The soldiers on the ship say they will never, ever set foot on land and are demanding to be taken back to Greece – that's what I heard.'

Panagiota squinted at the mass of people camping on the shore. She was surprised but didn't give it much thought. There was something about the crowds – the bare-bottomed children; the young women with heads covered by black kerchiefs – that scorched her heart, but at least they had escaped from their villages and made it this far. They were safe now. They could stay there until the war was over and everything was calm, then go back to their homes. The weather was good, Smyrna was bountiful. Or if they wished to leave, they could get on the ships that would come from Greece and leave. *Mana Ellas* would save her children. And in the meantime, there were many charitable people like Adriana's family, and churches and schools, that would take care of them.

Like the genie in Aladdin's lamp, love had been summoned from its hiding place in the corner of Panagiota's heart and was now suffusing her whole being. Her eyes saw only beauty and goodness. And lines of Greek soldiers marching towards the docks. She didn't notice their skeletal bodies, the wounded chests beneath their torn shirts, their bloodied feet in holed boots, their crippled legs that they dragged along with great difficulty, their lustreless eyes, their lice-infested hair and beards. She saw only what reminded her of Stavros.

Three times she took steps towards tall men with green eyes, and each time Adriana grabbed her wrist and pulled her back.

'Panagiota *mou*, what would Stavros be doing here? Why would he be among the soldiers getting evacuated? His home is here. He wouldn't come down to the quay. He'd go straight to his mother's house like Minas did.'

Adriana was right, but Panagiota had a feeling – and if she'd thought about it a little, she'd have realized that she'd always carried this feeling in her heart – that Stavros would leave her. His volunteering for the army had made her miserable but at the same time had confirmed the old suspicion that pierced her heart like a thorn: it was her fate to be abandoned. She could not have known that this feeling was a result of events that had been set in motion long ago, years before she was born, and that had been passed to her from another, had seeped into her essence. With a logic that was both simple and limited, she considered cause and effect to be entirely contained within one's own lifespan and so believed that this fate was the outcome of some deficiency in her character or something she'd done wrong. She thought that she deserved to be abandoned because she wasn't good enough, or smart enough, or pretty enough or whatever it was she needed to be.

Now, as she searched with anxious eyes for Stavros among the soldiers streaming towards the ship anchored in front of Punta, from a dark crevice of her subconscious a voice was whispering that she was about to be deserted once more. Drawing a handkerchief from her breast, she wiped the sweat from her brow and took her friend's arm. The two girls left the chaos of the Punta dock behind them and walked towards the Café de Paris. The quay was full of ladies swinging their hips and showing off their tightly corseted waists as they paraded along the waterfront. Their wide-brimmed hats were trimmed with ribbons that were tied under their chins in bows, in colours chosen to match their parasols.

There were no parasols to twirl for Adriana and Panagiota, nor hats on their heads. At any other time, Panagiota would definitely not have come down to the quay dressed as she was, but today she was following along with her friend and had had no time to change. She was wearing a loose-fitting blue dress that she'd had on while helping her mother in the kitchen. The skirt came down to her ankles and her hands still smelled of onions. Her big toe stuck out like a small hill at the tip of her pink satin shoes. Even when she took the shoe off, the mound didn't disappear; it was imprinted on the shoe. Uneasily, she grumbled, 'Let's not sit down at the Café de Paris. Let's eat our ice creams while we walk around.'

'Whatever you want, Panagiota *mou* – it's your birthday!' said Adriana with a wink.

Her friend's good humour had returned. Splendid! A walk on the quay cured all. With gratitude, Panagiota watched the blue water sparkling in the sunlight. The hills on the horizon spread over the sea like supine whales. Sailing boats rocked in front of colourful fishing boats and from far away came the familiar chug-chug of a motorboat. The setting sun, as round as a cannonball, was turning everything it touched to gold. Her heart filled with happiness.

Her darling Smyrna!

The duty of this most beautiful of all cities was to remind people, even in their most sorrowful moments, of the beauty of the world. She wanted to hug Adriana. Minas had returned, Stavros was on his way home – everything was going to be wonderful!

They walked arm in arm with light steps, ice cream cones in their hands. As they passed the Théâtre de Smyrne, they raised their heads to read the wide black letters spelling out the name of the film across the arched entrance: 'Tango de la Mort'.

Adriana licked her lemon and cherry ice cream and poked her friend. 'Did Pavlo take you to the cinema, girl?'

Trying to hide her smile, Panagiota made a tour around her ice cream cone with her pink-tipped tongue.

Adriana squealed in excitement. 'Look at you – you're blushing! He took you, of course! You, naughty girl! Oh, who knows what those dark seats saw.'

'Adriana!'

'Come on, come on, *ela filenada*. You're not going to keep

secrets from me, are you? Tell me, how far did you let him go? He is your fiancé after all, right? Did you pay a late-night visit to a dance hall or what?'

'Adriana!'

Now that Adriana had got started, she wouldn't stop. 'He must have taken you for a ride in a carriage, yes? And of course he chose a covered carriage, right? Wait! Wait, don't tell me, let me guess. You went from here to Kokaryali in a covered carriage. And when you got there, you ate red mullet at one of those cafés in the sea, dangling your feet in the water. Oh, the shore there smells so deliciously of sea urchins and mussels! Then, let's see... maybe to the meadows. Naturally, as a good Smyrna girl, it was your duty to show your guest from Ioannina the picnic places. And since you'd gone all that way, you couldn't return without first alighting from the carriage and taking a walk to get some fresh air. Such a beautiful spot, with the mountains covered in olive groves and fig trees, the occasional solitary house, an abandoned barn... and beds of hay in the barns. Yes?'

'And how do you know all of this?'

Panagiota asked this question, which was supposed to be her counter-attack, in a tone that told Adriana she'd guessed everything exactly right. Both of them began to laugh. As she nibbled the tip of her ice cream cone, Adriana made up a song about love in the hay and began singing it at the top of her voice. Panagiota hid her face in her hands.

They were walking towards the harbour and had almost reached Kraemer's.

'*Aman, aman...*
Making love in the haystack
Wrapped up so tight!'

'Adriana!'

'Making love in the haystack
All through the night…
Aman, aman.'

Panagiota cut her short by grabbing her wrist. Adriana was just about to object when she noticed that her friend's face had suddenly lost all its colour. She stopped singing and turned to see what Panagiota was looking at.

Hundreds of soldiers were packed onto the wharf. From somewhere in the mass confusion, Pavlo emerged, dressed in a spotlessly clean khaki uniform, and came running towards them. A large cloth bag the same colour as his uniform was slung over his left shoulder; in his right hand he carried a small grey bag with his initials embroidered in red thread in the corner. Weaving between the soldiers and the villagers, he arrived at Panagiota's side. Sweat was dripping from his cheekbones; his forehead shone like a mirror.

'Panagiota! Where have you been, for God's sake? I've been searching for you for hours.'

Panagiota had never seen him this agitated, but she was upset that he'd scolded her in front of her friend. So what? Couldn't she even go out for an ice cream with Adriana? Her mother had let up, but now this Pavlo was going to start? And he hadn't even wished her a happy birthday. Raising his chin as if she was smelling the air, she turned her face towards the sea. Adriana had walked away to leave the two of them alone. She'd found a relative fishing in front of Kraemer's and was chatting with him.

'As you see, I am here. What's going on?'

'Panagiota *mou*, listen to me now. Okay, my darling? Are you listening?'

His huge hands squeezed Panagiota's shoulders until they hurt. She scowled, but he paid no attention.

'I have arranged a fishing boat to take you to Chios. It will leave at midnight tonight from the outer harbour. The fisherman's name is Panagiotis – he knows your father. Be at the outer harbour at midnight on the dot. He will light three candles on his boat as a sign. Okay? *Endaksi?*'

Panagiota nodded distractedly.

'Now, *omorfula mou*, my beautiful one, run home immediately and gather up everything you have that is of value. Don't take too much. Jewellery, *parades*, cash, gold hidden in jars, that's all. Leave your rugs, candlesticks and weapons. Lock all the doors securely, lower the shutters and fasten them from the inside. Your father should also lower the shutters of his shop and put locks on them. He should leave nothing valuable there, not even in the storeroom at the back. Do you understand? Panagiota, are you listening? Why aren't you paying attention? Giota, *agapi mou*, my love, this is important. You are listening, aren't you? This is a matter of life and death.'

Panagiota nodded again. Her ears were ringing. She was vaguely listening to him.

He set his bag on the ground and took her two hands in his. His puppy-dog eyes gazed directly into his fiancée's, black beneath her thick lashes.

'My love, as you can see, they're evacuating us. We're all going. If we stay, we'll be taken prisoner. From this evening, not a single unit of police officers, gendarmes or civilian guards will be left in Smyrna. Can you imagine how much danger that will put you in? You cannot stay here another night. A great catastrophe may be upon us. Listen to me now, my one and only. When you get to Chios, do not linger. Arrange an immediate passage to Piraeus. You understand, don't you? I will be waiting for you at Piraeus. In case something happens, I've written here my address in Ioannina. Even if I'm not there, my family will be expecting you, all of you. Be careful not to lose this piece of paper, okay, Giota *mou*? Darling, are you all right? Your face is so—'

Suddenly a loud commotion was heard from the port. The refugees, who'd been sitting around semi-conscious amid the sacks, camels, carts and belongings they'd brought from their villages, were on their feet, shaking their fists in the air and booing someone in unison. Adriana and her fisherman relative had stopped chatting and were looking at the boat preparing to raise its anchor at Passport Pier. Pavlo stood beside Panagiota to get a better view of what was happening.

Aristidis Stergiadis, High Commissioner of Smyrna, who for the last three years had been in charge of the city, was making his way through the crowd; with confident, dignified steps, he ignored the arms raised in anger, the curses and jeers, the screams of fear and fury, and strode on towards the motorboat which would take him to the British ship waiting for him in the bay.

Lost in thought, Pavlo put his arm around Panagiota's waist. She drew away, discomfited. What if Stavros should appear? What if he came and found her in another man's arms? She twiddled the ring on her finger. The shouts of the crowd jeering at Stergiadis intensified. The Europeans sitting at the tables outside Café Ivi stood up to see what was going on.

Pavlo's eyes were fixed on the manoeuvres of Stergiadis's ship. He didn't notice that Panagiota had slipped out of his arms. The vast majority of police and civilian security forces whose duty it had been to keep Stergiadis safe and protect the populace of Smyrna were leaving the city. The few that remained were just enough to guard the largest firms and the consulates and orphanages. Pavlo's superiors had informed them that from now on the Allied soldiers would protect only their own citizens. The American soldiers who swaggered around the streets had been alerted and would be leaving the poor girls and women who trailed after them in the lurch. He looked at the hordes of people gathered at the shore. The people who minutes earlier had screamed with all their might at the boat carrying Stergiadis to the British battleship, that stern-faced man who'd ruled the city for three years, were now silent, glancing at each other with eyes full of fear.

'What will happen now? If the Turks come, who will protect us?'

The piercing whistle of a ship tore through the silence. It came from the direction of Punta. Pavlo grabbed Panagiota's hands. Then the hands were not enough – he took hold of her shoulders and pulled her to his chest, burying himself in her face, her neck, her hair, breathing in the jasmine scent of her skin. When he unwound his arms, tears were streaming down his cheeks.

'Giota *mou*, my darling, may God keep you safe.'

The throngs of soldiers surging towards the ship that was urgently blowing its whistle took the young lieutenant with them. In his spotless khaki uniform, Pavlo was being dragged away from Panagiota. Easily distinguished among the capeless, lice-infested heads of the others by his carefully waxed and combed hair, he turned for one last look at his fiancée. Then, leaping up into the air so as to be visible above the taller soldiers, he pointed with one hand to an imaginary wristwatch and with the other to the dock in the outer harbour. He was reminding her of the fishing boat he'd arranged to take them to Chios. His clean, freshly shaved face and his eyes the colour of milk-chocolate shone with the innocence of love.

Panagiota was ashamed of herself for feeling nothing for this sensitive boy. Involuntarily she touched her lips with her fingertips and blew him a kiss. Settling his cape over his head, Pavlo smiled almost as if he was laughing, and was then quickly swallowed up by the crowd, disappearing from sight.

Black smoke from the ships on the horizon trembled in front of the red sun as it dipped into the sea. Panagiota raised her hands and looked through them at the light reflected off the water. The veil separating her from other beings had lifted; her fingers had become transparent and shimmered like light, like heat, like sound. They were vibrating in front of her like delicate waves. There was a supreme order in the world and each person had their own place in it. She was never going to be separated from her place in Smyrna. All at once the curtains in front of her eyes were parted. The past and the future appeared crystal clear in her mind. The gates of paradise would soon close; and while everyone else would be locked outside, she would be left behind in a land of loss. This was how she envisioned the story that was her life. This was how her fate had been woven.

Her eyes filled with tears.

While she was removing from her finger the thin gold ring with her name and Pavlo's engraved on the inside, two big teardrops rolled from her cheeks onto the pink satin shoes.

Last Encounter

They found Avinash Pillai dead in his house in Tilkilik one morning. When the fifth of the month came and Avinash had not rung his bell, the owner of the house, accustomed over thirty years to receiving his rent regularly on the first of each month, became suspicious. They entered the house using the spare key and found the elderly Indian man's body, wrinkled like a prune, seated cross-legged on a cushion in front of the fireplace. He was wearing baggy trousers that came down to his knees and there was no belt around his waist. His white hair fell across his chest, and both his chest and his head were bare.

They did not understand immediately that he was dead because he was sitting as if lost in meditation. It was strange. There was no decay, no stench. It was a while before they realized he wasn't breathing and his body was cold.

The voice on the other end of the telephone that one of the children at the Mansion with the Tower was holding to my ear told me all this in one breath. There had been only one telephone number on his desk among the chaotic jumble of notes, old newspapers, shop signs saved from the fire, faded photographs, and officially translated and stamped journals. And that number was ours at the Mansion with the Tower.

I wrote down my response on a piece of paper which I thrust into the child's hand. The two of us were at home alone. He read it out: 'Please call the British Consulate.'

It wasn't up to me to bury Avinash Pillai! He wasn't my relative; he wasn't my anything. He was a nutcase pushing a hundred who'd never stopped wandering the streets in search of anything that might remind him of his old lover. According to him, he was looking for me. Wait a minute, what were his words exactly? That he had never stopped searching for me. And that if he'd found me in time, he would have taken me to Paris, to Edith.

Not interested.

I'd had my share of deaths. And lives. There was no point ruining my peace of mind with another life's dreams.

Besides, what would have happened if he'd taken me to Edith? I would have died in Paris in 1944. Edith lived in a building that was destroyed not by Hitler but by the British and Americans when they bombed Paris. Furthermore, it was a poor neighbourhood.

I don't know what Edith was doing there. I didn't ask. Probably her brother-in-law Philippe Cantebury had finally managed to kick her out of the business and take away her partnership privileges. Anyway, even he had lost his offices, and his deeds and bonds and so on in the Great Fire, and their houses had been confiscated. They never came back to Izmir. Even though these details didn't interest me in the slightest, Avinash insisted on sharing them with me. That night – he made sure to mention that it was 21 April – Edith was asleep in her apartment near Porte de la Chapelle. Avinash wasn't with her. Even as she aged, that ill-tempered woman wouldn't consider living in the same house as Avinash. Decades had passed since then, but the former spy was still sad when he said that. When a person's heart has been scratched, like a broken record they get stuck and can never move on.

That it was a British plane and not a German one that had dropped the bomb on Edith's building was salt to the wound for Avinash. At this point in the story, he bowed his head, as if he were responsible.

'Hey you! God's son of India! Why should you, of all people, feel responsible?' I did think of saying that, but then it occurred to me that because this Avinash had been a spy – retired now, of course – there was a possibility that he'd known that the British were planning to bomb an important arms depot in the 18th Arrondissement, where Edith lived. Why were the British and Americans bombing Paris anyway? That also didn't interest me. Hadn't I personally experienced how those monsters could switch sides like backgammon pawns during a war?

And also, what did I care about Edith Lamarck?

If Sumbul had been alive, she would have listened avidly to the story of Edith's body being torn to shreds by British bombs. And she would have cried copious tears. But, listen, things were different by the time Avinash told me this story. A half-century had passed since Sumbul had hanged herself in the Mansion with the Tower.

After Avinash lost Edith, he set his heart on finding me. He believed that I was Edith's daughter. 'Believe' is not the right word: the clever spy was not in the slightest doubt. If I had a little patience, he said, I too would believe it by the time he got to the end of his story. So be it. Since he wanted it so badly, I let him tell the story.

If I'd wanted to object, what could I have done – pushed the white-bearded granddad down the stairs?

We were sitting across from each other in my tower, he in a rocking chair with a wicker seat and wooden back, I on Sumbul's old bed, whose pink paint had peeled away long ago. An electric fan was between us, though it made not the tiniest difference to the hellishly hot tower. From the small barred window behind me came the screams of seagulls and the chug-chug of fishing boats. You could hear the whistles of the Karsiyaka ferries and the zoom of warplanes heading to Cyprus. The television downstairs had begun playing military marches nonstop, which drove me crazy.

Having lost Edith, Avinash came to Izmir and moved into a hotel room. It was the year the Americans flattened Japan. Another September. He didn't remember the date, but it was a dark, moonless night. The misery of the Second World War had made the world forget the First. He tried to talk about it to a few of the old people in the coffeehouses and bazaars, but as soon as they heard the 'G' of either 'Great Fire' or 'Greek', they'd get up and move to another table. Avinash was bemused by this. It was as if the whole city had suffered universal amnesia. They gazed at him with vacant eyes, as if the old Smyrna had never existed, had not been burned to the ground, had not lost half its population. Most of the churches had been destroyed, schools had become Turkish, and all the old records, ledgers and deeds had been incinerated. Our old neighbourhood had been put up for auction. When nobody bought it, they turned it into a park.

When Avinash understood that the past had become a secret here, a taboo subject that could never be talked about, he went to Greece. He went round asking for me in the squatter neighbourhoods where fugitives from Smyrna, Aydin and the interior of Asia Minor had settled.

'Thank goodness I had in my hand your name and the name of the neighbourhood in Smyrna where you'd lived,' he said, reminding me of our first encounter at the quay. 'I wasn't feeling my way in complete darkness. It didn't take long before I found someone who knew you and your father.'

The refugee settlements around Athens, Piraeus, Faliro and Kastella had popped up like mushrooms. It was to these shanty towns that the refugees from Smyrna had fled, cobbling together huts made out of bricks and tin and wooden fruit crates, painting them white and covering the roofs with tar paper. Sewage flowed openly through the middle of some of them.

In the settlement called Nea Smyrna people made do with curtains rather than doors in their houses, but in the courtyards of each house they still managed to raise spindly little plants in tin containers. Here was a pot of basil, there a pot of carnations. One portion of the water they drew from the community well was for themselves, the rest was for the flowers and trees that reminded them of the life they'd left behind in the fertile soil of old Smyrna.

The residents of Nea Smyrna welcomed Avinash with open arms.

In contrast to the people back in Izmir, here everyone remembered old Smyrna. Like a sweet dream, they held the memory of it in the centre of their hearts. Seeing Avinash, the men in the coffeehouse stopped their backgammon game midway through; women, old and young, brought chairs out in front of doors that opened onto sewage-smelling courtyards and offered the former spy whatever they had to hand. Although more than twenty years had passed since the Great Catastrophe – they referred to what had happened during those horrifying days as the Great Catastrophe – some still asked when they would be permitted to return to their homes. In lowered voices the men would urge Avinash, 'Mister, tell us which political party we should vote for to get us sent back to our country.' Some could not accept that they had left their rose- and jasmine-scented city forever and that their life would continue in this sewage-smelling settlement on the outskirts of the city of Athens.

Suddenly, Avinash paused and I realized that he had some information concerning me. It wasn't his own crazy, nonsensical story this time. It was something about my life, the life I had once lived, something to do with the people from that life. I sat up straight, opened my eyes. The light in my dim tower changed suddenly. Finally, he started speaking again.

'In the settlement of Nea Smyrna I found your father.'

I was confused. Who did he mean by 'my father'? Did he mean the one who repaired the cars Edward Thomas-Cook brought from England, the one who seduced Edith while he was giving her driving lessons, the boatman Ali from Chesme? Or did he mean Grocer Akis, whom I knew as my father all my life? It was quite possible, according to the story this senile spy was telling, that Juliette Lamarck had had my real father taken out by Cakircali's gang. Which meant that it was Akis that Avinash was speaking of. My lips began to tremble.

'No, I did not meet him in person. Mr Prodromakis died the year that I arrived there. I spoke with his neighbours. When he came to Greece, he settled first in Faliro; then he moved to Nea Smyrna, where he remained for the rest of his life.'

The trembling spread from my lips and took over my whole body. I held on to the iron bedstead to stop myself from falling over. It was the first time in fifty years that someone had brought me news from the life I had buried in the cemetery at Daragaci. My father had survived, had made it to Greece, had lived all alone in a squatter settlement, and had then died there. Where was my mother while all this was happening? Avinash must have read the question in my eyes, for he bowed his head. He swayed back and forth in the rocking chair. His body was so diminished, his feet didn't reach the floor.

I got up from the bed, walked over to the rocking chair, grabbed hold of his wrinkled chin and turned his face to mine. The rocking ceased abruptly. The saggy flesh under his chin made Avinash look like a turtle. The only connection with that handsome, exotic-looking man I'd hit in the testicles in front of Kraemer's a half-century ago was the spicy scent of distant lands that emanated from his skin. My eyes were bulging. I stared into his café-au-lait eyes, over which a dull curtain had fallen. Since he had come to tell me the truth, he was obliged to tell me what had happened to my mother – not Edith Lamarck, but the one who knew me as her daughter, who held me close to her heart, who raised me. Katina Yagcioglu.

'The neighbours I talked to in Nea Smyrna said that Ms Katina, that is, your mother... unfortunately...' He tried to escape my gaze by twisting his head towards the hatch that opened onto the stairs leading down from the tower. I held his chin and again turned his wizened face to mine. The curtain of death lowered itself over his eyes.

'Your mother, unfortunately... did not survive the Great Fire.'

When I let go of his chin, the chair rocked back and forth a few times. Avinash was gripping its arms in fear. I kicked the slippers off my feet, lay back on the bed and lost myself looking at the scrap of Sumbul's pink sash that still hung from the beam. Another warplane zoomed by above us. I closed my eyes and thought of Akis, in a settlement outside Athens, grieving for the rest of his life; of Katina swallowed in flames; of the lives and dreams destroyed by war; of my youth, also destroyed by war. For some reason I mourned most deeply not for my mother, who died in the most painful way imaginable, but for my father, who lost everyone he loved on earth and died all alone in exile.

By the time Avinash began to speak again, the sea breeze had picked up and my tower was filled with the rosy light of evening. The neighbours in Nea Smyrna had been unanimous in claiming that Grocer Akis's daughter, like her mother, had died in Smyrna. Some had seen me being lifted up by a Turkish officer and thrown over the back of his horse just as I was about to jump into the sea. They had raped me behind Gumruk, as they had the other girls, then slit my throat.

That's what they told Avinash.

A woman who had been raped many times by soldiers but had managed to stay alive said that she'd been at my side when they cut my throat. When I pictured my father all alone in that settlement imagining such scenes, I again began to cry.

My God! Who deserved that much pain?

After hearing those stories, Avinash returned to Izmir and rented that old house in Tilkilik, where years later his body would be found in front of the fireplace. Apparently, he wanted to die in the city where he had met his one and only love, where he had spent the best years of his life. But death forgot him, just as it has forgotten me.

A quarter of a century passed and still Avinash had not died.

Almighty God had not taken his soul because the universe was waiting for the coincidence to arise that would bring him to me. That's what he said. If he wasn't a nutcase, then what was he? But as it turned out, that crazy theory of his proved to be true. One spring morning, the day after his ninety-fourth birthday, Avinash Pillai left his house in Tilkilik and was on his way to the coffeehouse beside the Hatuniye Mosque, when he ran into Gypsy Yasemin. The peddler wasn't at all surprised to see him; in fact, it was almost as if she'd been waiting for him, there, in that deserted passageway behind the mosque.

'Well, you have finally come, Avinash Efendi,' she said. 'Please, follow me.'

As I've said, Avinash was pushing a hundred at that point. His spine was as crooked as the handle on a walking stick. His hair was still long but bore no trace of his erstwhile black curls and fell down his back like a silver rat's tail. As for his beard, it was down to his belly. He was skinny, as puny as could be; you could count the ribs beneath his shirt. They probably treated him like a white-haired crazy in those old neighbourhoods. He still attended the music sessions at the Dervish lodge, he said. I thought the Mustafa Kemal Pasha had ordered all those lodges closed, so either there were still some underground meetings or our Avinash really had lost his marbles. He also claimed that he'd walked all the way here, to the Mansion with the Tower, from there, following behind Yasemin. Yasemin wasn't any younger than he was, so I don't know how they managed to get here from Tilkilik.

I'm not minded to believe any of that Gypsy Yasemin

nonsense, but I can't think of any other way to explain how, out of the blue one morning, the former spy finally found me. He'd spent thirty years searching for me without success, pounding the streets, interrogating old Smyrna residents in the suburbs of Piraeus and Athens, leafing through church records and population registers. If you asked Avinash, he'd say that Yasemin's was one of those deaths that had to wait so that I could learn my story. Ah, Panagia *mou*, Mother of God! Where is this story straight that I should say this part is crooked?

On that day, just before dawn, when Midwife Meline returned from the Lamarck mansion and ran with the baby swaddled in her arms from the Greek Orphanage on the corner of Hadji Frangou to the French Hospital, Yasemin had been one of the gypsies reading fortunes on the corner of Chan Street. Avinash was impressed that the old gypsy had made the connection, but Yasemin had simply snapped back, 'I added two and two and got four. Why are you surprised, Avinash Efendi?' Avinash, however, maintained that Yasemin had used supernatural powers to determine how the story would end. I think the ancient spy had gone bananas. Anyway, thanks to Juliette Lamarck having acted on a last-minute whim – a whim that would cost her her life – he knew that an orphanage was involved in the story. Yasemin filled in the blanks. Everything slotted into place.

But let me not speak ill of the dead. He put a lot of effort into getting me to believe this story, which I thought was total nonsense at first. Because Edith stuffed all of Juliette Lamarck's journals that had been kept in a locked box into a suitcase at the last minute while she was running from the fire, those journals have survived to this day. There were also photographs that had been taken over the following years in Paris, and diaries full of confessions that the woman had written as she got older. All of the letters and the diaries that survived were brought to the tower.

After Edith died, Avinash contacted her closest friend from the school in Paris, Feride. He even visited her at her home in Istanbul. Feride was aware that during Edith's Christmas vacation in 1904, which was extended for two months because of her father's illness, Edith had had a secret affair with a car repairman in Bournabat named Ali. She was pregnant when she returned to school. By May of 1905, her stomach had begun to show even under the loose school uniform and the nuns packed her off to Marseille, where she boarded a boat for Smyrna. Feride was with Edith at that time. In later years the two friends kept in touch with letters and visits. Feride was sure that Edith's daughter had died at birth. Avinash did not contradict her.

In truth, there was no need for Avinash to have brought all those sacks of letters and notebooks to my tower. The photographs that he took out of a leather case and placed in front of me were enough to prove his story correct. The young woman in the photograph taken in a studio against a backdrop of deer and trees was me. I even found myself thinking: I don't remember that white scarf at all. Wondering in which year and at which studio I'd had it taken, I turned it over and saw the date, 1903, written in pencil. The young girl looking at me from between the faded cardboard with torn edges was Edith Lamarck.

The resemblance continued in photographs my mother had had taken during her years in Paris. In particular, in a photograph taken at a café during the war, every line and shadow of the face was exactly the same as the face in the mirror that Avinash placed in my hand. In one of the photographs Edith was smiling in such a way that all her teeth were visible. There was the exact same gap between her two front teeth that I had been so ashamed of when I was young and had always tried to cover with my lips.

Thank you, *Maman*.

Okay. I accepted it. Now I knew. So what were we supposed to do? Was I surprised? Was I upset? A half-century had passed since the early morning Sumbul found me in her garden. Ever since that day, I had lived in that Turkish house as the silent Scheherazade. I was sixty-nine years old. Sumbul had died. Hilmi Rahmi, unable to bear her absence, died shortly thereafter in the grip of a feverish illness. After all that time, so what if the past, my identity, my mother and my father were not as I'd thought?

I had already died once, on the night when I lost everything, and was reborn. So if Avinash Efendi had added to my past one more death and one more rebirth, what did it change?

I am Scheherazade, Hilmi Rahmi's mute concubine, whom he saved and then abandoned to loneliness. I will continue to wait calmly and silently for my death in my tower overlooking a city which has lost its memory.

Not counting that one time, when he was dying and I whispered my name in Hilmi Rahmi's ear, I had not spoken a single word in fifty-two years. After all that time, I wasn't about to open my mouth and tell Avinash what was on my mind. The nasty spy nodded his head as if he'd read my thoughts. He had done his duty. Death could take him now. He could surrender himself peacefully. From his case he brought out a thick, leather-bound notebook, the one in which I am now writing these words, a gold-plated fountain pen and a box containing hundreds of ink cartridges. Attempting to straighten his crooked spine, he got up and walked round the bed to the tower's small window. Back then, they'd not yet demolished the stone house in front of the tower or erected an apartment block in its place, so you could still see the sea from the window. Without taking his eyes off the glittering water, which had turned a magenta colour in the setting sun, he spoke.

'Those people who saved you and took you in did not give you the name Scheherazade for nothing. Until you tell this story, death will not come knocking at your tower.'

For the first time since I had opened the door to my tower and seen his face that morning, I smiled. If I could have spoken, I would have said, 'My dear Avinash Bey, you are mistaken. Scheherazade tells her story to keep herself alive, not to allow death to visit.' Actually, I didn't need to speak. Like Sumbul, Avinash could read my mind. He understood the shame I would feel, as one who had managed to survive, if I were to take it upon myself to speak for the dead. Still, he left the brown leather notebook and the fountain pen on the table, then picked his hat up off the faded pink iron bed rail where he'd hung it that morning and placed it on his head.

Just as he'd done a half-century earlier when we met on the quay, he brushed my hand with his fleshy purple lips as he murmured, 'There will come a day, Panagiota, when you will be so constrained by the dark eternity in which you have hidden yourself, where you hear no voice except that within you, that as Scheherazade longed for life, you will long for death. That will be the time to tell your story.'

Part V

PARADISE LOST

The Silence of the Church Bells

When Hilmi Rahmi returned home, everybody, even Mujgan, who was in mourning for Huseyin, rejoiced. Ever since he'd ridden up Bulbul Street in his spotlessly clean colonel's uniform on his shiny black horse, the house had been filled with laughter and tears, tears and prayers.

It wasn't only Bulbul Street. All the Turkish neighbourhoods had been celebrating. From Konak to the Caravan Bridge, everywhere was decorated as if it were a holiday. Red flags hung from shops, from the doors of houses, off balconies; red ribbons were tied around lampposts and the necks of carriage horses. Children had put on their holiday clothes and were singing and dancing in the streets; women opened their hands and gave thanks to Allah for creating Mustafa Kemal Pasha, then hugged and kissed each other, crying with joy. The sound of drums and pipes reverberated from the steep, narrow, labyrinthine roads around the cemeteries. In wealthy homes, gramophones played cheerful records. Young girls holding baskets full of flowers threw roses in the path of the soldiers marching down Hukumet Avenue.

The three-year Greek occupation had ended. Smyrna had become theirs again.

Sumbul wore a purple silk dress she'd taken out of the trunk. For the first time in years, she'd woken up in her husband's arms. Hilmi Rahmi had lost weight, and aged somewhat, but he'd proved he was still a strong and healthy man by making love to his wife many times, despite his exhaustion.

Even though Sumbul tried to hide her happiness so as not to make Mujgan sad, when she came into the kitchen with her blonde hair cascading over her shoulders, all the women of the house, from Nanny Dilber to Great-Aunt Makbule, knew at one glance that she'd had a night filled with pleasure. Her cheeks were flushed as if she'd just come from a steam bath, and a deeply peaceful glow had settled in her green eyes. When the image of Hilmi Rahmi in that fancy dark green uniform came into her mind, the delights of the night played over her body and a spontaneous smile lit up her face, like a new bride.

The night before, when she was helping Hilmi Rahmi to undress, he'd told her that the uniforms had been given out the morning before they entered the city. They had come as gifts to Mustafa Kemal Pasha's officers from the Bolsheviks. Someone from one of the influential Levantine families in Bournabat had had the uniforms tailored for the officers and then sent to the frontlines. His boots were jet black like his fez and came up to the knees. His silk necktie was the same red as the star and crescent embroidered on his fez. The tailoring of his jacket was perfect, with not a button missing. Hilmi Rahmi couldn't stop talking about the strength and nobility of the horses which had been a gift of the Italians to the Pasha's army.

Like a child who'd received a prize after a difficult examination, he had forgotten the painful war years passed in hunger and thirst. He just kept describing to Sumbul the pomp of their entry into Izmir.

'Captain Serafettin was at the front, and we made such an entrance at the quay, Sumbul, on our splendid horses. We showed the whole world what a well-disciplined army we are. Everyone exhibited great restraint and when the Christians fled from our horses, we calmed them by repeating over and over, "Do not be afraid, do not be afraid, do not be afraid." Just wait until Kemal Pasha comes to Izmir and you will see how well-trained his soldiers are. He made those mountain villagers into an army and defeated the infidels. My Sumbul, we are going to create a brand-new country. The Pasha has a great vision. We will be a European nation. I am going to take you to Kraemer's and to dances at Kordelio. You won't hide in a corner drinking beer; you will wear low-cut gowns and dance. Why do you lower your head? Do you think I don't know that you want to get all dressed up like those European ladies and promenade? Come on now, get up and I will show you how we will dance together at the balls!'

As Sumbul wandered around the kitchen, she hummed the song that was being played in all the cafés that year, 'Le tango du rêve'. Then she sang 'Izmir'in Kavaklari'. She lifted the lids of the pots bubbling on the stove to check on the food they were preparing for the feast in honour of Hilmi Rahmi's return and Izmir's independence. Her father-in-law Mustafa Efendi would also attend. She heard her sons' voices outside the kitchen window. Cengiz and Dogan had put on boots under their baggy trousers and were waiting for her at the courtyard gate that opened onto the street. She threw a robe around her shoulders and joined them.

When he saw his mother, Dogan gave an excited yelp. 'Mummy, you are coming with us, aren't you? To see Kemal Pasha?'

Sumbul leaned down and straightened the wide red sash

around her younger son's waist. When she saw that there was a crown of flowers under his fez, she smiled indulgently. 'Who put that crown of flowers on your head, I wonder?'

'It was Ziver,' his elder brother Cengiz interjected, before Dogan could answer. 'He made it himself. I wouldn't let him put one on my head. Flowers don't look good on a man's head.' He looked to his mother for approval.

Releasing Dogan, she turned to her elder son. His crimson fez was too big for his shaved head and came right down over his slightly protruding ears. Unlike his father, Cengiz was short and chubby, with languid round green eyes. As she gazed at her sons, her heart filled with love. She wanted to take them in her arms as she had when they were babies.

'Come, let me hug you boys. Today is our happiest day.'

'Yes, because our father has returned!' said Dogan, as if reciting a lesson he had memorized.

Hearing the lack of genuine feeling in her younger son's voice, Sumbul reminded herself that Dogan didn't really know his father at all. For the past nine years, ever since Dogan was born, Hilmi Rahmi had been at one battlefront after the other. Dogan had grown up without a father.

'Not because of that, stupid,' Cengiz scolded. 'Today our Kemal Pasha is coming to Izmir. Today is our independence day. That's what our mother said, isn't that right, Mother?'

Dogan tugged at Sumbul's robe. 'Mummy, you are coming to see Kemal Pasha, aren't you?' he repeated.

'Of course I'm coming, child. I want to see Kemal Pasha too. We'll all go together – your Aunt Mujgan, the girls, your father, Ziver, Nanny Dilber, maybe even Aunt Makbule. We're just waiting for your father and grandfather to finish their coffee. Why don't you run to the men's quarters and see if they're ready.'

Dogan had just opened his mouth to say he didn't want to go into the men's quarters when a commotion broke out in the street. Women were screaming, drums were booming, and children were running beside the drummer shouting, 'He's coming! He's coming!'

Cengiz rushed to the gate. 'Mother, Kemal Pasha is coming! Hurry!'

The door to the men's quarters opened. Mustafa Efendi came out first, leaning on his cane, followed by Hilmi Rahmi, standing tall in his immaculate uniform. Seeing her husband with his cartridge belt and sword at his waist, Sumbul felt that silly grin creeping across her face again. Her insides fluttered; it was as if she were a fifteen-year-old girl and not a thirty-five-year-old woman.

Mujgan's daughters and Nanny Dilber flew out from the kitchen. At the last minute, Mujgan had changed her mind and decided to stay at home with Aunt Makbule. She couldn't bear all that rejoicing while she was crying bloody tears inside. So as not to leave the women at home alone, it had been agreed that Ziver would stay with them. Hearing this, the poor Ethiopian boy looked crestfallen, but as Hilmi Rahmi mounted his handsome black horse that had been tied up in the courtyard, he promised he would take Ziver to Konak to see Kemal Pasha later.

Mustafa Efendi, the women and the children joined the crowds going down Iki Chesmelik Street towards Konak to the accompaniment of the drum and pipe band. Hilmi Rahmi dug his spurs into his horse and headed off to take his place in the cavalry unit that would line both sides of the Caravan Bridge as Kemal Pasha's cavalcade entered the city.

Every road leading down from Hukumet Street was blocked by a mass of people. Mustafa Efendi indicated with his hand that he could go no further and sat himself down on a stool in front of one of the shops decorated with red flags in the Kemeralti Bazaar. Since his wife Sidika Hanim's death, the poor man had aged a great deal. Sumbul told the children to stop. It would not be appropriate to leave their grandfather and go down to the quay without him. Cengiz pouted. He wanted to at least cross the street to where the men were standing; from where they were, they couldn't even see the street.

Students from a girls' school, dressed in black uniforms and waving flags, passed in front of them. Their teachers, in long black robes, were prodding them from all sides to keep them in line. When Cengiz saw his neighbourhood friends on the pavement across the street, dressed as he was in jacket and trousers with dark purple fezzes on their heads, he mixed in with the girl students and crossed over without saying anything to his mother.

Sumbul realized immediately that her son had given her the slip. She pushed through the throngs of women to get to a spot where she could keep an eye on him. Dogan, frightened by the crowd and the noise of the drums, was glued to his mother's skirts. Mujgan's daughters edged their way to the front with their baskets so that they could throw flowers on the road as the procession passed. Sumbul noticed that they had a picture of Kemal Pasha pinned to the breasts of their capes. She also noticed that Nanny Dilber's forehead was shiny with sweat; taking a fan from her handbag, she passed it to her. She wiped her own face with the edge of her robe, which was the colour of pomegranate flowers.

When the five cars comprising Mustafa Kemal's cavalcade finally appeared at the top of the avenue, shrieks of joy rippled through the crowd. Cengiz was standing with the other boys closest to the road and Dogan was crying for his mother to pick him up so he could see. As the sparklingly clean black cars covered with olive branches drove past, roses rained from the sky. With one voice, the crowd roared, 'Long live Ghazi Mustafa Kemal Pasha!'

Sumbul didn't get to see Kemal Pasha sitting in the back seat of the open convertible at the rear of the cavalcade. Her view was blocked by the heads of the women in front of her and by the cavalry lined up on both sides of the road with their sabres crossed. But that didn't dampen her excitement; her heart was bursting with pride and hope as she studied the piercing blue eyes that stared out at her from the portrait on the giant cardboard placard that two girls in the front row were holding up. How handsome he was.

Women in the front who'd had the honour of catching sight of him whispered, 'He's lost so much weight, his cheeks are hollow. But he still looks magnificent.'

'He hasn't touched a drop of alcohol in a month and he didn't allow his soldiers to drink, either.'

At the back, old people opened their hands to the sky, praying for Mustafa Kemal's health and prosperity, and thanking Allah for bringing them independence.

Dogan hadn't climbed into his mother's arms soon enough and so had missed seeing the Pasha. Aware that his brother, on the opposite side of the street, had had the best view, he began to cry. Behind the women, Mustafa Efendi was leaning on his cane as he sat hunched over on the stool in front of the shuttered shop. Sumbul thought that he might be finding it all too much – the crowds, the noise and the heat. As the cavalcade of shiny black cars inched its way down towards the sea, she motioned for Nanny Dilber, Cengiz and the girls to get ready to leave. Holding her father-in-law's arm, she got him to his feet.

As they walked up Hukumet Avenue to Iki Chesmelik, Cengiz pulled sulkily at his mother's robe. He wanted to follow the convoy down to the quay. Sumbul looked desperately for Hilmi Rahmi among the soldiers showily riding around on their horses, but she couldn't see him through the crowd. 'Your grandfather's not well, son,' she said, prizing Cengiz's fingers from her robe. 'Let's take him home, then you can go out with Ziver, down to the quay. Okay?'

Cengiz kicked at a stone by way of reply.

When they'd pushed their way through the throngs of people drunk on victory and arrived at their house on Bulbul Street, they found Hilmi Rahmi at the entrance to the courtyard. He looked very upset about something; his face was set in a frown. Handing his horse over to Ziver, he walked to the door.

Cengiz had been imagining the moment when he would tell his father about coming eye to eye with Kemal Pasha, but seeing him distracted and silent, his confidence faltered. Still, he put on a brave face and raced up to his father.

'Father, I saw Kemal Pasha – and he saw me! He looked straight into my eyes – his eyes are like the sea, deep blue – and then he lowered his eyebrows the way the women teachers at school do. He was so serious.'

Hilmi Rahmi pushed his son aside, ignoring the pleading look in the boy's eyes, eyes that were the same green as his mother's, and went into the men's quarters. A now tearful Cengiz came to his mother's side, and Sumbul, who'd observed the change in her husband with concern, took him in her arms and whispered, 'Your father is thinking about his brother, your Uncle Huseyin, who was killed in the war.

Let him go to his room and rest for a bit. Later he'll talk to you about Kemal Pasha. Now go and tell Ziver that you and he should get down to the quay. The girls will want to go too, I'm sure. Don't miss the Pasha's speech. Listen well so that when you come back you can repeat it for me, word for word. Okay? Don't forget your flag.'

Sumbul breathed a sigh of relief when Mujgan's daughters and Cengiz left the courtyard with Ziver. Her ears were ringing. It was so hot. Maybe she had heat stroke. She went to the women's quarters. Without stopping by the kitchen, she made straight for the spacious salon, took off her robe and shoes and lay down on the couch.

'Mummy, is Father going to shoot Uncle Kostaki with his pistol?'

Sumbul was startled. She had dozed off, forgetting her younger son Dogan, who was waving his sword at imaginary enemies in a far corner of the room. 'What's happened, my Dogan?' she asked anxiously. 'What's made you think that?'

Even from where she lay on the couch, she could see that her son's eyes had welled up. Suddenly she was worried. Had the humpbacked confectionary seller Kostaki, who came past the mosque every day with his rooster-shaped, red, yellow, orange and green lollipops, done something to Dogan?

'Son, come and sit here with me. Did Uncle Kostaki do something to make you unhappy?'

Dogan scampered across the rug in his bare feet to where his mother was sitting. Sumbul took a handkerchief from the bosom of her dress and wiped his runny nose, then raised her purple silk sleeve so that Dogan could settle under her armpit like a cat, as if he were an extension of his mother.

'Dogan, darling, tell me, why did you think your father would shoot Uncle Kostaki?'

The boy felt safe under his mother's arm. '"Father will kill all the infidels with his gun," that's what my brother said. I asked him, "Even Uncle Kostaki?" and he said, "Yes."' He straightened up and turned his small face to hers. 'Please, Mummy, tell Father not to shoot Uncle Kostaki. He always gives me lollipops when he passes the mosque.'

He buried himself in his mother's silky armpit once again and began to sob. Sumbul decided she would give Cengiz a good beating when he came home, but then her heart softened as she reminded herself that her older son was caught up in the euphoria of victory, that was all.

'Your brother was joking, son. Your father killed the enemy with his gun, but he wouldn't shoot people who weren't soldiers. Thanks be to Allah, we won the war. We got rid of the enemy who were occupying our land. Now we can live as we did in the past. Uncle Kostaki will stay here as our neighbour for the rest of his life, giving you rooster-shaped lollipops.'

'Mummy, is Uncle Kostaki an infidel?'

Sumbul leaned down and buried her nose in her son's chestnut-coloured hair. The smell of mastic and lavender had seeped from the pillows into the curls flattened by his fez. She poured kisses onto his head and squeezed his little body tight until he had had enough.

From outdoors came the clatter of plates, forks and glasses on the table that Nanny Dilber and Mujgan were setting in the shade of the chestnut tree. Leaning her head back on the couch, Sumbul closed her eyes. What could Hilmi Rahmi be doing alone in the men's quarters? On this happy day, a splinter was still pricking her heart. Why? Was her soul so greedy that it could never find peace? Surely not. On the contrary, after the night of lovemaking in her husband's arms, she felt like a satisfied cat. Izmir was back in Turkish hands. In Mustafa Kemal their country had a progressive, European-style leader at the helm. This filled her with pride, joy, and excitement. Hilmi Rahmi had said they would go to balls like European husbands and wives, would dance together as they did. Sumbul could not believe that something like this would happen in her lifetime, but she was still pleased that her husband could imagine dancing with her in the European style. In her mind she saw herself playing the piano in Plovdiv while her mother and father waltzed in the ballroom of their mansion.

'I'm so hungry,' Dogan mumbled, walking his soldier-fingers across his mother's stomach. 'If there's extra, can I have two helpings of quince dessert?'

The silence at dinner, which they ate all together under the chestnut tree after the evening call to prayer, suited Mujgan perfectly. The festive mood in the neighbourhood had brought home the fact that her husband had been killed not by the infidels but while fighting against the army of the Ottoman sultan, who opposed Kemal Pasha's National Struggle for Independence. The cheerful celebrations and victory yells, rather than alleviating her pain, were making it worse. The patriotic fervour that she had defended throughout the War of Independence now felt hollow in her husband's absence. The thing they called a country didn't fill even a corner of the great emptiness she felt inside. How was she supposed to feel any bond with those stupid people out there when her life had been deprived of its most precious connection?

As the revelry outside continued, Mujgan's sorrow and anger intensified.

The sun had set. In the evening breeze, the scent of roses wafted over the dinner table. Nanny Dilber lit the lamps she'd hung in the branches of the chestnut tree. The sound of drums and pipes still echoed on the street, and through the open window of the owner of the gramophone they could hear martial music, folksongs, opera melodies and even the tango. From time to time youths passing through Iki Chesmelik would yell out in celebration, to be met with either scolding or applause from neighbours who'd brought their chairs out in front of their houses.

The boys raced to finish their food so that they could go out and join in the revelry as soon as possible. Dogan even forgot about that second dessert. While Nanny Dilber was serving the coffee, Sumbul asked if she could let the boys go out onto the street with Ziver to supervise them. Hilmi Rahmi said no.

The boys looked to their mother with both disappointment and hope as Hilmi Rahmi and Mustafa Efendi took their coffee into the men's quarters. Sumbul sensed that the dinner table had been quiet not out of respect for Huseyin but rather because of something that had happened in the city earlier that day. She paid no attention to the boys' pleas. 'You heard with your own ears that your father does not permit you to go out. What can I do?'

After finishing his coffee, Hilmi Rahmi went to his bedroom, put on his tall black boots and slung his cartridge belt over his shoulder. Where was he going so late in the evening? Sumbul's heart was thumping with fear. Hilmi Rahmi frowned. Looking into the mirror, he straightened his red necktie and pulled at his moustache. Sumbul took the lamp at the head of the bed and placed it on the small table in front of the mirror.

'Sumbul, I have forbidden my father to go to the European neighbourhood. Word has been passed to Madame Lamarck's daughter's house too. Madame Lamarck sent all the servants working in the mansion in Bournabat away except my father. How thoughtless! Is an old man to act as an armed guard? Father was very insistent, but eventually he agreed to stay here.'

'You did well. He should stay with us for a time and rest. Today was difficult for him. I thought he might collapse at one point. But why has Madame Lamarck come into the city? Is Bournabat not safe? What's happening in the European neighbourhoods?'

Hilmi Rahmi had taken an ivory comb from his pocket and was smoothing back his light-chestnut hair in front of the mirror. Sumbul took his black fez from on top of the trunk and held it ready for him. He placed it on his head, took his watch from the pocket of his jacket and checked the time.

'Wife, everywhere is in chaos right now. I heard that there's been fighting in Bournabat – nothing to do with us, but Greek soldiers fighting among themselves, settling old scores. A noisy row between supporters of Venizelos and supporters of the Greek king. Such quarrels don't concern us any longer. I spoke with my superiors a little earlier and it seems I must be on duty for a few more days. I will leave my father in your care. Do not go out into the neighbourhood at all until I return. You should send Ziver to the market and have him buy a week's provisions. Do not leave the house.'

'But…' Sumbul knew that with such a festive atmosphere

on the streets, it would be impossible to keep the boys inside. Turkish soldiers had liberated the city, so why the need for such caution? And was she about to be left on her own again? She hadn't had enough of her husband yet. Her eyes filled.

'Are there weapons in the house?'

Sumbul sniffed. For so many years she'd not shed a single tear. She'd been patient. But now, in front of her husband, her vulnerability was coming to the surface. Ashamed of herself, she turned her head.

'There's a double-barrelled shotgun in the well. And an old Greek Mauser rifle. When we were here on our own, your father thoughtfully brought us a Russian Nagant revolver. We hid that too. That's all. Huseyin took the rest.'

'Any shells?'

'A few. What's going on, for God's sake, Hilmi Rahmi? Are we not safe? Are Greek gangs going to come and ransack our houses? I thought they'd all been evacuated, or are some of them still here? Are they going to burn this city as well before they leave?'

Hilmi Rahmi looked at his wife with love. Standing there in front of the door in her purple silk, with her curly blonde hair falling over her shoulders and her green eyes wide with fear, she looked like a fairy in the dim light of the lamp. She was even more beautiful than he remembered. His heart tightened at the thought that he would not be sleeping by her side that night. He straightened his back and reminded himself that it was his duty to keep the city and its people safe. Waving his hand in the air, he tried to dispel the dark possibilities that came to his mind. It was probably because of these possibilities that Nureddin Pasha had called his officers back to work.

He buckled on his brown leather belt and embraced Sumbul. 'You are safe, wife. As long as we're in this city, you're safe. No one is going to burn our beautiful Izmir or ransack our houses. Everyone can continue going about their business.'

They walked out to the courtyard together. The streets had finally quietened, and night had settled over the city. The full moon had risen behind Kadife Kale in all its splendour, preparing to bathe the bay in its silver glow. The courtyard was filled with the intoxicating smell of honeysuckle that had been warmed by the sun all day. Sumbul passed her fingers over the scented flowers twining up the wall.

With one hand holding his horse's reins, Hilmi Rahmi scanned the courtyard. 'As a precaution, lock the gate behind me – I know how to open it from the outside. Take the shotgun out of the well and keep my father's Russian Nagant to hand. Do not open the gate to anyone asking for shelter, even neighbours.'

Sumbul's eyes widened in surprise. 'Even women and children?'

When Hilmi Rahmi didn't answer, something else occurred to Sumbul. 'Or are you worried that our own soldiers might ransack the city? But didn't Kemal Pasha declare that anyone who so much as laid a finger on the possessions, lives or honour of the Christians would be sentenced to death? In which case, who would dare?'

With a nervous expression on his face, Hilmi Rahmi passed his palm over his horse's glossy black coat. He didn't tell his wife that Metropolitan Bishop Chrysostomos, the highly esteemed leader of the Greek Orthodox community in Smyrna, had been killed by a lynch mob in Konak. They had first gouged out the old man's eyes with a pair of barber's scissors, then cut off his ears and his nose. After which, to make an example of him, they had dragged his dying body through the streets, before finally throwing his corpse outside the city.

He turned his hazel eyes to the sky, where the moon was shining like a jewel. He didn't mention how on cold nights at the front hungry soldiers used to dream of looting the houses of infidels as revenge for the tortures they were suffering. Hilmi Rahmi remembered how disgusted he'd been when the officers had related how on those lonely nights the young men torn from the heart of Asia Minor would huddle together for warmth around a fire, rubbing their hands and talking of the beauty and immorality of infidel women and how, if they won the war, they would have the right to make those women do anything they wanted.

The horse whinnied impatiently. Solitary clouds scudded across the starry sky towards the sea.

'No one. No exceptions.'

'But—'

'Sumbul, to save the lives of our children, you must follow what I say to the letter. I entreat you. Just do as I say and ask no more questions.'

Sumbul lowered her blonde head and looked at the long shadows in the garden lit up by the full moon. Hilmi Rahmi went through the wooden gate, mounted his horse in one smooth movement, turned the animal with a tug of the reins in the direction of the Jewish neighbourhood, and, without looking back at his wife, disappeared from sight behind the cemetery.

As she locked the gate behind him, Sumbul had the feeling that nothing would ever be the same again. She suddenly realized what it was that had been making her so uneasy the whole day, like a thorn pricking her heart. It was a Sunday, and for the first time ever since she'd arrived in the city as a fresh young bride, not one of the church bells in Smyrna had rung.

The Copper-Coloured Cloud

Adriana's mother, the washerwoman Sofia, shook her head as she gathered in her laundry from the line. The sheets she'd scrubbed with soap and bluing had suddenly turned black. Soot was raining from the sky.

'Adriana, *kori mou*, you'll have to wash these again tomorrow, *endaksi*? They're covered in soot – I don't understand why.'

Adriana nodded from her chair in the corner of her father's cabbage patch. Sofia didn't want to add to her daughter's troubles that evening. Adriana was very sad. Before daybreak that morning, Minas had snuck onto an American ship transporting tobacco to Alexandria and escaped. Protestant missionary friends who'd given him American comic books as well as other books to read had saved his life.

The previous day, word had spread that the Turks were rounding up all Greek males between the ages of eighteen and forty-five who were still in the city and taking them as prisoners of war. Rumour had it that several had already been hunted down in the basements and attics of their mothers' houses where they'd been hiding.

Minas didn't wait to find out whether the rumours were

true or not. He went straight to the cinema where some Americans had set up camp; he was already known there because he'd been to one of their missionary meetings, and that really paid off now. If he converted to the Protestant faith, a tall man with a red moustache told him, they would send him to university in America. The man didn't drag his feet: that morning, before dawn, he'd taken Minas to the port. Following an argument with the ship's captain, who was unhappy at being roused from his sleep, Minas was taken down to the hold and hidden behind crates full of tobacco.

Minas hadn't had time to say goodbye to Adriana, but he wrote a note while he was in the hold and pressed it into the hand of an Italian sailor who was loading more cargo onto the ship. The sailor, may God bless him, immediately stopped what he was doing and went off to find Adriana at the address Minas had directed him to.

Panagiota, sitting beside Adriana in the cabbage patch, was no longer praying that Stavros would return. The last Greek ship evacuating soldiers had left the harbour. If Stavros came back, he'd be taken prisoner, and then who knew where he'd be sent, what suffering and torture he'd be subjected to. It was much, much better to die a hero on the battlefield than to be taken prisoner. She was consumed with fear and regret; her heart felt like it was in a clamp, being squeezed ever more tightly. She should have escaped to Chios five days ago, on the fishing boat Pavlo had arranged, and saved herself and her parents. There was no knowing now whether they would live or die.

From the quay came a roar like a wild animal dying in agony.

'Panagiota *mou*, it's late,' Sofia called out from over by the washing. 'You should go home now. Your mother and father will be worried.' Hearing machine gun-fire in the distance, she crossed herself three times. It was rumoured that Metropolitan Bishop Chrysostomos had been flayed. Her fingers trembled as she collected the clothes pegs.

'I'm waiting for my father, Auntie Sofia. He doesn't want me to be out on the streets by myself. He's gone to Uncle Petro's and will stop by for me on his way home.'

Sofia raised her head and looked at the darkening evening sky. A copper-coloured cloud appeared from the direction of Basmane.

Grocer Akis and the other men of the neighbourhood were sitting in Warehouseman Petro's garden, which was near Adriana's house. They were discussing what to do. They too saw the reddish cloud above the city.

'The quay is so packed that if you dropped a needle it wouldn't hit the ground,' Petro said. 'There are thousands of people on barges lined up alongside the dock. White-bearded old men and grandmothers are sleeping on the streets – homeless, helpless, still waiting for boats to come from Greece. The boats came, yes, but who did they take? Only those working for the commander of the occupying forces and the Greek central bank, along with strongboxes of money. There are swollen corpses floating in the water now, and just a couple of steps away, mothers are giving birth. There are outbreaks of cholera and typhus. Things are so desperate, we shouldn't just be thinking of ourselves – we should go down there and help, take in a family each, feed them bread and soup.'

'My wife has been feeding two families in our garden for a week,' said Adriana's father. He was known as Gypsy Mimiko because he was tall and lean, with straight black hair and dark skin. 'They walked all the way from Manisa on bare feet. Children, elderly grandmothers... We share our bread with them.'

'Good for you, Mimiko! And bravo to Kyra Sofia. We should all be following your example.'

The men pivoted in their chairs and looked at him with admiration.

Gypsy Mimiko turned his thin face to the ground. He looked a bit like a pigeon, with his small head and his beaky nose that jutted straight out from his forehead. Of all the men there, his was the poorest family, and the biggest, with eight children. He played a new instrument called the bouzouki in taverns and his wife Sofia took in washing. Even so, they were the only ones who'd thought to open up their home to the destitute refugees.

'They cook shish kebab and beans right in front of those poor wretches and then ask for money. That is inhumane!' grumbled the ironmonger Androulis. 'I saw them this morning when I went down to the quay. Barbers have set up chairs and are giving shaves in the middle of the street.'

Like it or not, the mention of villagers getting shaved in the open air brought to the men's minds the image of their beloved Metropolitan Bishop Chrysostomos, forced into a barber's apron in Konak and then having his beard ripped off and his eyes gouged out.

Akis's heart was as heavy as an ingot.

'They pulled the Armenians out of their homes and slit their throats. They raped all the girls and women.'

Mimiko's yellowish face went even paler. He had five daughters.

Seeing him shake, Akis placed a hand on his shoulder and said in a voice which was unconvincing even to himself, 'They will not touch us, Mimiko, my friend. The Armenians opened

fire on Turkish soldiers from the Church of St Stepanos. That
was their punishment. We are sitting quietly in our homes. The
danger has passed. We have to be smart, get reaccustomed to
Turkish rule and not be taken in by the tricks of an adventurer
like Venizelos. The European newspapers are all saying this.'

He glanced round Petro's garden for a newspaper, as if
there were any among them who could understand a French
newspaper. Seeing that no one, including himself, was
comforted by his words, he got up.

'Come, gentlemen, let us get to our homes. Our women
and daughters should not be left by themselves. We will meet
again tomorrow morning and talk.'

They all rose and began making their way back to their
homes in the streets around the square. The evening had
turned purple. Venus appeared then disappeared in the sky
of the setting sun. Akis and Mimiko followed the wall and
turned into their small neighbourhood square. It was usually
full of people at this time of the evening, but tonight it was
completely empty, blanketed in unaccustomed silence. The
bakery was still baking bread, but the coffeehouse was closed,
the table and chairs under its arbour upturned.

Mimiko bought five loaves of bread to feed the refugees
in his garden as well as his large family. Tearing off the heel
of one, he handed it to Akis. Steam spiralled up from the soft
white dough. As he chewed the bread, Akis raised his head to
the twilight sky and thought for a moment that everything
would again be as before. The reddish cloud over Basmane
seemed to have got closer.

'Kyr Akis,' Gypsy Mimiko said, speaking in a low voice,
as if he was afraid of the grocer, who was both respected
by everyone in the neighbourhood and famous for his burly
frame and his roar. 'You know best, of course, but I say let's

hide our daughters before the gangs come to ransack our neighbourhood. Let's not let what happened to the Armenians happen to us. They broke down their doors and forced their way in at night while everyone was sleeping.'

Akis scratched his black beard. He hadn't shaved in four days. He was planning to go down to Fasoula in the morning and get a shave, if he could find an open barber's shop.

'Do you have any suggestions?'

'I heard from the refugees that people are hiding their daughters in the tombs at the Daragaci graveyard. The bandits, gangs and soldiers are apparently afraid of going into the Greek Cemetery.'

'They're putting their daughters in graves? *Ti les vre*, Mimiko? What are you saying? Have we sunk so low? This is what war does, turns human beings into monsters.'

When they arrived at Mimiko's house on Katipzade Street, they could hear gunshots in the distance. As the two men passed through the garden gate, they were both thinking the same thing – which was why they were reluctant to look at each other. If the sound was coming from far away, it meant it wasn't their family but some other family. Thanks be to God.

They found Adriana, Panagiota and the other children sitting at the table under the mulberry tree eating olives and growler fish. The barefooted refugee children had adjusted to their new home, having been there a week now, and one had even crawled into Adriana's lap. In the light cast by the lamp that was hanging from one of the mulberry branches, Mimiko saw that his daughter's eyes were red from crying. Beside Adriana sat Tasoula, one size smaller; across from them were the twin girls, and four-year-old Irini was on Sofia's lap.

The boys were ashen-faced; they too had heard the rumour

that Greek males would be taken as prisoners of war. In the eyes of the Turks, they were all traitors who had taken up arms against their country. But Mimiko's sons hadn't gone to war; they'd never even held a gun in their hands. God willing, this was only a rumour. The youngest boy had just turned fifteen; the eldest, Aristo, was twenty-one and last Easter had got engaged to a girl from Agios Voukolos. There was still room for new dreams. There had to be.

Hadn't the European newspaper written that the danger had passed, warning people not to fall for the tricks of ridiculous politicians again? God forbid! thought Gypsy Mimiko. They would never trust outsiders again; they'd seen how they all just packed up and left. Mimiko and his friends were the ones who'd stayed, he thought bitterly, and now they were considered the traitors. He tried not to think about the Metropolitan Bishop, for fear of weeping in front of his children. Despite the urging of the Europeans, the man had not run away but had stayed in Smyrna to protect his community.

Sofia's hands were trembling as she cut the melon.

'I'll come again tomorrow,' said Panagiota at the gate, hugging her friend. Then she turned anxiously to her father. 'I can come, can't I, Papa? Will you walk me here again?'

Akis nodded. During these sad, tense days, it was better that Katina and Panagiota spent their time in busy households; he felt easier taking them to a friend's house than leaving the two of them on their own in the house on Menekse Street. They turned into the square. Katina had joined the women looking after Auntie Rozi at her home next to the coffeehouse, and as Akis and Panagiota passed, they picked her up.

When they got home, Panagiota and Katina set the table. They ate, dipping the bread Akis had brought from the bakery into the juice of the beans cooked at noon. None of them had any appetite and no one felt like talking.

'I saw a red cloud over Basmane,' said Katina, her eye on a stray piece of lace hanging off the edge of the couch in front of the bay window.

'I saw it too. Auntie Sofia said soot had rained down on all her washing.'

The two of them turned and looked at Akis, thinking he might be able to explain the cloud and the soot. Seeing his daughter's wan face, Mimiko's advice came to the grocer's mind. So the refugees were hiding their daughters in the cemetery at Daragaci, huh? He'd have to bring this up with Katina when they went to bed. Or would that be frightening the poor woman for no reason?

With nothing else to do, they went to bed early. Perhaps sleep would ease the weight of the fear pressing on their hearts, at least a little bit.

Fire

Midwife Meline's house on Nevres Street was the first to burn. Thank goodness that when the flames raced through the wooden door, already smashed open by rampaging soldiers, and hungrily attacked the wooden staircase, nobody was at home. After that, fires broke out simultaneously at different spots in the streets around the Church of St Stepanos, bursting into flames at the same moment, like fireworks being set off. People who'd been hiding in attics, cellars and basement apartments ran screaming into the streets like rats leaving a sinking ship. Some of them had their throats slit right there; some managed to disappear among the European groups protected by foreign sailors and got down to the quay; some died halfway there.

Avinash, who'd been dozing on a sofa on the top-secret floor of the British Consulate reserved for the Queen's spies, opened his eyes. The shouts and yells of the hundred thousand people massed on the quay had made it almost impossible to sleep, but he must have nodded off for a couple of minutes. From behind the closed shutters he tried to work out what he was hearing, and smelling. Someone was screaming, 'Fire!' He opened one of the shutters. The roaring of the crowd intensified. The wind had changed direction and gathered force; it was now blowing from the hills to the sea. If a fire had broken out in the upper neighbourhoods, it would take less than fifteen minutes for the flames to reach the hundred thousand on the quay.

Glancing up, he saw that the consulate employees working in the building next door had gone out onto their roof to observe the fire. Below the window, a young girl turned to the family she was dragging along with her and shouted, 'We're all going to die! They're going to burn us all to death.'

Avinash flew outside. Hurrying past the crying, shouting people trying to climb over the ornamental wrought-iron gate of the consulate, he ran into Ingiliz Iskelesi Avenue. The crowds camped on the waterfront were staring at the hills in despair, but the Turkish cavalry holding the southern and northern ends of the harbour weren't letting anyone through; there was no way they could escape. He turned around and without slowing his pace ran up Sari Street and then Maden Street, past the Italian Girls' School with its courtyard full of people whose eyes were popping with fear, and on to Fasoula Avenue.

Yakoumi's Pharmacy had been ransacked. When Avinash saw that the front window had been smashed to pieces, he came to a standstill; he felt as if he'd been stabbed in the side. The shop was empty. Bottles, tubes, needles and medicinal powders were scattered everywhere. For a moment Avinash considered going in through the broken-down door and grabbing a bottle of the rose oil that the elderly pharmacist guarded with his life, but time was short and his sensitive nose told him that all the bottles of oil had been smashed long ago. Taking a deep breath, he carried on running.

The fire was roaring now, as if it were a river rushing

towards the sea. Avinash thought he heard a church bell ring in the distance, then something collapsing with a resounding crash. With all its might, the wind was blowing the flames from the hills to the sea; the blaze was raging through the Greek and European neighbourhoods. The glass windows of some of the fashionable shops on Fasoula had been shattered and their contents raided. The looters had strewn whatever they considered to be worthless across the glass-splattered pavement – toys, dresses, rolls of fabric, rugs, books, all smeared with blood. Avinash ran on, not looking, not thinking; numb.

The roar from the quay, as if in competition with the roar of the fire, was getting louder and louder. '*Kegomaste! Kegomaste!* We're burning up!'

He was drenched in sweat. The city had become a huge oven. The streets were deserted and shuttered, but the courtyards of the schools and churches were packed with evacuees. Avinash was breathing steadily now as he ran, but suddenly he couldn't decide which way to go.

He saw old grannies being carried on the backs of young men, young girls with chic leather suitcases in their arms, sewing machines being shouldered, women dressed only in thin nightgowns but with fancy feathered hats on their heads. These were not refugees who'd walked barefoot and bareheaded all the way from their villages; these were residents of the city who'd fled into the streets as flames engulfed their houses. Neighbourhood squares that connected several streets were littered with tables, stools, mandolins, sieves, coffee grinders, pots, pans and much else besides.

When he finally got to Vasili Street, he was as wet as if he'd been swimming in the sea. He found Edith in the garden. She had plaited her hair and wound the plaits around her head.

She was applying vinegar compresses to the forehead of a young girl lying on a makeshift mattress. The whole garden, even the pool, was filled with sitting, crying, moaning people. As yet they were unaware of the fire. Standing at Edith's side was a tall man in baggy trousers holding a gas lamp; presumably the girl's father. When Edith looked up from where she was kneeling, the lamplight was in her eyes and at first she couldn't make out Avinash (or at least that's what Avinash hoped). 'What do you want?' she asked in a cold, harsh voice. The black circles under her eyes were a sign that she'd not slept for several nights.

There was no time to argue. Avinash grabbed her arm, pulled her up from the ground and dragged her towards the house. 'Quick, gather up anything of value. You must be really quick. We're leaving – they're burning down the city.'

Edith was momentarily dumbstruck. But what she saw in her lover's face made her turn and run up the stairs. Avinash followed. While she was filling a suitcase with jewellery and clothes, Avinash was drawn to her library. Edith had many valuable books, bound in leather and with their titles embossed in gold. Russian and French classics, American literature… He took a few in his hands, then put them down again. He was in no state to carry books on his back.

As he was replacing one of them, a photo of Edith as a young girl fell out from between the pages. It was from a long time ago, before they'd met. She was wearing a white dress and had the hint of a smile on her face, and she was positioned in front of a fancy studio backdrop of deer and trees. With a spy's reflexes, or perhaps a lover's, he tucked the photo into the sweaty pocket of his waistcoat.

Edith had gone back down to the garden. 'Leave everything and run to the quay,' she shouted in her deep voice. 'The fire is coming. Get ready to run. Quickly! Do not dawdle. You must go to the waterfront immediately, all of you – now! Yes, now! *Tora!*'

Her butler Christo and the other servants had already returned home to their families. Juliette, together with Jean-Pierre and his family, had taken refuge in the French Consulate three days ago. Citing the refugees in her garden, Edith had stubbornly disregarded her mother and Avinash's insistence that she go with them.

When they reached the quay, neither Avinash nor Edith could believe their eyes. There were ten times more people than when they'd last been down there. They were all but stacked on top of each other, their arms raised in the air as if asking God for help. Whenever anyone saw a horse and rider approaching, they hid their daughters. Hundreds of people were trying to crowd onto boats at the shore. Some of the boats capsized right away. The oars of those that stayed upright were being pulled hard in the direction of the European ships anchored some distance away. The surface of the sea was littered with bloated bodies. Boys from the Muslim neighbourhoods were jumping into the water with knives in their hands, cutting necklaces and rings from necks and fingers and stuffing them into their pockets. The soldiers holding the two ends of the harbour did not interfere.

Avinash helped Edith into a British motorboat that was waiting just beyond the barricade set up by the cavalry. Without wasting any time, the captain turned the bow towards the dark waters of the open sea and started the engine. Hearing the engine, people charged out into the road from where they'd been hiding in dim corners of nearby restaurants, forgetting about the cavalry, the barricade and the machine-gun fire. Edith screamed at the sight of them, seized the rudder from the captain's hands and gestured frantically and wordlessly at the desperate people on the shore, as if she were mute.

The collar of the captain's white uniform glowed in the darkness. 'I am sorry, Miss Lamarck,' he said coldly, 'I am under strict orders from my superiors not to take anyone except British citizens and their families on this boat.'

'Fuck you, you animal! Don't talk to me of your superiors.'

Like a wild tiger, Edith launched herself at the captain, screaming curses she had never before uttered. She was going to throw him into the sea with the bloated corpses and fill the boat with refugees. She could hear the poor souls yelling their entreaties, could hear their children wailing. She and the captain struggled. The small boat rocked from side to side.

With one swift movement, Avinash grabbed her in his strong arms and squeezed until she was still. The captain grumbled and went back to his rudder. After straightening his collar, he took a cigarette from his waistcoat pocket and lit it.

'Goddamn you, Avinash!' Edith shrieked as she wriggled to escape his arms. 'Goddamn all of you! What are you doing, abandoning all these people? They will burn to death here! Don't you see? Let me go. I will go back. Let me go! I don't want to leave. Don't take me away. *Merde!* Don't put me on a goddamned British ship. Take me back to Smyrna. *Emmène-moi à Smyrne!*'

Avinash did not loosen his hold. The bow of the motorboat sliced through the water, away from the screaming herd.

Having used up all the swearwords in all the languages spoken in Smyrna at that time, Edith, sobbing, surrendered to her lover. 'Avinash, I beg you, do not take me away from here! Leave me here. Let me burn with these people. I belong here.

This city is my country. Having seen what I've seen, I do not want to live as a ghost who's been rescued.'

Her sobs ceased abruptly and from her throat came a hoarse sound like a yelp. She covered her mouth with both her hands. The motorboat was now far enough from the shore that she could see the full horror of what was happening to Smyrna.

From within Avinash's embrace, Edith stood rigid and stared at the land they had left behind as if spellbound. Flames swelled like a pack of rabid dogs, a red monster with four huge arms opened wide, taking the city into its fiery clutches. Trying to protect her, Avinash hid her face in his chest, but Edith pushed his hand away and turned towards the city. The sharp lines of her face softened in the red light reflected off the water; she looked like the girl in the photograph Avinash was carrying in his waistcoat pocket. Without taking her hands from her mouth, she blinked several times. Two teardrops rolled slowly down her cheeks onto her lap.

The fire reared up from the city's hills like an ocean wave, preparing to swallow beautiful Smyrna and its children in one gulp.

They had reached the *Iron Duke*. A crowd of people packed into a small boat had seen a rope ladder being thrown over the side of the British battleship and had begun rowing with all their might towards it. Waving their arms, they were shouting something with one voice, though it was impossible to understand what.

Edith hung onto the rope ladder with the last of her strength as she transferred from the motorboat and made her way up the side of the battleship. Midway up, she stopped, looked back, and came face to face with a two-year-old baby who'd been thrown to her.

'Take this baby with you, lady! Save my child, madam, *se parakalo*, madam!' The mother's screams split the sky.

The cloth wrapped around the child had fallen open as she was thrown, leaving her naked, dirt-encrusted body exposed. There was a delighted expression on her tiny face as she flew through the air, and when her eyes were on a level with Edith's, she opened her mouth to laugh. Perhaps she remembered happy days when her father had tossed her into the air like this and caught her as she fell.

Edith let go of the ladder with one hand to catch the little girl, lost her balance and almost toppled backwards into the sea. As the baby plummeted towards the water, the tiny child's laughter turned to tears. She hit her head on the side of the rowing boat and disappeared underwater. With a shriek, the mother jumped into the sea, brought her baby's bloody face to the surface and kissed her. Then, with her daughter in her arms, she sank into the depths.

As Edith watched this horror unfolding from halfway up the rope ladder, the other people in the rowing boat paid not the slightest attention. They were entirely focused on trying to climb the ladder themselves, pushing and shoving each other as they struggled to grab onto it. The captain of the motorboat Edith had fought with earlier had taken an iron pipe from under the rudder and was now smashing their hands, forcing them to drop off the ladder and into the water one by one. Seeing this, Edith stopped climbing. This time she really was going to strangle the captain. But as she tried to descend, her hands slipped and she fell into Avinash, who was on the bottom rung. 'If you don't hurry up,' he said, 'many more people will lose their lives because of the false hope this ladder is giving them.'

As soon as the two of them stepped onto the deck, the

ladder was hauled up and pails of boiling water were hurled over the side onto the heads of the people in the rowing boat, to get them away from the *Iron Duke*.

Edith was breathing fast as she made her way to the front of the ship and leaned on the iron railing. She could not bear what she was seeing. If she jumped overboard from there, would she die immediately? Even from that distance, she could feel the heat of the flames. If her forehead was beaded with sweat, the crowds on the quay must have been suffocating. People were leaping into the sea, ten to twenty at a time. Some had grabbed hold of the iron mooring rings used by the fishermen and were managing to keep their heads above water, but Turkish soldiers were hitting their hands with iron pipes as they passed, just as the British motorboat captain had. The hands that let go of the rings stayed on the surface for a while, gesticulating in the air as if bidding farewell to the crowd. Then they sank out of sight, disappearing into the dark void.

Avinash came up behind Edith, put his arms around her waist and wet her neck with his tears. They could hear all too clearly the howls coming from the shore. From everywhere, sirens wailed and bells in church steeples rang as they burned, but nothing could suppress the screams rising from the quay. Neither of them had ever in their lives experienced such acute sorrow or despair. They clung to each other to keep themselves upright. In the ballroom of the *Iron Duke* a military band had begun playing a polka. The insatiable flames jumped from the beautifully ornate Théâtre de Smyrne to the Café de Paris and from there to the Kraemer Palace. As the hotel's roof collapsed, the majestic building vanished forever.

Bread-Baker's Square

Panagiota woke to the sound of dogs barking. There were screams and other noises coming from the square. Was there a fire? She ran from her bedroom to the bay window in the living room.

Yes, fire! Oh, my God! It had engulfed the Armenian district and was now heading straight towards them. The flames, whipped up by the wind, were licking the rooftops and the church domes like a many-tongued monster, twisting into houses and coming out of windows as bright red smoke, then rising into the sky as a copper-coloured cloud.

Muhtar, the neighbourhood's beloved dog, passed under the window. Holding his short tail high and with his nose lifted to the red sky, he was racing from Menekse Street to the square, barking all the while, as if he was on a very important mission. Five yellow dogs followed behind. Birds, thinking the bright sky portended daybreak, had begun to chirp in the branches of the lemon tree under the bay window. Cats were abandoning the rooftops in droves.

Panagiota ran barefoot to her mother and father's bedroom.

Katina jumped out of bed. Akis grabbed the revolver at his bedside.

'What's happening? Are you all right, *kori mou*? Is there someone at the door? Have they come to ransack our house? *Kala ise*, daughter – did they do something to you?'

Gun still in hand, Akis pulled his trousers on over his pyjamas. Katina had begun digging inside the pillowcase for her gold, unaware that Akis had already taken it and hidden it in a sack of wheat. People were screaming outside.

'There's a fire, Papa!' Panagiota shouted. 'Fire, Mama! We have to leave – quick, or we'll burn to death!'

Akis abruptly stopped buttoning his trousers. A fire, huh? This was actually good news in a way, because it meant the gangs hadn't come to loot the neighbourhood. They all rushed to the bay window. Half of the sky had turned orange, and the houses across in the Agia Katerina neighbourhood were bathed in a tangerine light, as if the sun was rising.

Akis made some swift calculations. 'It's spread from Basmane up to Agios Dimitris. What bad luck – the wind's changed direction, so it's coming towards us now. Still, we have time.'

Turning away from the window, he glanced at Panagiota, trembling in her thin white nightgown. In the reddish light, with her slender white body and her black curls falling over her breasts, she looked like a Chinese porcelain figurine. Her hair was sticking to her neck and chest, sweaty from her uneasy sleep. How delicate and beautiful she was; how vulnerable.

'*Kori mou*, go quickly to your room and get dressed. Cover yourself well. Wear a cloak if you can, something to hide your hair and even your face.'

Panagiota's teeth were chattering. Akis took her in his arms and squeezed her thin form tight, as if he were wringing it. 'Nothing will happen, my beautiful daughter. I'll be right beside you. Come, *ela*, run now and get dressed. I'll go and see where your mother is.'

Her father smelled of olive oil, bluing and flour.

Panagiota stood for a long time in front of her cupboard, looking at her dresses. She took out a few, held them up to her body, rejected them and threw them onto the bed. To anyone unaware of the situation that night, she'd have looked like a normal girl who couldn't make up her mind what to wear for a stroll along the quay. Finally she chose an old grey dress that reached down to her ankles. She'd seen that some of the women camping at the quay were wearing trousers and now she understood why. Because they were more difficult to remove, trousers were a deterrent: the soldiers and bandits would go for an easier target instead. Her trembling got worse. No, now was not the time to think such thoughts. Her father, the great Akis, would protect her. No one would be able to lay a finger on her.

The whole neighbourhood had gathered in Bread-Baker's Square. Adriana, her brothers and sisters, her mother and father, Fisherman Yorgo, his wife Eleni and son Niko, old Uncle Christo, Warehouseman Petro, Akis's coffeehouse friends, the women Katina chatted with in front of her door – all of them had turned their faces to the dome of the sky, half of which was red. They were carrying out rugs, radios, framed pictures, photograph albums, sacks of flour. Gypsy Mimiko was trying to say something to Akis from over by the coffeehouse, but his words were lost amid the crackle of the approaching fire.

It had never occurred to Panagiota that a fire might sound like the thundering rush of a great river. The howling of the flames suppressed everything else – the sobbing and shouting of the people in the square, the rumble of buildings collapsing, the barking of the dogs, the chirping of the birds. The only other sound was the continual tolling of a distant bell, from the steeple at the Church of Agia Ekaterini perhaps, its urgent, unceasing ringing more insistent than the sirens of the fire department, its entreaties enough to freeze a person's blood. Then the flames must have reached it, for the huge church bell rang out one last unearthly shriek, and fell silent.

'I hear sirens,' said Katina.

She and Panagiota were clasping each other tightly. The heat was unbearable. Their foreheads and necks were wet; sweat trickled between their breasts like ant trails. Katina was wearing all her jewellery and all the jewellery from Panagiota's dowry chest under her dress. She unhooked the delicate gold chain and crucifix from around her daughter's neck and put it around her own neck. Women were being robbed of their jewellery in the middle of the street, and she couldn't bear to think of anyone touching Panagiota. She remembered what Akis had told her about the cemetery at Daragaci before they went to bed.

People were shouting, 'To the quay, the quay! Everyone run to the quay. Quickly!'

'Auntie Rozi? Has anyone seen Auntie Rozi? She's trapped in her house like a prisoner – someone needs to rescue her.'

The streets suddenly filled with people – hunched over, eyes wide. The refugees who'd been sheltering in the churchyards at Agia Ekaterini and Agios Dimitris were fleeing the flames and had made it this far. Some were carrying bundles on their backs, others had grannies and grandfathers in their arms. They were dumbstruck, running from hell.

Seeing them, Katina remembered the dream she'd had during Panagiota's birth. As she'd hovered between life and death that night, she'd found herself in a place full of flames, where people, horses and other animals were dying in agony. She'd thought it was hell, but now she understood that it was this very night that she'd seen.

She sensed that death was imminent. One of the two of them would die this night. She begged the Holy Mother Mary to take her own life and spare Panagiota.

A young priest came past, from the direction of the French Hospital, with a line of people trailing after him. Katina dashed over to join them, pulling Panagiota along with her, but Akis grabbed his wife's wrist and stopped her. 'What are you doing, *vre* woman? Following a priest on such a day – do you want to get us all killed?'

They'd got as far as the bakery. The deliciously sweet smell of bread lingered still. Panagiota couldn't believe that it was only a few hours earlier that she and her father had stopped there and bought two loaves. Then they'd sat in their living room with the bay window and eaten that bread dipped in bean juice. It was like a slice of time from another life.

That girl was not her. That girl had a future she could dream about; she was a fool who didn't realize the value of what she had. Raising her head, she glanced over at Menekse Street at the far end of the square; at the house where she'd spent her childhood, her entire life; at her father's grocery shop. She would give anything to go back a few hours, back to the moment when she'd sat with Akis and Katina at the dinner table, content in the unshakeable belief that the life they knew so well would remain as it was forever. She would never again tire of that life, even if one day passed without a grain of difference from the last. With deep sadness, she realized that she had lost the most precious of all things. That life was over. No matter how this night ended, they would never again peacefully sit and eat bread dipped in bean juice in their house with the blue door.

The great roaring noise had got louder. The fire was getting nearer; soon it would engulf them all. Suddenly from the direction of Agios Tryphonas came the thrum of hoofbeats. Everyone began rushing into the side streets, yelling, 'The Turks are coming!' Akis gestured to Gypsy Mimiko with his head and the two men, their faces as red as sour cherries, both grabbed their wives and daughters by the arms and began to run in the opposite direction of the quay, towards the British Hospital. The way was dusty and smoky. Adriana's little sister Irini was crying in Adriana's arms. Aristo was carrying Auntie Rozi on his back.

As she jumped over the railway track, Panagiota's dress got caught on a loose nail and she fell and hit her forehead on the wooden track. Katina screamed. Panagiota immediately tried to collect herself and stand up, but her head was reeling. 'I'm fine, *Manoula*. Keep running.'

A warm trickle of blood was running down from Panagiota's cheekbone. Katina pressed the hem of her skirt to her daughter's face. Then suddenly she let go of the skirt and, sobbing, embraced Panagiota. Mother and daughter stood glued together in the middle of the winding railway track, under the red sky. Katina knew she was holding her daughter in her arms for the last time. When they finally separated, she took off the sapphire ring which her mother had given her and slipped it onto Panagiota's slender white finger. Her mother had told her that the stone brought good fortune.

Akis, Mimiko, Sofia, Adriana and her sisters and brothers were waiting for them on the road to the Greek Cemetery. The wire fence surrounding Panionios Stadium had been broken through in many places and the grandstands and playing field were filled with refugees. Right behind it, encircled by sturdy cypress trees, the graveyard awaited them, calm and silent. Together, they passed through the stadium, where Minas the Flea had once upon a time performed wonders on the football field, and entered the realm of death.

Nightmare

Although Hilmi Rahmi had spent more than half his adult life on battlefields, he had never before witnessed humanity gone so wrong. Maybe it was the heartless power of the fire and the sea; maybe it was because the tragedy was taking place in Smyrna, where he'd been born and raised, where he'd played on the streets, where he'd brought his young bride; maybe it was the sheer number of people – there must have been half a million, including the Christians who'd fled from their fire-ravaged neighbourhoods – squeezed into an area the size of his palm between the flames and the sea, piled one on top of the other on barges.

Whatever the reason, Hilmi Rahmi was never able to forget the scenes he witnessed on the quay in Izmir on the night of 13 September 1922. The screams of the women continued to tear at his ears and chill his blood in his nightmares. Every night as he drifted off to sleep, he relived that momentary flicker of hope and despair in the eyes of the drowned just before they sank. Eventually, the intense fever of shame which rose from his subconscious seeped into his internal organs and brought about his own death.

The heat on the quayside was unbearable. The wind was

madly blowing the fire from the hills to the sea and the stench of burned flesh from the streets and the water was making everyone vomit, civilians and soldiers alike. Many soldiers had covered their mouths and noses with wet cloths, including Hilmi Rahmi. The side streets, squares, courtyards and school playgrounds were filled with the corpses of men, women, children, cats and dogs. At the quay, pigeons whose hearts had stopped in the heat and seagulls with their wings on fire fell patter, patter to the ground.

Hilmi Rahmi's horse was nervous. It kept trying to throw him off its back and escape to somewhere calm and cool. At the same time as attempting to control his horse, Hilmi Rahmi was also inspecting the evacuees crammed into the boats. Twenty, thirty people at a time were boarding the rowing boats they found. If they were lucky, the boat would carry them out to the side of a European ship, after which they'd be at the mercy of the ship's captain. Many rowing boats capsized before an oar even touched the water, sending every last one of its desperate passengers to the bottom of the dark sea.

A command had been issued by his superior officer to capture any Greek male between the ages of eighteen and forty-five who was trying to flee. 'Those delinquents will stay here to rebuild the villages and cities they have razed and destroyed, the railways they blew up. No one will escape without paying the price. Catch them all and line them up in front of me. Shoot those who do not surrender. They deserve it, the thugs.'

There was no need to waste ammunition on the men who'd come from mountain villages far from the sea. They didn't know how to swim. When they jumped into the water, their clothes dragged them down and within five minutes they'd sunk to the seabed and were gone. The ones who'd grown up by the shore and knew how to swim were shot as they began to swim towards the European ships.

The crews on the European ships were no more merciful than the soldiers on the shore. Hilmi Rahmi saw with his own eyes two battleships flying foreign flags refuse rowing boats which had approached them to ask for sanctuary, then throw buckets of water over the heads of those who persisted. Very rarely would a ship put down a ladder for an approaching rowing boat and pull the women and children up on deck.

Like the civilian robbers who were looting the city, the privates, corporals and sergeants of Kemal Pasha's army were out of control. A week ago, these perfect soldiers had been well behaved, but as soon as they got to Smyrna, all military discipline and moral codes were forgotten. Aping the gang leaders, they ransacked houses and shops, murdered people in the middle of the street and raped Christian girls and women in public places – all under the eyes of the European generals watching through binoculars from the decks of their ships.

Smyrna was even bigger, richer and more abundantly provisioned than they had imagined. And with no gendarme installations currently in place, no police to arrest them and no courts to pass judgement, this brief window of time was their chance to make their dirty fantasies a reality. All the suffering they'd endured through the war and all the depredations that they'd witnessed – villages incinerated, women and children hacked to pieces by Greek soldiers – had fired them with a lust for revenge. They were taking out all their hatred on innocent civilians, paying no heed to morals or conscience. The great generals had turned Smyrna over to these outlaws as they met in mansions in Bournabat, busying themselves with the troublesome problem of Istanbul.

Hilmi Rahmi wiped the sweat from his neck. His handkerchief was already as wet as the red cloth he'd tied over his mouth and nose to filter out the stink of the dead. A little earlier, Captain Mehmet, who'd been riding beside him, had felt faint and had tumbled into the crowd below him. The poor people on the quay, thinking he'd jumped down to grab one of their girls, had screamed and covered their children with their bodies.

They'd had to pour a pail of water over Mehmet's head to revive him. From where he lay, the captain was muttering, 'What's the point of just saving one or two of them? Best not to get involved.'

While Hilmi Rahmi was occupied with Mehmet, Brigadier Sadullah – jacketless, hatless, sweaty – cantered up. Paying no attention to the milling crowd, he pointed his bayonet at a young girl cowering behind her grandfather. 'That's the one I want,' he shouted. 'The chubby one. Bring her. I'm going behind the customs building. Choose one for yourself, Colonel! These days will not come again.' He galloped off through the crowd towards the port, forcing at least twenty people to leap into the sea to avoid being trampled. Machine-gun fire immediately raked the water.

Hilmi Rahmi was nauseated. As he remounted his horse, he wished that he too might faint. Maybe Mehmet had been faking. Unbefitting of a soldier though that was, Hilmi Rahmi could understand why.

He looked over at the poor girl hiding behind her grandfather. Her shirt was stained with blood. Her hair was like a bird's nest on top of her head, and her arms were covered with festering scratches. What kind of creature could look at this child and feel lust?

Sensing his eyes upon her, the girl desperately bowed her

head. If she behaved docilely, perhaps he would let her go after finishing his business. A woman from Aydin whom she'd met on the quay had told her that after twelve soldiers had raped her, one after the other, they'd dragged her to an empty backyard and gone away. As they left, they'd spat in her face, saying, 'Compared to what your people did, this is nothing.' The woman had almost wanted to run after the soldiers and embrace them for not having killed her.

The devastation that Hilmi Rahmi saw around him had to be the work of the devil. So this was what happened when man lost his faith and his conscience; when he broke his bond with himself and with God. He turned into a monster cut loose from his chains, a base creature, a slave to lust, greed, anger and cruelty.

He remembered how just a week ago he and Brigadier Sadullah had came upon a village where Greek soldiers had filled the mosque with men and set it alight. The brigadier, whose mouth was right now salivating at the pleasure he would get from torturing the poor girl shivering behind her grandfather, had held the body of a little girl from that village, ten or twelve years old, in his arms and sobbed as blood emptied like a river from between her legs. Who knew how many Greek soldiers had raped her. How could a person unable to hold back his tears at such horror just one week later torture another soul whom Allah had created? What kind of power was it that turned a person into the lowest and most cruel of living beings?

The portholes of the battleships anchored in the harbour were reflecting the flames devouring the city. Hilmi Rahmi anxiously turned his head to the hills where his house was located. The fire had not spread to the Turkish district. It was as if there were an invisible barrier between the districts. The flames had raced through the Armenian quarter and then stopped where the Jewish quarter began, as if cut with a knife. Not one spark had fallen on the Turkish neighbourhoods. Thanks be to the Creator, thanks be to Allah.

He was ashamed to be thinking of his own family when hundreds of thousands were dying in agony in front of his eyes.

American philanthropists had finally got Nureddin Pasha and their own superiors to agree to send one rescue ship to the quay. The crowd, fighting among themselves, surged towards the dock where the ship was anchored. American sailors were trying to impose some order by hitting people on their backs, shoulders and heads, but they couldn't control a hundred thousand people engaged in a life-and-death struggle.

'Women and children only! Women and children only!'

There was no way that all of them could get on the ship and be saved. Hilmi Rahmi was pleased to see that the girl Brigadier Sadullah had chosen was not where he'd left her. Had she managed to board the ship? It was impossible to distinguish any single individual among the vast sea of desperate people massed before him.

Some who looked as if they were sleeping had already died. If he could only save one life from this multitude of shame... Just one life among the hundred thousand. It might not change the world, but for that one person it would make a world of difference. A family with two children was running towards the rescue ship from Parallel Street. The woman was carrying a baby, the man was holding the hand of his little girl, whose legs had been burned, pulling her along. As Hilmi Rahmi made a swift movement towards them, he heard, amid the flames and the screams, the officer holding the northern end of the quay order the man to stop.

'Halt and surrender!'

The man didn't hear him, or he heard but didn't obey. Life was two strides ahead, on the American ship. The second he took that step forward, towards life, dragging his daughter with him, a bullet pierced his heart. He and his wife fell to the ground together. A second bullet had targeted her. The little girl cast a fearful glance at her dead parents. Then she picked her baby brother up off the ground, ran through the flames and jumped onto the ship.

Hilmi Rahmi stopped his horse halfway there. His heart felt heavy, as if it had dropped to his stomach. He was probably about to vomit.

He would not describe to Sumbul, Cengiz or Dogan the scenes he had witnessed. Definitely not. He would do whatever he could for them not to have to carry this shame. He would excise the events of these days from his past and throw them away. If necessary, he would deny them or lie. But would the new country, whose birth was awaited with such excitement and enthusiasm, be built on the premise that this river of blood had never happened, on a lie disconnected from the past? Was the future to be made of this?

Since his face was already wet with sweat, when tears rolled down his cheeks, no one understood that this young colonel, whose duty it was to squeeze infidels into an area hotter than an oven, between the flames and the sea, was crying for his lost city and for his dreams turned to ashes.

Confession

Edith was no longer sobbing in Avinash's arms on the deck of the *Iron Duke*. She was rigid inside, a large part of her soul lost to the fire. In the ballroom of the navy ship the military band was still playing polkas and waltzes to suppress the screams rising from the shore, but the faces of the people sitting at the tables set with white tablecloths were as dark as an awful winter's day.

The news that the ship would soon be approaching the port to rescue refugees had comforted their uneasy hearts somewhat, but Edith could see from where she stood that only a tiny fraction of the massive crowd would be able to get on the *Iron Duke*. The throng seemed to spread without end along the length of the shore, and those obliged to stay put would have to carry on waiting, in fear of the flames, the dark water and the machine-gun fire.

Wood from burning houses was bursting into the sky like fireworks. Without taking her eyes off the terrible spectacle, Edith began to speak, in a voice devoid of emotion.

'I had a baby, Avinash.'

The shoulder she was leaning on stiffened.

The wind circled around them, howling in her ears.

'It was a few years before I met you. She died the night she was born; I didn't even see her face. I'd fainted. My mother took her and buried her in the cemetery of the Catholic church in Bournabat; that's what she said. Because the baby wasn't baptized, there was no name, and no grave where I could have placed flowers.'

Turning, she looked into Avinash's eyes.

He was shocked. All that time he'd spent searching for details about Edith's life before he met her – how was it that pregnancy had never entered his mind? How was it that no one had even hinted that Edith had given birth? People mentioned that she had thrown herself into the bohemian life in Paris, had become the mistress of an artist, had had affairs with women, but they had never said a word about a pregnancy. He felt betrayed – not because Edith had been with another man before himself, but because everyone in Bournabat had colluded in hiding this baby from him.

As if she understood what he was thinking, Edith continued, 'No one knows. Only me, my mother, and the midwife who delivered the baby, Midwife Meline.'

Avinash looked confused.

'When my pregnancy became obvious, the sisters at the Catholic school I was attending in Paris immediately shipped me back to Smyrna. They sent my mother a telegram. She met me at the port and bundled me into one of those carriages with closed curtains, like Turkish ladies use, where you can't be seen. She'd arranged everything very carefully. When we arrived at the Bournabat mansion, she didn't even give the butler a chance to see me before she shut me up in the turret.'

She turned her face towards her beloved Smyrna, which was glowing like a giant orange.

Avinash was appalled. 'How long did you stay there?'

'Until I gave birth. Exactly three months, one week and five days. My little girl was born on the night between the sixth and seventh of September and died in the morning. If she had lived, she would be seventeen now.'

Avinash stood with his mouth agape. He repeated his question, hoping he had perhaps misunderstood. 'Your mother held you prisoner for three months in the turret of the Bournabat mansion?'

Edith nodded.

'How cruel. How brutal.'

As he said these words, the screams followed by machine-gun fire rising from the quay brought the same thought to both their minds: they had no right to talk of 'cruel' or 'brutal' behaviour.

Avinash turned Edith's face to his. 'I am so sorry, my darling. What a difficult time that must have been for you; what a sad loss. I did not know anything about this.'

Tears which she'd thought had dried up began streaming down Edith's cheeks again. It was the first time she'd revealed her secret to anyone. She had written a short note to her classmate Feride, saying that the baby had been born dead, but she hadn't told her friend of the suffering she'd endured throughout the summer, nor of her powerful suspicion that her mother had had Ali killed by Cakircali's gang.

Avinash took her in his arms and held her tight. Edith rested her head on his shoulder and closed her eyes. All the losses formed a knot inside her. As the insatiable flames reduced her beloved Smyrna to ash in front of her eyes, she surrendered to the choking sobs.

★ ★ ★

While Edith was standing sobbing on the deck of the *Iron Duke*, the gates of the French Consulate on Limanaki Street opened and a stream of people exited through them. Among them were Juliette Lamarck, her son Jean-Pierre, his wife Marie and their children Daphne and Louis. The group was lined up in twos. At their head was a naval officer with a French flag in his hand, and to either side were French soldiers clearing a path through the crowds for them. They walked in the direction of Passport Pier, where a motorboat was waiting.

Marie, dressed in a spotless cream suit, was at the back, holding her two children's hands. In front of her walked Juliette with a large straw hat on her head, looking as if she was going to Kordelio for a swim rather than escaping from a fire. She was clutching Jean-Pierre's arm. Louis had refused to leave his cat in Bournabat, so they'd brought the animal with them in a birdcage, and the boy was now taking tiny steps so as not to startle his pet. His mother kept urging him to hurry, but he just grumbled and continued the argument with his sister that he'd begun inside.

No one from the French group was able to remember in what order events happened when they got to the motorboat waiting in the inner harbour. A month after the Great Fire, when the family were reunited in a hotel room in Paris, Jean-Pierre struggled to explain it all to Edith. His tongue was tied from shock and sorrow, and his account was muddled, but Edith and Avinash were able to put the pieces together.

Just as Juliette Lamarck was stepping onto the motorboat with the French flag flying from its bow, she drew back, freed her hand from her son's arm and ran from the port into the flames, shouting, 'My grandchild! I must save my grandchild!' She began asking people on the quay where the orphanage was located and made such a strange spectacle, in her straw hat and stilettos, that even the Turkish soldiers left their posts and came over to her.

Finally, from among the wretched crowd, a woman came forward. Without taking her eyes off the officers, she pointed towards a place northeast of the quay. Jettisoning her hat, Juliette began to run in the direction the woman had indicated. Jean-Pierre turned to hurry after her but was stopped by Marie. The motorboat that was to take them to the ship the *Pierre Loti* was about to depart, and the captain could not guarantee them a passage if they missed it. With difficulty, his wife and children persuaded Jean-Pierre aboard.

As the boat pushed its way past the bobbing corpses and out into the forbidding sea, they caught a last glimpse of Juliette Lamarck, racing through the crowd in the direction of Punta. Leaping like a deer over the prone bodies of those who were sick or had fainted, she passed the ruined Kraemer's, the Théâtre de Smyrne with its roof on fire, and the American Consulate, where it looked as if hundreds of fireworks were exploding all at once, and plunged up Bella Vista into one of the many flaming side streets. Then she disappeared from view.

How did Juliette know that Midwife Meline had left the baby at that orphanage? Did her guilty conscience get the better of her, prompting her to find the midwife and question her? Did the owner of the donkey that had carried Meline to Smyrna go gossiping, and did his words reach Juliette's ears? The answers to those questions were consumed by the fire, as was Juliette Lamarck.

When Jean-Pierre was eventually able to return to those miserable, fire-ravaged ruins, to that place which could not even be called the ghost of beautiful Smyrna, he could find neither the orphanage nor the neighbourhood in which it had been located. The crowd on the quay had dispersed, leaving only bloodstains and headless, handless, fingerless bodies floating in the sea.

No one had any information concerning Juliette Lamarck.

Well before the meeting of the Lamarck family – minus Juliette – in the hotel room in Paris, before he'd heard about what had happened to Juliette, Avinash knew, as he stood on the deck of the *Iron Duke* in the ominous red light that was obliterating Smyrna, that Edith's baby had not died.

While he was stroking his sobbing lover's hair with one hand, with the other he had taken from his pocket the photograph of Edith as a young girl which he had found in the library earlier. The child was alive. In Smyrna, which was dying in the roaring claws of the fire, a fire that was growing brighter, Edith's daughter was caught somewhere between life and death.

Daragaci

The Greek Cemetery at Daragaci was packed. Families had raised the marble lids of their graves, taken out the coffins and hidden their girls in groups of twos or threes in the empty holes. Then, with everyone weeping, they closed the heavy marble lids again and left the girls in the graves.

Katina, holding Panagiota's hand tight, ran up to Akis, who was walking in front. 'This is not our family cemetery – what will we do? If only we'd gone to Chesme. And it's quieter there too.'

Akis didn't answer. Both their sets of parents were buried in Chesme. Maybe their families still living there had put their own children in the graves. What times these were.

Gypsy Mimiko was in charge. He had obviously planned this out long ago and he was now striding through the weeping and wailing crowd with resolute steps, clearing a path for his family and Akis, Katina and Panagiota behind him. There were people opening graves everywhere.

A woman in a black headscarf was beating herself and sobbing at the head of her husband's grave. 'Come and save us now!' she shouted. 'An army of soldiers passed over your daughter. They tore the child to pieces. Where are you now when we need you so much?' She hammered at the white marble tombstone, which responded to her pain with sombre silence.

The woman looked like the mother of Panagiota's friend Elpiniki. Panagiota tried to get Katina to stop. 'Mama, wait. That woman is Kyra Rea, I think.'

Katina did not stop. 'Forget about that now, *kori mou*. Keep walking.'

Tiny Katina had turned into a raging bull. Chin held high, she strode forward into the heart of the cemetery, dragging Panagiota behind her with superhuman strength.

Elpiniki had fled to Athens with her Greek lover. Long before this disaster, when it had become obvious that she was pregnant, her lover had put her on the first boat to Greece. Elpiniki's mother had taken her younger daughter Afroula and gone round the streets surrounding the square announcing to everyone like a town crier that Elpiniki was no longer her daughter. Everyone knew that once the baby was born, Kyra Rea would forgive her, but when she'd walked around the neighbourhood with Afroula ringing a bell, they'd pretended to agree with her by coming to their windowsills and clicking their tongues.

Since Elpiniki was in Athens, the daughter who'd been raped had to be Afroula. Afroula was not even fourteen yet. Panagiota hurried on.

When they got to the edge of the cemetery overlooking Paralikopru Road, they stopped. To their left a woman was giving birth on top of a family grave; other people were burning bones to boil water. Immigrant Turkish boys from Crete were selling water and oil at exorbitant prices. Some of them were carrying trays with photographs of Mustafa Kemal and miniature Turkish flags. Wandering around amid the graves, ornate statues and crosses, they were yelling at the tops of their voices, 'Buy these flags and pin them on your collars and no one will touch you! Save your lives!'

Gypsy Mimiko glanced around at the statues, the inscriptions on the gravestones, the cypress trees and the gravel – taking his bearings. He counted the graves to his right, walked to the third one and knelt down. Adriana's twin sisters followed behind their father like wind-up dolls. He stood up, a triumphant smile on his small face, and raised two shovels in the air, showing them to Akis.

'They're right where I left them, thank the Lord.'

The twins hugged their father's long legs.

'We'll hide my little girls here, and we'll dig a hole for the older ones in the *kinotafio*, the mass grave for the bones of the dead. No one will think of looking for them there. Come on, boys, give us a hand to raise this slab.'

Panagiota and Adriana looked at each other fearfully. Mimiko's sons rushed to help their father move the heavy marble.

'There must be another empty grave,' Katina whispered to Akis. 'How can we bury our child in the earth with all those bones? Come, let's have a look.'

'Are we at the market bargaining for fruit and vegetables, woman?' Akis roared. 'Don't you see how many families are kneeling around every single cross?'

It was true. The cemetery was full of families fighting each other. On discovering that someone else had commandeered the grave that belonged to them, they were yanking out the girls hidden there and replacing them with their own children. The nineteen granddaughters of one woman were slugging it out with their fists at the bottom of their grandmother's grave.

Mimiko, wiping the sweat from his forehead with his

shirttail, came to stand between Katina and Akis. 'Kyra Katina, the land behind this patch of heather is allocated to the *kinotafio*, the ossuary. Trust me, it's the safest place. Even if they do dare come into the cemetery, they won't think of looking there.'

After they'd closed the marble lid on the little girls, Mimiko and Akis grabbed the shovels and began digging. The women went onto the heather patch to gather laurel leaves and grass to cover the opening which would be left for the girls to breathe. Katina wouldn't let go of Panagiota's hand. When the men unearthed a bag of bones, Adriana's teeth began chattering. She reached for Panagiota's other hand. Her skin was like ice, but she leaned into her friend's ear and murmured, 'It will be like burying ourselves at the beach, like we used to do when we were little at the Diana Baths. Just like that.'

When they had dug a hole big enough to hold both girls, they helped Panagiota and Adriana down into it. 'It would be best if you lay facing each other,' said Mimiko. 'Hold your hands under your chins, so you can dig your way out if you need to.'

The girls lay in the hole like twins in their mother's womb, with their knees drawn up to their stomachs and their fingers under their chins, as if they were praying. As the men shovelled the earth back on top of them, Katina and Sofia knelt and placed handkerchiefs over their daughters' faces, making the sign of the cross three times as they did so.

Panagiota, acutely aware of how upset her mother was, tried to comfort her, as she always did, disregarding her own fears. 'Don't worry, Mama dear,' she said from behind the handkerchief. 'No one will find us here. And we're not alone. If we get bored, we can talk to each other.'

Still on her knees, Katina prayed that God would protect

her good-hearted child. The wind carried the tang of scorched wood, molten metal and boiling flesh; the cypress trees swayed in the darkness, as if trying to give meaning to all the smells. Women were screaming from the direction of the street.

Quickly, they closed the hole, covered the vent with dry twigs and laurel leaves, and scattered the bag of bones they'd excavated.

'We can't stay here. We'll attract attention,' said Mimiko. 'Let's go back into the middle of the cemetery.'

'I'm not moving from here!'

'Kyra Katina, for the sake of our daughters, we need to mingle with the crowd.'

'No! Impossible. *Ohi!* You go and mix with the crowd. I will stay here to keep watch over my child.'

'Katina *mou*, when the bandits see you keeping guard, you think it won't whet their appetite? *Ade, ade.* Let's get out of this heather. We won't take our eyes off them. Come.'

With difficulty they pulled Katina out of the heather and over to the middle of the cemetery. She collapsed beside a marble gravestone and began to cry. Sofia, with her little daughter Irini in her lap, sat beside her, holding her hand. No one paid any attention to them among all the other sobbing, moaning women. Everyone was entreating God, Mother Mary, and every known angel and saint to protect their own daughters.

Someone screamed from the edge of the cemetery, 'The gasworks is on fire! It's about to explode. We'll all be burned to death!'

From beneath the dark earth, Panagiota flinched. Her neck was itching terribly from the leaves and grass covering their heads. She tried to make out Adriana though the white handkerchief that smelled of mastic. She could hear women shrieking – some were giving birth; others were escaping the fire. Families were combining forces and shifting the heavy stones again, getting their daughters out of their hiding places and fleeing from the cemetery.

The gasworks was one street below the cemetery. Panagiota scratched at the earth with her hands and tried to move her legs, but the soil was pressing down on her like a heavy blanket. She was suddenly overtaken by panic. How would they get out? If the gasworks exploded and fire spread through the cemetery, they would suffocate to death. Pulling the handkerchief off her face, she shouted into the leaves, 'Adriana, we have to get out of here. *Ade!* Move your hands and feet and dig. Adriana! *M'akus?* Do you hear me?'

The two friends began to twist and turn like worms in their earthen hole. Dust, dirt, leaves and weeds stuck to their sweaty foreheads and necks. The world was loaded upon them like a nightmare. They were trapped. Forgetting that they were in hiding, they moaned, yelled and howled with all their might, like wild animals. But their screams were heard by no one.

Nearby, Mimiko was trying to soothe Katina, who was out of her mind with worry.

'Kyra Katina, the fire's a long way away. Even if it does get nearer, it won't cross the railway track. Look, you can see the gasworks chimney from here – there's no fire there. People are shouting because they're panicking. Trust me, this is the safest place to be – for us and for our daughters.'

Katina was in no state to listen to any more talk. She grabbed the shovel that Mimiko had dropped beside a grave, and when Akis made to stop her, she swung it at him. 'If you come any nearer, you'll end up worse than these stinking corpses! *Katalavenete?* Do you understand?'

478

Akis had never seen his wife like this. He followed her to the heather patch.

'Fire! Fire! We're all going to burn to death. *Kegomaste!*'

Katina shovelled the earth out of the hole and Adriana and Panagiota staggered out. A flood of people was stampeding past them through the heather, heading for the stadium.

'Run, Panagiota! Run, *kori mou*!'

Panagiota turned around, trying to see her mother and father among the growing throng of people racing for the stadium. Katina was short, but she could always spot her father's burly frame in a crowd. As she stopped to look for them, someone crashed into her from behind and she stumbled, hit the wall beside the railway track and fell. Her dress was ripped and her knee was bleeding. She tried to stand up. People were streaming past from her right and her left. Some tripped over her and fell flat on their faces, others trod on her and carried on.

When eventually she managed to grab onto the wall and pull herself up, she heard her mother's increasingly shrill voice.

'Run, Panagiota *mou*. Run, *yavri mou*! Run to the quay!'

The human tide, twisting like a snake, paused for a moment in front of the train station. A black cloud had settled on the narrow residential streets ahead, obscuring everything. Which way were they supposed to go? Panagiota stumbled into Bournabat Avenue, which happened to be right in front of her. She could hear the roar of the fire in the distance. Somewhere beyond the streets that crossed the avenue – was it far away, or near? – houses and churches were collapsing, scattering sparks as they fell, one after the other.

A group passed her, dived down Vasili Street and turned in the direction of Panagiota's neighbourhood. She couldn't see

Adriana or her parents. She only hoped they would find each other at the quay.

A young man from up front shouted out, 'Go from Parallel Street to Punta – the fire won't get as far as Punta!'

The very young and the very old fell by the wayside, and no one paid them any heed. A large group started down the avenue. One of Panagiota's shoes got stuck in the tram rails; she carried on running with one foot bare. The smoke rolling down the street was creating clouds darker than the night, causing people to completely lose their sense of direction. A fat man who was running in front of Panagiota stopped suddenly – at the corner of Parallel Street, probably – and everyone behind him bumped into one other. Panagiota again tripped and fell, hitting her head on the pavement. She squealed with pain as blood dripped from her temple.

The people at the front began dropping to the ground, exposing the people behind them to a hail of bullets from men with machine guns who were holding the street corners. Were they bandits, or soldiers or gang members? Panagiota was now sprawled in a lake of blood. She squinted through half-closed eyes. The gunmen were coming towards her, emptying the pockets of the dead as they went. Her teeth were chattering; her whole body was shaking like a leaf. In just a few seconds they would realize she was alive. She was at the back, near a corner. Slowly she withdrew her bare foot from under the dead body of the fat man. The looters were hurriedly snatching up the riches from the fallen, tearing off the jewellery that women had hidden under their dresses. She would have to act quickly.

She waited until all the men were leaning down, then with a massive effort she sprang to her feet like an arrow and, limping, plunged left, disappearing into Mesudiye Avenue under a cloud of black smoke. Behind her a voice shouted, 'Catch the whore! Make her pay!' But when her pursuers got to Kosma Street, none had the courage to jump into the vast, open-mouthed oven that greeted them.

Panagiota ran into the heart of the fire. She ran and ran and ran.

At first she ran slowly. She felt sick; her lungs were choked with smoke and she had to stop to cough. Nails and shards of glass sliced through her bare foot. Then her lungs cleared and she ran faster, faster, becoming one with her surroundings, losing herself in the light, the noise, the wind. Her legs, which had felt as heavy as an ingot under the thick blanket of soil, now felt as weightless as a feather, flying her forwards, on and on. The streets to her right and left glowed orange; the sky was a copper bowl. The skirt of her dress caught fire at Tercuman Street. Flames licked her legs, but she didn't feel them any longer. Nothing got through to her – not the stench, nor the din nor the horror. She was going to die. Oh, Mother Mary, what a great relief it was to have accepted death! If only she'd known this earlier. Some of the streets to her right, lined with warehouses, hadn't been touched by the fire's deadly tongues, but she didn't even consider going down them. There was no stopping her now. She had become the wind. She was Smyrna's mischievous wind, smelling of roses, salt and seaweed, a cure for all ills.

What gentle comfort the prospect of imminent death brought amid such horror. If only she could tell the crowds on the quay to quickly surrender themselves to death. Death was freedom!

A building collapsed to her left, scattering sparks into the sky like fireworks. Without slowing down, Panagiota glanced over at the sign on what remained of its wall. It was one of the fashionable boutiques. Goodbye furs and muffs and lacy underwear, and hats from Paris. May all the stuff that had promised a happier life burn in this hell. There was only one happy life, and that life was in the little house with the blue door. It was hidden in the pot of beans they dipped their bread in. It was sitting at Katina's knees on the couch by the bay window; it was in Grocer Akis's spice-scented hands caressing her chin; in the brief touch of Stavros's knee under the table. Since that life had now disappeared, let all the hats, corsets, muffs, cafés, and hotels with ballrooms burn. Let them all turn to ashes.

A coal-black horse thundered out of a side street. With his legs aflame, he looked like a mythical creature. Like Panagiota, he too was galloping into the heart of the fire. Seeing her, he reared and whinnied with pain. They ran together down Bella Vista Avenue, which had become a corridor of fire. Panagiota found she could run as fast as the horse. Oh my God! Of course, *vevea*, she was the queen. She was Smyrna, the single-breasted Amazon warrior who had founded the city four thousand years ago. This was, of course, the horse that Smyrna had ridden bareback. After thousands of years they had found each other. Without slowing, she turned and smiled at the horse. The horse neighed. They were united, complete. If she were to get on his back, she would feel even more complete.

She laughed out loud.

The creature, half horse, half fire, and the goddess with skirts ablaze burst onto the bright orange quay at Bella Vista at the same moment. Their faces were crimson, and white halos encircled their heads. People screamed at the sight of them and huddled even closer together. There was nowhere to escape to.

The incandescent pair reached the middle of the quay and stopped, glancing first at the dark water and then at each other.

The girl smiled.

The horse neighed.

The decision had been made. As one, they moved towards the water.

Hilmi Rahmi pulled at his horse's reins. It resisted, whinnying, but the colonel paid no attention. He was staring at the mythical pair as if bewitched. Never in his life had he encountered such beauty.

Unbelievable as it may have been, when the fire horse and the girl with her skirts ablaze appeared, the air no longer stank of scorched flesh but was suffused with the scent of Bournabat jasmine. It seemed that, amid the monster conflagration swallowing his beloved city, there was still a place for hope and beauty. Thanks be to God! Hilmi Rahmi's soul brimmed over with gratitude, his heart with love. If God was taking everything from him and offering him in return only this one scene to watch for eternity, he had no hesitation in consenting.

The fire horse and the girl with her skirts ablaze must have come from another world; perhaps like the phoenix born from its own ashes. Maybe they were angels, sent from Allah to put an end to this mad massacre. For there was not a trace of fear or pain on either of their faces. The girl with the crown of sparks around her head was more enchanting than an angel and was smiling at the horse. But what could one say about the smile on the horse's face?

The horse, scattering fire, moved towards the sea. The people on the quay cried out and raised their arms in alarm. The girl ran after it. The flames had spread from her skirts to her arms and hands; to her hair and her shawl. She did not notice.

Hilmi Rahmi spurred his horse forward.

Everyone turned and stared at the cavalry officer galloping towards the girl.

She flew over an old man lying on the ground. With scorched hands, she gathered her burning skirts. Her legs were festering wounds. The soldier's eyes shone as if lit by electricity. People moved aside. The girl lifted her bare, bloodied foot and leapt into the darkness, ready to join her beloved horse, already deep in the murky water.

Everyone watched as the girl hung in the air like a bird of fire, suspended over the ghastly sea.

And then, through the gloom, an arm reached out. The bird of fire was caught mid-air. Paying no mind to the flames which leapt at his skin from the waist he'd grasped, Hilmi Rahmi threw Panagiota across the back of his horse. The animal whinnied and tried to buck the flaming creature off his back. Panagiota screamed with all her strength. '*Ohi!*'

The crowd closed their eyes.

'Do not be afraid – *min fovate. Kala ise.* Do not fear me.'

As they galloped away, the hundreds of thousands on the quay parted just as the Red Sea waters had parted for Moses. The mothers and fathers who were watching all had the same thought: if that soldier had grabbed someone else's daughter, then their own daughter was safe for now. Ashamed of themselves, they turned and stared at the black sea that had silently closed over the fire horse.

Hilmi Rahmi spurred his horse. The *Iron Duke*, having taken on its load, was reversing out of the port. Sirens were wailing painfully. As he felt the heat of the girl's body against his back, Hilmi Rahmi's heart opened so wide that he began to laugh out loud. He was weak with happiness. The crowd drew back even further to make way for the officer who had obviously gone crazy.

He wanted to embrace the angel behind him, to kiss her and hold her and tell her that he would keep her safe, that he would love and protect her for the rest of his life. He had saved a life – a whole life! But what was one little life in the face of the monumental tragedy of hundreds of thousands? Captain Mehmet, who'd fainted earlier, had posed that very question. According to him, it was better not to interfere with whatever fate awaited these miserable souls.

As Hilmi Rahmi entered the labyrinthine streets of the Turkish district where not so much as a spark had taken hold, still carrying the half-conscious Panagiota on the back of his horse, he continued to laugh and shake his head. 'You are wrong, Mehmet,' he said, repeating the same words over and over. 'You are very wrong. A life saved is worth a world.'

Angel Fingers

I was lying on soft, moist earth in a dark garden. Silken fingers wandered across my face. I had fallen into paradise. Paradise smelled of honeysuckle and ripe mulberries, like my lost city. Through the leaves above me, I could see stars in the copper-coloured sky.

Smiling at the stars, I closed my eyes.

I was spreading into the earth in waves, becoming one with everything I touched. I realized that the spirit does not rise into the sky as the Holy Book says but ripples out into space in circles, as when a stone splashes into water. Grasses and flowers, worms wriggling under my wounded, expiring body, sparrows singing to the stars in the branches of the mulberry tree, roots reaching out underground – my soul embraced and was embraced by every living thing within its ever-widening rings. We synchronized vibrations; we were one.

When I was a little girl, my brothers used to throw me up in the air and catch me, making my insides jump. On the one hand I was afraid; on the other hand, I wanted them to continue. As my soul left my body, I had that same sort of feeling. I was afraid of falling and tried to hold on to life with my last breath, but I also felt light and fully trusting of the hands into which I was surrendering myself.

Soft angel fingers caressed my face. It was like hot halva melting in my mouth. Paradise had to be a field of honeysuckle because the angel's fingers smelled so fragrant.

Lips sweeter than sugar touched my earlobes. I giggled.

'Princess... Princess, open your eyes... Princess Scheherazade, wake up. Wake up and tell me a story.'

I tried to open my eyes. My big brothers had called me princess. *Prinkipisa, prinkipisa*. They must have come to take me. I had been granted the most beautiful death. How lucky I was! I wanted to tell my dearest mama that my death was not something to grieve over. Take off your black robe, Mama. My brothers have come from heaven to get me. I raised my arms.

In some far corner of paradise, a door slammed.

An intense, heavy pain leaked from my arms into my consciousness. I tried to get up.

'Dogan! Dogan!'

From somewhere in the distance, a woman was shouting. I wanted to tell her that there was nothing to be afraid of. If only people could experience death just once in their life, they wouldn't waste a single day on earth fearing it. Life is a dream, a short holiday, a break from reality. Death is the only reality.

'Dogan, come here quickly!'

The sweet lips whispering in my ear withdrew. But I had been going to tell him a tale. A tale about Queen Smyrna and her horse. In the place of angel fingers stroking my cheek came a banging and a clattering. The copper sky masked by leaves was now masked by something else. I tried to move my head.

'Dogan, go inside the house and don't come out!' shouted the same woman, now much closer to me. My soul made more circles, spreading into her vibrational space, our waves uniting like two rivers merging. Already I loved this woman I had not yet met. If only whatever was in front of my eyes were pulled away and I could see her. I heard the click of a rifle being loaded.

When I awoke, I was no longer in paradise. I was lying on a couch. My legs, my arms, my neck were burning up. My heart ached worse than my flesh. So this was the pain one feels when being born into this life. No wonder our first reaction is to cry. I moaned.

'Shhh, shhh,' said someone. An angel with blonde hair. She was rubbing ointment on my arms.

Life was such a warm and painful thing.

I wanted to be taken back to the garden. I wanted to die again as soon as possible. My brothers were waiting for me. I could still feel those little angel fingers wandering across my cheeks. Maybe I still wasn't very far from heaven. Maybe if I tried hard enough, I could slip out of this old, scorched dress and, circling, circling, become diffused into the universe, united and complete.

Whispers. Whispers whispering.

'Mummy, she is Scheherazade, isn't she? The one Nanny Dilber told us about in *One Thousand and One Arabian Nights*? Dunyazad's sister. Look at her hair, her eyes, her lashes. What do you think? Will she tell me a story?'

'Dogan, darling, Scheherazade is sleeping now. We must let her rest.'

'But she will when she wakes up, won't she? Mummy, did she get burned? Why are her hands and legs red like meat?'

'Shhh.'

They said I slept on that couch for forty days and forty nights. Sumbul kept watch at my side, soothing my blisters with ointment. Every morning she would go down to the quay, mingle with the crowds and ask about my mother and father. But all she received in return were the empty stares of people whose souls had been stolen by hopelessness.

As I slept, my beautiful, complicated, labyrinthine city burned. Sailors on ships out at sea mistook the smoke shrouding Smyrna for a giant mountain. Journalists in distant countries reported the news, and photographs of our ghost city became headline stories.

When the fire was finally extinguished, the quay was still jam-packed. Hundreds of thousands of people who only a week earlier had planned to welcome the homeless villagers under their roofs and feed them were now themselves homeless. So much was lost during those days: great fortunes, the fruits of an immense amount of labour, so much beauty and so many lives. In time, ships came, swept up women and children, and left. Men were marched into the interior and shot in the mountains. What remained were waters clogged with corpses and a city in ruins.

For forty days and forty nights Hilmi Rahmi did not return to his home on Bulbul Street.

Little Dogan would slip out of his bed at night and come and sleep beside me. In the mornings, he would run barefoot to the kitchen and relate the dreams he'd had while sleeping at my side. 'Scheherazade tells wonderful stories, Mummy. There's a queen and a horse and gods and a cloud. The horse smiles and the cloud talks.'

They hastily started rebuilding the city. Agia Katerina, Agios Dimitris, Agios Tryphonas, our neighbourhood, Frank Street and the joyful world of the quay had all been reduced to ashes. They smashed our houses, our bakeries and our little squares to dust and built huge roads on top of them. There was no one left to call it Smyrna any more. In one night, hundreds of thousands of citizens who had lived there for centuries disappeared into nothingness. After forty days and forty nights, no one honoured them. Church bells were silenced forever. It was only the ghosts that roamed the ruins that remembered the past.

And me.

They say that when Hilmi Rahmi came back home after forty days and forty nights and saw me lying unconscious on the couch in the women's quarters, he collapsed on the rug with the bird and fish designs and cried like a child. Sumbul took him in her arms, rocked him, kissed him, comforted him. When I opened my eyes for the first time, that was how I saw them, on the floor, embracing.

They never spoke of how I came to their house on that cursed night, how I fell into their garden through the gate which was locked from the inside. Hilmi Rahmi carried my secret until the end of his life. Not minding my muteness, my past, they enfolded me into their hearts and their home.

That day I was born again.

They named me Scheherazade.

Epilogue

This morning, for the first time in many years, I came down from my tower. Walking along the corridor of the Mansion with the Tower, which smelled of sun-warmed wood, I went into my old room.

Ipek was staying in there, in my old room. Sumbul's grandchild's grandchild. She appeared one day with a huge rucksack on her back and settled into the abandoned Mansion with the Tower, which had fallen into decay because the heirs somehow hadn't been able to agree on how to share it. She sent away the woman from Turkmenistan her grandfather had hired to take care of me. Now it was she who cooked my food, scrubbed my parchment-like skin with soap and a sponge, and rubbed herbal oil into it. She saw my muteness, which intimidated other people, not as a handicap hidden in my mouth but as a loss I was mourning. Not only did she not find my silence strange, but, like Sumbul, she could read my thoughts. And her curly blonde hair, chubby pink cheeks and languid green eyes were exactly like Sumbul's. She didn't know this, because other than myself there was no one left in the world who remembered Sumbul. In all her living days, they never took the poor woman to a studio for a single photograph.

Ipek and I had been living on our own under the ruined roof of the Mansion with the Tower for quite a while.

She was still asleep, bathed in the sweet September sun that was seeping through the closed shutters. Her golden curls were spread over the pillow, her pink lips were parted and she was snoring lightly. Who knew what gentle dreams she was enjoying. I sat down on the edge of her bed with the thick leather notebook in my hand. At the head of the bed was the walnut bedside table left from the former owners. For some reason, neither the grandchildren of Sumbul and Hilmi Rahmi nor those grandchildren's grandchildren had ever thought to change the furniture in the house. Ipek's bedroom still had the original matching set of heavy walnut bed, wardrobe and chest of drawers. As soon as I went into the room, my nostrils were assailed by the smell of the past. Who says furniture doesn't breathe?

When she opened her green eyes and saw me sitting on her bed, she smiled without raising her head from the pillow, as if I came down from my tower every morning to wake her.

'Good morning, Aunt Scheherazade!'

Since Dogan, all the children of this house have called me 'aunt', for some reason.

'What's that notebook in your hand, Aunt Scheherazade?'

She reached out and I handed her the leather notebook full of pages that had swallowed the ink of my fountain pens. Ever since Avinash Pillai's last visit I had been writing constantly. I don't know that 'writing' is quite the right word. The words just came out of my deep silence and scattered themselves on the paper. Forty years have passed since then. Forty years might seem like a lifetime, but for people like me who have knocked back a whole century, forty years is as short as the breath it would take to read this story.

At first she flicked through the pages indifferently, but then her fingers began moving with curiosity and excitement. She sat up properly, buried her elbow in the pillow and turned the pages with a rustle. As she attempted to read the text I had written in four different alphabets and three different languages, she faltered, tilted her head and looked at me in amazement. After forty years of service, the notebook was falling apart. At least let her rough fingers not crumble it to pieces now.

'What's this, Aunt Scheherazade? Where did you learn to write Arabic? What are these letters – are they Greek? Ah, I have a Greek friend who's moved here. Can I take it to him and get him to read it? And here you've written in French – you!'

The Sumbul-faced child had pushed aside the covers and was sitting cross-legged in the middle of the white sheet, squirming. Then, all at once, she stopped fidgeting. An odd thing happened. She lifted her small nose and sniffed the air. It was as if a stranger, a third person, was in the room with us. She waved her hand in front of her face, trying to catch a beam of light.

'Aunt Scheherazade?'

'What, *yavri mou*?'

The green eyes in her chubby pink face widened, just as Sumbul's had done when she was listening to stories about Edith Lamarck. She cocked her head as if straining to hear a sound from far away.

'Aunt Scheherazade!'

I was startled. She'd shouted that very loudly. I turned and stared fearfully at the corridor. There was nothing there. The two of us were, as usual, alone in the vast mansion. Or had Sumbul's ghost appeared to the child? God help us! The girl was gazing at my face as if bewitched.

The sound she'd heard was not that of a ghost.

'You're speaking, Aunt Scheherazade! You're speaking… I mean… I mean, you're speaking with your own voice! Not your inside voice but your outside voice. Oh, I can't believe it. *I-can-not-be-lieve-it!* Are you really speaking or did I dream it? Say something else!'

I bowed my head and stared at my stomach as if she'd said, 'There are horns sticking out of your belly, Aunt Scheherazade.' Then my hand went to my throat. My voice? Had I really spoken?

'What are these writings in your notebook?' Ipek said again, as if it was her questions that had unravelled the knot caught in my throat for a century.

The answer came into my head, but my voice caught the sentence in the air and released it into the room. 'This, Ipek *mou*, is the tale of a young girl who was born three times before she was eighteen. It is yours to take care of.'

My hand was still at my throat. Anxiously I turned towards the corridor. My heart was beating so rapidly, I thought it might stop altogether. I wanted death to find me in my tower, in my bed with the peeling pink paintwork. Avinash's prediction was about to come true:

'Those people who saved you and took you in did not give you the name Scheherazade for nothing. Until you tell this story, death will not come knocking at your tower.'

I reached for the hidden doorknob in the wall with the rose-patterned wallpaper.

It was hard to believe, but my voice had not changed at all!

Was it because it hadn't been used, or what? It was still the innocent, deep bass of my seventeen-year-old self.

Ipek's green eyes widened even more. Holding my notebook to her chest, she jumped off the bed. She was wearing pyjamas with lambs on them. I had my foot on the first step of the stairs going up to my tower when she caught my hand. Light was streaming down the empty stairway, and with the shadows falling on her face she looked exactly like Sumbul. When she began to speak, it was in the same nurturing and determined voice.

'No, you cannot die! No, no, no! Not yet. Your voice just came out for the first time this morning. You definitely can't die – you have so much to tell. Come on, let's go out and celebrate the birth of your voice. Let me take you to the quay and we'll have breakfast there, by the sea. You'll talk; I'll listen. I'm so hungry – are you hungry too? No, no, don't even think about it. You can't go up there any more. Wait here. I'll be ready in two minutes. From now on, no more going up to the tower. Wait for me in my room.'

She led me back down the stairs to the corridor and closed the door hidden behind the wallpaper. After looking in surprise at the padlock which Hilmi Rahmi had installed on the door when he'd carried Sumbul up there, as if seeing it for the first time, she reached out and clicked the padlock shut, sealing the tower forever. Then she raced down the corridor to the bathroom in her lamb pyjamas.

I went and stretched out on my old narrow bed with the walnut headrest where, every morning after I returned from Hilmi Rahmi's room, I used to replay over and over in my imagination every detail of our lovemaking. I buried my nose in the pillow. Ipek's skin smelled exactly like Sumbul's, of honeysuckle and cinnamon.

Even though the key that Hilmi Rahmi had once, with his own hands, placed around my neck still hung there, I knew I would never again go up to my tower. Silent Scheherazade might lie down in her tower to die, but I, who had regained my speech, would return to life.

The moment I took my first step into the street from the garden of the Mansion with the Tower, a burst of life flowed into the blue veins beneath my thin and wrinkled skin, like an injection from Ipek's palm into mine. The immense sky was bright blue. Seagulls fluttered off from the roof of the mansion, shrieking, and cats yowled after them. There was music and laughter from the side streets. Arm in arm, taking tiny steps, we walked to the quay. A yellow dog with a short tail followed along behind us.

'Everything! I want to hear everything from the beginning,' Ipek said as we sat down.

I tried to work out where we were. The smiling waiter, who had furnished our table with tomatoes, olives and various cheeses, said that the place used to be the Tayyare Cinema, and before that it was the Cinema Pallas. In 1923, for the first time a Muslim woman had performed on stage there. The building had hung a sign in her memory and the street was named after her.

I turned and looked fearfully at the sea. It had not taken on the colour of the lives it had swallowed. The water still sparkled as blue as could be. It seemed the sun was more merciless, nervous. There was a slight whiff of coal in the air. Two laughing girls passed arm in arm in front of us. They were eating ice cream. Their skirts were well above their knees, their plaits loose. Somewhere in the distance a merry song was playing.

Ipek wasn't interested in what the waiter was saying. She was following my gaze, looking at what I was looking at.

'Isn't it a magnificent city, though? There's something in the air, in the wind, that takes away a person's troubles, reminds you of everything beautiful in the world. Do you know what I think? You can't kill the spirit of this city, no matter what you do. You can set it on fire, tear it down, evict all of its people and import others in their place, but that love of freedom, that vivacity will always resurface. Don't you think?'

My eyes filled with tears.

'Auntie dear, it would be best if you read your notebook to me, from the beginning. You could translate the Greek and French sections into Turkish. Your voice will warm up, become attuned.'

It seems that when there is an ear that wants to listen, one's voice will find a way to speak out. As I turned to the first page of the notebook, I leaned across the table towards Ipek. The eyes inherited from Sumbul blinked their encouragement. I coughed, put on my glasses, which were hanging from a chain around my neck, and placed my finger on the first sentence.

All of a sudden, confusion descended. Like a well-trained dog waiting for his master's whistle, the wind came out of whatever hole it had been hiding in when it heard my voice and whirled around our table. Unaware of its own strength, it rummaged through the pages of my notebook. The short skirts of the girls eating ice creams as they passed swirled in the air, and the men in the next-door coffeehouse stared at the girls' legs over their glasses of tea. Waiters ran to catch a huge umbrella that was flying towards the sea.

With one hand gripping her wide-brimmed straw hat, Ipek looked with trepidation at the notebook. The wicked wind had already grabbed some of its faded and tattered pages and blown them away.

I waved my hand unconcernedly, took off my glasses and let them swing at the end of their chain. Inhaling the salty, seaweed-smelling air, I closed my eyes. My voice, a memento from Edith Lamarck – that deep, distinctive, bass voice – rose, independent of me, and brushed the skin of Ipek's beautiful face.

'My birth, on a sweet, orange-tinted evening, coincided with the arrival of Avinash Pillai in Smyrna.

'According to the European calendar, it was the year 1905.

'The month was September.'

The wild wind, waiting at my side, carried my voice and the stories in it to the east and to the west, to eager ears in the far corners of the earth, just as it had whisked away the pages of my notebook. Beside the familiar waterfront of my lost city, from the ashes of silent Scheherazade, like the phoenix I was reborn once again.

Glossary

(Fr.): French; (Gk): Greek; (Tur.): Turkish

aga (Tur.) landlord; man of power and/or wealth

agapi (mou) (Gk) (my) love

Agia/Agios (Gk) Saint (f./m.)

amanedes (Gk) songs of lamentation from Asia Minor

Asia Minor land mass that lies to the east of the Bosphorus
and constitutes the majority of modern-day Turkey; also
known as Anatolia

baglama (Tur.) stringed instrument used in folk music

Bey (Tur.) Mr

borek (Tur.) filo-pastry pie stuffed with cheese, spinach or
meat

Circassia formerly independent country in the north
Caucasus located in present-day European Russia

Committee of Union and Progress reformist party affiliated
with the Young Turks and supporting policies of
Turkification that resulted in the ethnic cleansing of the
Christian population of Asia Minor

Efendi (Tur.) Sir

ela (Gk) come on

endaksi (Gk) okay

Enver Pasha a leader of the Committee of Union and
Progress

evzones (Gk) Greek soldiers in the traditional uniform of
white skirts and pointy-toed shoes

filenada (Gk) girlfriend

foustanella (Gk) the white skirt worn by Greek soldiers

Ghazi (Tur.) honorific title accorded to a Muslim fighter
against non-Muslims

halva (Tur.) dessert made with tahini or semolina

Hanim (Tur.) Mrs

hookah see *waterpipe*

Izmir the Turkish name for the city of Smyrna, in universal
use since 1928

Izzet Pasha Smyrna's Turkish governor in May 1919

Kala ise? (Gk) Are you well?

kalimera (Gk) good morning

kalispera (Gk) good afternoon

kinotafio (Gk) ossuary

koliva (Gk) boiled wheat berries with spices and sugar
made for the souls of the dead

kori mou (Gk) my daughter

kuluraki (Gk) Greek bagel

Kyr (Gk) Mr

Kyra (Gk) Ms or Mrs

Levantines people of European descent living in the eastern
Mediterranean or Levant

lokum (Tur.) Turkish delight

mademoiselle (Fr.) miss

makari (Gk) hopefully

malaka (Gk) idiot

Mana Ellas (Gk) Mother Greece; Greece the motherland

Manoula (Gk) Mother dearest

mari! (Gk) hey you! (for women)

Megali Idea expansionist political project that aimed to create a Greater Greece by incorporating all significant Greek populations formerly living under Byzantine and later Ottoman rule

Metropolitan Chrysostomos the Greek Orthodox metropolitan bishop of Smyrna between 1910 and 1914, and again from 1919 until his death at the hands of a lynch mob in 1922

mou (Gk) my

Mustafa Kemal Pasha military leader in Turkey's National Struggle for Independence and subsequently the founder of the modern Turkish Republic; also known as Ataturk or Father of Turks

National Struggle for Independence Turkish War of Independence fought against the army of the Ottoman Empire and subsequently also against French, Italian and Greek troops following the 1918 Treaty of Sèvres; the longest of the battles is known as Greco-Turkish War of 1919–1922

Nizam-i Djedid Army reformed and professionalized army of the Ottoman sultanate

Nureddin Pasha Turkish Governor of Smyrna from 1922

ohi (Gk) no

okka (Tur.) Ottoman measurement equivalent to about 1.2 kilogrammes

oriste (Gk) please; welcome

palikaria (Gk) young men

Panagia (Gk) Mary, Mother of God; Maria, Mother of Jesus Christ *parasang* (Tur.) the distance travelled in one hour, equivalent to about six kilometres

pasha (Tur.) title given to a high-ranking Turkish officer

raki (Tur.) sweetened alcoholic drink, often anise flavoured

se/sas parakalo (Gk) please

signomi (Gk) I'm sorry; excuse me

Stergiadis Greek high commissioner of Smyrna from 1919 to 1922

subye (Tur.) beverage made with crushed almonds and/or melon seeds

Thee mou (Gk) my God

Theo(s) (Gk) God

Treaty of Sèvres 1920 treaty following the First World War in which many territories of the defeated Ottoman Empire not inhabited by Turkish people were ceded to and occupied or administered by the Allies

Turkos (Gk) Turkish man

Unionists see *Committee of Union and Progress*

Usta (Tur.) Master

Venizelos prime minister of Greece from 1910 to 1920 and 1928 to 1933; supporter of *Megali Idea* policies

vevea (Gk) of course

vre (Gk) you, bro

waterpipe (also, hookah) tobacco pipe with a flexible tube that draws the smoke through water contained in a basin

yahni (Tur.) stew of meat, fish or vegetables made with onions, tomatoes and olive oil

yavri mou (Gk) my child